FIRESTONE

Sarah Fisher

Book Two in the Dragonscale series

First published in Australia in 2018 by Sarah Fisher

Copyright © Sarah Fisher 2018

Website: www.sarahfisherauthor.com
Email: sarah@sarahfisherauthor.com

ISBN: 9780648182405 (paperback)

 A catalogue record for this book is available from the National Library of Australia

Disclaimer
This is a work of fiction. Names, characters, places, incidents and events, other than those clearly in the public domain, are fictitious and any resemblance to actual persons, living or dead, is entirely coincidental.

To my father, Ray and my brothers, Cameron and Daniel

Acknowledgements

It takes quality people to produce quality work, so a special thank you to my editor, Patrice and graphic artist, Lucy.

A huge thank you also to Judith and Maree who poured through drafts, offering invaluable insights to help me develop and tighten my narrative.

And to Angus, for his unwavering support of my writing journey.

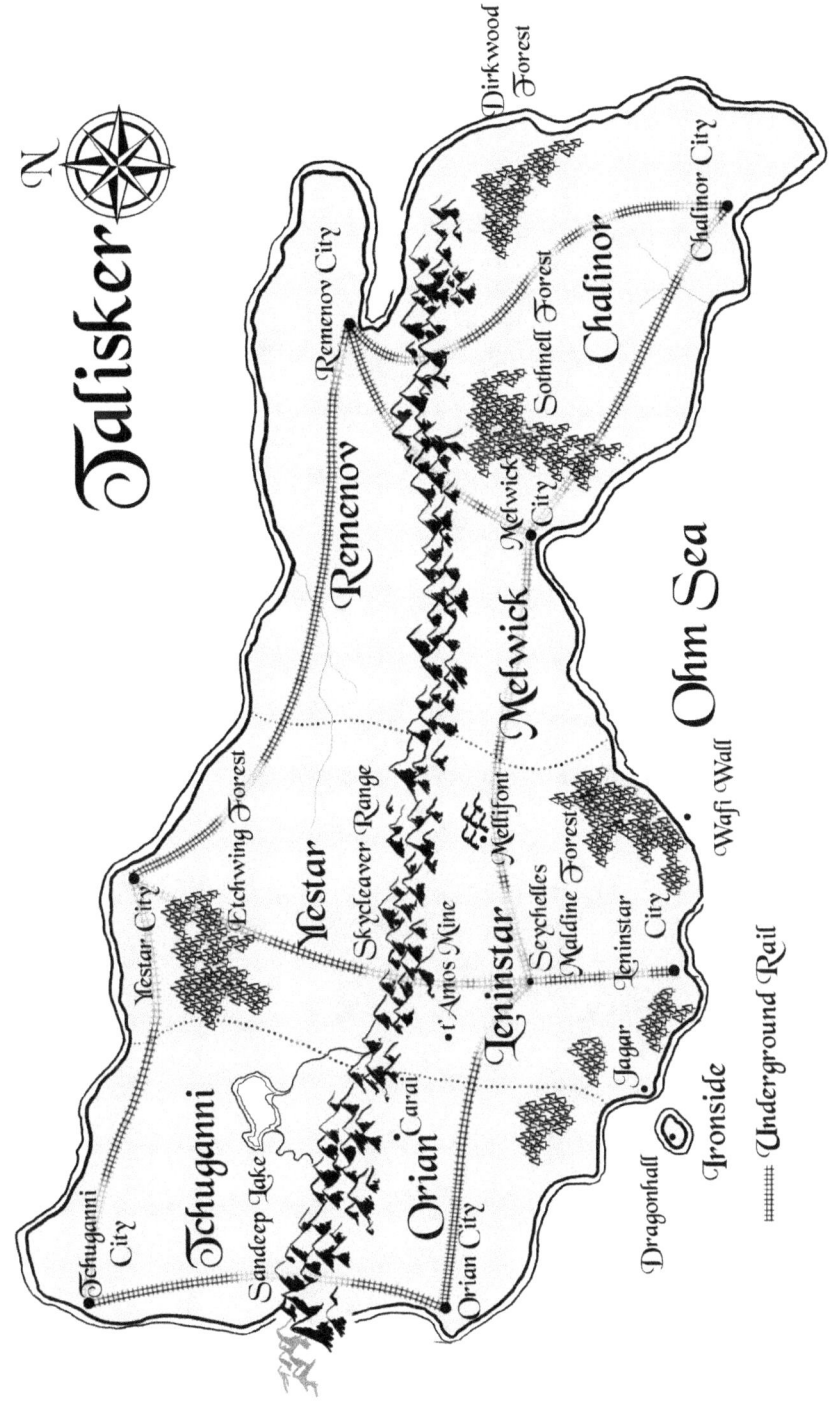

Characters

Royals

King Tambian, Leninstar
King Henrik, Orian
King Mallory, Melwick
King Tara, Chalinor
King Arissa, Remenov
King Franco, Ylestar
King Ulster, Tchuganni
Queen Rosemary, Leninstar
Princess Catriona, Leninstar
Prince Vernon, Leninstar

Goblins

King Nerili
Shar, King's guard
Liah, King's guard
Frost, King's guard
Jacin, King's adviser
Gisa, King's adviser
Rankin, King's adviser
Ulan, King's adviser
Grave, Army Commander
Iron, Army Commander
Princess Severine
Prince Sandor

Academy adepts

Professor Noah Chord, viola
Major Sachin, flute
Major Maggie, clarinet
Major Anok, lyre
Doctor Alan, recorder

Others

Raven Chord, Leninstar's Army
Commander
Emir Delorian, King Tambian's
adviser
Jaxon, Emir's brother
Gillette, Emir's nephew
Montana, High Priestess of
Talisker

Chapter 1

As the door hinge shrieked its displeasure, Noah looked up from her sewing table.

'Someone should oil that,' Gillette said as he dumped his school satchel on the floor.

'Probably,' Noah said, 'but if it squeaks then no one can sneak up on me.'

The boy's face crinkled into a frown. 'You're the king's tailor, Noah. How many people want to sneak up on *you*?'

'You'd be surprised,' Noah said, returning her attention to hemming the queen's new gown.

'I could oil it for you,' Gillette said. 'I could do it right now, in fact.'

'Do you have homework?'

'Not much.'

'Wouldn't you rather get that out of the way first?'

Gillette opened one of the doors on Noah's sewing cabinet. 'It won't take long. I'll just use a bit of sewing machine oil and it'll be good as new.'

Noah shrugged. 'Okay.'

Having found the oil he needed, Gillette wound his way back to the external door of Noah's studio and got to work.

Noah watched as he oiled the lower hinge first. 'What is your homework?'

'Something boring.'

'Boring how?'

Satisfied with his work on the bottom fitting, Gillette turned his attention to the top one. Unlike most ten-year-olds, he didn't need a stool to reach the hinge. He'd sprouted over the summer, and though he sometimes had difficulty coordinating his rapidly growing limbs, he revelled in being the tallest in his class.

'This is the main offender,' he muttered.

'Boring how?' Noah said again.

'We have to tell the story of Talisker's creation in our own words.'

Noah waited to see if there was anything else.

'If Chase was here, I'd pay her to write it,' Gillette added.

'Don't you think your teacher would notice the difference between a story by a professional writer and one by a fifth-form boy?'

Gillette swung the door back and forth. 'Perfect,' he said. 'Not a sound.'

Noah sighed. Her last day on homework duty promised to be less fun than being stabbed in the eye with a fork. *Emir should be doing this,* she thought. *He's the uncle.*

Gillette recapped the bottle and returned it to the cupboard before taking a seat next to Noah.

'I reckon that's worth five dinah,' he said.

Noah glanced at him. 'Maybe so, but don't think I'll be paying you. Palace maintenance – you'll have to talk to the king about that. You can ask him at dinner tonight if you like.'

'I'll do that,' Gillette said. 'I'll just make sure I get to him before you start throwing prawn shells at him.'

Noah turned to him. 'I have a needle in one hand and a pair of scissors within reach of the other – much more dangerous than prawn shells. Do you really want to go there?'

'Oh come on, Noah. Everyone loves that story.'

'No. Not everyone,' she said as she tied off the thread with a double knot.

'Raven tells it best,' Gillette said.

Noah rolled her eyes. She didn't see what all the fuss was about. She hadn't done it on purpose. Everyone knew peeling prawns was tricky. Twisting off the head first without spurting goo everywhere was the first challenge. And she'd passed that test. She'd removed the legs and peeled away the shell from the body without incident too. The last step was the problem – squeezing just above the tail to press out the last bit of meat. As she'd squeezed, her fingers had slipped, firing the tail across the table and hitting King Tambian in the eye. *Raven tells it best.* Her brother embellished the story with each telling. The last version made it sound like an assassination attempt.

Glaring at her young charge, Noah said, 'You're not going to live to see dinner at this rate. Go and get your homework journal.'

'I don't want to do my homework,' he grumbled.

'Well, that's up to you,' Noah said, 'but you know you don't get to see your father tomorrow until it's done.'

She re-threaded her needle as Gillette drummed his fingers on the table.

'Will you help me write it?' he said.

'No.'

His eyes widened. 'But you have to – you're my *favourite* aunty.'

'Two things – I *don't* have to and I'm *not* your aunty.'

'But Emir is my uncle so that makes you—'

'Your uncle's girlfriend,' Noah finished.

He folded his arms across his chest. 'You're mean.'

'You started it,' Noah said.

'What?'

'You brought up the prawn thing. That was mean.'

Gillette laughed. 'Okay, so we're *even* then.'

'Maybe.'

'We *are* even,' he said, 'so now will you help me with my homework?'

'I have to finish this hem so I'm not writing it for you.'

Gillette jumped off his seat to retrieve his journal. 'That's okay. You just tell me what to write and I'll write it.'

'How about … you tell me what you know about how Talisker was created and I'll try to spice it up a bit?'

Gillette settled himself back on his stool and opened his journal. 'So there were two gods who were brothers and they had a fight about something and then a dragon ate the evil one and the good one built a world around the dragon – and the evil god too obviously, because he was in the dragon's belly.'

Noah checked her watch. 'Dinner's in three hours. We'll never make it.'

'Don't be like that …'

'Do you even know any of the names?'

'Of course I do!'

Noah waited.

'Elani is the good god, Jong is the evil god and Xan is the dragon,' Gillette said.

'Good. Now let's start where Jong is fighting Xan.'

'But that's near the end of the story. Why aren't we starting at the beginning?'

'Because Chase says you should start with action,' Noah said. 'Now, you like sword-fighting, right?'

Gillette puffed out his chest. 'Yes, Ma'am I do! Raven is teaching me and I practise every chance I get.'

'Have you ever imagined fighting a dragon?'

He shook his head.

'Well that's what you're going to do,' Noah said. 'You're going to imagine that you're Jong—'

'Why do I have to be the bad guy?'

'Because he's the one who fights the dragon,' Noah said. 'Now close your eyes and I'll help you get into character.'

Gillette wriggled on his seat as he closed his eyes.

Noah cleared her throat. 'Now imagine you're sheltering in an abandoned castle on a faraway world. The weather is terrible – the wind is howling, driving icy wind through the gaps in the stone where the mortar has long since deteriorated. There's no life left on the planet, which is no surprise to you. This is yet another of Elani's failed creations. It sustained life for a few millennia but when the weather system failed, life disappeared.'

Gillette opened one eye. 'But it might come back,' he said hopefully.

'That's what Elani would say,' Noah said, 'but you're Jong. That's not the way Jong thinks – he's the master of destruction.'

'Oh. Right.' He closed his eyes again.

'So you're getting cranky because your trusty dragon, Xan went off hunting on a nearby world and has not yet returned. You're keen to destroy this world and move on but you can't do that until you have transport. When Xan finally does arrive, you're even more annoyed because she's brought Elani with her.'

'Am I still inside the castle?'

'Yes.'

'Are they inside the castle?'

'No,' Noah said, 'they've just landed outside. You're looking out a window. What would you say?'

'*Elani! Get your own dragon!*' Gillette cried, punching the air with his fist.

Not quite what she had expected. Noah checked her watch again. 'And?'

'*What are you doing here?*'

'That's better,' Noah said, 'now I'll be Elani.' She lowered her voice. *'Xan asked me to come. Why don't you come out here so we can talk?'*

'*Talk? Okay, let's talk.*' Gillette opened his eyes. 'I think I'm getting this, Noah. Now, I'd go outside and confront them. They'd try to kill me—'

'*Xan* would try to kill you, remember? Now that Elani has shown her beautiful places she's angry at Jong for all the destruction they've caused. She thinks she needs to destroy her master to save Elani's creations.'

Gillette frowned. 'Yeah. Okay.'

'What's wrong?'

'I'm thinking about my sword ... if I was a god, would I really fight with a sword?'

'Your teacher said you could write it in your own words didn't he?' Noah said.

Gillette nodded.

'Well, if nothing else,' Noah said, 'at least your teacher will know you wrote it.'

Snatching up his pencil, he said, 'This is going to be the best sword-fight ever.'

'So remember that during the fight, you need to show the reader what they're fighting about. We started where the action is, but you need to weave in the background information.'

'Do dragons talk?'

Noah shrugged. 'Up to you.'

Gillette held his pencil out like a sword. 'This dragon is going to talk.'

With a nod, he set about his task and stuck at it for almost an hour. When he was done he pushed his journal across the workbench to Noah.

'All done?' she said.

'Yep. Read it.'

Noah squinted at the page. 'Do you have something against punctuation?'

'The teacher said it had to be in my own *words*,' Gillette said. 'If he wanted punctuation too, he should have said so.'

Finding no suitable response, Noah started reading …

♪♫

Jong drew his sword as he stomped across the frozen ground towards his brother.

'What's going on here?' he demanded.

'I won't be part of your destruction anymore, Jong,' Xan said.

'But I am your master,' Jong said. 'If I say you must, then you must.'

'I am no longer your servant,' the dragon said.

'Why not? We've been destroying failed worlds – like this one – for ages. Why the change of heart?'

Elani spoke. 'They weren't all failed, Jong.'

'Life could come back here,' Xan said. 'There is hope. That's what Elani has showed me.'

Jong spat. 'Life? Hope? Absolute rubbish!'

'You should change your ways, Jong,' Elani said. 'This is your chance to be a creator rather than a destroyer. Work with us.'

'Us? *Us!*' Jong screamed in rage. 'There is no US!'

'Calm down,' Elani said.

'Fight me,' he said, challenging Elani with his lethal sword.

Elani shook his head. 'No. I won't fight.'

Anger exploded inside Jong and he lunged at his brother. 'If you won't fight, then you will DIE!'

Xan stepped in between the two gods. 'Stop!' she commanded.

Jong slashed at the dragon and his sword scraped across her scales. Sparks flew. The god overbalanced and fell over, skidding on the icy ground. He stood up. He was really angry now.

'Jong, you don't need to do this,' Xan said.

Jong set his stance and raised his sword ready to strike. 'Stand aside, Xan. This is between me and my brother.'

The dragon crouched. 'If you want him, you'll have to get through me first.'

'Okay,' Jong said and thrust his sword at her shining scales.

Xan swiped at him with her claw, easily blocking him. Jong kept his balance. He slid one foot across the other as he looked for a better position. He needed to find a soft spot to strike. Unfortunately it was cloudy so he couldn't use the sun to blind his opponent. Xan lashed out with her talons and Jong parried. *Be patient,* Jong told himself.

Jong and Xan circled each other while Elani watched on. Jong kept his sword raised as Xan swished her long tail. Suddenly, Xan crouched and then sprang at Jong. *At last,* Jong thought. He ran forward and caught the dragon by surprise. As Xan landed, Jong raised his sword over his head and it pierced the dragon through her shoulder joint. Jong twisted and wrenched his sword, trying to cut off Xan's front leg. The dragon roared in pain as she collapsed on the ground. Jong jumped out of the way just in time and then stabbed Xan in the eye.

But Jong underestimated the dragon. Xan flicked her head up and he was thrown into the air. Up and up he went, still clutching his sword … and then down and down again. He looked down and screamed. The dragon's open mouth was below him.

When Jong landed in Xan's mouth she swallowed him instantly and then collapsed on the ground again.

'Help me,' she said to Elani. 'Jong is still fighting. Help me to stop him escaping.'

Elani patted the dragon's head. 'I will put you to sleep and then remake this world around you, Xan,' he said. 'You will be safe and Jong will not escape. And even better – your blood and scales will warm up this world and life will return.'

Xan wheezed a puff of smoke. 'Do it,' she said. 'Do it.'

And that is how Talisker was created.

The end.

♪♫

'What do you think?' Gillette said.

Noah turned to him. 'It's wonderful, Gillette. Exceptional actually.'

'Did you like the swordfight?'

'Very detailed,' Noah said. 'I think you should show it to Raven.'

'I will,' he said, eyes gleaming. 'Is there anything in the story you'd change?'

Noah picked up the pencil and drew a line through the word 'end' and replaced it with 'beginning'.

Gillette picked up his journal and reviewed Noah's amendment. 'Neat,' he said at last. Hugging the book to his chest, he added, 'I can't wait to show this to Dad when he gets home tomorrow. He's going to be really proud of me.'

'He definitely will be,' Noah said. 'He'd probably really like it if you'd bathed too.'

Gillette shook his head. 'You don't *actually* think that's going to work, do you?'

Noah sighed. 'It was worth a shot.'

Chapter 2

With a furtive glance around the king's banquet table, Noah picked up the prawn from her plate and twisted off its head. To her left, Emir was instructing Gillette in the finer points of cutlery use at royal dinners. On her right, Major Sachin folded napkins into animal shapes while ignoring a lecture from Alan on the mathematical structure of onions. Across the table, King Tambian and his wife shared a joke while Raven poured Princess Catriona another goblet of mead.

I'm safe, Noah thought as she peeled off the shell. *No one will notice.*

She glanced up at the elaborate candle chandeliers that loomed over the table. A hundred little flames danced on their wicks, twinkling merrily as they robbed the parlour of the darkness that was proper at this hour of the evening. *Bright little thieves stealing the darkness,* Noah thought.

'Noah, let it go,' Emir said quietly as he wrapped his hand around her wrist. 'You know what happened last time.'

'It's too good to waste,' Noah replied, squeezing the prawn tail gently to get the last of the juicy flesh. 'And anyway, what are the odds of hitting the king a second time?'

Emir looked past Noah. 'Sachin,' he said, 'you heard me warn her, right?'

'Yep,' Sachin replied, putting his goblet down on the table. 'I heard you. It's funny, isn't it? You're the Royal Adviser – the king's confidante – but your own girlfriend won't listen to your advice.'

'That's a bit harsh,' Noah said defensively as she placed the prawn tail on her plate. 'I listen.'

'Sometimes,' Emir said.

'To be honest,' Sachin said, 'I was hoping for a repeat performance. The look on King Tambian's face last time was priceless.'

Noah looked across the table at King Tambian who was chuckling at something his queen had said. A stray prawn tail would erase that grin instantly. At least if it were to happen again, there were fewer witnesses this time.

'Flicking prawn tails at the king is no laughing matter, Major Sachin,' Emir said.

Noah groaned. 'For the thousandth time … I didn't do it on purpose. They're really slippery and when you squeeze them …'

Sachin patted her arm. 'Yes, yes, Noah,' he said. 'So you say.'

King Tambian stood up, drawing the attention of his guests. 'A toast,' the king declared, raising his goblet with a hand that trembled on account of his advancing years. 'To Noah.'

'To Noah,' the guests echoed.

'Just to clarify,' Sachin said, 'are we toasting her improved prawn-peeling technique?'

The king looked at the adept from Mellifont for a long moment. 'If only we were,' he said in a gravelly voice. 'For that, Major Sachin, I would not have required your presence.'

'Right, Your Highness,' Sachin said. 'Understood.'

Noah smiled to herself. Sachin's extraordinary musical talent came at the expense of manners. He'd achieved the rank of Major when he was just eight years old, something unheard of on Talisker before that. Now, at twelve, he was a highly respected member of the Academy but outside Mellifont, most people, including King Tambian, found him forthright to the point of abrasive.

'Good,' the king said. 'Now Noah, last night I was reflecting on your time with us. You've achieved so much in the fifteen months you've been here. And through your achievements, you've changed Talisker dramatically. In fact, it's difficult to think of anyone who's had as big an impact on this world as you have.'

Noah felt the heat rise in her cheeks as she waited for a wisecrack from Sachin. Nothing came. *Typical,* she thought, *when I need him to say something to take attention away from me, he doesn't do it.*

'You are a wonderful tailor, Noah,' the king continued. 'Your designs are stylish yet practical – I love not ever having to worry about what I'm going to wear. Beyond that, I'm amazed that you have kept my family clothed while attending to other matters of such importance. Tonight we celebrate you attaining the rank of Professor of Raiki. Combining your studies at the Academy in Mellifont with your duties here has no doubt been difficult, but your talent and hard work have paid off. Congratulations.'

'Hear, hear!' Queen Rosemary said.

'Hear, hear!' the other guests echoed.

The king stroked his white beard. 'And if that isn't reason enough to celebrate,' he said, 'thanks to you, Noah we now have a massive piece of firestone.'

'Almost,' Alan interjected.

All eyes went to the Academy's chief auditor, who tried – and failed – to hide behind the turkey leg he'd been gnawing on. It was an ambitious feat. The turkey would have to have been elephant-sized to hide Mellifont's pudgy bean-counter.

'Almost?' the king said.

Alan's mouth opened and closed several times before his voice cooperated. 'W-well we haven't qu-quite g-got it yet,' he stammered. 'I mean, we *nearly* have it – the lift is scheduled for next week – but we don't quite have it … yet.'

Waving his hand, the king said, 'Fine. Thanks to Noah, we *almost* have a massive piece of firestone.'

As Alan fidgeted with his napkin, Noah felt sorry for him. He didn't mean to be irritating. It was just a natural talent.

'Your work as Dragonsbane after the debacle with Orville Kurz saved us all,' King Tambian said. 'The way you and Dr Grainger re-established the dragonsong's equilibrium after the destruction of Talisker's keys was astonishing. And the fact that, in the course of your work, you located a piece of firestone is nothing short of a miracle. Past Dragonsbanes have been aware of firestone buried deep in our world but none have been able to describe its position as precisely as your perception has allowed you to do. Your affinity with firestone is a blessing to us all. We, and future generations of Taliskerans, are in your debt. This firestone will power our electricity network for centuries to come.'

The king smiled warmly at Noah.

Noah nodded at her boss. 'Thank you, Your Highness,' she said, 'but can I say, I couldn't have done any of this without the support of the people at this table. I am very lucky to have such wonderful people around me. On Earth, I was a deaf orphan. The only family I had was a dog.'

Noah looked at Raven.

'I'm glad you came here too, Sis,' Raven said. 'I mean, being a dog was fine but I like being a person much better.'

He turned his gaze towards Princess Catriona. Noah resisted the temptation to roll her eyes. Her twin was smitten with the strawberry-blonde princess and while she seemed to like him too, Noah was certain there'd never be anyone Catriona would love more than herself.

Unable to contain himself, Alan said, 'And I bet you're excited about studying to be a doctor now, Noah! Of course, you know that I'm happy to mentor you through that process.'

'Yes,' Noah said with a smile. 'I *do* know that, Alan. You've only told me about a thousand times.'

'Yes, yes,' he said. '*So* exciting.'

'*But* I'm going to take a break from my studies,' Noah said. 'I have plenty to do here and I want to take some time to master what I've learned so far.'

'Well, whenever you're ready, I'm your man,' Alan said.

'I'll remember that,' Noah promised.

'Perhaps you could play something for us, Noah,' Queen Rosemary said.

'It would be my pleasure,' Noah said.

She reached under the table to retrieve her viola. Unable to find enough real estate on the food-laden table to place the weathered black case, she handed it to Emir. Noah's heart thumped as she ran one hand over the scuffed leather before opening it. Memories of her late mother flashed in her mind as she lifted the instrument from its cradle and nestled it under her chin. Noah inhaled deeply of the fragrant saffron oil that gave the viola its deep orange hue and retrieved her bow.

'Noah, do you take requests?'

Noah's gaze landed on the boy seated next to Emir.

Queen Rosemary scolded him. '*Gillette!* Have you no manners?'

'It would seem not,' Noah said as she put her bow to the strings.

'He doesn't lack manners …' Princess Catriona said.

Gillette sighed. 'Thank you.'

'… it's a sense of occasion he lacks,' she finished.

The boy frowned. 'Oh, thanks so much.'

'He does lack manners as well though,' Emir added.

'Hey!' Gillette cried indignantly. 'You're my uncle! You're supposed to say nice things about me.'

Emir tousled the boy's hair. 'Only if they're true.'

'Oh fine,' Gillette said, throwing his hands in the air. '*Please*, Noah, do you take requests?'

'Only if your request is for *Ayuna de chanzè*,' Noah replied.

'Which one's that?'

The queen put her index finger in front of her lips. 'Oh Gillette, please just be quiet and listen.'

The boy settled into silence as Noah drew her bow across the strings to begin the lively folk piece. Though the piece was technically challenging, she relaxed and let the music cascade from her strings. She'd practised the piece so often that it was likely everyone in the palace was sick of hearing it, but no one would say so tonight. Becoming a Professor of Raiki was a great honour; she could play whatever she pleased in celebration.

Warm applause absorbed the final note.

'That's a lovely piece, Noah,' Queen Rosemary said. 'I'll never tire of it.'

'Aren't *you* lucky,' Raven said.

Noah scanned the dinner table for something to throw at her twin. No sooner had she spotted the prawn shell than Emir whisked the plate out of her reach.

'You're *not* throwing that at your brother,' he said.

'What makes you think—'

'I know you, Noah,' Emir said.

'And you say *I* have no sense of occasion,' Gillette said. 'You'd think someone *her* age would know better.'

'She *does* know better,' Emir said with a sideways glance at his girlfriend.

Noah ignored Emir's comment. 'What do you mean "someone my age"?'

'Seventeen is *way* old, Noah,' Gillette said. 'You should start acting your age.'

'Seventeen is *not* old,' Princess Catriona said. 'And if you say that again, pipsqueak, I'll lock you in the dungeon for the night.'

Noah resisted endorsing the princess's sentiment about age; it was disconcerting enough to agree with Catriona let alone to be seen doing it publicly. Noah had found little common ground with the princess. Catriona relished every opportunity to press her seniority – in both rank and age. The two months that separated them might as well have been two decades.

'No one is being locked in the dungeon tonight,' King Tambian said with a stern look at his daughter. 'Perhaps we could return our attention to the main act for the evening? Major Sachin, would you do the honours, please?'

Sachin pushed back his chair and stood up. 'Thank you, Your Highness. I would be delighted. As you all know, after Orville destroyed the twelve keys, the way raiki is performed on Talisker has changed. When we retrieved the twelve pieces of firestone from the original keys, each of the seven states was given one piece and the remaining five pieces went back to Mellifont. They were cut and reforged into ten sliders. All adepts in Mellifont have instruments that use sliders – sliders made from a range of materials. With the ten *firestone* sliders, we can share them around – we're no longer restricted to having set keys. Although we only have ten at any one time, we can change the mix and share the responsibility.'

'And when we have our share of the *new* firestone,' Alan cut in, 'we'll have more sliders and therefore more keys available to us.'

Sachin's shoulders slumped and Alan realised what he'd done – again.

'Sorry,' Alan said. 'I am *so* sorry. It's just I get so excited.'

Sachin sighed. 'Yes, we know. Slider please.'

From a pocket in his trousers, Alan produced a red velvet pouch and a clipboard.

'For you,' Alan said as he placed the pouch in Sachin's hand. Without waiting for acknowledgement, he whipped a stylus from his breast pocket and looked at his watch. '8:25 pm,' he murmured as he made the appropriate entry on the form on his clipboard.

Sachin opened the pouch and put his fingers inside. The stateroom was silent as everyone watched him draw out a long silver chain. The highly polished, rope-braid necklace glinted in the candlelight as it snaked its way out of the pouch. Noah clutched her hands over her heart when the locket at the end of the chain appeared.

'Noah,' Sachin said as he placed the locket in her hands, 'inside this locket is your piece of firestone – the one that made the 13th key – which has been refashioned into a slider.'

Gillette spoke up. 'I thought only Majors could use firestone,' he said.

'That is usually the case,' Sachin replied, 'but Noah is different. She defeated Orville with the 13th key, she retrieved all the pieces of firestone from the lava pit where he destroyed the original keys, *and* she used firestone to help restore Talisker's dragonsong. Her affinity with firestone – dragonscale – is well-recognised and the Council at Mellifont endorses her to retain this piece that was entrusted to her family by the Descera.'

Gillette appeared to consider Sachin's words. 'Sounds fair,' he said at last.

'Noah,' Sachin said, 'do you promise to use the firestone in accordance with the Council's by-laws and for the greater good of Talisker?'

Mesmerised by the fine engraving and rolled edges of the locket, Noah said, 'I promise to use the firestone in accordance with the Council's by-laws and for the greater good of Talisker.'

'Sachin?' Alan whispered.

Without taking his eyes off Noah, Sachin said, 'Not yet, Alan.'

'*And,*' Noah added, 'I promise to sign all Alan's paperwork and show appropriate respect for the serial numbers of the property issued to me.'

The auditor relaxed visibly at her words. 'I should think so,' Alan said. 'I don't want a repeat of the wristband fiasco.'

Noah couldn't suppress a smile. It appeared that Alan would never forgive her and Sachin for swapping their Academy-issue wristbands. Sachin had been trying to save her life but that wasn't a good enough reason for Alan. He was the perfect auditor. His devotion to numbers left room for little else in his life – like personality and social grace. He had a singularity of purpose that was as admirable as it was exasperating. Almost.

'Are you going to try the slider, Sis?' Raven said. 'The suspense is killing me.'

'Certainly am,' Noah said, looping the silver chain over her head and then opening the locket.

The fingernail-sized piece of firestone lay embedded in a silver slider. Looking into the oval stone, Noah felt she was staring into the depths of the cosmos – swirls of azure, green, gold, red and mauve glimmered in the potent piece of dragonscale. Like the viola, the stone had belonged to her mother. Noah had worn it in a ring for years as a keepsake after her mother's death, unaware of its significance and power. But her time on Talisker had taught her about the power of firestone and she was relieved to have the stone back.

With great care she removed the slider from the locket and pushed it gently into its custom-made slot in the bridge of her viola. Now the instrument was not just a means to make beautiful music but a tool to manipulate Talisker's dragonsong. She'd spent a month developing this tonic, and though it was for visual appeal rather than healing, she felt the composition reflected her growing raiki skills.

'First, I will dim the lights,' Noah said.

A handful of notes was all it took extinguish all the candles, plunging the room into darkness. Several of the dinner guests gasped.

'Do you not know what *dim* means, Noah?' Princess Catriona said. 'You really *should* know given that you're—'

'That's enough, Catriona,' Tambian said. 'Noah, please continue.'

'Thank you,' Noah said.

The first note of her composition sent a shiver through her as the firestone in the bridge caught the string's vibration. The music that underpinned Talisker was now hers to command – a great privilege and tremendous responsibility. To Noah, tonight's ceremony was not about being ostentatious; it would be subtle yet symbolic. As she wove her melody, a small ball of light appeared above Raven's head to an appreciative gasp from her audience. Gillette squirmed in his chair, barely able to contain his excitement. Noah installed a light above him next to keep him occupied.

Once everyone was illuminated with a glowing nimbus, Noah moved into the next phase of her performance. The lights stretched and swirled, slowly at first and then more rapidly as the tempo of the tune increased. Sachin's light tailed Alan's, whose light raced Emir's, while the lights of the royal couple slithered and intertwined.

'Gillette, can you juggle?' Noah asked.

His eyes widened as he shrugged. 'I don't know.'

'Try,' she said as she split his light into three glowing spheres.

'They tickle,' he said, grinning as the balls came to rest on his hands.

He threw one ball into the air, quickly followed by a second one. Before he could toss the third one, the first ball demanded his attention again. As he flicked it up again he proclaimed, 'I'm doing it! I'm juggling.'

Noah looked at Emir. He smiled his approval but nodded in Catriona's direction. Noah winked at him before using her music to fuse the princess's light with Raven's to make a heart shape – the perfect diversion to stop the royal heir pointing out that Gillette's juggling prowess was not actually of his own doing. She let the juggling continue for a few more moments before whipping all the lights skyward.

As the melody changed again, the lights joined to make a large halo above the dining table. Noah employed a series of higher notes to make the halo constrict. The ring of light continued shrinking until a single ball hovered over the table. As the piece reached its climax, the glowing nimbus ballooned in size, its rapid growth mirroring the now frenetic tempo. Noah stopped, bow poised. Eyes closed, she counted her heartbeats … on the fifth beat she unleashed her final two notes.

The light obeyed her, showering a hundred sparks neatly onto the wicks of the candles on the chandeliers. Everyone applauded as Noah lowered her viola.

'Very tasteful,' Queen Rosemary said. 'Simple yet elegant.'

'Something she'd do well to reflect in other aspects of her life,' Catriona said.

With effort, Noah held her tongue. Though the Council's by-laws strictly forbade the use of raiki to resolve petty grievances, she enjoyed the thought of creating a tonic that fused Catriona's lips permanently.

Deciding not to acknowledge the princess, Noah turned her attention to the queen. 'Thank you, Your Highness,' she said.

'Noah,' Alan said. 'Can you sign my paperwork now?'

Extracting the firestone slider from her instrument and securing it in her locket, Noah said, 'I'll sign the paperwork. Do you think we could do it without you hassling me about the thesis thing?'

'I'll stop hassling you when you agree to do it,' Alan said with a shrug. 'It's actuarially very simple.'

The queen frowned. '*Actually* is how that word is pronounced, Dear,' she said.

'*Actually*, Your Highness,' Alan said, 'I was attempting a bit of auditor's humour. An *actuary* is someone who compiles and analyses statistics. I would love to be an actuary. I dream about it … dealing with numbers all day in the most intimate way …' After a momentary pause, he continued, 'The word *actuarially* is the adverb related to the noun *actuary*.'

The queen's frowned deepened. Noah wasn't sure what distressed Queen Rosemary more, the thought of Alan's quasi-amorous fascination with numbers or the fact that she'd been given a grammar lesson by Mellifont's auditor.

'Alan,' Noah said, 'how about I sign those papers for you now?'

'Oh, that'd be super,' he replied, almost dropping his clipboard in his rush to get out of his chair.

'Here,' Sachin said, 'you can have my seat.'

'Great,' Alan said, barely waiting for the Major to vacate the ornately carved chair before planting himself on it.

'Don't get too comfortable,' Noah said. 'It's not a permanent arrangement.'

'I need to be comfortable,' he said. 'There is a fair bit to go through here.'

Noah sighed. 'Just tell me where to sign.'

'You need to read all the conditions,' Alan insisted.

'Life is too short to read all the conditions,' she said.

'Look,' Alan said, 'the legal team went to *a lot* of trouble to write this whole new section for *your* firestone slider. You're the only one who *owns* a piece of firestone – everyone else has to lease theirs.'

Noah's eyes narrowed. 'Surely all they'd have to do is take out the lease clause. They wouldn't actually have to write a whole new section?'

'And that's why you're not in the legal team, Noah. It's *your* firestone, true, but there is the issue of setting it in the slider. You need to acknowledge the owner of the patent that makes the slider possible. You need to agree not to—'

Noah raised her hands in surrender. 'Okay, I'll look over it. Just … stop talking.'

As Noah steeled herself to read a sentence or two of unintelligible legal jargon, Gillette yawned. 'Emir, I'm tired.'

'Okay, let's get you to bed,' Emir said. 'Your dad will be back tomorrow – we don't want you all tired and cranky now, do we.'

Gillette shook his head. 'I need my beauty sleep.'

Noah's eyes went straight to Emir and her quick reaction was rewarded. The look on his face was priceless.

'Beauty sleep?' Emir said. 'Really?'

'Really,' Gillette said as he slid off his chair and walked around the table to Noah. 'Night, Noah,' he said, patting her on the head.

Swatting his hand away, she said, 'Night, Gillette. See you in the morning.'

Emir bowed to the king. 'Excuse us, Sire.'

Tambian nodded. 'Goodnight, Gillette,' he said.

'Night, Your Highnesses, night all.'

Noah watched them leave and wondered how long it would take her to divest herself of Alan and join Emir in their quarters.

'So, Noah,' Alan said, 'are you sure you don't want to at least start *thinking* about a thesis topic?'

Noah winced. 'Alan, don't start.'

'Oh come on. We'd be great together. I've analysed it numerologically. It's meant to be.'

In her peripheral vision, Noah saw the queen shudder.

'I'm just not a numbers person, Alan,' Noah said. 'Fashion and music – that's pretty much me.'

'I know,' Alan said. 'But I will provide all the numerical expertise – you won't have to worry about that part. I'll have it covered.'

Noah signed the last place with a cross that she could find on the paperwork and handed it back to the auditor. 'Can we talk about this another time?'

Alan smiled hugely. His eyes disappeared and his nose looked even more snout-like. Noah cringed. She had the urge to stick an apple in his mouth and put him on a spit.

'Another time,' he said. 'I'll hold you to that.'

He put out his hand, which Noah accepted reluctantly. When he released his grip on her, he gathered up his clipboard and stylus and stood up.

'Well, my job here is done,' he said, 'so I will bid you all a good night.'

Once everyone had responded in kind, he waddled towards the door.

'Well, it's been a lovely evening, Noah,' Queen Rosemary said, 'but I think it's—'

Two guards burst into the stateroom, knocking Alan onto his backside.

'What is this?' Tambian demanded, rising from his chair. 'Is that any way to enter a room?'

'Apologies, Your Highness, forgive our intrusion,' one guard said as his companion struggled to pull Alan up off the floor, 'but we have come in haste, bearing an *urgent* message. You are required in the mine control room. There has been an … incident at t'Amos.'

Rising to his feet, the king said, 'What kind of incident?'

The guards exchanged a look. The older one spoke. 'You need to hear it from the mine controller.'

Chapter 3

'It's got to be an accident,' Alan said, wringing his hands, 'but what kind of accident?'

'Speculating isn't going to help,' Noah said, as she threaded a new spool of pale pink cotton onto her favourite sewing machine. 'We need to wait until Emir gets back.'

'I hope he gets here soon.'

'I wouldn't count on it,' Noah said. 'I suggest you get busy.'

'What can I do?'

Noah pointed to the sliding clothes racks that took up the entire northern wall of her well-ordered studio. After her appointment as the king's tailor, the palace carpenter had cursed her for the whole six weeks he'd spent designing, re-designing and constructing the mobile shelving system to her exacting specifications. She'd learned some very evocative epithets in their time together as he strove for new and emphatic ways to assure her that what she wanted was not actually possible.

'There is heaps to do in there,' she said. 'Take your pick.'

Alan's eyes widened. 'All these outfits are for the royal family … you would trust me with them?'

'Yes,' Noah said without hesitation. 'I've seen your knitting. It's of an incredibly high standard. I think you have a talent for needlework.'

'I am incredibly good at knitting,' he said without a shred of modesty. 'I guess I could do something. What are you working on?'

'Princess Catriona's new ball gown.'

'Looks extravagant.'

Noah looked at the river of pink silk that cascaded from her machine. 'It is extravagant,' she admitted.

'I'm not sure I'm at that level,' he said.

'You could always go outside and find Kane. I'm sure he'd love someone to play with.'

Alan frowned. 'It's dark out there.'

'He doesn't care. He'll play fetch anytime.'

A cold, wet nose against her arm alerted her to her Alsatian's arrival.

'Kane!' Noah cried. 'Where did *you* come from?'

Alan laughed. 'It's like saying his name makes him appear.'

Noah looked at her dog. 'Don't *do* that! You just took ten years off my life.'

The canine danced around in circles, hardly an act of contrition.

'Sit.'

Woof!

The Alsatian complied reluctantly and resorted to his ultimate weapon – looking immeasurably cute. Tongue lolling out the side of his mouth and his dark brown eyes shining brightly in the lamplight, Kane was a wound spring. His tail swished back and forth across the parquetry as he waited for the attention that was his due. Knowing that any further work on the new ball gown would have to wait, Noah stood up, leaving the silk spilling over her workbench frozen in time. Experience had taught her that attempting to whisk away the endangered garment would not deter her beloved pet; it would simply create a new form of entertainment for him.

'I'm going to take him outside,' Noah said as Kane dashed to the oak door – all that stood between him and freedom.

'Okay. I think I'll find something to do in here.'

'There is mending on the far shelf if you want to start there,' Noah suggested.

Alan waved. 'Right you are.'

Noah rested one hand on the recently-oiled wood while she released the iron bolt with the other. Her fingers tingled with the music in the timber. Despite the tree having been felled many years ago, its music survived in the wood, still vital – though few besides Noah would be able to detect it now. She let her hand linger, enjoying the warmth and calm the music brought her.

When she pushed the door open, Kane scooted through. She followed him out into the courtyard, the cool air embracing her tenderly. Dawn was still hours away but the two moons, both near full, provided ample light. Kane bounded along the cobblestone terrace that ran adjacent to the palace wall towards the sprawling expanse of manicured lawn while Noah wandered into the olbery. The nine magnificent olbera trees that ringed the courtyard outside her studio looked as spectacular at night as they did during the daytime. Though the moonlight didn't show the vibrant magenta and gold blooms to their full, the reflection off the large glossy leaves turned the intertwined canopies into a glowing silver crown.

She picked up a stick and threw it. Kane bolted after it.

Whatever had happened at t'Amos, Noah hoped that Emir's brother was okay. Jaxon was due home tomorrow and she didn't fancy having to tell Gillette that his father had been hurt … or worse. She pushed the thought aside. Hopefully it was just a problem with the equipment scheduled to perform the lifting of the firestone.

Kane returned with the stick wedged in his mouth. Dutifully, Noah took it. This time she hurled it towards the orange grove. *He's got me well trained,* she thought as she watched the stick arc in the moonlight. Kane was back within seconds and Noah threw the stick again. The game of fetch continued until the stick was slick with slobber and Noah could no longer bear to touch it.

'Noah?'

'Here,' she called, spinning round to see Emir making his way out of her studio with Alan in pursuit. 'What news?'

'You'd best sit,' he said, gesturing towards the stone bench in the centre of the olbery.

She sat, dreading what she was about to hear. Alan sat on one side of her with Emir on the other.

Without preamble, Emir said, 'The mine has been raided by goblins. They have commandeered the firestone and taken hostages.'

'Jaxon?' Noah said.

Emir nodded. 'He's among them.'

'Goblins,' Noah said. 'I hate goblins.'

Noah shuddered as memories of her first encounter with the grotesque creatures swam in her mind.

'Me too,' Alan said. 'They're the scourge of Talisker – repulsive and brutal. The hostages will not last long in their charge.'

Noah put her hand on Emir's knee. 'Are you going to tell Gillette?'

'Yes,' Emir said, his face grim.

Noah studied him. As always, Emir was calm despite the circumstances. It would take a miracle to save Jaxon and the other miners from the goblins, and if they couldn't, Emir would lose a brother and Gillette would be an orphan.

Fighting to focus on the big picture, Noah said, 'What's the plan?'

Kane galloped down the path and skittered to a halt in front of Emir. He sat down, craning his shaggy head for a pat.

'A full meeting of the Sovereign States Alliance in an hour,' Emir said as he stroked Kane's ears.

'Can I come?' Alan asked. 'I'd *love* to see Talisker's seven kings in one room.'

'No, Alan,' Emir said flatly. 'This is not a circus. The Alliance has a serious job to do. They need to come up with a united response to this attack.'

Noah raised her eyebrows. 'Good luck with that,' she said. 'They don't agree on much these days. I'm sure the only reason all the kings are here for the lifting of the firestone is because they don't trust each other to share it equally.'

'Noah, Tambian wants you there,' Emir said.

'Me?' Noah said. 'What am *I* going to do? And what will the other kings say?'

'Each king may bring whatever staff he or she deems necessary.'

'But I'm a tailor.'

'You're Dragonsbane, Noah. You're the 13th key. You know things about firestone.'

'This is about goblins, not the firestone,' Noah countered.

Alan's eyes widened. 'Are you going to tell them Noah is the 13th key?'

Emir stared at him but said nothing.

'Right,' Alan said after a long moment. '*That's* still a secret then.'

Noah nodded.

Alan smiled. 'That's good. I like the little club we have at the moment. I like knowing something that six of Talisker's kings don't know.'

'Being Dragonsbane won't be enough,' Noah said. 'They won't accept me.'

'You can go as Montana's assistant,' Emir said.

'Montana?' Noah said. 'She's here?'

'She'll be here soon,' Emir said.

'Technically the high priestess isn't part of the Alliance,' Alan said. 'Will they accept *her*?'

'Montana has faithfully served as Talisker's spiritual leader for over three hundred years, and no one's questioned her before,' Emir said.

'Could that change?' Alan asked.

'Not today, I don't think,' Emir said. 'Today, the kings are focused on goblins, hostages and the firestone. They won't want the distraction of arguing with the high priestess about her attendance at the meeting.'

'And besides,' Noah said, 'she's part elf and has her own army. Who'd argue with her?'

Alan frowned. 'I wouldn't put it past the *northern* kings, Noah. You know how contrary they've been lately.'

'Montana is *very* persuasive,' Noah said. 'They won't put anything past her.'

Chapter 4

Noah watched the kings from her seat under the window. The four kings present in the palace library were seated and talking among themselves at one of the three long tables. Tambian's collection of journals, books, scrolls and maps was assembled around the walls rather than on free-standing shelves on the floor as was customary in Leninstar's public libraries, and their collective, ancient knowledge seemed to watch over proceedings in silent judgement. Moonlight streamed through the window above her and glinted off the brass handles of the ladders opposite her. Noah considered climbing a ladder and finding something to read to keep herself occupied while she waited for the others to arrive, but decided against it.

When the oak doors at the far end of the room opened, Emir and Raven entered but there was no sign of the high priestess. Noah waved to them. Emir nodded to her before taking his place beside Tambian.

Raven walked over to his sister and sat beside her. 'Montana'll be here shortly, then we can get started.'

'I thought all the kings would be here, ready to start when she arrives.'

Raven's dark eyebrows arched. 'Come on, Sis, you didn't really think that, did you?'

'Well, it would make sense.'

'Of course it would make sense,' Raven said, 'which is exactly why they're *not* here. The northern kings don't worry about what's sensible. They're only worried about themselves.'

'It certainly seems that way.'

The library doors opened again, interrupting their conversation. This time the high priestess entered. Everyone stood.

'Morning all,' Montana said with a wave. 'Sorry I'm late.' Surveying the room, she added, 'Please tell me the others are on their way.'

A herald scuttled towards the door. 'Yes, Ma'am,' she said. 'I'll summon them now.'

'Good,' Montana said, making her way towards the conference table where four kings waited.

The high priestess stopped at the table only briefly before making her way to Noah. As Montana approached, Noah marvelled at her youthful complexion which, by virtue of her elfin heritage, betrayed only a fraction of her true age. Three hundred years in the top job and not a wrinkle to be seen. Her long auburn locks, untainted by even a hint of grey, were braided and coiled behind her head just above the collar of her lilac cloak.

The high priestess embraced her warmly. 'Good to see you, Noah. I'm sorry I missed your dinner. I really wanted to be here.'

'You don't need to apologise,' Noah said. 'I'm just glad you're here now.'

Montana released her. Turning to Raven, she said, 'Good to see you too, Commander.'

Raven smiled and wrapped his arms around her. 'Don't think I'm going to miss out on a hug. You can't play favourites.'

'I wouldn't dream of it,' Montana said.

Satisfied he'd made his point, Raven let her go. 'Well, girls, I'll leave you to catch up. I'll go and see what the others are up to.'

He put his fist over his heart and bowed his head to the high priestess before making his way to the table.

Montana looked around her. 'This is a big room; it's a pity it's not big enough to hold all the egos that will be in here.'

'I doubt there is a room of that size on all of Talisker,' Noah said. 'I can't believe they're being so petty. Lives are at risk.'

'Yes,' Montana agreed. 'This is a far cry from the Alliance of old. Back in the day, the seven kings were united in purpose and deed. When they came together great plans were made. There was camaraderie and respect, and their focus was on bettering their kingdoms and the lives of their subjects. Now there is deep division among them. Politics and intrigue have usurped diplomacy and reason. If they cannot unite in the face of this threat, I fear the Alliance will finally fold.'

Noah took a deep breath. 'Surely that won't happen.'

Montana turned and put her hand on Noah's shoulder. 'Do not think that just because it has endured for two thousand years, that it will remain. The division between the northern and southern states is growing. This firestone they have found could be a blessing or a curse. While I long to see the Sovereign States Alliance return to its former glory, I hold little hope that it will.'

'Don't say that. If you have lost hope, how are the rest of us supposed to keep faith?'

Montana squeezed her shoulder. 'I'm sorry, Noah. I feel that I can share my private thoughts with you and sometimes I forget that I shouldn't. Forgive me, I am old – self-indulgent. Melancholy stalks me.'

Noah regretted her remark. In Montana's long reign as high priestess, she'd had countless followers but few close friends. To protect her position, herself and those she cared for, she'd always kept her own counsel. Noah treasured her friendship; the last thing she wanted was to discourage Montana from speaking openly.

'Nothing to forgive,' Noah said as the library doors opened again, this time to reveal the three northern kings and their advisers.

King Arissa of Remenov, the youngest and only female of the trio, led her male counterparts. Noah watched the three kings as they strode to the table where their colleagues waited.

'That's our cue,' Montana said. 'Let's get a good seat.'

As they walked to the main table, Noah said, 'You know after all this time, I still can't get used to female kings. On Earth it is simple – men are kings, women are queens.'

'Of everything you've had to contend with since coming here, Noah, I'm surprised this sort of thing would bother you. I think it's very sensible. The ruler, whether male or female, is the king. If their spouse is female, they have a queen. If their spouse is male, they have a consort.'

When Noah sat down, King Arissa was the only one left standing. Her amber eyes blazed and layers of white face powder did nothing to conceal the heightened colour in her cheeks. Noah judged the king to be only in her early twenties, despite her bio claiming she was thirty-eight. Any ill-gotten credibility this obvious lie earned her quickly evaporated when she spoke.

'How did this happen?' King Arissa demanded.

Noah winced. King Arissa reminded her of a sulky teenager. Noah glanced around the table. The three female and four male kings had their advisers seated to their right. *I look like the high priestess's adviser,* she thought. Raven, like the other kings' soldiers, stood behind his liege. An overwhelming urge to flee surged through Noah. She didn't belong here – she'd rather have been anywhere but in this room. She'd rather have bandied thesis ideas with Alan than attend this meeting.

'This meeting will now commence,' Tambian declared. 'As you all know, the t'Amos mine has been overrun by goblins. They have commandeered the firestone and taken hostages. Our task is to formulate our response.'

'Again,' King Arissa said, 'I ask – how did this happen?'

'The goblins accessed the mine through secret tunnels,' Tambian said.

'So why weren't these tunnels guarded or blocked?' Arissa said.

'Because they were *secret* tunnels,' Tambian said coolly, 'meaning we didn't know about them.'

King Henrik of Orian massaged his temples as if he might reverse the effects of time and worry, and return the two silver streaks that marred his wavy ebony locks to their former shade.

'We have long known that the goblins are masters of the underground,' Henrik said. 'Their slinking ways make them well-suited to a life skulking around in the bowels of the world. Their knowledge of the ancient Desceran cities and tunnels is their one advantage over us.

This was most likely a newly-constructed tunnel – one purposely built to access the firestone.'

Chalinor's long-serving matriarch, King Tara stood up. 'I think we are wasting time if we focus on *how* it happened,' she said. 'We need to focus on what we're going to *do* about it. Retrieving the firestone and the hostages is in *all* our interests.'

A chorus of ayes rippled around the table.

Arissa glowered. 'What do the goblins want?'

'They demand a share of the stone in exchange for the hostages,' Tambian said.

Everyone spoke at once.

'No chance—'

'Outrageous—'

'Over my dead body—'

'Do they truly think we'll bargain—'

'I wouldn't give them a share for a thousand hostages, let alone twenty—'

'Silence!' Tambian growled.

'How much do they want?' Arissa asked.

'They want a share in accordance with how we've negotiated our seven-way split,' Tambian said.

'At the moment, they have the whole thing. Why do they want a split?' King Franco asked.

All eyes turned to the young king of Ylestar. Noah suspected that he was used to attention – especially from women. With his smooth, olive complexion and piercing green eyes, King Franco wouldn't have been out of place in a romance novel.

'They obviously can't use the firestone,' Tambian said. 'Maybe they want to bargain for access to our electricity network.'

'Be damned if I'll let those barbarians get their hands on electricity,' King Franco said.

'Here, here!' more than a few agreed.

'This firestone is the key to our electricity network,' Franco said, slamming his palm on the table. 'Nothing can jeopardise that. *Nothing.*'

'It's the last thing I want to see too,' King Henrik said. 'We need to get that stone back.'

'And the hostages,' Emir added.

'Of course it would be ideal if we could have both,' King Ulster put in, 'but the firestone is the priority. Twenty lives compared to hundreds of years' worth of electricity for everyone ... it is an easy equation.'

Noah's fists clenched at Ulster's words. She'd never warmed to the octogenarian King of Tchuganni and she wasn't alone. Though he was the senior king at the table, just out-ranking Tara, he was the least respected.

Melwick's king joined the conversation. 'We should be focusing on the hostages first,' King Mallory said. 'The goblins can't hurt the firestone and they won't risk destroying it since they want a share of it. I say we promise them a share so we get our hostages back.'

'Give them nothing,' Arissa countered. 'We should storm the mine site and retrieve the stone and whatever hostages we can.'

Mallory didn't speak but there was an obvious rebuke in her smouldering brown eyes.

'What if it isn't electricity they're after?' Franco said. 'What if they want to use the power of the firestone against us – as a weapon to destroy us. I agree with Arissa. We don't negotiate with goblins. What we need is a show of force – put the barbarians in their place.'

'I concur,' Ulster said.

'If we storm the mine, they will kill the hostages,' Tambian said.

'If we allow them a share of it,' Ulster said, 'I guarantee we'll lose a hell of a lot more than twenty hostages.'

Thinking of Jaxon and unable to hold her tongue any longer, Noah said, 'If we are prepared to sacrifice our people for a piece of stone, how are we better than the goblins?'

Arissa glared at her. 'Who are you to speak here?'

'Noah speaks as my assistant and as a Dragonsbane of Talisker,' Montana said. 'She has a right to be heard – and she has made an excellent point. If we do *not* put our people first, we *are* no better than the goblins. As High Priestess, I remind you that the Score dictates that we care for those who suffer. If we fail in this duty to our fellow human beings, we risk compromising the dragonsong.'

'It's not that simple, High Priestess,' Ulster argued. 'What if this is a trap? Part of some grander plan to overthrow us?'

'You give the goblins too much credit,' King Mallory said. 'They aren't that sophisticated. They seek to destroy us, yes, but they can only do so with swords and brute force. They have no talent to use the power of the firestone.'

'They've commandeered the stone,' Arissa reminded her.

'That doesn't mean they can manipulate its power though,' Henrik said.

'We cannot let them take the firestone,' Franco said. 'They will destroy us all. Under Nerili, Carai has grown bold. This is the one group we should not underestimate.'

'Who is Nerili?' Noah asked.

'A goblin leader,' Henrik replied. 'Carai is an underground goblin city in Orian. My soldiers have been trying to pinpoint its location to destroy it, but so far no luck. Nerili – he calls himself King Nerili – is much slipperier than any goblin I've ever encountered.'

Franco slammed his palm on the table. 'They kill your men, Henrik; they take your women as slaves. Now, they have our firestone.'

'They have no capacity to use it,' Henrik argued.

'But they *will*,' Ulster said. 'I say *we* use it against *them* first – teach them a lesson they won't forget.'

Into the prickly silence that followed, Noah said, 'As a Dragonsbane of Talisker, I remind you that firestone *cannot* be used as a weapon. This Alliance has agreed that firestone will be used only to produce electricity and to advance the Academy's use of raiki for the good of this world.'

'Given the circumstances, I say we revisit this,' Ulster said. 'It is clear that the goblins are more of a threat than we'd realised.'

'Regardless of the threat the goblins pose, we will not revisit this issue,' Tambian said. 'The use of firestone for destruction has consequences far beyond our war with the goblins and as such, we cannot entertain its use as a weapon. I would take this opportunity to remind members of the Alliance that there are penalties for using firestone this way.'

Noah looked at Montana. This was the division in the Alliance that the high priestess had spoken of. The northern states' desire to use the firestone to eradicate the goblin scourge had put them at odds with their southern colleagues. Three against four was a tight margin on such an important issue.

'I have a suggestion,' Montana said. 'Will the Alliance hear it?'

'I would like to hear it,' Tambian said.

Leaning forward in his seat, Henrik said, 'And I.'

'I will listen,' Tara added.

Mallory nodded her willingness to hear what the high priestess had to say while Arissa waved her acknowledgement.

'Might as well,' Franco said, folding his arms across his chest.

'Go ahead,' said Ulster.

'We should send a delegation to t'Amos to speak with the goblins face to face. It should be clear that we are prepared to negotiate but that any hostages or negotiators who are harmed – before, during or after negotiations – would render the negotiations null and void and the goblins would feel the full might of a human military response.'

'No,' Arissa said. 'We must not negotiate with goblins.'

Montana didn't acknowledge the young king, instead waiting for the others to respond.

'We would have to be assured that we'd be negotiating with this – Nerili,' Tara said.

'Well, if we're within arm's length of the goblin king, I say we run a sword through him and be done with this nonsense,' Ulster said.

Tambian frowned. 'They will simply find a new king and we'll have full-scale war on our hands. We'll lose a lot more than twenty hostages.'

'We've been at war with the goblins for two thousand years,' Franco said. 'In case you don't remember, the whole reason this Alliance exists is because of the goblins – the human race's united response to their arrival here. No one before us has managed to succeed in getting rid of them. Maybe this is *our* chance to wipe them out for good.'

Tara sighed. 'As Tambian said, we risk many more casualties that way.'

'We are already at war,' Ulster growled. 'We have been for millennia – the number of casualties is beyond counting. I know it sounds callous to risk these twenty hostages but what of the countless thousands that have perished at the hands of goblins in the past? Are their lives worth less? Do we not owe them to eradicate this curse? This is a sign,' he said, using his cane to push himself to his feet. 'This is a sign for us to act and to exterminate the barbarians for all time. High Priestess, it is naïve for us to think we can negotiate with these creatures. How can we expect them to honour an agreement? They have no honour; they don't know what it means.'

Noah glanced around the table. Arissa and Franco nodded their agreement while Tambian, Henrik and Tara wore their concern openly. Mallory was unreadable, her thoughts and emotions securely locked down behind her dark complexion. Most of the advisers gauged reactions around the table – with Emir the notable exception. His eyes were on Montana.

As Noah watched him, he leant over to whisper to Tambian. The king stroked his white beard as Emir spoke. When he finished, Tambian nodded.

'What is your decision?' Montana asked. 'Will we send a delegation to negotiate the release of hostages and the firestone? Those in favour?'

When four hands went up, King Arissa swore.

Franco spoke first. 'I pity whoever is going,' he said. 'They're as good as dead.'

'I am happy to chair it,' Montana said, 'as an independent intermediary.'

'I will go,' Tambian said. 'I would like to see this Nerili face to face.'

'And I,' King Henrik said.

King Mallory raised her hand. 'Count me in,' she said.

Both Ulster and Franco shook their heads.

King Tara said, 'I will remain here with Arissa, Ulster and Franco in your absence, Tambian.'

King Tambian nodded. 'That is good,' he said. 'I will take Emir with me.'

'So what will you offer them?' Arissa asked.

Tambian glanced at Emir. 'We will draw up an agreement offering them access to our electricity network in exchange for the safe return of the hostages and firestone.'

'They will get a share of the firestone over my dead body,' Arissa declared.

Tambian appeared to consider her words. Noah wondered if he thought it was an offer.

'We will offer them access to the electricity *network*,' Tambian said, 'but not a physical share of the firestone. If it's electricity that they want, it's electricity they'll get – but *no* firestone.'

Franco leaned forward. 'Do you think they'll accept it?'

'I don't know,' Tambian said, 'but we'll call their bluff. And if we appear to be negotiating, it might be enough to get us at least some of the hostages back.'

'I like it,' Mallory said. 'Let's draw up an offer.'

As King Arissa objected again to the idea of making any offer to the goblins, Montana leant in close to Noah. 'Noah, I want you to come with me to t'Amos.'

Noah recoiled in shock. '*What?* Why?'

'You're our firestone expert. It would help our negotiations if you were there. It sends a message that we are serious.'

'Dr Grainger should go,' Noah said. 'As Dragonsbane *and* a Doctor of Raiki, he's more qualified than me.'

'I'm also worried that the goblins might try to hide the firestone from us.'

'It's pretty big – even Grainger couldn't miss it.'

'Noah …'

'Montana – don't get me wrong – it sounds like great fun, but I just don't think I'm the right person to go.'

'Because?'

'Well, for one thing, I hate goblins.'

'We all hate goblins,' Montana said. 'Next?'

'Emir will object to me going.'

'Yes, he will, but I outrank him.'

'You'd go over his head?'

Montana smiled. 'I hope it won't come to that. To be honest – it'd be nice to have the support of a friend. And you're the best qualified for that.'

Noah groaned. 'Emir will still object.'

Patting Noah's hand, Montana said, 'Thanks, Noah. I really appreciate it.'

Chapter 5

Gillette frowned. 'But why do you *both* have to go?' he said.

Noah poured boiling water into the teapot, leaving Emir to answer Gillette's question.

'We think we have the best chance of rescuing your dad if we both go,' Emir said.

Gillette pushed his half-eaten plate of lavender marmalade scones aside.

'But what if you both die?' he said matter-of-factly. 'Then who'll look after me?'

'Raven will,' Noah said.

Staring at the remains of his breakfast Gillette said, 'When do you leave?'

'Tonight,' Emir said, 'after we tuck you into bed.'

'Can I come?'

Emir didn't hesitate. 'No.'

'Why not?'

'Firstly, because you have no skills that would be advantageous in our negotiations and, secondly, because the goblins would most likely see you as excellent leverage and take you hostage as well.'

Gillette nodded, though Noah wasn't sure that he actually understood what Emir had said. She had a suspicion that as long as the answer wasn't 'because you're a kid', he would accept it.

'I don't want to be an orphan,' he said.

Noah sat on the stool next to him and put her hand on his arm. 'We're going so you won't have to be.'

'Promise you'll bring Dad back,' he said.

'I can't do that,' she said softly. 'This situation is very difficult but we are taking the best people. If it is in our power to rescue him, we will.'

Gillette stared at her. 'If you're taking the best people, why isn't Raven going?'

Noah held his eye. 'Do you want the adult answer or the kid answer?'

'The adult answer,' he said.

'I can give you the adult answer,' she said, 'but if you need to discuss it with anyone after Emir and I have left, you can only talk to Raven about it. Okay?'

'Only Raven,' he said.

Noah nodded. 'Well, you know that all the kings are here in Leninstar City because King Tambian invited them all to be here for the lift. But now some of those kings disagree with this plan to deal with the goblins and that makes them a bit dangerous to have around, especially when King Tambian is going to the mine site.'

'Why doesn't he kick them out then?' Gillette asked.

'It is likely that would upset them even more,' Emir said, 'making the situation worse. And that's why Raven needs to be here. We're relying on the Royal Guard to keep everyone safe.'

Gillette pursed his lips. 'I'm going to practise my sword drills with Raven.'

'Make sure he teaches you to *think* as well,' Emir said. 'Being clever and having a cool head are just as important as being good with a sword.'

Raven chose that moment to appear in the kitchen doorway. Dressed in his full livery, he called, 'Morning all.'

Emir and Gillette stood up as the army commander strode across the room. Raven put his fist over his heart and bowed his head to Emir who returned the salute in kind. Noah smiled as her brother and Gillette then exchanged the same formal greeting.

'Hey, Sister,' Raven said, kissing Noah on the forehead.

'Hey, Brother.'

Raven looked at the counter. 'Whose breakfast is that?'

'Mine,' Gillette said.

'Why is it still on the plate rather than in your stomach?'

Gillette's shoulders sagged. 'I don't feel like eating. My stomach is all squirmy.'

'Well, you can't do sword drills if you haven't eaten enough,' Raven said, crossing his arms across the *infini* insignia on his leather breastplate.

Gillette reached for his plate. 'This is going to be the *best* fun.'

Raven's hand came down on the boy's shoulder. 'This is not a game, son – not something to entertain you for the day. This is serious business and I'm doing a serious job. Do you understand?'

'Yes, sir,' he said, scone in hand.

'I can't protect you twenty-four hours a day. You need to be able to look after yourself – and maybe others as well.'

'I understand,' Gillette said. 'Are you going to teach me to be clever too?'

Raven smiled at him. 'That is part of my plan. I'm glad you know that you need to be smart. That's good. Now take your scones and go and wait outside for me.'

Giving the traditional salute, Gillette said, 'Yes, sir.'

They all watched Gillette race out of the kitchen.

Raven stared at Noah. 'You better get this mess sorted out quickly. I don't how long we'll be able to keep this place contained.'

'Railcar out tonight, we'll be there midday tomorrow,' Emir said. 'Negotiate and then return by railcar. Hopefully we'll only be gone two days.'

'I hate to think what your terrible trio can dream up in that length of time,' Raven said.

'As long as you keep Franco busy in the barracks and Catriona tails Arissa for kingly tips, we should be okay,' Noah said. 'Surely Ulster can't do too much damage on his own.'

Rubbing his chin thoughtfully, Raven said, 'Cate's not overly fussy for her assignment, you know.'

Noah kept her thoughts to herself, leaving it to Emir to respond. 'She doesn't have to like it,' Emir said. 'It is what her king requires of her. It is his order.'

'But your idea?'

'Irrelevant.'

Raven let out a long breath. 'You better look after Tambian, my friend. If Cate becomes king, she will make your life a misery.'

'Noted,' Emir said dispassionately.

'I'll see you at dinner,' he said, saluting them both.

'Yes, you will,' Noah said.

Her stomach tightened in a knot as she watched her brother leave.

♪♫

Noah clenched her teeth to avoid inadvertently biting her tongue as the railcar rattled its way towards the t'Amos mine. Though primitive compared to the trains she had been used to on Earth, the mine railcar was the pinnacle of locomotive engineering on Talisker. Holding her handkerchief over her nose and mouth, she longed for the upgrade to electric rail. The celebrated coal that fired the engines and allowed speeds of up to seventy kilometres per hour wasn't content to confine itself to the engines. The wooden carriages had been lined with canvas to filter the worst of the soot but the black dust was unrelenting.

Flat-topped wooden chests ran the length of both walls of the carriage with another line down the centre. The padding tacked to the tops of the chests did an admirable job of protecting against splinters, but failed spectacularly in providing any real cushioning. Noah shifted in her seat trying to re-establish blood flow to her left buttock.

'Comfortable, Noah?' King Tambian asked, raising his voice to compensate for the clattering of the railcar.

Noah shook her head. 'Not really. I'll be glad to get off.'

'Well, in about an hour, you'll have your wish.'

Noah looked at her watch, though the insipid lighting in the carriage made it difficult to read. *Seven hours down,* she thought, *one to go.* She considered the group around her. Three kings and Talisker's high priestess sat across from her. Three royal advisers, including Emir, sat beside her. Though she'd worked in Tambian's palace for over a year and spent time with all of them, it still felt strange that she was accepted as part of such an elite group.

'Do you think Nerili will accept the offer?' Noah asked.

'I think he'll want to change it,' Tambian said.

'He'll want to add clauses to guarantee rights for his own ... citizens,' Henrik said.

Citizens, Noah thought. It was the word they'd agreed to use instead of 'barbarians' in their negotiations with Nerili but she couldn't get used to it. Citizens were people – humans – something goblins clearly were not.

'What do you know about the goblin king?' Noah said.

'Not much,' Mallory admitted. 'Like all goblins, he's secretive. And of course, his citizens go to great lengths to protect him. That makes it hard to get information about him.'

'He's made a bold play at the mine,' Noah said. 'He must be pretty confident that they can defend the firestone.'

'Either that, or he's really confident we'll agree to his demands to share it,' Montana said.

'What do you think makes him so confident?' Noah asked.

Tambian answered her question. 'That's what we're hoping to find out. This meeting is basically a reconnaissance mission. It's our best chance of getting some information we might be able to use to regain control of the mine.'

Noah put her hand on Emir's knee. 'We can't afford to fail. Gillette shouldn't lose his father too. He barely remembers his mother. It just wouldn't be fair.'

'Life isn't always fair, Noah,' King Tambian said.

'Yeah, I know *that*,' she replied, 'but being orphaned isn't something I'd wish on anyone.'

Gillette was not much older than she had been when she'd lost her parents and though they'd been dead for over eleven years now, she well remembered the pain of losing them.

'Well, if it is to be, he will be lucky to have you and Emir around,' Montana said gently.

'Let's just make sure that doesn't happen,' Emir said.

Tambian stood up. 'I'm going to check in with the soldiers. Anyone care to stretch their legs?'

Henrik and Mallory nodded their agreement and stood to follow the senior king to the adjoining carriage. Their advisers joined the procession, though being significantly older than their bosses, they were much less steady on their feet.

With more room on the seat Noah swivelled and lay down, resting her head on Emir's lap. She smiled at him as he put his hand on her forehead.

'Considering the group we've got here, I think we've given ourselves the best chance of success,' Montana said.

'I agree,' Noah said. 'Leaving the trouble-makers at home is definitely to our advantage.'

'Now, now, Noah,' Montana chided. 'Ulster, Arissa and Franco do have some legitimate concerns.'

'Maybe,' Noah said, 'but I don't trust them.'

'Because?'

'Because they're willing to sacrifice their own people.'

'War is a tough business, Noah.'

Noah frowned. 'You're taking their side?'

'No,' Montana said, 'I wouldn't be here if I was. I'm just saying, we have lost many people in this war. I can understand them wanting to end it with a decisive victory.'

'I can too,' Noah said quietly. 'We just want to get Jaxon and the other hostages out safely first.'

'We all want that,' Montana said, 'but you need to remember, Noah, kings think differently. They have to consider the big picture – and this is a very complicated picture.'

'Yeah, I know,' Noah said. 'I'm very thankful I'm not a king. I'm not made to make decisions like that. You might remember that I didn't want to come along – and that's why.'

Changing the subject, Emir said, 'I am interested to meet this goblin "king". Under Nerili, this group of goblins has become a real threat.'

'They seem more organised,' Montana said.

Emir rubbed his chin. 'It's more than that. They show … restraint. That's something we haven't seen from goblins before. Usually, it's attack, kill, pillage, take prisoners and retreat. This is different. They have a strategy and they appear to want to negotiate.'

'How does that make them more of a threat?' Noah said.

'Historically, they've been brutal, vicious and relied on their knowledge of the underground to escape,' Emir said. 'It's been simple and effective. If they're becoming more sophisticated though, it's going to be even more difficult for us to end this war.'

The conversation about goblins continued until the railcar started to slow.

'I'll be glad to get back above ground and wash my face,' Noah said as the brakes squealed their protest. 'My eyes are killing me.'

Before anyone could respond, a chest two down from Emir crashed open.

'You think *you're* uncomfortable?' Princess Catriona said as she struggled to extricate herself from the chest. 'How do you think *I* feel?'

Noah, Emir and Montana gaped at the unexpected sight of the dishevelled princess.

Catriona wobbled and grabbed for the side of the chest. 'Bit of help?' she asked tersely.

No one moved. The shrieking brakes provided the only answer until the connecting door to the next carriage opened and King Tambian froze in the doorway.

'Hello, Father,' Catriona said, stepping out of the chest now that the train had stopped. 'I've come to help.'

The king turned around to face those behind him in the adjoining carriage. 'Go out that way,' he said. 'Have the soldiers assemble the horses and meet us at the lift.'

Turning back to face his daughter, Tambian strode into the carriage and stopped in front of her. He glared at his daughter. Noah measured the king's heartrate by the pulses in the veins at his temples. She wouldn't have been surprised to see steel melt under that kind of scrutiny, but Catriona stood unflinching.

When at last Tambian did speak, it wasn't to his daughter but to Emir.

'Tie her up,' King Tambian said. 'We need to get going.'

Emir saluted. Catriona glared at him. 'You'll not lay a hand on me,' she said haughtily. 'I am the heir to the throne of Leninstar.'

Emir looked at Tambian.

'She defied a direct order from her king,' Tambian said. 'She is a prisoner. Use whatever force you deem necessary to detain her.'

The king turned, marched to the door and yanked it open. He stepped out without looking back. Noah looked at Catriona, almost feeling sorry for her. While the princess sorely needed to be put in her place, Noah hadn't actually wanted to witness it. Raven had said that Catriona wasn't happy about shadowing King Arissa in her father's absence, but Noah hadn't suspected she'd go to these lengths to avoid her assigned task.

Catriona looked around her. Since Emir and Montana outranked her, Noah was the obvious target.

'Don't you have anything better to do than stand there gloating?' she demanded.

Noah's empathy dissolved and she counted to three before she responded. 'I'm not gloating,' she said evenly. 'In fact, I'm not even inter-ested in you. I'm worried about my brother. You were supposed to keep Arissa busy. By coming here you've made Raven's job more difficult and more dangerous. If anything happens to him, I will hold you personally responsible.'

Noah turned to Emir. 'I'll wait for you outside.'

She walked to the door and jumped out into the voracious dark-ness of the tunnel. She couldn't see the ground but the crunch under her boots told her it was gravel. To her right, near the railcar's engine, the soldiers' torches gallantly battled the blackness, but victory was far from certain. Noah squinted, trying to gauge the distance between her and them. She shivered. The sooner they were above ground again, the better she'd like it.

At the sound of crunching gravel behind her Noah spun round, but the darkness revealed nothing. She cursed under her breath.

'That was impressive,' Montana said.

Noah frowned. She was relieved it wasn't Emir who'd caught her cussing – he'd certainly have reprimanded her. Montana usually ignored it; she'd certainly never complimented her on it.

'Really?' Noah said.

'Absolutely,' the high priestess replied. 'You really put Catriona in her place.'

'Ahh,' Noah said, belatedly recalling what she'd said to the princess.

'You did very well,' Montana said. 'Almost like Emir would have done it.'

'Almost?'

'Well, *no one* is quite as composed as Emir.'

'*Almost* is good enough for me,' Noah said. 'I'll take it.'

Montana slid her arm around Noah's. 'Let's join the others.'

Allowing the high priestess to lead her, Noah asked, 'Is someone going to stay here and guard her?'

'I think Tambian will leave a couple of his soldiers here.'

'Can we spare them?'

'Time will tell.'

Although they still had a five-hour ride above ground on horseback before they reached the mine, Noah's stomach fluttered at the thought of meeting the goblins. The contingent of twenty that was supposed to visit t'Amos would likely now be eighteen.

'Let's face it, though,' Montana said, 'if the goblins' intention is to capture us … they'd take twenty people as easily as they'd take eighteen. I don't think two people will make much difference.'

'I guess not. Are you nervous?'

'Yes,' Montana admitted.

'You don't sound like it.'

'I can't afford to. We can't show any weakness, Noah. Nor can we appear aggressive or emotional. This meeting needs to be very calm and controlled.'

Noah chewed her lip. 'Calm and controlled … not what I'm known for.'

'Just do what you did inside there with Catriona,' Montana said. 'That was perfect.'

Chapter 6

Behind King Tambian, Noah reined in her horse in a cloud of dust, her heart hammering in time with the hoof beats around her. The gigantic elderwood stakes of the t'Amos fort loomed overhead as the rest of the party pulled up around her. This site northwest of Seychelles had once been a quarry and the limestone dust stirred up by the horses swirled gloriously in the midday sun. Two goblin guards stood either side of the main gate, swords and shields in hand. Their large wooden shields bore a bronze inlay of an olluka tree. Noah looked right to the bastion at the far end of the front fence. At least half a dozen goblin archers stood guard in the hexagonal palisade.

'Welcome to t'Amos,' the guard to the left of the gate said.

The guards wore leather breeches and jerkins – a far cry from the loincloth-wearing creatures Noah had encountered before. But their improved fashion sense did nothing to enhance their appearance. They still looked like the aftermath of a thermostat malfunction in a wax museum.

'It seems highly inappropriate that you welcome us to our own mine,' Tambian said.

'I have my orders,' the goblin said.

Tambian sniffed. 'Indeed. Where is Nerili?'

'*King* Nerili awaits you underground,' the guard said. 'His personal guards will escort you to him.'

'How many?' Tambian asked.

'Three.'

'Only three?'

'Three,' the goblin replied.

'Then let's proceed,' Tambian said.

'Not so fast,' the goblin said. 'Only the kings and the high priestess may go down the mine – each with one assistant – and only the kings and high priestess may be armed.'

'And what of our companions?' Mallory demanded.

The goblin looked at her. When he spoke, his voice was calm. 'Your horses will be stabled and your soldiers can reside in the kitchen until you return.'

'They will keep their weapons,' Henrik said, a statement rather than a question.

The guard nodded once. 'Yes.'

Tambian looked to his fellow kings. Henrik and Mallory both nodded their acceptance of the terms.

'We will proceed,' Tambian said.

The goblin turned. 'Open the gates,' he called.

Noah's horse sidled left as the winches behind the walls ground into operation. She patted the stallion's neck as he shook his head to protect his ears from the hair-curling whine of the hoists. The wooden doors parted slowly and Noah strained to peer into the gap, eager for her first glimpse of the famous mine. Despite her trepidation at dealing with goblins and the worry about the hostages trapped below, the lure of actually seeing the firestone she had located excited her. She wondered if she would get a chance to see it.

Emir pulled up beside her as she stared through the breach. 'You ready for this?'

'Ready as I'll ever be,' Noah said. She examined the walls again. 'The fort is bigger than I'd imagined.'

'Yes,' Emir said, rubbing his chin. 'In hindsight, maybe we'd have been better off spending more effort fortifying the underground.'

The massive walls surrounding the fort had successfully protected the mine precinct from human thieves and bandits as well as a handful of goblin raids, but had failed to account for the goblins' knowledge of secret underground tunnels. When the gates were fully open, the goblins signalled for the contingent from Leninstar to dismount and follow them.

As Noah led her horse over the threshold, she shivered. She didn't know if it was her imagination or not but the air seemed cooler inside the compound, like walking into a crypt.

The mineshaft entrance punctuated the centre of the compound like a giant navel, and a dozen armed goblins circled the gaping hole. Scanning the perimeter fence, Noah noted the stone buildings with thatched roofs that lined the eastern and western walls. The stables and equipment sheds were easily identifiable. Noah guessed that the long, squat structure on the western wall was a dormitory while the one next to it was the kitchen. Another bastion stood diagonally opposite the one they'd passed as they entered, occupying the north-western corner of the compound with silent menace.

A door to the building closest to them opened and a stream of goblins emerged. They too wore jerkins and breeches like their comrades at the front gate and were similarly armed. When they reached the group from Leninstar, three goblins stood to the front while the others formed up in four rows of six behind them.

The middle goblin in the front row addressed them. 'I am Liah.' He motioned to his left. 'This is Shar and this,' he said, gesturing to his right, 'is Frost. We are King Nerili's personal guards and will escort you underground to meet with him. Your kings and high priestess will come with us. Please move to one side.'

Two goblin soldiers came forward to take the royal horses.

'We will stable them,' one of the goblins said to Tambian.

As Tambian, Henrik and Mallory relinquished their horses and moved to one side with Montana, Noah studied Nerili's guards. They were tall – at least a head taller than Emir – and powerfully built. Though their faces showed more symmetry than other goblins Noah had encountered, she still struggled to not gag at the sight of them. Beady, dark orbs like the chunks of coal she'd used to decorate snowmen as a child were pressed either side of a massive wedge of a nose. Long pointed ears stuck out perpendicular to their bald heads. But it was their teeth – their fangs – that were truly terrifying. Seeing them, Noah understood the goblins characteristic speech impediment. The necessity of keeping their tongues well behind the sharp points meant that pronouncing an 's' sound was problematic and sounded more like 'sh'.

Liah spoke again. 'The attendants who accompany you must surrender their weapons.'

Noah and Emir unbuckled their sword-belts, as did Mallory's and Henrik's advisers. They handed their swords to the next two goblin guards that presented themselves. Handing her sword to a goblin made Noah queasy. While these ones showed uncharacteristic civility, she knew the brutality goblins were capable of.

'Now,' Liah said, 'your soldiers will see their horses to the stables and then they will be escorted to the kitchens. It is King Nerili's intention that no blood be spilled here today, but that will be up to you. As a show of good faith, your soldiers will retain their weapons. But I give you this warning – any attack initiated by you will be met with a swift and bloody response. Do I make myself clear?'

'Very clear,' King Henrik said. 'Though we give you this warning – if *you* attack *us* we will provide a swift and bloody response.'

Liah nodded once. 'I think we understand each other. Let us go.'

Noah took a step closer to Emir. 'That's a big call.'

'What's that?'

'That we understand each other,' Noah said.

Emir looked at her. 'May I give you some advice, Noah?'

'It's okay,' Noah said, 'I know what you're going to say.'

He raised an eyebrow. 'Yes?'

'That I should keep my mouth shut for the duration of this visit.'

'Yes,' he said. 'That pretty much covers it.'

'I make no promises.'

'I didn't think you would.'

As Leninstar's soldiers departed for the stables with their horses, most of the goblin guards followed them. Only Liah, Shar and Frost remained.

Shar spoke for the first time. 'I will tell you that King Nerili will also be armed. So four of *you* will be armed, four of *us* will be armed. Are you willing to proceed?'

'Yes,' Tambian said. 'Let's go.'

'Follow us,' Shar said.

He and Liah turned, leaving the company to follow them to the shaft. Frost brought up the rear.

Liah opened the gate to the wooden platform. 'This lift will take nearly an hour to get us to where our king awaits.'

Trapped on a lift with three goblins for an hour, Noah thought as she shuffled aboard. She made a solemn promise to herself that she would not complain about the sooty railcar ride on the way back to Leninstar.

Frost put his hand on the metal lever. 'Once the hoist is in motion, we must continue at least until the first stop – about two kilometres down. Are you ready?'

The three kings looked at each other and nodded.

'We are ready,' Tambian said.

Noah braced herself for the inevitable lurch as the platform began its descent. She looked at Montana whose face was a mask of calm. Perhaps sensing Noah's scrutiny, the high priestess turned to her and winked. Noah forced a smile, wondering what was going through Montana's mind. For three hundred years, the high priestess had promoted harmony in accordance with the Score – Talisker's spiritual book. She'd never negotiated with goblins before though. Meeting with a goblin king was new territory.

Noah wondered what story they'd have to tell when they returned to Leninstar. If they returned to Leninstar.

♪♫

The highly decorated goblin stood when they entered the underground mess. He wore a coiled silver crown on his bald head. A long, blue velvet cloak, pushed back over his broad shoulders revealed tailored and embroidered hide breeches and a jerkin. Silver bands encircled his fore-arms while a long sword in a jewelled sheath hung from his right hip.

Noah suppressed a shudder. She was glad Emir was at her side. He'd had plenty of practice fighting goblins. If things went sour, he'd be indispensable – even without his sword.

'I am King Nerili of Carai,' the goblin said. 'I thank you for coming.'

Montana responded on behalf of the group. 'I am Montana, High Priestess of Talisker,' she said. 'With me are King Tambian of Leninstar, King Mallory of Melwick and King Henrik of Orian.' The three kings nodded in turn as they were announced. 'We have also brought our assistants – Noah Chord, Emir Delorian, Yuri Gemmel and Daved Li.'

The goblin king gave a curt nod. 'I assume my guards have introduced themselves to you.'

'Yes,' Montana replied. 'They have.'

'Then might we get started straight away?' Nerili said.

'I would see the hostages first,' Tambian said.

'I expected you would,' Nerili replied. 'Follow me.'

The group followed the goblin king to the far end of the mess hall. He opened the wooden door to reveal a corridor. The corridor was punctuated on either side with more wooden doors.

'They are here in the dormitories,' Nerili said as his three guards positioned themselves at even intervals along the passageway. 'Feel free to open any door. You may open all of them if you wish, but only two at a time.'

Tambian looked at King Mallory. 'Montana and I will take this side,' he said, pointing to his left. 'You and Henrik take the other side.'

'Of course,' Mallory said.

Noah stood behind Tambian as he pulled back the bolt on the first door. The king pushed the door open. Noah peered into the dim interior. Far too much was being asked of the lone candle inside. Though the room was small, it was a lot to expect the candle to spread its luminance that far. The miner lying on his cot opened his eyes. On recognising his visitor, the young man leapt from his bed and bowed to his king.

'Your Highness,' he said. 'My apologies. I wasn't expecting you.'

'At ease,' Tambian said. 'What is your name?'

The young man stood up. 'Simon, Your Highness.'

'Are you well, Simon?'

Despite the grime smeared across his face and the dark rings under his eyes, Simon said, 'Well enough, Sire. I have been fed and watered and my'—he glanced at the bucket in the corner—'facilities have been attended to. Are you here to take us home?'

'We're working on it,' Tambian said. 'Is there anything you need?'

'It'd be nice if they put the locks back on the *inside* rather than the outside …' he said with a wry smile.

Montana said, 'I see you've kept your sense of humour, Simon.'

Simon shrugged. 'It's about all I've got here at the moment, Ma'am.'

'Stay strong,' Montana said. 'We're going to check on the others.'

Simon bowed before lying back down on his cot. Tambian closed the door and Frost slid the bolt across, checking that it was secure.

As they moved on to the next door, Noah fell in beside Emir. 'I hope we see Jaxon,' she said.

'Well,' Emir said, keeping his voice low, 'if he's on this side, we'll see him. Tambian will open every door.'

When Tambian opened the fourth door, they found Jaxon sitting on his cot.

Noah slipped past Tambian. Jaxon looked from face to face as he stood up. 'I must be dreaming,' he said. 'You can't all really be here.'

'We're here,' Emir assured him.

'You're taking us home?'

'We're here to negotiate,' Emir said, embracing his brother. 'Once we know everyone's unharmed, we'll get started.'

Jaxon frowned. 'How's Gillette?'

'He's worried about you but he's putting on a brave face,' Noah said. 'Raven is keeping him busy.' She looked him up and down. 'So how are they treating you?'

'Better than I'd expected,' he said. 'When I saw those goblins swarm into the mine, I thought I was done for, for sure. But they haven't laid a hand on me. I've even been fed.'

Noah said, 'That's because they want something.'

Jaxon nodded. 'A share of the firestone. I know.'

'I am glad you are well, Jaxon,' Tambian said, 'but we'd best keep moving – hopefully we'll be back soon with good news.'

Jaxon bowed. 'Thank you, Your Highness.'

As the king turned to leave, Noah hugged Jaxon. He put both his arms around her and rested his cheek on top of her head. With the side of her head pressed against his chest, Jaxon's elevated heartbeat echoed in her ear. He took a deep breath and exhaled slowly.

'I am glad you're here,' he said as her released her.

'I wish I could say the same,' Noah said, 'but it's creepy down here.'

'It's only creepy because there are goblins here now,' Jaxon said. 'It was fine before.'

'Noah,' Tambian said, 'we must keep moving.'

Noah pulled back and looked Jaxon in the eye. 'We're doing everything we can.'

Tambian continued along the corridor, speaking to every hostage in turn before returning to where Nerili waited.

'Are you satisfied they are unharmed?' Nerili asked.

King Tambian looked to his fellow kings who nodded.

'Yes,' King Tambian said. 'But before we discuss the terms of their release, I would see the firestone.'

'It is a ten-minute hoist ride,' Nerili said.

'Yes,' Tambian said. 'I understand that.'

Nerili nodded to his guards. 'Prepare the hoist.'

The three goblins saluted and left.

The goblin king made a sweeping gesture with his arm. 'After you,' he said.

King Henrik led the way this time while Noah waited with Montana until last. As they walked through the tunnels, Noah marvelled at the effort and ingenuity that had allowed the miners to tunnel down this far to reach the firestone.

Nerili dropped back to walk alongside her. 'You must be very proud, Noah.'

Her heart thudded in her chest. 'I'm not sure what you mean.'

'You must be proud that the firestone you found is almost ready to be lifted and put to good use.'

Noah risked a glance in his direction. *How does he know I found the firestone?* she wondered.

'You're surprised I know you're the one who located it?'

Unwilling to admit it, Noah said, 'I just hope that it *is* put to good use. I am worried that it might be used the wrong way.'

'Yes,' Nerili said. 'I think you're right to worry about that.'

Noah held his gaze for a moment before the goblin strode ahead to catch up with Tambian.

'What do you make of that?' Noah said to Montana when he was out of earshot.

'I'm not sure,' Montana said, 'but I don't think he'd openly admit that they'd misuse it. More likely he thinks that *we'd* use it against *them.*'

Once they were all on the platform again, Liah set the hoist in motion. Adrenaline surged through Noah. She was only minutes away from seeing the biggest piece of firestone ever found on Talisker, in very unlikely company. Trying to be discreet, she looked at those around her as the lift passed the four kilometre mark. Emir looked composed as always, as did Montana. Though Tambian, Mallory and Henrik were grim-faced, they maintained a calm demeanour. She looked at Yuri and Daved who, as expected, wore the facades of veteran advisers. Catching Yuri's eye, Noah smiled at her. The old woman gave her a nod as Noah turned her attention to the goblins. Considering the barbaric creatures she'd encountered in the past, it was difficult for her to see a king and three elite guards. So far they'd shown no hostility, but Noah wondered how long it would last.

The lift stopped and the gate squeaked as Nerili opened it. He took one of the oil lamps and stepped off the platform, following the narrow passageway to the left without looking back. The group walked single file along the tunnel for about a hundred metres before a light twinkled tantalisingly ahead in the gloom. At the end, the tunnel widened slightly but even crammed shoulder to shoulder, only half the company could view the firestone at a time.

Nerili stood back to let Tambian, Mallory and Henrik past.

'Noah,' Tambian said, 'come here.'

Noah squeezed past Montana, Yuri and Daved and took Emir's hand as she got to him.

'Come with me,' she whispered to him.

Emir nodded.

Noah's skin tingled as she took her place next to her king.

'Wow,' she said, clutching Emir's hand a little tighter.

The massive pear-shaped piece of firestone lay on its side in a pit on the floor. The excavation of the dirt and stone around it was almost complete. Noah tipped her head to one side. She estimated that the stone was longer than she was tall and were she to try wrapping her arms around it, her hands wouldn't meet on the other side. As she gazed into the stone, she felt like she was looking into forever – seeing all of time. *If I could decipher the patterns in the stone,* she thought, *I would understand* **ALL.**

Letting go of Emir's hand, Noah took a step forward and knelt in front of the firestone. Tentatively, she reached out towards it. When she was within a centimetre of touching the dragonscale, Noah hesitated. The colours inside the firestone shifted, then swirled. Disoriented, Noah closed her eyes and took a deep breath. She was aware of her blood, felt its rising heat as it tracked faster and faster through her veins. *I'm the 13th key, firestone is in my blood.* Noah opened her eyes. She looked at where her hand should have been but she couldn't see it.

I can feel it, she thought as she balled her hand into a fist and then waved it about. *I know it's there.*

Emir distracted her. 'Noah?' he said, catching her wrist. 'Did you burn yourself?'

She stared at him as he knelt beside her and sandwiched her hand between his.

'No,' she said, putting her other hand on top of his. 'It just felt … strange.'

His eyes searched hers. 'I think that's enough for today,' he said. 'Your sensitivity to firestone makes you vulnerable. I think it was unwise to bring you this close to it.'

'I really wanted to see it though,' Noah said, letting him help her to her feet.

'Well, you've seen it now. Time to go.'

'What happened to her?' Nerili asked. 'Is she hurt?'

Montana moved to stand beside Noah. 'She'll be fine,' she assured the goblin king. 'We just need to move her away from the firestone.'

Nerili tapped his talons on his sword sheath. 'Are all Dragonsbanes this sensitive to firestone?'

'Given that we've never had one this close to a piece of dragonscale this size, it's difficult to say,' Emir said.

'I suppose,' Nerili said, 'anyone who can perceive the location of a piece of firestone so accurately from so great a distance, must be *particularly* sensitive.'

Noah shivered. *She* was in no danger from the firestone but the same couldn't be said for her secret.

'This is a powerful stone,' Noah said, 'and I won't be the last to feel its effects. Take it to Mellifont and I'd bet one out of every fifty adepts would have a similar reaction.'

Tambian stared at her for a long moment before turning to Nerili.

'I am satisfied that our people are unharmed and the stone is intact,' he said. 'It is time to discuss terms.'

'Okay,' Nerili said. 'Shall we return to the mess hall?'

Tambian nodded. 'Yes.'

Chapter 7

Noah put her tray of fruit and nuts down on the table and Emir placed a loaf of bread on either side. Yuri and Daved distributed goblets and water pitchers while Nerili's guards farmed out plates and knives. The food was basic, a reflection of the circumstances. This was neither a celebration, nor a meal to be savoured. This was necessary sustenance for negotiations between sworn enemies. Survival food. Simple fare – easy to swallow, which was more than could be said for the discussion to come.

Noah took her seat beside Montana at the long table, which could have seated another eighty or ninety people by her reckoning. Liah sat across from her with his fellow goblins. *Them against us,* Noah thought as she picked at some fruit and nuts and put them on her plate. She wasn't hungry – nerves suppressed her appetite – but she needed to stay sharp.

Tambian spoke first. 'We have come to reclaim our people and our firestone,' he said. 'What is it you want?'

'I seek a share of the firestone for my state,' Nerili said.

'We don't recognise your state,' Henrik said.

'I'm aware of that,' Nerili said, 'but if you want your stone and your people back, I'm sure you could find a way around that.'

'What do you want the firestone for?' Tambian asked.

'Electricity,' Nerili said.

'But you have no infrastructure,' Mallory argued.

'Not yet,' Nerili said, 'but that is our goal.'

Tambian reached into his pouch and took out a folded piece of parchment. 'If that is indeed the case, then this is our offer,' he said, handing the paper to the goblin king.

Without taking his eyes from Tambian, Nerili accepted the paper and unfolded it. Only when it was flat on the table did he look at it. Noah knew that every move Tambian made was planned and calculated. Handing Nerili the document was no accident. It was a test – a test to see if he could read. Noah watched him. Nerili scanned the lines from left to right. He appeared to be reading.

'For the benefit of my guards,' Nerili said, 'I will read aloud.'

'Fine,' Tambian said.

Nerili picked up the paper from the table and read.

Offer of access to Talisker's electricity network

Subject to ratification by a full meeting of the Sovereign States Alliance (the Alliance), the city of Carai is offered access to Talisker's electricity network on the following conditions:

1. *All firestone remains the property of the Alliance.*

2. *All infrastructure relating to electricity generation is constructed by, operated by, and remains the property of the Alliance. A monthly fee is payable in relation to this service. Carai agrees to pay the Alliance as per schedule attached (Appendix A).*

3. *All wiring from the generator is Carai's responsibility – construction and costs.*

4. *All electrical infrastructure and appliances in Carai are Carai's responsibility.*

5. *For points 3 and 4, equipment and appliances may be sourced from the Alliance for an agreed fee.*

6. *All goblin hostilities towards humans must cease. Any of the following will render the above offer null and void:*

   a. *Attempted theft of firestone by a goblin or goblins.*

   b. *Damage to electrical infrastructure (property of the Alliance) perpetrated by a goblin or goblins.*

  c. *Abduction and incarceration of any human by a goblin or goblins.*

  d. *Threats or injury to, or death of any human at the hand of a goblin or goblins.*

 7. *Any breaches of point 6 will result in cancellation of electricity supply.*

When Nerili was finished, he put the paper down. 'You don't want us to have a physical share of the firestone,' he said.

Montana spoke this time. 'That is correct,' she said. 'If you are true to your word and it is electricity that you want, then it's electricity you will get. That is our offer to you.'

Nerili tapped his talons on the table. 'Point 6 says that all goblin hostilities towards humans must cease. I would require a clause that makes the same demands of humans towards goblins – all hostilities must cease.'

'We can add that,' Montana said.

Nerili nodded before slicing a segment from an apple. He put it in his mouth and picked up the parchment again, studying it as he chewed.

'I think,' he said, 'that I would feel more comfortable if we had a physical share of the stone as well.'

'But if electricity is your goal …' Montana began.

'Electricity is our *primary* goal,' Nerili said holding up his index finger to emphasise his point.

'Perhaps you should enlighten us as to your *other* goals,' King Mallory said.

'Raiki,' Nerili said.

Noah leaned forward, resting her forearms on the table. 'Raiki?' she said. 'What do you know about raiki?'

Nerili's responses surprised her. This was not some witless barbarian with whom they bargained.

'I have scores of adepts in Carai, Noah,' the goblin king said. 'They use the same kinds of sliders that you would be familiar with from your time in Mellifont. As the adepts at the Academy do, we would like to use *firestone* sliders as well.'

Noah could feel Montana's eyes on her but she kept her gaze on Nerili. It was a legitimate reason to want a physical share of the firestone but she couldn't accept that goblins would be willing to use raiki, much less be capable of performing it. She wanted to dismiss his claim but she thought of Jaxon … and Gillette.

'If we were to add a clause to our offer for the use of firestone sliders,' Noah said, 'your … citizens would first have to train to the level of Major at Mellifont and then they *could* be issued with a slider.'

'With no limit?'

'There would be a limit,' Noah said.

'Of?'

Noah looked to Montana. 'The Academy is proposing ten Majors per state – as a long term goal.'

Montana nodded and turned to King Tambian. 'We could apportion on a population basis? Perhaps one or two?' she suggested.

Nerili snorted. 'You're not apportioning sliders on a population basis for *your* states. Why should we accept this?'

King Henrik put up his hand. 'We haven't actually offered you anything yet. How do we know you wouldn't use its power against us?'

'Likewise,' Nerili said. 'How do *we* know it is not your intention to use it against *us*?' He leaned forward. 'This is part of our motivation for commandeering the stone. Yes, we want a share of it but we also want an assurance that it won't be used against us.'

'We said we'd update our offer,' Mallory said, 'to include a clause that required humans to cease hostilities against goblins. That's our assurance.'

'That will be little comfort when we're all dead,' Nerili said. 'With that amount of firestone you could wipe us all out. No, you can offer what you like but we do not trust you to keep your promise.'

'Well,' Tambian said as he rubbed his silver beard, 'it's obvious that you would trust our promises about as much as we would trust yours – not at all.'

'Correct,' Nerili said. 'Promises are empty. I see only one possibility.'

'What's that?' Tambian said.

'That you recognise the goblin state of Carai and admit us to the Sovereign States Alliance,' Nerili said.

Noah stared at the goblin king as she awaited Tambian's response. She hoped Tambian didn't say, 'Over my dead body'. Down here, that might be considered an invitation.

To Noah's surprise, Mallory was the one to respond.

'Why would you seek to join the Alliance?' Mallory asked. 'The only reason I can see is that you want to bring us down from within. Why should we agree to that?'

Noah looked at the King of Melwick, wondering if she had foreseen Nerili's proposition.

'That is not our goal,' Nerili said. 'We want peace.'

'And why should we believe *that*?' Henrik said. 'Goblins have been butchering our people for centuries.'

'And the same can be said of you,' Nerili said. 'Our races have been at war for over two thousand years. There have been heavy losses on both sides. We see this firestone as an omen – a chance for peace and freedom. If we are united in one Alliance, there will be no more war.'

No more war. It was a grand idea. It seemed too good to be true. Noah's mother had told her that if something *seemed* too good to be true, it probably *was* too good to be true.

'We cannot grant you that today,' Tambian said. 'This would require a full meeting of the Alliance.'

'Send a message from the control centre to your fellow kings,' Nerili said. 'Have them join us here as a matter of urgency.'

Montana spoke. 'A summons of this type will win you no favour,' she said. 'The kings should return to Leninstar. This requires delicate negotiation.'

'Ask them to come here for the lifting of the firestone,' Nerili said.

'They will suspect a trap,' Emir replied. 'After two thousand years of war, do you really think all Talisker's kings will congregate in one place that is under goblin control?'

'I will release five of the prisoners as a show of faith,' Nerili said. 'The rest will be released once negotiations are settled on our joining the Alliance.'

The kings bristled. Mallory spoke. 'Do you think bullying us like this is the way to win favour? You say you want peace, but this is not what I see.'

'We have no other options, Your Highnesses,' Nerili said. 'Is there another way we could win favour? Please, tell me.'

'Release all the hostages,' Tambian said.

Nerili frowned. 'And trust you? There is no trust here – on either side. No, we do not trust that you will negotiate with us further if we release all your people now. You can take five hostages now … or fifteen if you're willing to leave Montana and Noah here.'

Stay here? Noah stared at the goblin. *Did he really just say that?*

'What fresh treachery is this?' Henrik demanded. 'What makes you think we'd agree to that? Explain yourself!'

Nerili nodded and waved demonstratively. 'I understand your reluctance to admit us to your Alliance. You think of us as mindless barbarians, vicious beasts. I think you need to see what my state has to offer. I plan to take Montana and Noah to Carai – to show them around. Then, I will personally escort them back to Leninstar. They can report what they saw and we can negotiate further.'

'You planned this all along,' Henrik accused. 'You planned to take more hostages – high profile hostages – at this meeting.'

'I planned to negotiate a *swap*,' Nerili said.

'*You're* going to come to Leninstar?' Mallory asked.

'Yes,' Nerili replied, 'and I expect to speak before a full meeting of the Sovereign States Alliance.'

'Will you guarantee their safety?' Tambian said.

Nerili tapped on the table. 'No.'

One of Tambian's eyebrows arched. 'No?'

Nerili shook his head. 'There are no guarantees, but you should understand this – it is my intention to join your Alliance. I will do any-thing – *anything* – within my power to achieve that. I need them back in Leninstar *alive* to report what they've seen. There is *nothing* more important to me than that.'

'When do you plan to be in Leninstar City?' Tambian asked.

'Ten days from now,' Nerili said. 'It's three days from here to Carai, four days from there back to Leninstar. That leaves three days in my city. That will be long enough.'

Tambian sat perfectly still. 'We will take five hostages in return for your consideration of our offer to join the electricity network.'

'I will go to Carai,' Montana said.

'Montana, you …' Tambian began.

The high priestess smiled.

'… are impossible,' he finished.

Montana was not subject to any king's order. If she wanted to go, no one could stop her.

'I will stay instead of Noah,' Emir said.

'No,' Nerili said. 'Noah is the one I need.'

'Why?' Emir asked.

With a fearsome talon, Nerili traced a figure of eight on the table. 'She is best qualified to judge and report on our raiki facility.'

Noah inhaled deeply. This was worse than she'd imagined. More annoying than the fact that they discussed her as if she weren't here, was the fact that she couldn't speak in her own defence because she didn't know what to say. She didn't want to go to Carai, but she didn't want Montana to go alone either.

'Noah,' Tambian said. 'Do you want to go to Carai?'

Noah froze. *Is he actually giving me a choice?* she wondered. *He's the king. He could just order me to go. Or order me not to. I think I liked it better when he talked about me like I wasn't here.*

Noah looked at Emir. 'No,' she said slowly. 'I don't want to go to Carai.'

Nerili tapped on the table. 'Well, that leaves—'

'Noah,' King Tambian said, raising his hand. '*Will* you accompany Montana to Carai?'

Folding her hands in her lap, Noah avoided Montana's gaze. The high priestess had asked her to come to t'Amos as a friend, but could she expect Noah to follow her into a goblin city? As high priestess, Montana's duty was to Talisker. As King Tambian's tailor, Noah's duty was to the royal family's wardrobe. Montana was a seasoned fighter. Noah was not. If they got into trouble in Carai – which was highly likely – Noah would be more of a hindrance than a help. *It's not logical for me to go,* she thought.

'Noah?' Tambian said.

Noah sighed. This wasn't about logic. 'I'll go.'

Tambian nodded. 'Ten days,' he said. 'We'll see you in Leninstar in ten days.'

Chapter 8

Emir put his hands on Noah's shoulders. 'Noah, why?'

'You know why,' she said.

While the hostages were selected and released for return to Leninstar, Noah had a precious few moments to spend with Emir.

'You're impossible, you know that?' he said. 'And what if Jaxon isn't one of the men released?'

Noah didn't think Jaxon would be released but didn't say so. If Nerili were keeping so few hostages, he'd certainly keep the ones that would give him the most leverage. 'There'll still be more going home than there would have been.'

'And two more staying,' he said, taking her hand and squeezing it between his. 'How do you expect me to walk away, get on the railcar and leave you here?'

Noah didn't say anything – even if there was anything she could think of to say, it wouldn't have got past the hot lump in her throat.

Eventually, she managed to say, 'How about a hug?'

Emir pulled her close to him. She closed her eyes, enjoying the warmth of his body.

Without releasing her, he said, 'What happened to you down there? With the firestone, I mean.'

A picture of the massive piece of dragonscale flashed in Noah's mind. Her skin tingled. 'It was strange,' she said. 'Did you see the colours in the stone move?'

'No,' he said. 'I didn't see them move.'

'To me, they were swirling and the light was pulsing.'

'Interesting.'

With her head against Emir's chest, she listened to his heartbeat. The syncopated rhythm soothed her. 'Could you see me?' she asked. 'All of me?'

Pulling back, he said, 'Yes. Why would you ask that?'

'When I put my hand up in front of the stone, I couldn't see it. It was invisible. I could feel the firestone in my blood. It was racing through my body, reacting to the dragonscale. I could see the firestone but not me. It's like my body wasn't there – wasn't real enough to see – only the firestone.'

Emir exhaled slowly. 'The 13th key.'

Noah nodded.

'Lucky no one else saw that,' he said.

'Yeah, I know. That'd be game over.'

Montana arrived with one of Nerili's guards as her shadow. 'Bad news,' she said. 'Jaxon isn't going home today.'

Noah swore. 'Can we see him?'

'Yes,' Montana said. 'Come on.'

Noah and Emir followed her to Jaxon's dormitory. Liah waited at the door; he unlocked it as they approached. The goblin soldier said nothing as they entered.

Jaxon stood up and looked at them in turn. 'I'm not going home today, am I?'

'No,' Emir said.

Jaxon rubbed his unshaven face with his miner's hands. 'How many?'

'Fifteen.'

'So there are five of us left then.'

'Seven,' Noah said.

Jaxon frowned. 'Seven? I thought there were twenty of us. Have you changed the way we do maths since I've been here?'

'There *were* twenty,' Montana assured him, 'but Noah and I are joining you.'

Jaxon's eyes widened. 'You … and Noah are prisoners here now too?'

Noah, Emir and Montana nodded in unison.

Jaxon scratched his head. 'You know I think you guys are great, but I'd have to say – your negotiating skills could do with some work.'

'Thanks,' Noah said. 'Your honesty is really refreshing.'

'Well, it'll be nice to have more friends around,' Jaxon said.

Montana and Noah looked at each other.

'What?' Jaxon said. 'What was that look for?'

'We're not actually going to be *here*,' Noah said. 'Nerili is taking us to Carai.'

'Teacher's pets?'

'Hardly,' Noah said. 'Nerili wants to join the Alliance.'

'What! That'll *never* happen.'

'You'd think not,' Noah said, 'but he thinks if he can convince Montana and me that the goblins are civilised, that we will support his bid.'

Jaxon shook his head. 'That's ridiculous!'

'Ludicrous,' Noah said. 'I can't imagine what he'd have to show us for us to agree to that.'

Jaxon's eyes flicked between Noah and Montana. 'Why do they want to join the Alliance?'

'They say they want peace,' Montana said.

'And what do you think?'

Montana shrugged. 'I don't think they want peace.'

'What then?' Jaxon said.

'I don't know,' Montana admitted, 'but we're hoping to find out. No doubt Nerili will show us what he wants us to see. We need to find out what he *doesn't* want us to see.'

Jaxon looked at Emir. 'You're going home?'

'Yes.'

'Take care of Gillette for me – tell him I miss him.'

Emir nodded. 'I will.'

Liah appeared in the doorway. 'Time to go.'

Emir embraced his brother. 'We'll get you home.'

'Soon, I hope,' Jaxon said.

When Jaxon was the only one remaining in his cell, Liah locked the door. He motioned to Noah and Montana. 'Follow me.'

The goblin walked to the other side of the corridor and indicated an empty dormitory. 'This is now yours, High Priestess,' he said.

Montana nodded. She turned to Emir and offered him Leninstar's traditional salute, which he returned in kind.

'I'll see you in ten days,' Emir said.

'Ten days,' Montana echoed before making her way into her dorm.

'And you're next door, Noah,' Liah said.

'Got it,' she said without looking at him.

Emir put his hand behind her neck and bent down to kiss her. Noah's skin tingled and this time it wasn't the firestone.

'It's going to be a long ten days,' he whispered.

'Yes,' she said. 'I'll miss you.'

'I'll miss you too.'

He kissed her one more time before turning to leave. Noah watched him as he walked down the corridor towards the mess hall. Aware of Liah's scrutiny, Noah kept her eyes ahead. She remembered how she'd responded to Catriona in the railcar and employed the same detached composure. When Emir was gone she turned and walked into her cell, closing the door behind her.

Noah lay down on the cot against the far wall and found the thin mattress surprisingly comfortable. *It's not supposed to be a prison,* she reminded herself. *It's supposed to be a miner's home away from home.*

Settling herself, Noah let her mind relax. Though she had plenty to worry about, she needed a reprieve. She coaxed her mind into a trance and once there, she tested her surroundings. Few knew of her ability to perceive the world's music and to keep her secret, she didn't use it often. Now seemed like a good time to blow off the cobwebs though to see what she could learn about the mine site. Without the aid of her viola or firestone slider, she released her perceptions into the surrounding earth.

Deeper and deeper she went, listening to the ancient music of the underground. She located the central shaft of the mine and followed it to the firestone below. Tempted to linger on the massive piece of dragonscale, Noah forced herself to branch out to find what else was around.

'Hello?'

Noah stopped. Did she really hear a voice? She waited.

'I know you're there,' the voice said. 'Identify yourself.'

Noah sat up on her cot. Searching the dimness in her cell for the source of the voice, she answered, 'I'm Noah, who are you?'

'I am Xan,' the voice said. 'What are you, Noah?'

Noah's heart raced. 'Xan?'

'Yes,' Xan replied. 'What *are* you?'

'I am human.'

'That doesn't sound right,' the dragon said. 'Are you sure?'

'Pretty sure. Aren't you supposed to be sleeping?' Noah added.

'I am sleeping,' Xan said. 'That's very curious.'

'What is?'

'Goodbye, Noah.'

'Goodbye? No … *wait!* I want to talk to you. Xan?'

Silence.

'Xan,' Noah said again. 'Xan, please talk to me. Please? Xan?'

Noah shivered. *Did that just happen? Have I lost my mind?* She shook her head, trying to restart her brain. Nothing. Noah opened her locket and extracted her slider. She lay it on her palm, looking for inspiration. As far as she knew, no human had ever communicated directly with Xan. Even when Orville Kurz had almost succeeded in waking the dragon in his quest to destroy Talisker last year, there was not a peep. *That should have got her attention if anything was going to.* And in the aftermath, when she and the most talented adepts from the Academy in Mellifont had united to repair the damage, still nothing. Noah's hand trembled. *I don't know what's worse,* she thought – *that she spoke to me in the first place or the fact that she doesn't want to talk to me anymore.*

As she pondered Xan's motives, movement on the bed beside her caught her attention. Noah scrambled off the cot and snatched the candle from the table. Turning back to the bed and brandishing the candle like a sword, she saw an ear twitch on a ball of striped fur nestled on the pillow.

Noah exhaled slowly. 'And here I was thinking that this couldn't get any worse.'

The cat opened one eye. 'It's good to see you too, Noah.'

'Are you here to get me out?' Noah asked as she put the candle back on the table.

'No. Locks aren't my thing,' Brinn said, inspecting one of her paws. 'No opposable thumb.'

'Great, so you're just here to keep me company?'

'Hardly.'

Brinn sat up and stretched. Noah watched, wary. In the low light, the cat's tiger-like markings seemed even more menacing.

'So what do you want?'

'It's not what *I want*,' Brinn said, 'it's what the *world needs*.'

'And that is?'

'For you to get rid of that piece of firestone.'

Noah clutched her locket. 'Why?'

Brinn's eyes blazed. 'Not *your* piece, Noah. The *big* piece. The one that they're about to dig out.'

'*What?*'

'You need to make that piece of firestone disappear,' Brinn said. 'It's too big – too dangerous.'

'You've got to be kidding. I can't make it disappear.'

'You have to,' Brinn insisted. 'The world isn't ready for a piece that size.'

Noah stared at the cat as her anger grew. At last she said, 'Why are you telling me this *now*? You can appear and disappear whenever you like – why come now? Why couldn't you have warned us before if it's so important?'

'I've been busy.'

'*Busy?*' Noah balled her hands into fists. 'Busy? For a *year*?'

Brinn cocked her head. 'Is that how long it's been since I saw you last?'

Noah nodded.

'Well, in that case,' Brinn said, 'yes – I've been busy for a year.'

Noah unclenched her fists and covered her face with trembling hands. She shook her head.

'And, in fact,' Brinn continued, 'I'm still busy. But to answer your question about why now … it's because *you* have got Xan's attention, Noah.'

'Me?'

'Were you not just talking to her?'

'You were eavesdropping?'

The end of Brinn's tail twitched and Noah knew that was the only response she'd get. *This is why I'm a dog person,* she thought. In Noah's view, all cats were contrary, haughty, and self-centred, but Brinn took cat-ness to the extreme. Cats didn't talk, but Brinn did. Cats didn't appear and disappear at will, but Brinn did. Cats *acted* like they knew everything, but Brinn seemed to *actually* know everything. Rules were beneath her. Even rules of nature.

'Do you not remember what Orville did with thirteen *small* pieces of firestone?' Brinn said. 'Do you not remember how close he came to waking the dragon?'

'I remember,' Noah said testily.

'That was thirteen *small* pieces – this is one *massive* piece.'

'There are laws about who can use it and how it can be used,' Noah said. 'The Alliance has consulted the adepts in Mellifont and it's going to be strictly monitored. It'll be safe.'

'Safe? Really? It hasn't even made it to the surface yet and already it's under goblin control *and* you're talking to the old girl.'

'It'll be fine,' Noah said. 'The Alliance will …'

'Will what?'

Noah didn't answer.

'Get rid of that stone, Noah,' Brinn said. 'Whatever it takes.'

'You're not going to help?'

'I just did. I told you what you need to do.'

'I couldn't do it by myself – even *if* I wanted to.'

'You don't have to *want to*, Noah. It needs to be done and you're best qualified to do it. You're a Dragonsbane of Talisker – do your job.'

'Why don't you go and hassle Dr Grainger?' Noah asked. 'He's Dragonsbane too.'

Brinn growled. 'Because, as the 13th key … you're best qualified. As distressing as that is to me, that is the reality.'

'Nerili is taking Montana and me to Carai. How am I supposed to do anything about the firestone from there?'

'You'll have to find a way.'

'Very helpful,' Noah said. 'Thanks.'

'Well, you've got lots to do,' Brinn said. 'So I'll leave—'

'Is there a prophecy about this?'

The cat's eyes narrowed. 'What?'

'Last time I had to save the world it was because there was a prophecy. Is there one about this?'

'Perhaps it's the same one,' Brinn said at length. '*The thirteenth key the world shall need, for evil to be brought to heel. One of two, the Dragon's bane must rise; and the music wield.* The evil *this time* is that piece of firestone. And you're the 13th key, so sort it out.'

Noah blinked. Brinn was gone.

'Fabulous,' Noah said to the candle. 'That's just fabulous.'

Chapter 9

I need to get out, Noah thought. *If I don't get out of this carriage soon, I'm going to scream.*

'Not far to go now,' Nerili said. 'Were there less traffic, I would show you the tunnel. Here the roadway is about thirty metres wide, enough for at least eight lanes of carriages, and the ceiling is about ten metres above us. It is a wonder of Desceran engineering and the magic of the old ones still shines – the walls glow silver to light our path.'

'Another time perhaps,' Montana said.

How any magic could endure goblin occupation was beyond Noah. If Nerili's carriage was any indication, the stench alone would be enough to unravel any spell. It was a vehicle worthy of a king, but for the smell. Everything – polished wooden panelling, woven carpets, gold-trimmed velvet curtains and padded seating – reeked of rancid flesh and after three days trapped in the putrid odour, Noah ached for a chance to scrub her skin to make sure she didn't suffer the same fate.

'I suspect this Desceran city is much different to the ones you're used to,' Nerili said.

'No doubt,' Noah said, thinking of Leninstar's elaborate subterranean city. 'The ones I've been in weren't full of goblins.'

Nerili rested his hand on his sword hilt. Perhaps out of habit, perhaps as a warning.

'We chose a city away from the main tunnel network that links your seven royal cities,' Nerili said.

'If this tunnel is as large as you say,' Montana said, 'it couldn't be far from the main line between Seychelles and Orian.'

'It actually was connected at one stage, but we sealed it off.'

Noah suppressed a shudder. The thought of goblins defiling an ancient Desceran city was outrageous.

The mystical Descera had wrought an underground empire across Talisker that predated the appearance of humans by hundreds of millennia. Manipulating the dragonsong using spells and charms, they'd spent many centuries building more and more elaborate cities. But in the end, their extravagance had paved the way for their downfall. They'd taken *from* the dragonsong but hadn't taken care *of* it. By the time they realised they needed to replenish the dragonsong, it was too late for them. Noah pondered the Desceras' fate. *At least they left us the twelve keys so we didn't make the same mistake,* she thought.

As the carriage slowed and turned, she wondered what the Descera would have done if they'd had one big piece of firestone rather than thirteen small pieces. Did they not know of larger pieces or did they specifically not use them? Brinn's words haunted her. *It's too big – too dangerous. Sort it out.*

Voices outside distracted her from pondering Brinn's ultimatum further.

'We're going onto a restricted road,' Nerili explained, '*my* road actually. We'll go to my palace first and have dinner there. We'll start our tour tomorrow morning. You may open the curtains and shutters now if you wish.'

Noah parted the drapes.

'This tunnel's quite narrow,' she said as the carriage again picked up speed.

'Yes,' Nerili said, 'dual carriageway only here.'

Noah found it difficult to imagine two carriages passing here but kept her skepticism to herself. Instead, she passed the last few kilometres of their journey lost in the silver glow of the tunnel walls.

Eventually the carriage came to a stop, rocking slightly as Nerili's three soldiers climbed down. The door opened. Nerili motioned for his guests to exit. Noah and Montana did so, grateful for a chance to stretch cramped muscles.

'What do you think of the karesh?' he asked, referring to the hairless, dog-like creatures pulling the carriage.

Clasping her hands in front of her, Montana said, 'They certainly have stamina.'

'Better than horses down here,' Nerili said. 'You'll have noticed that the air is thinner the deeper we get. Horses don't cope well but the karesh – they run all day.'

Noah avoided looking at the naked critters. The goblins had fitted them with wool-padded harnesses to protect their smooth skin from chaffing and blistering, but she'd have made them little vests to wear at the very least.

Scanning the tunnel, Noah counted eight wooden doors on either side. One of the doors to her right opened, leaving a gap like a lost tooth. Several goblins emerged. After saluting the king they attended to the karesh who, despite three days on the road, still had the energy to leap about to lick the faces of their keepers.

'Follow me,' Nerili said.

Liah took his place beside his liege as Noah and Montana fell in behind. Shar and Frost brought up the rear as they entered a narrower tunnel. *It's more like a corridor,* Noah thought. After the clattering of the three-day road journey, the eerie quiet here unsettled her. The floor was smooth and soft, and absorbed the sound of their footsteps. She shivered at the thought that she was walking on the same ground that the Descera had trod. The tunnel ended at a spiral staircase.

'I hope you like steps,' Nerili said.

Noah let Liah take the lead. She gave him a few steps head start before mounting the staircase herself, but tripped on the third step. She put her hands out to break her fall but crashed heavily on her left knee.

'Ouch!' she said.

'Are you alright?' Nerili asked.

Noah turned and sat on one of the narrow steps, inspecting her knee. 'Skin's not broken,' she said, rubbing it briskly. 'I'll be fine.'

'Take your time,' Nerili said.

Noah stood up. 'I'm fine. Keep going.'

The party continued up the stairs. Noah tried to ignore her aching knee, but each entryway they passed made that task more difficult. At the seventh doorway, Noah said, 'Can we not take this exit?'

'You can,' Nerili said. 'Would you like to help with the laundry?'

Though tempted to escape the punishing ascent, Noah declined the invitation and coaxed her legs into action again.

'Here,' Liah said finally, deviating to his right and pulling aside a sky-blue curtain to reveal an archway.

The guard motioned for her to go through. Noah nodded, unable to find enough breath to acknowledge him.

'This is my library,' Nerili said, entering the room behind Montana.

It hardly needs an introduction, Noah thought. Although the room curved away in both directions so the full extent of the room was a mystery, books choked the walls. Polished wooden tables and chairs sat on tapestry rugs on the floor between the shelves. Nerili had proven his ability to read so Noah knew his collection wasn't just for show.

The goblin king pointed to an external door. 'There is a balcony,' he said. 'It will give you a view of the city. Please.'

With Montana at her side, Noah walked to the door and stepped outside.

Her voice barely above a whisper, Noah said, 'What do you see, Montana? I don't think I can trust my eyes.'

'I don't know that I trust my voice to do it justice,' Montana replied.

'Many Desceran cities are nestled among the branches of olluka trees,' Nerili explained. 'This chasm allows us only a glimpse of this tree's true majesty. Its branches twist through the earth for hundreds of kilometres all around. Somewhere to the west, its massive trunk sits and its roots go to the centre of the world where the great dragon sleeps. As you can see, even though there is no sunlight down here, there is still light. Olluka means flame tree. The trees are rooted in lava and its heat travels through the wood and the surrounding earth, not only providing warmth, but also light.'

Noah whistled into the dry air of the underground. Stepping forward, she leaned on the railing, looking out into the vast expanse before her. She studied the branches that snaked around the cavern. *We're in the canopy of an underground olluka forest,* she thought. *The Descera excavated this section to make their city.* High overhead, branches coiled and intertwined, creating not only an intricate and beautiful pattern for their underground sky, but also providing a protective shell over the city. The undulating floor below was carpeted with thousands of double-storey brick buildings. Lights twinkled in the windows and on the carts that rambled along the roads and laneways. As Noah's eyes devoured the alien subterranean landscape she picked out parks and playgrounds, markets and factories. No matter which direction she looked, the city teemed with life.

'What you can see here is only a portion of the city,' Nerili said. 'We can see more from the other side of my palace but even then, not all is visible. The farmlands are far beyond the mountains behind us.'

'Mountains?' Montana said. 'That's unbelievable.'

'When the Descera fashioned their city, they wanted it to reflect their favourite landscapes above ground. They had no love for flat ground.'

'It looks like they used some of what they excavated to make bricks,' Noah said.

Nerili nodded. 'Yes. When we came, we continued their practice.'

'How long have goblins been in Carai?' Montana asked.

'About twelve hundred years,' Nerili said.

'How many are here?'

'About five hundred thousand.'

Five hundred thousand. The number swirled around in Noah's head, making her dizzy.

To steady herself, she looked up at the palace behind her. It was carved out of a gargantuan branch that protruded from the city floor. Noah inspected the wood. The textures and colours of the tree branches captivated her, filling her mind with design ideas for Queen Rosemary's next state dress. The smooth rust-coloured bark was punctuated with a kaleidoscope of coloured lichens. Some of the lichens clung to the branches in flat patches while others clumped in polyps. Others stretched out finger-like projections, with the rest dangling lazily downwards.

'Come,' Nerili said. 'Let us take a rest before dinner. No doubt you would both like a bath?'

Noah and Montana nodded.

'Liah will show you to your rooms.'

♪♫

It felt good to be clean again and Noah looked forward to a sit-down meal. She glanced at Montana as they followed Shar through the palace corridors. As usual, the high priestess was the epitome of calm. Noah returned her attention to the olluka passageways, trying to draw into herself some of the ageless music from the wood. *It wouldn't even notice us,* she thought. *Our lives are so fleeting and small.* Even the ancient Pyranhi, the diminutive immortals who roamed the deep underground eons before the Descera, came late in the lives of Talisker's olluka trees. The trees thrived on elemental power – feeding on lava, the blood of Xan, deep in the earth.

Noah took a deep breath as the sound of conversation intruded on her thoughts. Light and laughter spilled into the corridor through an open doorway ahead on the left. The dining room, Noah guessed.

When Shar reached the doorway, he stood aside to let Noah and Montana pass.

Noah scanned the table as she entered, finding Nerili at the far end. He beckoned to her.

'Come,' he said, 'I have seats for you here.'

Noah walked along the near wall towards the goblin king while Montana rounded the end of the table and followed the far wall. Liah pulled out the chair at Nerili's left hand and nodded to Noah. With her heart thumping in her chest, she allowed the guard to push her chair in as she sat. Across the table, Frost did the same for Montana.

'Allow me to make introductions,' Nerili said. 'Montana, Noah – I have three of my four counsellors here this evening. Rankin of the Irangi clan, Gisa of the Ilian clan and Ulan of the Tyler clan.'

The three goblins waved in turn as they were announced. By their dress, Rankin and Gisa appeared to be female. Both wore floral headscarves while Ulan had a narrow black band across his forehead that was tied in a knot behind his bald head.

'Unlike your kings,' Nerili said, 'I do not put my trust in a single adviser. I have four masters on whom I rely for counsel. You will meet Jacin – Gisa's brother – later.'

Noah and Montana nodded to the three advisers.

'And these two youngsters are my children,' Nerili said. 'Severine and Sandor.'

The young girl stood up. 'We are twins,' she announced, 'but I – Severine – am the eldest. I will be the next King of Carai.'

She bowed her head solemnly before taking her seat again.

'Princess Severine,' Montana said, 'though there is wisdom in your eyes that seems at odds with your youthful complexion, I hope your ascension to the throne is not too soon.'

Severine nodded. 'I am in no hurry for the throne. I have no wish to lose my father too.'

Happy to let Montana ply diplomacy, Noah searched the face of the young prince. Did his scowl signify jealousy? Was he even scowling? His disproportionate goblin features made it difficult to tell. And what had happened to their mother?

Nerili tapped his skewer on his goblet, the metallic clank drawing his guests' attention. 'By the grace of Elani, let us feast,' he said.

Noah watched as everyone bowed their heads briefly and she followed their lead.

To her surprise, Noah recognised most of the food on the table. Though breads and pastries were notable absences, roasted meats and vegetables, nuts and fruits were abundant.

'Help yourself,' Nerili said.

Noah picked up her skewer and knife and selected items from the platters closest to her. Gisa tapped her lightly on the arm and held a platter towards her. 'Try some of this,' she invited. 'It's smoked eel – a goblin delicacy.'

'Eel?' Noah said as she eyed the headless ribbons of dark, oily flesh. 'Down here?'

'They're from the sulphur pools deep down,' Gisa explained. 'Just have a little taste – too much might make you sick if you're not used to it.'

'You wear your skepticism openly, Noah,' Nerili said, 'but you needn't worry. We are careful where we fish – these eels are not contaminated with ilanxis worm.'

Noah took a small piece of the cured flesh. 'Ilanxis worm? What's that?'

'It is a parasite, found deep underground,' Nerili said. 'The worm lays its eggs in the sulphur pools and the eggs are eaten by gurum – little crustaceans that thrive in the toxic subterranean pools. Eels then eat the gurum. Once the worm eggs hatch inside the eels, the worms burrow their way out through eels' skin into the sulphur pool and the cycle starts again.'

'Sounds gruesome,' Noah said.

Nerili shrugged. 'It doesn't harm the eels – the exit wounds heal – but if goblins eat them, the results are devastating. The worm releases a poison that unhinges the mind and rots the skin. Goblins affected by ilanxis worm are wild, deranged – beyond reason. They don't recognise anyone – not even themselves. And there is no cure.'

As Noah wondered just how different an ilanxis-affected goblin was from any other goblin, she wrapped the piece of eel in a cabbage leaf.

'Mead?' Gisa said.

'Is there water?' Noah asked.

The goblin nodded and selected another pitcher from the table. She filled Noah's goblet.

'My brother, Jacin, wanted to be here tonight,' she said. 'He is desperate to meet you.'

Noah's stomach tightened. The calm acceptance of her presence here only highlighted to Noah that Nerili and his advisers had plotted this visit. They were all in on it and it didn't bode well that one was particularly keen to meet her.

'All in good time,' Noah said.

To Noah's surprise the goblin giggled.

'I mustn't say too much,' she said. 'He made me promise not to give anything away.'

Noah groaned inwardly. Too much of this kind of talk and she wouldn't be able to force any food past her lips. She glanced at Montana who didn't appear to be having any trouble.

The high priestess looked up and nodded. 'I recommend the pheasant, Noah.'

As Noah picked at her food, she considered her knife, wondering if the palace staff would notice its absence. It was a serious blade with uses far beyond the dining table. Noah quickly dismissed the idea though. Nerili was no fool.

'Would you like to know what we've got planned for you?' Nerili asked.

Noah dropped her skewer and it clattered loudly on her plate. She looked up and caught Prince Sandor's eye.

'Nervous?' he asked with a sly smile. 'You should be.'

Nerili glared at his son. 'That's enough out of you,' he growled.

'Humans best be careful here is all I'm saying,' Sandor said defiantly.

Collecting her cutlery, Noah said, 'I'm always careful.'

Sandor scowled at her as she returned her attention to her plate.

Nerili nodded to Frost who stepped forward and grabbed the prince's tunic at the shoulder.

'Let's go,' the guard said.

Prince Sandor collected his plate with one hand and reached for his knife with the other.

'Just the plate,' Frost said.

Sandor sighed and allowed himself to be escorted from the dining room. Noah got the impression it was a ritual. He did look back when he got to the doorway, but it wasn't at his father, she noticed. Sandor spent his last glance on Ulan.

'My apologies,' Nerili said. 'My son has suffered for lack of his mother. My Queen, Angie, died giving me my children.'

Noah barely heard Nerili's words; her attention was on Ulan. She'd have to watch him. Goosebumps pricked her skin all over. She'd have to watch *all of them*, she reminded herself.

Clearing his throat, Nerili said, 'Now, about your schedule for the next few days – first up tomorrow we'll go to the temple. I've organised for you to visit a factory, our raiki precinct and our Parliament building. I will also take you out to the farmlands.'

'I look forward to seeing the temple, certainly,' Montana said.

Nerili nodded. 'I thought you would.'

'And who will be chaperoning us?' Montana asked.

Wiping his mouth with a napkin, Nerili said, 'I will.'

'Just you?'

Nerili met her eye. 'And my guards.'

'Don't you have more important matters to attend to?' Noah asked.

'No,' Nerili said. 'There is nothing more important than gaining Carai a place in the Sovereign States Alliance.'

'And your … subjects support that?'

'Support continues to grow among my *kin*, but there is still much work to do,' he said.

'Starting at home?' Montana ventured.

Nerili's eyes flashed but to Noah's surprise, Severine responded.

'My brother is a simpleton,' Severine said dismissively, 'but he can be trained.'

Ulan came to the Prince's defence. 'Leave the boy alone – he's eight years old.'

'As I am,' Severine said with a level stare at the adviser across the table.

A cold knot smouldered in Noah's stomach as she considered the conflicting allegiances in Nerili's house. Rankin and Severine had chatted between themselves for the duration of dinner, and there was clearly a comradeship between Ulan and Sandor.

Noah skewered a morsel of pheasant and popped it in her mouth. The sooner dinner was done, the sooner they could retire for the evening. Sleep would be impossible but that was the least of her worries. *I just hope we survive the night,* she thought.

Chapter 10

Noah's relief that they had survived the night was short-lived. It hadn't been nearly long enough since their last carriage ride. *I wonder if anyone has ever died from the smell in here?* she thought. As they rattled their way to the temple, Noah felt around the edge of her headscarf to check no errant locks of hair had escaped.

'Is the glamour holding?' Noah said.

Nerili nodded. 'You two are the spitting image of Rankin and Gisa.'

As much as Noah deplored glamours, she'd made an exception today. She and Montana needed to disguise themselves in public and a glamour was the only option; hooded cloaks were too conspicuous. *I can't believe I've had to stoop to this,* she thought. *A year studying raiki, learning complex tonics that will heal people and here I am spinning glamours like a charlatan.* She just hoped that they held. Unlike the robust tonics she'd learned, glamours were fragile, flimsy spells. There'd be no repairing any lapses in public.

As Gisa, the goblin garb Noah wore was surprisingly comfortable. The loose woollen pants and matching long-sleeved tunic were light and cool. She looked down at her hands, the only skin visible besides her face. They appeared rough and gnarled and her talons, if they'd been real, would have easily pierced flesh.

The carriage slowed as the muffled sound of bells reached Noah's ears.

'Our temple,' Nerili announced. 'Are you ready?'

Noah nodded at Montana when the carriage stopped.

'We're ready,' Montana said.

Nerili gestured towards the door. 'After you.'

Noah and Montana stepped out to find Liah and Shar waiting. Pipe music filled the air, signalling the commencement of the morning service. They'd arrived late intentionally to minimise interaction with others. Noah smothered her surprise as she attempted a casual inspection of the temple's exterior. A massive sleeping dragon greeted her.

'Xan,' Noah whispered. *Will you talk to me here?*

Carved out of an olluka branch, the dragon's head rested on the temple threshold. The top of the eyebrow ridge came up to Noah's waist while the tips of its upward-curving horns peaked above her head. One was left to imagine that the rest of the body lay curled around the branch. An enormous wing was the only other feature visible from the street. From its main wing claw high above, the spar bones arched down to the ground with the outer one almost touching the dragon's nose – hiding its face like a sleeping dog with its paw over its nose. The webbing between the bones was carved in loose folds and the fine blood vessels that interlaced the membrane had been etched in red ochre.

'We revere the great dragon, Xan as the Descera did,' Nerili said. 'This temple honours her. Come and see inside.'

The interior of the temple made the outside look plain. The asymmetrical cavern resembled the body of the dragon upon whose bones the world was built. Stylised rib bones arched up to meet the central spine that curved around in a semicircle to mimic the dragon's sleeping form. Rubies, topaz, emeralds, sapphires and amethysts formed intricate mosaics on the walls depicting the story of Talisker's creation. Beyond the pulpit, a mosaic immortalised the desolate figure of the god, Elani, weeping at the ultimate sacrifice of the great Xan as she sought to destroy the evil god Jong.

'Sit,' Shar said quietly.

Noah looked around. Nerili had taken a seat near the door. She slid onto the pew next to him leaving enough room for Montana.

The temple was packed. As the music died down, a lone goblin in the front row stood and walked to the pulpit. He was tall and weedy, with white tufts of hair sprouting in patches over the lumpy landscape of his skull. *I hope that's hair,* Noah thought, *and not some kind of fungus.* Like Nerili's guards, his ears stuck out rather than up, but unlike the guards his were lopsided; his right ear was noticeably higher than the left. His black cassock was unadorned save for a red cord around his waist.

'My kin,' he began as he opened the tome on the lectern. 'Welcome.'

Noah marvelled at the acoustics. Given the goblin's slight form, his voice had no right to make the length of the grand temple, but it was as clear as if he'd been sitting next to her.

'It is my honour to read to you today from this great book,' he said, patting the page reverently. 'As always, we are thankful for the wisdom of the ancients – the Pyranhi – who passed on their lore to the Descera, who in turn gifted it to us. Today's scripture concerns freedom …

'A travelling elf comes across a farm one day and finds a teenage girl strapped to a harrower, ploughing a large field. Aghast, the elf rushes to her aid.'

'My dear,' the elf says, 'let me cut your bonds so that you are free.'

'No, no,' the girl protests, 'do not cut me loose! I have all the freedom I need.'

'You are shackled to a machine,' the elf replies. 'How is that freedom?'

'I am free to think my own thoughts all day out here,' says the girl. 'If you want to free someone, go and find my brother. He is not free to think his own thoughts – his tutor fills his mind with *knowledge.*'

Perplexed, the elf continues on towards the farmhouse. In a room at the back of the house the elf finds a young boy being rapped over the knuckles by a waspish-looking tutor-woman.

'Do it again!' the tutor demands.

'Stop!' the elf says as she jumps in through the window.

'What's this!' the tutor says. 'We're busy. Go away!'

'This boy should be free to think his own thoughts,' says the elf. 'Stop filling his head with what's in yours.'

'My lessons finish at sunset,' the boy says, 'then I am free to eat what I like for dinner and watch the stars for as long as I want – all night if I want. *That's* freedom. If you want to free someone, go and find my baby sister. She is stuck in a cage.'

With eyes wide, the elf goes in search of the baby sister and she finds her in a nursery. The toddler is standing in her cot, fists wrapped around wooden bars, screaming. The elf plucks the toddler out of the cot but before she can escape, the farmer enters the nursery.

'What are you doing elf?' he demands. 'Give me my baby.'

'This baby should be free,' the elf says, 'not locked in a cage!'

'Free? Free to do what?' the farmer replies. 'Free to crawl into the kitchen and burn herself on the fire? Free to crawl out and drown in the dam? Or maybe free to crawl out into the paddock and be trampled by a horse?'

The elf frowns. 'I travel the roads as I please and it pains me that others don't have the freedom I have. Your elder daughter is strapped to a harrower.'

The farmer nods. 'But she doesn't have to be. She understands that if we don't harvest enough food during the growing season, that we will not have enough to eat in the winter. She chooses to lend a hand so the family doesn't starve.'

'Your son is stuck in lessons all day,' the elf argues.

'He dreams of going to school one day,' the farmer replies, 'so that he may choose a job that he wants.'

Reluctantly, the elf puts the baby back in the cot. 'But this is not freedom,' she says softly.

'And you think you're free?' the farmer asks.

The elf looks up, surprised. 'Of course,' she says. 'I go where I want, when I want.'

The farmer nods. 'Are you free to go without food and water?'

'Well, no,' the elf admits. 'I need food and water.'

'Are you free to go without clothes? Without shelter? Or fire?'

'No, I need those things too,' the elf says.

'So you are not truly free then,' the farmer surmises.

'Well if I'm not free, who is?' the elf asks.

The farmer smiles. 'Good question.'

Montana lent in to whisper in Noah's ear. 'They have a copy of the Score.'

Noah nodded. She'd recognised the story.

The goblin at the lectern continued preaching into the congregation's rapturous silence but Noah turned her attention to the temple. *This shouldn't be here. How is it all still intact – the gemstones, the artwork?* Few creatures followed a moral code and the goblins' apparent interest in the Score didn't fit. Noah frowned. The Score promoted peace and harmony between people and respect for the natural world. Yes, the book was here but goblins weren't known for peace and harmony. Quite the opposite.

As she teased out her ideas, a prickly sensation crept up her spine. *Someone's watching.* Noah sat very still, scanning the temple. Apart from the goblin at the front everyone else had their back to her, but she couldn't shake the feeling someone was watching her. She looked down at her hands. The glamour was wavering. She stared for a long moment, her mind scrambling through the implications. If someone here could pierce her glamour, that meant they had some knowledge of the world's dragonsong. But not just knowledge of it, they could manipulate it. She and Montana were in danger.

'We need to go,' she said to Nerili.

Without looking at her, Nerili put his hand on the back of the pew in front of him and Shar was on his feet instantly. Noah nudged Montana.

'Follow Shar,' she said quietly.

Montana nodded and did as she was told. Noah slipped out after her. With Nerili at her back, she hoped their disguises would hold until they reached the carriage. Forcing herself to keep the pace Shar set, she adjusted her headscarf to obscure her face just in case. Liah fell in beside her when they reached the temple door.

'Put your hand down,' he said.

Freedom, Noah thought. *Am I free to defy him?* Butterflies fluttered in her stomach. She was free. She could run right now, bolt across the street and disappear into an alleyway. Then she'd be able to do her own investigating in Carai. Nerili wanted to show them the best parts of Carai so she and Montana would report back favourably to the Alliance. Montana had other ideas. She wanted to find human slaves.

Freedom. Noah knew she was free to run but Liah was also free to chase her down and drag her back. The butterflies ceased stirring. She lowered her hand and held her breath as they approached the carriage. Frost was in the driver's seat and the karesh were dancing about in anticipation of a run. Shar opened the door and Nerili stood aside, ushering Noah and Montana ahead of him.

Noah stumbled as she entered, landing face first on the carpeted floor. She crawled on hands and knees to clear the doorway so the others could follow her inside. She noticed her hands. They were her own.

Taking his usual seat, Nerili said, 'Want to tell me what that was all about?'

Montana put her arms around Noah. 'Leave her alone,' she said curtly.

As the carriage lurched forward, Noah said, 'Someone saw me.'

'Who?' Nerili asked.

Noah clutched Montana's arm and shook her head. 'I don't know.'

Chapter 11

Noah studied another swatch of material in the folio she'd been given at the textile factory they'd visited after the temple the previous afternoon. Nerili had chosen to ride outside with his guards today, so for the next half hour there was no need to keep up appearances for which Noah was grateful. She turned the pages, enjoying the simple pleasure of touching beautiful fabrics. The goblins' manufacturing process had done nothing to diminish the natural melody of the fibres. The subtle music that ran through the materials was cheery and pure.

Nerili wanted a trading partnership with Leninstar. This hefty tome was the first step. On her return to Leninstar, she was expected to petition King Tambian to source fabrics from Carai. An economic link with one of the current members of the Alliance would enhance Nerili's chances of admission.

'I thought you'd be more excited about seeing a raiki facility,' Montana said.

Noah closed the book and ran her hand lightly over the wooden cover. She'd gotten little sleep overnight. Even though guards had been placed outside her bedchamber, she'd lain awake waiting for Prince Sandor or Ulan to come for her.

'Again, we'll only see what Nerili wants us to see they're using raiki for,' Noah said. 'I'm more worried what *else* they might be doing with it.'

'At least we don't need our disguises there.'

'No, plenty of time for that this afternoon.'

Like yesterday, Nerili had two destinations on today's schedule. After they'd toured the Raiki Research Centre this morning, they'd be off to Carai's Parliament for the afternoon.

'Take a deep breath, Noah,' Montana advised. 'You need to be calm.'

'I am calm,' she said without conviction.

The high priestess raised an eyebrow. 'You're fidgeting. You're not calm.'

Noah put her hands in her lap.

'You're still worried about who saw through our disguises yesterday,' Montana guessed.

'Yes. It was someone with talent – I'm worried we might run into them at the facility today.'

'I would have thought that was a good thing.'

'A good thing?'

'Wouldn't you rather know who it is?'

Noah let out a long breath. 'I guess so.'

'You need to keep your mind open as well as your eyes, my friend.'

When Noah met her eye, Montana smiled. *Mind open, eyes open.* Noah's eyes were definitely open but she longed for the chance to snoop around to find human slaves. But it was looking increasingly unlikely that she'd get the opportunity.

When the carriage stopped, Frost opened the door. Montana nodded to Noah.

'I'm ready,' Noah said.

Nerili waited for them at the carriage door. 'Let's go.'

As Noah approached the five-storey building, the brick façade seemed to mock her. She frowned. Montana was right. She did need to keep an open mind. Even though she was surrounded by goblins of questionable motives, she was a Professor of Raiki. This was the one place she needn't feel overwhelmed.

Liah pulled the wooden door aside but there was barely room to step inside. Goblins filled the foyer. Silence fell as Noah stepped over the threshold. The mass shifted slightly, allowing her to take several steps but with so many in the room, space was a slippery commodity. For more space to open up in front of her, the space behind her needed to be filled. And the mob filled it. Noah glanced back. She saw Nerili and his guards at the doorway but Montana had disappeared.

Nerili opened his mouth but whatever he was about to say was lost as the mob erupted into a gibbering throng. The crowd surrounded her. They jostled her to the left and she almost lost her footing. Grabbing the nearest limb, Noah managed to keep herself from falling to the ground.

As Noah battled to stay upright, a shrill whistle split the air and threatened to do the same to her eardrum. She clamped her hands over her ears as the goblin crush eased slightly. Nerili's guards closed in, collaring the offenders one by one and shoving them aside. Within seconds, Liah, Shar and Frost ringed Noah while the crowd tittered beyond the goblin barricade.

Nerili's voice rang out. 'Jacin!'

Between the guards' shoulders, Noah saw a hand go up at the back of the crowd. 'Here.'

'Come forward,' the king commanded. 'The rest of you will clear a path.'

A path appeared instantly and to Noah's surprise, the face that revealed itself was human.

'My apologies, Your Majesty,' the young man said with a deep bow. 'The acolytes are an overly enthusiastic lot.'

'Enthusiasm is fine,' Nerili said, 'but if I see another display like that I'll lock up every last one of you. Is that clear?'

'Yes, Your Majesty,' the crowd chorused.

Nerili turned to the young man. 'Master Jacin, this is Noah Chord and the High Priestess, Montana.'

The man's wide smile revealed a perfect set of white teeth, a rare sight in this city of fangs and discoloured molars. His dark locks were cut short at the back but grew longer on top, a strategically placed pin keeping the hair at the front from falling over his honey-brown eyes.

'A pleasure to meet you, High Priestess,' he said, bowing his head.

'Master Jacin,' Montana said, returning the gesture.

Turning to Noah, he said, 'And it's an honour to meet you at last, Professor Noah.'

'Just "Noah" is fine,' she said, unsettled that he knew of her recently-attained rank, 'and you don't need to bow like that. Please stand up.'

She extended her hand which he clasped warmly.

'It's an honour to be in the presence of such a skilled and highly-ranked adept,' Jacin said. 'I've been dying to meet you – so jealous that my sister got to meet you first. She hasn't half been rubbing it in either.'

'Your sister?'

Jacin smiled. 'Gisa.'

'*You're* Gisa's brother?'

Jacin nodded.

Noah turned to Nerili. '*This* is your fourth counsellor?'

Nerili nodded.

'But he's human.'

'Well, you're half right but we'll get to that later,' Jacin said.

Noah turned, searching his face for clues. Then she looked at the vest he wore bearing the insignia of a flute. 'How did you come by that uniform?'

His smiled broadened. 'I was a member of the House of Wind, as you were,' he said. 'In fact, I was there the night Sachin introduced you as his candidate to find the 13th key.'

Noah stared at him. 'Really?'

'Yes, it was amazing,' Jacin said. 'I will never forget it.'

'I don't doubt it,' Noah said. 'It's not every day you get to see someone die onstage.'

'You only *half*-died,' Jacin said. 'The story is legend. Sachin's genius is unparalleled.'

'I wonder if you'd say that if he'd half-killed *you* without asking your permission.'

Though she'd grown to love Sachin in the year since, she still hadn't quite forgiven him for half killing her – even if it was to save her from being imprisoned by Orville Kurz.

'Well, you're alive now,' Jacin said, 'and that's the main thing. And, may I say, I'm really looking forward to getting your feedback on what we're doing here as we tour the facility today.'

Noah's chest tightened. 'There are many at the Academy who are better qualified to be here than me.'

Jacin smiled. 'You don't need to be modest here.' Offering her his arm, he said, 'Shall we?'

Noah shot a glance at Nerili who nodded his approval. She linked her arm with Jacin's.

The swarm of goblins fell back as Jacin led Noah to the heart of Carai's raiki facility. As Montana fought her way to be at her side and Nerili and his guards took their positions, Noah prayed that Jacin didn't know about her firestone slider. She wasn't prepared to give it up – not even for a look.

'This first level is where we make our instruments,' Jacin said as they entered a room of craftsmen hard at work. 'In this room, flutes – my personal favourite. As well as metal flutes, we're making a variety of timber flutes too. Olluka is popular of course. We've discovered that different parts of the tree create markedly different instruments – the fullness of tone differs dramatically. So at the moment, we're investing most of our energy in researching the best wood source for our flutes.'

'Sounds interesting,' Noah said.

'It really is,' Jacin said. 'What do you think my chances are of getting Sachin down here?'

'Slim I would have thought,' Noah said. 'I don't know that visiting a goblin city is high on his list of priorities.'

'Well, I'll keep it on my wish list all the same,' Jacin said. 'If you follow me, I'll show you where we make the violas.'

Noah's pulse quickened. The viola was close to her heart and given the knowledge Jacin had displayed so far she wasn't surprised he knew that too. He pushed back a curtain to reveal another workshop where dozens of goblins plied their craft.

All of them looked up when Noah entered. Without any discernible cue, they made a guard of honour down the middle aisle, ushering Noah to the far end of the room. She obliged, flanked by Jacin and Montana. At the far end, a slender young female goblin – one who was easier on Noah's eyes than others she'd seen – nursed a viola. As Noah approached, the girl offered her the instrument.

'Will you play it?' she asked shyly.

Unable to resist, Noah took the viola, plucking each of the strings before putting it under her chin. The girl passed her a bow.

'What's your name?' Noah asked.

'Ginny of the clan Ng.'

Noah nodded. 'What is the bow strung with, Ginny?'

'Horse tail,' the girl said.

Without fear of ridicule or censure, Noah closed her eyes and played her favourite piece, *Ayuna de chanzè*. Each note melted from the instrument like warm caramel and Noah could almost forget that she was a hostage in a goblin city.

When she lowered the instrument, the room erupted in applause.

'That was inspired,' Jacin said. 'Simply inspired.'

Noah passed the viola back to its maker. 'That is a beautiful instrument,' she said. 'Thank you for letting me play it.'

Tears welled in Ginny's eyes and she took a long breath before she managed to say, 'It's yours – a gift.'

'No,' Noah said. 'I can't take this. It's yours.'

'I make lots of violas,' Ginny said. 'I would be honoured if you'd take it.'

Noah forced a smiled. 'Alright,' she said. 'Thank you – that's very generous.'

Jacin leaned in close to Noah. 'Come,' he said. 'There is still much to see.'

♪♫

'Top floor and last stop,' Jacin announced as they reached the top step. 'Our medical research lab.'

Dark blue curtains partitioned the floor space on either side of the central aisle. Keeping her voice low, Noah said, 'Do you keep patients here?'

Jacin nodded. 'We have twenty-three at present. These cubicles are where they rest and where we take our observations. There is a sound-proof booth at the back where we actually perform our tonics.'

Before Noah could quiz him about the tonics they performed, Nerili said, 'Montana and I will visit with the patients while Master Jacin shows Noah the treatment room.'

Without waiting for a reply, the king motioned for Montana to follow him.

Jacin took Noah's hand. 'Come with me.'

Each step she took towards the treatment room increased her anxiety. By the time they reached the door, she had to concentrate hard to control her muscles – she didn't want Jacin to feel her trembling. She glanced over her shoulder to make sure Shar and Frost were nearby.

'This door is solid wood,' Jacin explained as he heaved it open, 'and the panelling on the walls in here is the same.'

He disappeared into the room and Noah followed. Elaborate iron candelabras on the walls shed warm candlelight over the three low beds that stood like islands at evenly-spaced intervals down the length of the treatment room. On either side of the beds, carved wooden stools squatted on the dusty floor.

'What's on the floor?' Noah asked.

'Like the walls, there is wooden panelling on the floor, and like the walls, the floor has had olluka sap squeezed into the cracks to seal it and make it soundproof.'

'What about the dust?'

'Ground linseed. It preserves the olluka wood and enhances soundproofing by seeping into and filling all the natural spaces in the timber.'

'Neat,' Noah said.

'Very,' he agreed, 'but I'm sure that's not what you're most interested in here.'

Suddenly very aware that the door to the treatment room was closed with the guards on the other side of it, Noah turned to face Jacin. 'You're right,' she said. 'I'm particularly interested in who made those candelabras. I'd love a couple for my studio.'

He took the viola from Noah and put in on the end of the nearest bed. 'I will buy some and deliver them to you personally after you have returned to Leninstar,' he promised. Taking both her hands in his, he added, 'I've been looking for an excuse to visit.'

'Unless you're going to demonstrate a tonic for me, I'd say we're done here.'

'You're not even a bit curious?'

'About?'

'Me.'

'I am curious,' Noah admitted, 'but I'd be happier to talk about it outside.'

'You don't trust me?'

'No.'

'Why not?'

She looked down at her hands and then back at him.

Jacin smiled. 'We are just holding hands. Surely Emir would not be jealous?'

Balancing her weight and running through a series of defensive moves in her head, Noah hoped her surprise didn't show. 'This is not about Emir,' she said. 'This is about my personal space. I have a very big personal space.'

'Shame,' he said, drawing her closer and lightly kissing the back of each of her hands. 'I find it hard to resist a pretty girl.'

Noah felt her cheeks warming at the compliment, though she imagined that any human female would look attractive to him after living in Carai.

He released her.

'Leninstar has many pretty girls,' Noah said. 'When you deliver those candelabras, I will introduce you to some.'

He sighed and sat on the end of the bed. 'Alas, no matter how pretty they are – they won't have looks *and* talent. Not like you, Professor.'

Noah winced as she searched for a way to change the subject. Finally, she said, 'Where do you come from?'

'Sorry?'

'Where were you born?' Noah said.

'I was born here in Carai. The only time I've lived anywhere else was when I studied in Mellifont.'

Noah stared at him while she formulated her next question but he saved her the trouble.

'I'm a goman, Noah.'

She shook her head. 'A what?'

'A goman – half goblin, half human. I look human – like my mother – but my father is a goblin.'

'And Gisa …'

'Takes after my father,' Jacin finished. 'So I'll forgive you that you didn't see the family resemblance.'

'You're too kind,' Noah murmured, trying to think of a diplomatic question to ask about his parents. Unable to think of one she said, 'Why did you go to Mellifont?'

'Because I wanted to study raiki and because I thought I'd get away with it.'

'But Mellifont is full of adepts attuned to the music of the world and everything in it. If you are half goblin, how is it that no one there noticed?'

'They weren't looking for one.'

'Part of Mellifont's brief is to … control goblin populations,' Noah said.

'Kill goblins,' Jacin said evenly. 'Yes, I know. I never did that though. I wanted to study raiki to help my kin here. I did that. I went to Mellifont. I studied. I came home with knowledge. And now, if we can get a share of the firestone, I can start doing some real work here.'

Keen to avoid a conversation about firestone, Noah said, 'What do you mean "real work"?'

'Have you heard of the ilanxis worm?'

'Yes,' Noah said. 'Nerili mentioned it the other night at dinner. Sounds nasty.'

Jacin stared at her intently. 'It's worse than that. I've seen what it does … it's devastating.'

From his tone, Noah assumed someone close to him had been affected so she didn't press for details.

'Eel is a big part of our diet,' he continued, 'and eel fishing is a big part of our culture. Obviously the fishermen fish in specified areas and are careful to inspect their catch but occasionally the odd one slips through. I want to be able to heal people who are affected by it.'

'Surely prevention is better,' Noah countered.

'Obviously,' Jacin agreed, 'but if the worst should happen ... I've been working on a tonic for a year now, Noah, but I need firestone.'

Noah didn't dare breathe.

'I know you carry a piece,' he said. When she didn't reply, he said, 'Do you deny it?'

'No,' she said quietly.

'I will not ask you for it or try to take it from you, Noah, but I would ask a favour in return for my restraint.'

'What kind of favour?'

'Test me,' he said.

'Test you?'

Jacin picked up the viola Ginny had made and handed it to Noah. 'You have training. Test me to see what I really am. I want you to understand.'

'Why?'

'There are many of us, Noah – and we are growing in number. Being neither fully goblin or fully human, we don't "fit in". Our lives are ... difficult.'

Jacin pulled down the collar of the skivvy he wore under his adept's vest.

'Is that a tattoo?' Noah asked.

'A brand,' Jacin said. 'Just so everyone knows.'

Noah studied the mark. It looked like a cursive 'm' with an arrow on the exit stroke. 'Gisa?'

Jacin nodded. 'She has the mark too.'

'But you *look* different. That's part of why you went to Mellifont – to escape the taunts,' she guessed.

'The taunts I can take but the beatings ...'

'And that's part of your quest with the ilanxis cure?' Noah said. 'To gain acceptance?'

'King Nerili understands our plight,' he said, sidestepping Noah's question. 'He wants to make things right. Gomans have the potential to unite goblins and humans ...'

'But only if humans know they exist,' Noah said. 'That's why Nerili brought me here.'

Jacin smiled. 'Yes, that's why Nerili brought you here. You will verify it.'

He swung his legs up onto the bed and lay down, interlacing his fingers and bringing his hands to rest over his abdomen. Closing his eyes, Jacin said, 'Ready.'

Noah chewed her bottom lip as she placed the viola case on the stool by the bed and opened it. With her back to Jacin she took the firestone slider from her locket and put it into the bridge of the instrument. As she fumbled the slider into place, the pledge she'd made to Sachin swam through her mind. *I promise to use the firestone in accordance with the Council's by-laws and for the greater good of Talisker.* She decided not to count how many by-laws she might be breaking as she tucked the viola under her chin and retrieved the bow.

'You'll feel a tingling sensation,' Noah said, 'but it shouldn't be painful.'

'How long will it take?'

'Only a few minutes.'

'Take as long as you need,' Jacin said. 'It's important that you're thorough.'

'Right,' Noah said as she set the bow across the strings.

Noah brought an image of Sachin's face to mind as she began to play. *He would do this,* she thought. If it needed to be done, he'd do it and to hell with the by-laws. As a professor, she had a responsibility to the Academy. She couldn't shy away from it just because it made her uncomfortable. *You're a professional,* she told herself, *now do your job.*

Noah wove her tonic methodically. Every note was measured, every reverberation analysed. She tested him from his skin to his core in the most intense musical deconstruction that she'd performed. After several minutes, she lowered the viola.

Jacin opened his eyes and sat up. 'Well?'

Noah nodded. 'I can find goblin and human elements in your signature.'

Eyes twinkling, Jacin jumped up and strode across the room to the door. He pulled it open. Nerili stood on the other side.

Jacin bowed and stepped aside. 'Your Highness.'

Nerili's eyes went straight to Noah. 'And?'

'I've tested him,' Noah said.

'And?'

'I can find goblin and human elements in his signature.'

Nerili smiled as Noah wrestled her revulsion. She wanted to scream at him. *If your men would stop kidnapping and raping our women – this wouldn't happen!*

'Jacin, wait outside,' Nerili said without taking his eyes off Noah.

'But Your Majesty, I—'

'Wait outside,' he repeated, 'or I'll send you to … your room.'

Jacin sighed. 'I'll wait outside, Your Majesty.'

Noah frowned, the odd exchange taking the edge off her anger.

'Are you ready to change?' Nerili asked.

'Change?'

'You and Montana need to be Gisa and Rankin for our visit to Parliament this afternoon. I need to be seen with *all* my counsellors.'

'Where's Ulan?'

'He's just arrived.'

Ignoring her racing heart, Noah said, 'Well, we'd better find Montana then.'

Chapter 12

'A jousting arena that doubles as parliament? Very civilised,' Noah whispered to Montana as they took their seats.

The high priestess nodded but didn't say anything as she took her seat between Noah and Ulan.

'They only joust in the event of a tied vote,' Jacin said quietly.

To Noah's surprise, the public bleachers were packed. Either the goblins here had a keen interest in the parliamentary process or more likely, they were praying for a joust – free entertainment. The robed goblin on the dais banged his gavel on the bench.

'Be seated,' the chamber supervisor called, banging his gavel again. 'We are now in session.'

The seventy-two parliamentarians at the two long tables that ran the length of the jousting tracks did as instructed.

'Today,' the chamber supervisor said, 'we will hear final submissions for the One Citizen Project. I call on Ursis of clan Byron, to address the assembly as the project's sponsor.'

A goblin about a third of the way down the first table got to her feet. She wore a leather skirt bearing an embroidered leaf motif and a matching stole pinned at the front with a brooch that struggled to contain her ample bosom. Her right eye was higher than her left and her misshapen nose reminded Noah of a rotten apricot, but at least she wore a wig to conceal any other deformities.

'Gomans walk among us in Carai,' she began, reading from a sheet of parchment, 'and they have the right to feel as if they belong here. For too long, they have been discriminated against – treated as second class citizens. This must stop, and we have the power to ensure that it does.

'Yes, we are at war with humans and we cannot ignore this reality. The war goes on and we cannot – must not – shy away from it. But equally, we must not persecute our own. These are *our* children. And our children should revere us, not revile us. Can they revere us when we brand them like criminals? Can they revere us when we taunt them? Can they revere us when we bash them? Throw them out of our homes? Deny them an education? Deny them jobs? No, of course they can't.

'These are *our* children. Yes, they have human blood in them but it is our responsibility to teach them the right way to live. Do we want them thinking humans are better than us? That humans know how to live better than us? The Score tells us the right way to live. The Score tells us to take care of our kin.

'And there are some here who think that this "problem" should never have happened in the first place – some who think goblins and humans should not produce offspring. To those goblins I say this: if nature sanctions it then who are we to argue?'

As the goblin sat down to rapturous applause and whistling, Noah could feel her heart pounding in her chest. *If nature sanctions it?* Did she hear her correctly? Anger surged through her. *If nature sanctions it?* In her reading of the Score, Noah had found nothing that sanctioned kidnapping and raping prisoners of war.

The chamber supervisor was on the gavel again. 'Enough,' he cried. 'That's enough.'

When the din had died down sufficiently, he said, 'I call upon Leon of clan Hurne to speak on behalf of the opposition.'

A nuggety little goblin leapt to his feet and then up onto his chair. Noah wished he'd worn a full length cloak and perhaps a paper bag over his head.

'This is ludicrous,' he said, slamming a fist into the palm of his other hand. 'I call upon all true-hearted goblins to vote against this submission. This is a travesty! I, for one, cannot stand idly by while our ancient bloodlines are sullied with human filth. We should be proud of our heritage and stay true to our ancestors. Those noble goblins fought for our freedom and paid with their lives. Are we to show contempt for their sacrifice by consorting with the enemy?'

Out of the corner of her eye, Noah saw King Nerili's fists clench in his lap. She felt much the same way, though for a very different reason.

The little goblin continued his rant. 'And what of the half-castes themselves? While I pity them – they were given no choice about their creation – this outrage cannot be allowed to continue. We should compensate these *victims* – these tainted, pitiful creatures – though it is hard to imagine in what way we could possibly ease the burden of their ingrained human weakness and malice. But it should be done. And then we need to move forward. Let history show that today was the day when common sense and good judgement prevailed. Let history record that this parliament was the one that admitted to mistakes of the past and sought to set things right. Today we must outlaw breeding between goblins and humans! We must keep the goblin race pure!'

Noah thought she might actually be sick. In the goblin's speech she found her evidence of a commonality between humans and goblins. Bigotry. Hatred and prejudice flowed both ways – it seemed goblins and humans shared the same appalling character flaws. This goblin's prejudice against humans galled her but she knew humans held the same prejudice towards goblins. *She* held the same prejudice towards goblins. Though her revulsion for goblins seemed justified given their wanton slaughter of humans over centuries, it was going to be tough to look in the mirror from now on. Noah knew she'd see the repulsive little goblin leering back at her.

As if sensing her disquiet, Montana put her hand on Noah's leg and gave a little squeeze. Noah kept her eyes straight ahead, thankful for the glamour that concealed her face.

The chamber supervisor banged his gavel again. 'Charla of clan Nu to speak as an independent.'

The goblin that stood up wore her goman's brand like a challenge.

'I am a goman, Leon, and I am *not* going away.'

Applause rippled around the chamber, led by Jacin, and then swelled. 'Clap, Gisa,' he said quietly. 'She's one of *us*.'

Belatedly remembering her disguise, Noah fell into character, clapping alongside her brother.

'I don't want to be *compensated*, Leon,' Charla continued. 'I want to be *accepted*.'

Leon spat. 'I have no problem with you being accepted, Charla,' he said, 'just not here.'

'I must be accepted here,' Charla insisted. 'This is my home.'

When she offered nothing more, Leon sneered. 'Is that it?' he taunted. 'Is that all you've got to say?'

'Yes,' Charla said calmly. 'That's all I have to say.'

'A vote!' the chamber supervisor called.

Noah shifted in her seat. Compared to the other two speakers, Charla's address was astonishingly brief. Noah scanned the chamber. She was quite sure some of the parliamentarians had actually missed the independent's appeal.

The chamber supervisor stood up. 'Those in favour of the One Citizen Project, move to my right; those against, move to my left.'

The commotion on the floor was instantaneous. Goblins shot out of their seats and their fists flew as they fought their way to their preferred side of the chamber. Noah saw the ayes were in the majority but the nays still had significant support. About a third of the parliamentarians opposed the submission – not enough to force a joust today.

'The ayes have it,' the chamber supervisor announced.

The roar from the goblins in the bleachers was deafening. It was difficult to tell how many were for and against in the crowd, but fighting broke out all around.

Nerili hissed. 'We leave now. Move!'

♪♫

Noah watched Montana as Shar lit the torches in their bedchamber. After two exhausting days touring Carai, Noah was thankful they had only one day left.

'Will there be anything else?' Shar asked as he snuffed a taper with his fingers.

'No, thank you,' Noah said.

The guard nodded. 'I'll be outside for two hours and then Liah will take the guard.'

'Sure,' Noah said, following Shar to the door to hook the catch after him.

With the room secured, Noah said, 'Spill.'

Montana looked up. 'I'm fine.'

'Liar.'

Montana straightened in her chair but didn't speak. Noah waited. Maybe that was going a bit far. She imagined that the high priestess hadn't often been subjected to that kind of accusation during her three-hundred-year reign. But there was something wrong – she'd been quiet since the parliamentary proceedings – and Noah wanted to help. It hurt her that her friend wouldn't share her thoughts.

'I'm like them,' Montana said at last. 'I know how they feel.'

Noah knew she meant the gomans and though she wanted to object, she didn't interrupt.

'I don't know if it's worse to be banished, or to stay and be reviled,' Montana said. 'I don't remember my father. My mother and I were exiled from Aoratia when I was only days old. And my mother's been dead for over seven centuries now. Sometimes I think it would be nice to be among family. I guess you understand that too, Noah.'

'My situation's not the same,' Noah said. 'Both my parents were human – even if they did come from different worlds.'

'But you understand not … belonging.'

'Yes.'

'This will challenge the Alliance, Noah,' Montana said. 'The debate we saw this afternoon is equal to anything I have seen in the seven states. It was not just a question of law and order, but of morality. Carai's goblins are different.'

'And you liked the temple,' Noah said.

Montana nodded. 'Of course. But the parliament showed more. At the temple, they *read* from the Score. In their parliament, they are *actioning* it – or trying to. I wonder how the seven states would deal with gomans.'

'You're part elf, part human – and humans revere you as their high priestess.'

'That's different and you know it. Humans *like* elves.'

Montana went quiet again. Emboldened by what her friend had shared, Noah pushed a little further. 'Do you think your father knows that you're High Priestess?'

'I would think so. I hope one day – before he passes over – that he'll seek me out.'

'Passes over?'

'Elves live for a long time compared to humans, but we are not immortal. My father was young when I was born, just over a thousand years old, so he has a few thousand years left in him yet.'

'Can you not visit Aoratia?'

'My life is forfeit if I do.'

A knock at the door relieved Noah of the obligation of responding.

'I'll get it,' Noah said. Walking to the door, she called, 'Who is it?'

Shar's voice announced, 'Gisa and Jacin.'

Noah released the latch and slid the door aside. 'Come in,' she said.

The two goblin counsellors – *goman* counsellors, Noah reminded herself – swept into the room. She was relieved Ulan wasn't with them. Noah couldn't figure out what it was about Ulan that made her more uneasy than the other goblins, but he made her skin crawl. Whatever his relationship with the young Prince Sandor might be, Ulan was one of Nerili's counsellors, a trusted adviser, and though Noah didn't trust Nerili, she trusted he'd protect her safety to achieve his own ends.

'Noah!' Jacin said, kissing her cheek as his sister relatched the door.

Montana stood. 'To what do we owe this honour?'

Jacin took Noah's hands. They were warm and to Noah's chagrin, she felt the heat rising in her cheeks. He smiled at her.

'I'm here to break you out,' he whispered. 'You want to see more of Carai? I can show you.'

Noah gasped. 'How?'

Montana walked over to Noah and put a hand on Jacin's arm. 'Unhand her,' she said.

Jacin released his grip and held up his hands in surrender. Noah kept her eyes on his impish face. His honey-brown eyes gleamed in the torchlight.

'Noah, no,' Montana said. 'I forbid it.'

'How did you even hear that?' Jacin said. 'I whispered.'

Noah turned to her friend. 'We've spent two days seeing what Nerili wants us to see. We need to do our own investigating and this could be our only chance.'

'I'll take good care of her,' Jacin promised. 'I'll be her chaperone.'

Montana frowned. 'You work for Nerili – you're one of his counsellors – why would you do this?'

'He *employs* me,' Jacin said. 'He doesn't *own* me.'

'How will we get out?' Noah asked.

Jacin inspected his manicured nails. 'You're getting quite good at imitating Gisa.'

'You're too kind.'

'Today's attempt was certainly better than what you did at the temple,' he added.

Realisation washed over her. 'That was *you* watching me?'

'Yes,' he replied smugly.

Not knowing whether she should be relieved or not, she just said, 'Oh.'

'So are you up for a night on the town?' Jacin asked.

Before Noah could answer, Gisa spoke up.

'Noah will be in good hands, High Priestess and I'll stay here with you until she returns.'

'And if Nerili finds out?' Montana asked.

'I'll answer for it,' Jacin said.

Noah nodded. 'I'll get ready.'

'I'm coming with you,' Montana said.

'I can only take one of you,' Jacin said. 'One Gisa came in, one Gisa goes out.'

Montana stepped in front of Noah. 'Noah is only here because she is my friend, but this mission is my responsibility. *I* will come with you.'

Looking around the High Priestess, Jacin said, 'Noah?'

'I can do this,' Noah whispered to Montana.

Montana turned and put her hands on Noah's shoulders. Keeping her voice low, she said, 'What if it's a trap, Noah? What if he wants to get you outside, get you alone and then take your firestone?'

'Well, let's see.' Noah made a show of taking off her locket and handing it to Montana. 'Keep it here. Keep it safe.'

'Noah, this mission is my responsibility.'

'Yes,' Noah said, 'and if Nerili decides he wants to talk to one of us tonight – it's likely to be you. You need to stay here. Just in case.'

Montana shook her head. 'If anything were to happen to you …'

'If anything happens to me,' Noah said, glancing at Jacin, 'hunt him down and show him no mercy.'

Chapter 13

Her glamour in place, Noah unhooked the door latch with Jacin at her side.

Shar looked at them at they exited the bedchamber. 'Night,' he said.

Noah nodded her head to the guard as Jacin said, 'Night.'

The pair scooted along the passageways, greeting anyone they passed with a cheery wave. Each goblin they duped increased Noah's confidence in her disguise. Following Jacin's lead through the myriad corridors in the olluka branch palace, she contemplated what his motives might be. She had no right to trust him any more than anyone else in Carai. In fact, she should probably be more wary of him. Jacin had raiki training and had easily pierced her glamour at the temple. And he was willing to risk Nerili's censure by exposing his boss's hostage to great danger on the city's streets.

When they reached the reinforced doors that marked the boundary between the palace and the city beyond, Jacin knocked without hesitation.

A voice from outside said, 'Who wishes to leave the king's palace?'

'Jacin and Gisa,' Jacin called. 'We wish to go home.'

The iron-clad doors parted silently and two armed soldiers stood beyond the threshold.

In unison, Noah and Jacin said, 'Night.'

The soldiers nodded. 'Night,' one said. 'See you tomorrow.'

'Indeed you will,' Jacin said, taking Noah's arm and striding out onto the winding cobblestone path that led down to the city.

Once they were out of earshot of the soldiers, Noah said, 'It's weird that you say "night",' she said. 'Given that there's no sun underground – day and night are a bit irrelevant aren't they?'

'It is quaint, I guess but we need "waking" hours and "sleeping" hours. Day and night seems a good way to distinguish between the two.'

'Fair enough,' Noah said. 'Where are you taking me?'

'I'm thirsty. I say we get a drink.'

'What kind of drink?'

'There's an alehouse nearby.' He looked at Noah, a cheeky twinkle in his eye. 'You up for it?'

'Absolutely.'

They walked the busy streets arm-in-arm. Carts, carriages and barrows rumbled at speed along the main roadway, the drivers apparently unconstrained by the concept of lanes. To Noah it was like watching the on-douz – a spirited medieval chariot rally of supreme physicality. The overland race was now an historical curiosity to most in Leninstar but many relished the opportunity to preserve ancient traditions by competing in the annual event. Sentimentality aside, still more were lured by the prospect of the speed and danger that epitomised the race.

Noah tore her gaze from the mesmerising spectacle on the roadway to focus on her own safety. In this street, the foot traffic was as chaotic as the vehicle traffic. She had to avoid too much physical contact if her glamour were to remain intact.

'There,' Jacin said.

Noah looked at him and then followed his gaze. A tattered flag depicting a bunch of peaches hung from an iron bar just ahead.

'Does it have a name?' Noah asked.

'Bunch of Peaches,' Jacin said.

Sorry she'd asked, Noah followed him inside.

The goblin behind the bar waved as they approached. 'Two peach ciders?' the bartender called.

'You know us too well,' Jacin said. He pushed two coins into Noah's hand and added, 'Pay the man, Sis. I'll get our usual seats.'

The alehouse wasn't packed but Noah held her breath as she threaded her way to the bar. Her skin tingled, in small part from the glamour but mostly it was the thrill of doing something in Carai without Nerili or his guards looking over her shoulder.

Noah put the coins down on the bar and nodded to the barman as she collected the drinks. He saluted her before turning his attention to his next pour. Thankful he didn't want to engage her in conversation, Noah turned in the direction Jacin had gone. She caught sight of him in a booth near the window – a perfect vantage point to watch the comings and goings on the street.

Noah placed the drinks on the table and slid onto her seat.

'So where do you want to go tonight?' Jacin asked.

Noah sipped her drink. Even though this was the opportunity she'd been waiting for, she hesitated.

At length, she said, 'Somewhere Nerili doesn't want me to go.'

Jacin shrugged. 'I'm sure there are plenty of places he doesn't want you to go. Could you be more specific?'

'I don't know,' Noah said. 'I feel like he's showing me just the fragments of goblin society that the Alliance would approve of. I'd just like to see some other fragments … to present a more balanced view.'

'I wouldn't have picked you for a rebel, Noah,' he said, running his finger around the rim of his glass, 'but this could be fun. We could go to a few more bars, then head out to bet on some illegal cock-fights and – if you're up for it – we could go to a dance party after that?'

Noah stared at him. 'I can do all that at home in Leninstar.'

Jacin leaned forward and folded his arms on the table. 'I have no doubt, but I thought you wanted to see Carai – to get a balanced view.'

'Would you really take me to those places?'

'I promised Montana that I would chaperone you,' he said, putting his hand over his heart, 'so yes, I would. And I won't pretend that dancing with you – nice and close – isn't a *very* big drawcard.'

'You are unbelievably forward,' Noah said.

'Does that shock you?'

'I bet you wouldn't even know what to *do* with a girl if you managed to get your hands on one.'

Jacin winked at her. 'Will I get us another round of drinks?'

'Sure.'

He stood up. 'Don't go anywhere.'

As Noah scanned the clientele in the alehouse, a goblin at an adjacent table caught her eye. He winked at her and raised his glass. Noah froze. As Gisa, sitting at her usual table, how should she respond? Was the goblin a friend? Noah decided to go with a nod and a smile and a prayer that Jacin would return quickly with the drinks. To avoid any more eye contact with other patrons, she turned to the window and watched the antics in the street.

A full glass appeared on the table in front of her and Jacin took his seat.

'Why did you bring me out tonight?' she asked.

Unfazed, Jacin said, 'Because you wanted to come out.'

'But Nerili will be furious with you if he finds out.'

'Yes.'

'And that doesn't bother you?'

'Oh, he'll probably just send me to my room again,' Jacin said.

'He said that at the raiki centre this morning. What does that actually mean?'

'I'm for the dungeon again.'

'Again? You spend a bit of time there, do you?'

'There *is* now a cell with my name on it.'

Noah studied him. 'I don't get it. Why, if you have so much trouble following his orders, do you continue to work for him? And why, if he has to send you to the dungeon so often, does he continue to employ you?'

Jacin took a long sip of his cider. 'I work for Nerili because I support his stance on gomans and also his plan to join the Sovereign States Alliance for a share of the firestone,' he said. 'Nerili employs me for my raiki knowledge, but that doesn't mean he owns me.'

'You accused me of being a rebel,' Noah said, 'but it's actually *you* who is the rebel.'

'I'm not a rebel,' Jacin said. 'It's just that our agendas don't always align.'

Noah dropped her voice. 'And what is your agenda, Jacin?'

When he smiled, his eyes twinkled. 'To see you naked.'

Noah shook her head. 'You're impossible.'

'It's been said,' he admitted. 'Now drink up. Skuda is watching us and I don't want to talk to him tonight.'

'Who's Skuda?' Noah asked before chugging a few mouthfuls from her glass.

Jacin inclined his head. 'Two tables back. Red cape.'

'He winked at me before,' Noah said.

'He's a grub. Doesn't like gomans.'

'Ahhh. Well, he's up and—'

Noah stopped her commentary as Skuda made his way towards them.

'He's coming this way?' Jacin guessed.

'Mmm-huh.'

'Let me do the talking.'

'Mmm-huh.'

Skuda dragged a chair to the table, the unholy squeal it made threatening to unbind Noah's glamour. He put his half-empty pint-glass on the table and sat down. Even the yeasty smell of the murky ale couldn't cover the sour odour of the goblin and Noah kept her breathing shallow so she didn't gag.

'And how are my two favourite gomans tonight?' Skuda said.

'Leaving,' Jacin said coolly.

'Anything exciting happening at the palace?'

'Well, since we're not there, probably not,' Jacin said.

Skuda leered. 'You're a cocky little bastard, ain't ya?'

Jacin stood up. 'We're leaving.'

'I'm surprised to see you here – mixing with us commoners,' Skuda said, 'when the palace is entertaining such high profile guests. The high priestess is here, and some human.'

Skuda sat back in his chair, awaiting a reaction.

Ignoring the goblin, Jacin said, 'Gisa, let's go.'

Heart hammering, Noah pushed her chair back and got to her feet.

'You're quiet tonight, Gisa,' Skuda taunted. 'You don't look well.'

Focusing on the firestone in her veins to keep the glamour intact, she put her hand to her head. Jacin followed her lead.

'She isn't well,' he said. 'That's why we need to go. Excuse us.'

Skuda reached out for Noah's hand but Jacin was quicker, swatting the goblin's hand away.

'*DON'T YOU TOUCH ME, BOY!*' Skuda roared, drawing a knife from his belt and staggering to his feet.

Noah looked at Jacin who jumped up on the table.

'Come on Gisa,' he urged, waving his arm like a traffic warden. 'After you.'

She reacted instantly, joining him on the table and then leaping out the open window. Jacin landed beside her, took her elbow and steered her along the street.

'I want to meet your parents,' Noah blurted.

'Wow,' he said, without missing a step, 'and you think *I'm* forward. What would Emir say?'

'This isn't about Emir,' she said.

'So you keep saying,' Jacin said. 'Makes me dare to dream, Noah.'

Chapter 14

Jacin tossed a couple of coins into the driver's open purse. The goblin driver turned and winked, then focused his attention back on the road.

'We'll jump off just down at the corner,' Jacin said to Noah. 'The cart will slow down but it won't stop.'

Noah nodded. It was the first time Jacin had spoken since they'd boarded the cart near the alehouse and she'd found his silence disconcerting. She hoped that it was just prudent discretion rather than something more sinister. Would he take her to his parents? Could he? He'd said his father was a goblin but his mother was human. This could be what Montana was looking for. Evidence of human slavery.

'Now,' Jacin said, leaping off the cart.

Noah followed, thoughts of the afternoon's parliamentary sitting racing through her mind. For all the talk of gomans, there'd been no mention of the human women who'd mothered them. Noah felt a flash of anger surge through her. This *was* what she needed to see, but would Jacin let her see it? He'd said that his and Nerili's agendas didn't always align but could he afford to go this far?

As they walked along the quiet suburban street, far from the palace, Noah's mind raced. Like startled baitfish, questions darted about inside her head – chased by doubts cloaked in apprehension. But rather than give in to fear, Noah fanned her anger.

She glanced sideways at her companion. 'How much further?'

'Next block,' he replied without looking at her. 'Lose the glamour.'

Noah whistled a few notes to dismantle her disguise. 'Done.'

Jacin nodded as they crossed the street. 'Fourth house on the right.'

The squat brick cottages nestled side by side glowed warmly from within, light seeping from the open windows. The houses were set back a few metres from the road and the front doors were all on the right side of the buildings rather than in the centre. Jacin took her hand as he turned onto a brick path. With his free hand he reached into his pocket and pulled out a key. He slid it into the lock and the door opened without a sound.

Jacin turned to her, the mischievous gleam in his eye as bright as ever. 'Are you sure you want to do this?'

'Any option that allows me to keep my clothes on is a good one,' she replied.

'Such a shame,' he said with a shrug.

Noah followed Jacin into the kitchen where a goblin man and a human woman sat at the table with six children.

One of the boys, a goblin of about six, squealed when he saw Noah.

The man glared at Jacin. 'I've told you to stop disguising your sister – you know it wigs Evan out.'

'Not a disguise,' Jacin said, reaching over Evan and plucking a plum from the table. Patting the young boy on the shoulder, Jacin added, 'Gisa's still at the palace. This is Noah, from Leninstar.'

The human woman stood up and walked towards Noah as Jacin popped the plum in his mouth. All eyes around the table followed her.

'Noah?' she whispered. 'Noah Chord?'

Reflexively taking the woman's outstretched hands, Noah nodded. She glanced down but the woman's long sleeves meant Noah couldn't inspect her wrists for signs of ligature marks.

'This is my mum,' Jacin said. 'Amy.'

'Nice to meet you, Amy,' Noah said.

'I've heard stories about you,' Amy said. 'I'm from Leninstar … originally.'

Fighting to keep her face neutral, Noah said, 'Oh really? How long has it been since you were there?'

The goblin man stood up. 'Perhaps you'd like to take a seat, Noah?' he said, pointing to a vacant chair. 'We have a spare since Jacin has ditched his sister again. I'm Linus, by the way.'

'Nice to meet you, Linus,' Noah said politely as Jacin pulled out a chair for her.

Noah sat down. Jacin placed himself between her and Evan as Amy and Linus took their seats again. Smiling at the children, Noah saw that only one of them – a girl of maybe four – had human features like Jacin.

Linus waved a hand over the food. 'Help yourself to some dinner, Noah,' he said.

Noah looked at her plate. The place had obviously been set for Gisa. 'Thank you,' she said.

'Twenty-five years,' Amy said.

Noah looked up.

Amy smiled. 'It's been twenty-five years since I left Leninstar.'

Noah's stomach churned. She was desperate to ask Amy why she had left but there were children present. That question could wait.

'I haven't been on Talisker very long,' Noah said. 'I'm surprised you've heard of me.'

'It might surprise you to learn that we get much news of what happens on the surface,' Amy said. 'A girl who comes from Earth to become Royal Tailor and Dragonsbane of Talisker is big news.'

Embarrassed, Noah attempted a smile. 'Oh. Right.'

'So what brings you to our humble home?' Linus asked.

Noah considered her response. She couldn't tell him she was planning to find evidence of a human sex-slave racket. Nor could she tell him that she was trying to avoid a sleazy night on the town at his son's hand.

'I suffer badly from cabin-fever,' Noah said. 'Jacin offered to show me the sights.'

Linus raised an eyebrow. 'I wouldn't have thought this would be high on his list.'

Despite herself, Noah stifled a smile.

'We ran into Skuda at the alehouse,' Jacin explained. 'Even disguised as Gisa, it's too dangerous for Noah to be out.'

'Figures,' Linus said. 'Kids – time to get washed up for bedtime.'

All but one of the children scrambled from their seats to a room beyond view.

'Leif, go,' Amy said.

'I'm not a kid,' the boy insisted.

'Then keep eating,' Linus said.

Even his goblin features couldn't mask Leif's inner conflict. Leif clearly didn't want to eat but he didn't want to be banished from the table either. He reminded Noah of Gillette.

'Give me news of Leninstar, Noah,' Amy said.

Leif sighed. 'Alright. I'm going.'

Once he'd stormed out of the room, Amy added, 'Tell us about the firestone. Have you seen it?'

Noah's heart lurched. It wouldn't hurt to give them some information, she reasoned. And if she did, she might have more chance of getting the information she sought in return.

Jacin put his hand on hers. 'Please, Noah. Tell us.'

Pushing thoughts of Brinn aside, she said, 'Of course.'

For nearly ten minutes, she kept them enthralled with details about the mine and the electricity network the firestone would power.

'But have you *seen* the stone?' Jacin pressed.

'Indeed I have,' she said, and though she tried valiantly to describe it, when she was done she felt she'd done it a grave injustice.

'Sounds amazing,' Amy said. 'With electricity, Leninstar will be transformed.'

'As *we* will be if Nerili can negotiate a share for us,' Linus added.

Noah looked at Amy. 'Would you consider visiting Leninstar again?'

Amy shook her head. 'My life is here now. There is no going back.'

Noah searched for an appropriate question, but Amy saved her the trouble.

'You're curious,' Amy said. 'You want to know why I'm here.'

'It had crossed my mind,' Noah admitted.

Amy smiled as she looked at Linus. 'I was born in Leninstar, raised there, and married there,' she began, 'but my husband – Wess, his name was – was a brute. He beat me, almost daily. I slaved on our farm but whatever I did was never good enough. He always found something to thrash me for. One morning, I got up, packed my lunch and went down to the paddock as usual. But when I got there, I kept walking and walking and walking – as far from the farmhouse as I could get.

'At nightfall I stopped and lay down. I was so exhausted I slept through the night – untroubled by my pains, the cold or night prowlers. When I awoke, I was shocked to see a goblin sitting near me, watching me. It was Linus.'

Noah watched them smile at each other before Amy continued her story. 'His first words to me were "You're hurt". I couldn't deny it. I was covered in bruises and cuts and I had a broken arm – all courtesy of Wess. Linus offered to care for me and though I knew I should be terrified of goblins, I was in too much pain. I figured nothing could be worse than what I'd been through. He brought me here and cared for me until I was well again. We were married soon after and now we have eight beautiful children, including two sets of twins. I couldn't be happier. I will never go back to Leninstar. My family and friends are here now.'

Noah nodded, not knowing what to say.

'There are many women like me here, Noah,' Amy said. 'Many have come here – not just from Leninstar – and found happiness.'

Noah cringed when Leon – the nuggety little bigot in parliament – popped into her mind. She imagined him winking at her, validating her prejudice. She didn't want to be like Leon but the alternative was worse – believing that human women chose to be here.

'*Muuuum.*'

All eyes turned to see Evan standing at the end of the table clutching his blanket. Leif strode through the doorway as the younger boy lodged his complaint.

'Mum, tell Leif to stop making scary noises … I can't get to sleep.'

'I'm not doing anything,' Leif insisted. 'It's *him. He's* making the noises.'

'Am not!'

'Are too!'

'Am *not!*'

Out of the corner of her eye, Noah glimpsed movement at the window. She spun in her seat. A shadow flicked across the frosted pane. Followed by another.

'Shhhh,' Noah said.

Argument suspended, the sound of footsteps outside was clear.

Linus looked at Jacin. 'You've brought more friends?'

Thud. Thud.

'They're on the roof,' Amy said.

'Jacin!' a voice called. 'Come out and take what's coming to ya – and maybe we won't hurt anyone else.'

'Skuda,' Jacin said.

'What'd you do?' Linus asked as he pushed his chair back from the table and lumbered to his feet.

Jacin drew his sword. 'When we were at the alehouse, he tried to touch Noah. I swatted his hand away.'

Linus put his hand on Leif's shoulder. 'Get the little ones,' he said. 'Bring them in here. Quickly!'

Leif raced towards the doorway and disappeared. Linus strode to a chest and yanked open a drawer. He doled out blades like they were lollipops. Noah took a dagger and a pointed steel. Amy accepted a carving blade.

'Give me a dagger, would you?' Jacin said.

Amy passed the implement to her son and he tucked it into his belt.

Leif reappeared with his five siblings.

'You and Evan in the cloak cupboard,' Linus said to Leif. 'Little ones in the linen chest. Go!'

Amy grabbed as many little hands as she could and dragged them towards the chest. She wrenched open the lid as the youngest girl began to cry.

'Come on,' Amy said, reefing out a stack of blankets, 'it'll be like a cubby house.'

Noah raced to help clear the chest as more footsteps sounded overhead. When it was empty, she scooped up a little girl and put her inside.

'I'm going out there,' Jacin said.

'No,' Linus said.

'I'll lead them away.'

'There are too many of them. You might draw *some* of them – but we'll be left to deal with the rest.'

Chest secured, Noah sidled over to an open front window. 'Five out the front,' she said.

'There'll be at least that many out back,' Linus said.

'And there are at least three on the roof,' Amy added.

Jacin joined Noah at the front. 'They'll be archers.'

'We're trapped,' Noah whispered.

Jacin put his hand on her shoulder. 'Yes.'

'Will your neighbours come to help?'

'Unlikely. They won't want to draw trouble.'

Typical goblins, Noah thought.

Jacin turned to his father. 'You and Mum guard the back, Noah and I will make sure no one comes through the front.'

'And the archers?' Amy asked.

'They can't do anything while we're in here,' Jacin said.

Noah tested her borrowed blade. 'So we just wait and hope that they get bored and go away?'

'No,' Jacin whispered, peering out the window. 'I'm going out there.'

'But your father said—'

Without looking at her, he said, 'Skuda is not a patient goblin. More will come, Noah. And when they do, they'll storm the house and ...'

Crash.

Amy screamed.

'Look out!' Linus yelled, yanking his wife away from the window.

A rock lay on the floor under the shattered window. Noah watched in horror as a bottle sailed through the gap and smashed on the floor, spilling its contents in an oily slick. A goblin's sneering face appeared in the breach. He held a flaming torch.

'We told you to come out, Jacin and ya didn't,' he said. 'Don't say we didn't warn ya!' The goblin tossed the torch through the window. 'Death to the half-castes!' he chanted as he ran away. *Abominations!'*

Whoomp.

Noah felt the draught as the fire took hold, the flames sucking greed-
ily at the oxygen in the room. She leapt from her spot and dashed to the
chest where the children sheltered. Jacin was at her side. They opened the
lid and the terrified youngsters scrambled out.

'Catch them, Noah!' Jacin yelled.

Noah grabbed two arms and held tight. 'Got two,' she cried.

'They're smoking us out!' Amy said.

'*Burning* us out,' Linus said grimly as he pulled his sons from the
cloak cupboard. 'Leif, get the shields.'

Smoke filled the room, stinging Noah's eyes. 'What now?' she asked,
stifling a cough.

'We'll have to run for it,' Jacin said, 'but we'll all go together. If I
can get the lid off this chest, we can use it to shield the little ones from
the arrows.'

'And us?' Noah asked.

'We've got a few shields lying around – Leif will get the best ones.'

'Come on!' Linus called. 'We need to go.'

'Not yet,' Jacin said as he struck the chest's hinges with his hatchet
and tore off the lid. 'We need to wait until the last moment.'

'Why?' Noah said, hauling the children away from the advancing
flames.

'If the roof collapses, the archers will be stuffed. Take them,' he said
with a nod at the children, 'and wait at the door.'

Keen to put distance between herself and the hungry flames, Noah
did as she was told. Through the smoke, she saw Linus and Amy were
already at the front door shielding the two older boys.

Amid the crying and coughing, Noah heard Amy's voice. 'More are
coming.'

Noah squinted through watering eyes. Two carriages rolled into
view from opposite directions and stopped outside the Ilian house. *Jacin
said there'd be more,* she thought as goblins poured from the carriages.
We'll never get past them.

'So many,' Amy said.

'We stick together,' Linus said. 'Children in the middle under the
lid.' He passed a shield to Noah. 'Put that on your back ...'

Behind them, part of the ceiling crashed to the floor. Sparks spewed into the air, some landing on Noah's sleeve. One of the goblin youngsters squealed and swatted at Noah's arm. Noah wasn't sure if she was trying to extinguish the flame or release Noah's grip on her.

'Let's go!' Amy urged.

'Wait!' Jacin said, peering out the window. 'Something's wrong.'

Something's wrong? Noah thought. 'What's *not* wrong?' she said.

He put up his hand.

'Jacin! We really need to move,' Linus said. 'What do you see?'

All the children were crying now. If they didn't move soon, Noah's charges would slip from her sweaty grasp.

'The goblins are fighting each other,' Jacin said.

'We have allies?' Linus said.

'Couldn't say for sure,' Jacin replied, 'but we should run – capitalise on the confusion.'

'GO!' Linus roared.

Noah and Jacin took one side of the chest lid while Linus and Amy took the other. Leif herded the little ones underneath and pointed his sword at them. 'Stay under,' he commanded.

They ran outside. Noah checked herself, though her legs had more speed in them she needed to run in sync with the others. As goblins raced towards them, an arrow whizzed past her ear and another over her head. One sword-bearing goblin ran directly for her. Holding her dagger in her left hand, she clenched her jaw and braced herself for impact. He swiped at her and Noah blocked. Painful vibrations shot up her arm. An arrow zipped by her, lodging in the goblin's throat.

Lucky they're bad shots, Noah thought.

Skuda's voice cut across the mayhem. *'Death to the king who sullies our bloodlines!'*

Noah's head snapped to her right to see King Nerili striding towards them, a cordon of soldiers around him.

'I never thought I'd be glad to see him,' Noah said.

At Nerili's signal, his soldiers engaged the rebel goblins while he advanced on Noah. When he reached her, he grabbed her roughly by the arm.

'Let's go,' he growled.

'You have to help them,' Noah said.

'My soldiers will stay,' Nerili said, 'but we're going – *now!*'

'But—'

She saw his fist coming but wasn't quick enough to dodge it. Pain exploded in her head as blackness consumed her.

♪♫

Noah gingerly investigated the lump on her temple with her fingers. It had been three days since Nerili had struck her but the lump was still tender. At least the headache had subsided, despite the constant rattling of the carriage.

A shout of *'Whoa!'* from the driver distracted her. As the carriage slowed, Nerili put his hand on his sword hilt and looked at Noah and Montana. 'Get down,' he said.

Montana took Noah's hand and pulled her gently towards the floor.

As Nerili pushed open the door and got out of the carriage, Noah settled herself down beside Montana.

Montana smiled sympathetically. 'Stop beating yourself up, Noah.'

'How can I?'

After rescuing Noah from Skuda and his thugs at Jacin's house, Nerili had whisked them out of Carai. Montana had been waiting in the carriage. Noah hadn't seen Gisa, nor did she know if any of her family was still alive. While she wanted to direct her anger at Nerili for not staying to defend the family, she couldn't do it. She'd initiated the chain of events that had led the armed band to Jacin's house. Because of her, there was a good chance the Ilian family was dead.

At least, that's what her nightmares told her. The clattering of the carriage had made sleep difficult over the past few days but her sneaking subconscious had brutalised her at every opportunity with macabre and vivid visions of Skuda's work – Amy with an arrow through her throat, dismembered children. But Jacin had suffered most. All his skin had been removed before he died.

Noah clenched her teeth as nausea gripped her, making her head throb again. Amid a clatter of hoof beats, she heard a voice outside.

'Hail to the King!'

'What news?' Nerili replied, his voice like a simmering thunderstorm.

'I have to see what's happening,' Montana said, crawling to the window. She lifted the curtain a fraction and peeked outside.

Though Noah held her breath and strained to hear, she couldn't catch any of the conversation. She whispered to Montana. 'What can you see?'

'Three goblins,' Montana said. 'They're huddled around the king. I can't hear anything they're saying. Body language doesn't look promising though.'

After a few moments, the high priestess sat back down on the seat and patted the cushion beside her. 'There is no imminent threat,' she said. 'Come and sit, Noah.'

The pair sat in silence until Nerili returned. The carriage door flew open as the sound of hooves disappeared down the roadway towards Carai. Nerili lumbered back inside, his face pale.

'There is trouble at the mine,' he said as he took his seat.

'For whom?' Montana asked.

Nerili shot her a quizzical look.

'When you and your kin took over the mine,' Montana said, 'it spelled trouble for us. Now when you say there is trouble – I'm assuming you mean trouble for you?'

The goblin's eyes narrowed. 'There is trouble enough for all of us if what I'm told is true.'

'You have reason to doubt your messengers?'

'Not at all,' Nerili said. 'Only that their news is now hours out of date and the situation could have deteriorated further, although it is difficult to imagine how.'

'Are you going to tell us what happened?' Noah asked.

'The firestone is gone. Many of my soldiers are dead,' he said.

Noah's heart sank. 'And the hostages?'

'They remain.'

When he offered nothing further, Noah said, 'In what condition?'

'They were alive when the messengers departed,' he said. 'What we will find when we arrive, I cannot say.'

Noah said, 'How far out are we now?'

'About three hours.'

Montana said, 'How can the firestone be gone? Who took it?'

Noah thought about Brinn as Nerili tapped his knee with taloned fingers. 'Your kings took it.'

'How do you know that?' Noah asked.

'The assault force suffered some casualties,' he said. 'One of your kings is among them.'

Dreading the answer, Noah said, 'Who?'

He looked at her for a long moment. 'Your king,' he said. 'King Tambian.'

Chapter 15

Only when she stood over his corpse did Noah believe that Tambian was dead. No one had bothered to cover the body. The king lay on his side, his entrails and blood congealed on the dusty floor of the small chamber where the firestone had been. His sword lay beside him, his severed hand still on the hilt. Noah's stomach churned as she looked around her. Bodies littered the floor – in places, two and three deep, most of them goblins. Tambian's was the only body Noah recognised and she felt as if she might vomit.

'He wouldn't be a party to stealing the firestone,' Noah whispered. 'He wouldn't.'

'How Tambian came to be here is difficult to understand,' Montana said. 'There are many questions to be answered.'

Noah knelt down beside her king's body. She was aware of Nerili's gaze on her but her attention was on Tambian. His face looked peaceful. In light of his horrific injuries, she wondered how that could be. Whoever had disembowelled the king had been grotesquely thorough. With trembling hands, Noah reached out. A tear slid down her cheek as she took his remaining hand in hers. Something on his wrist caught her eye. She wiped away her tears to get a better look. Bruising. Dizziness washed through her. She closed her eyes briefly to steady herself. She looked again. Definitely bruising. She shifted her focus to the severed hand on Tambian's sword hilt, but there was too much blood for her to see anything conclusive there.

Noah looked up. 'Montana, can I have your cloak?'

Montana unclasped the clip at the neck of her emerald robe and let it slide from her shoulders. The high priestess laid it over Tambian's still form as Noah brushed away another tear. Noah had worked as the king's personal tailor for just over a year and he'd been good to her. He'd made her feel like part of the family – warts and all – even admonishing her for not being more tolerant of her pseudo-sister, Catriona.

'We will return the king's body to Leninstar,' Montana said to Nerili.

'Yes,' Nerili replied.

'You still want to join the Alliance?' the high priestess said.

'My goal has not changed,' Nerili said.

Noah stood up. 'Then let's get the hostages home.'

'No,' he said.

'Why not?' Noah said. 'The firestone was your big bargaining chip – and that's gone. The hostages have no value to you now.'

'That's not true,' Nerili said.

Noah glared at him. 'They have children at home.'

Nerili frowned. 'That is regrettable,' he said, 'but there is a problem with the hostages which means we cannot return them – especially if they have children.'

Noah's skin went cold. 'What kind of problem?'

'They've been infected … with ilanxis worm.'

'Ilanxis worm?' she said. 'How did *that* happen?'

Nerili shook his head. 'I don't know.'

Noah's fists clenched. 'Well, don't you think you'd better find out? You've clearly got some lunatic goblin running around here—'

'You think it's one of my kin?'

Noah's eyes widened. 'You don't? *We* don't have access to that kind of stuff! It's quite common in your part of the world though, I've heard.'

'We're looking into in,' Nerili said.

Noah rubbed her temples to shield her eyes. She didn't want him to see her tears. 'And you expect us to believe that?'

Nerili bent down next to Tambian's body. He lifted Montana's cloak and removed the severed hand from the sword, placing it gently beside the body. He picked up Tambian's sword and stood up. Gripping it by the handle, he proceeded to clean the crusted blood from the weapon with his own robe. As he worked, he said, 'Why should you believe me? Because it's the truth and because I have not lied to you, Noah.'

'I want to see Jaxon,' she said.

'I would advise against it,' Nerili replied.

Noah was insistent. 'I want to see him.'

When he finished cleaning Tambian's blade, he handed it to Noah. 'Perhaps later.'

'You're stalling.'

'We have lots to do, Noah. Our *first* priority is to contact Leninstar and make arrangements to return. Now go to the lift and send Liah and Shar to me. We will bring Tambian's body with us.'

With a silent promise to her fallen king that she'd find out what happened to him, Noah followed Montana to the lift platform. Montana gave the guards Nerili's instruction. Frost said nothing as he watched his companions go. Noah hoped they'd be quick; the stench of death was sickening.

To distract herself, Noah focused on one thing – Xan. She repeated the name over and over in her mind as she waited. It was probably too much to expect that the dragon would talk to her again but it was worth a try. Xan. Xan. Xan. It became a chant in her mind, the rhythm hypnotic and calming. If the dragon did talk to her, there'd be hell to pay with Brinn. *I'd even be happy to see the cat right now,* Noah thought.

When Nerili and his guards returned with Tambian's body, Noah gave up her quest. Nerili laid Tambian on the floor of the lift, his own cloak now in service as a shroud as well. Noah didn't ask about the severed hand. She assumed they'd have attended to it. For the duration of the half-hour journey to the control room, barely a word was spoken. Noah passed the time fretting about Emir, Raven and Gillette.

'Liah,' Nerili said when the lift stopped, 'you take Frost to the surface and check the fort. Report back here when you're done.'

'Yes, Your Highness,' Liah said.

'Shar,' the king said, 'you'll come to the control room with us.'

'Very good, Sire,' he said, opening the gate.

The soldier stepped off first and drew his sword. Nerili followed with Tambian's body in his arms. Noah walked alongside him with her king's sword at the ready. She longed to be above ground again – out in the open, under the sun. As she walked she tried to ignore the kilometres of earth over her head. When they reached the control room they found three weary-looking goblins who stood to attention when their king entered.

'At ease,' Nerili said, allowing one of his soldiers to help him lower Tambian's body to the floor. 'Connect the line.'

The stocky goblin nearest the device flicked the switch. A red light above it flashed. Noah watched, waiting for it to go green – the signal that the mine control room in Leninstar City was connected too.

'This device is impressive,' Nerili said as they waited. 'I think Tambian was wise to use his piece of firestone from Mellifont to power this machine.'

The communications line that linked t'Amos to Leninstar ran mostly through the Desceran tunnels that the railcar used. Only the sixty kilometres from the tunnel to the mine had had to be laid separately and while it had been a massive undertaking, it had proven indispensable. The firestone provided both power and a transmission frequency for the dots-and-dashes messages that went back and forth.

When the light went green, Noah's heart beat faster at the thought that Emir might be at the other end. She wondered what was happening at the palace in the wake of Tambian's death. Did they even know their king was dead?

Nerili gave his orders. 'Send this message ... *Nerili has returned. Where is firestone?*'

As the soldier complied, Nerili took a seat, and indicated that Noah and Montana should do likewise.

'You might as well get comfortable, ladies,' he said.

Given Tambian's fate, Noah was almost too afraid to hear the response from the palace. She steeled herself for bad news. She didn't think she could cope with any harm coming to Emir or Raven or Gillette.

The return message from Leninstar brought a small amount of relief.

This is Emir, Regent of Leninstar. We don't know the whereabouts of the firestone. If it's not at the mine, we believe it is with a rebel force. What news of my people at t'Amos? Is King Tambian there?

Nerili traced a pattern on the table top with one talon. 'Send … *Noah, Montana and I have returned to find King Tambian dead. The hostages have been poisoned but are alive. Send a railcar and we will return to Leninstar with your assurance of safe passage.*'

'Do you really think you'll survive Leninstar?' Noah asked.

'If your regent assures my safe passage, I will go … or should I doubt his word?'

Trying not to sound defensive, Noah said, 'It isn't Emir's word you need to worry about. You have many enemies in Leninstar. If Emir says you will be protected, you can be assured that every effort will be made to do so – but like you said yourself, there are no guarantees.'

Nerili was thoughtful. 'I wonder who is left in Leninstar. Tambian was here – would you like to wager who else?'

'You think Tambian led this?' Noah said.

Nerili exhaled sharply. 'I do not know who *led* it. Tambian *is* here though, that is clear. Would one king come alone? Who is party to this "rebel force" that Emir mentioned?'

'Emir only asked after Tambian,' Montana said.

'So *you're* saying Tambian led this?' Nerili said.

'No, no that's not what I'm saying,' Montana said. 'Emir said that if the firestone wasn't here, that it had gone with a rebel force. But then he asked if Tambian was still here – like he didn't expect him to be with the firestone or those who took it.'

'Sire,' one of the guards said, 'another message.'

'What does it say?' Nerili asked.

Will send a railcar once tracks here are repaired – two days' work at least. All must return.

Noah frowned. 'Ask what happened to the tracks.'

Nerili shook his head. 'That's not important right now.' To his soldier, he said. 'Send this message – *Hostages not safe to transport.*'

Nerili looked over to where King Tambian lay under his and Montana's cloaks, against the far wall. 'I think it odd that of the few human casualties here, that he was one of them – and that his body was left here,' he said. 'It feels staged.'

Noah hesitated a moment before sharing her observation. 'There is bruising on his wrists,' she said, 'like he'd been bound.'

'I noticed that too,' Nerili said.

'He was brought here against his will?' Montana guessed.

'Possibly,' Nerili said. 'So who would dare do that?'

Noah and Montana looked at each other. Noah had her suspicions but despite her distrust of the northern kings she couldn't bring herself to confide in Nerili.

'I'd put my coin on Arissa and Franco,' he said. 'If we find them, we find the firestone.'

'They were keen to raid the mine from the start,' Montana said.

Nerili sat up straight in his chair. 'Noah, can you tell where the firestone is now?'

The question caught her off-guard. 'What?'

'The firestone. You found it in the first place because you could sense it. Where is it now?'

'It's not quite that simple,' Noah said, frowning. 'When I found it, I was working with another Dragonsbane in Dragonhall with some … fairly sophisticated equipment.'

'Are you planning to retake it?' Montana asked.

'I want to demonstrate Carai's willingness to help *recover* it,' Nerili said.

'And we're supposed to think you're being generous rather than serving your own interests?' Noah said.

'At least we were willing to share it,' Nerili said evenly. 'That is more than can be said for your Alliance.'

Dispensing with formalities, the goblin at the message point interrupted with the next message.

Hale or not, all hostages must be returned. If anyone is unaccounted for, Nerili will be taken prisoner.

'He's direct, isn't he,' Nerili said.

'He can be,' Noah said. 'So what are you going to do?'

'We will go. And if Emir wants the hostages so badly, he can have them,' he said. Drumming his fingers on the table, Nerili added, 'Tell me about him.'

Noah's heart pounded. 'What do you want to know?'

'He is the regent. It is with him I will be negotiating for a place in the Alliance,' Nerili said. 'What can I expect from him?'

Noah battled to keep her face neutral as the realisation of Emir's current burden of responsibility hit her. Tambian had openly praised Emir's abilities. According to the king, Emir was the best adviser he'd had. And Noah didn't doubt it. Emir had a quick mind, was an excellent strategist and could remain calm in the face of any crisis. She'd often thought he would have made a great king, but that didn't mean she wanted him to be one – even act as one. Given Tambian's fate, his new role put him in great danger.

'You will get a fair hearing,' Noah said, 'but any decision he makes will be in the best interests of Leninstar. If he grants you safe passage, you will be protected. However, if your actions are contrary to the laws of the state, he will ensure you are dealt with accordingly.'

'How do you think he will react to the poisoning of the hostages?' Nerili asked.

'He's not going to like it,' Noah said, 'but it will count in your favour if you return them as directed.'

Montana spoke up. 'I would advise against … undue coercion.'

Nerili raised an eyebrow. 'What do you mean "undue coercion"?'

The high priestess looked at Noah and then back at the goblin king. 'If you're thinking of somehow using Noah or me to extort a decision from Emir, I'm telling you that will not work in your favour.'

'If you are saying I should not use the personal relationship between Emir and Noah to force his hand, you can rest easy. I will not do that.'

Nerili looked at the soldier at the controls. 'Send – *All will be returned. Advise when railcar is on its way.*'

'I still want to know why the tracks at Leninstar are damaged,' Noah said. 'It sounds like this isn't the only place that's seen trouble. I hope we're not stuck here too long.'

'Well, we have things to do,' Nerili said. 'If you want to see your friends, I will take you there. I still advise against it though. After that, Montana will attend to preparing Tambian's body for its return to Leninstar.'

Noah looked at where Tambian's body lay. Even though two cloaks now covered him, the image of what lay beneath was burned into her memory. Her stomach rolled violently. His family didn't deserve to see him like that. Montana would see to it that he was well-presented on his return.

Noah turned to the high priestess. 'I'll help you.'

'No you won't,' Nerili said. 'You've demonstrated you can't be trusted. You're going into a dorm.'

He's sending me to my room, she thought. If Jacin had survived the attack on his home, he'd likely be in his room by now too. Had he survived? Her mouth went dry, the metallic tang of guilt almost making her gag. Too tired and sick to argue, Noah nodded.

♪♫

Another blood-curdling shriek and Noah buried herself deeper in the blankets. Even though the woollen coverlets hadn't been up to the task of blocking out the agonised screams of the ilanxis-infected hostages for the past few hours, she continued to cocoon herself inside the bedcovers nonetheless. Eyes squeezed shut and teeth clenched tightly to avoid whimpering, Noah rocked from side to side – something that usually soothed her. It wasn't working today though. How could it?

She wished now that she hadn't insisted on seeing Jaxon. Images of him cascaded through her mind. He was barely recognisable. His skin was blistered and lumpy – where it hadn't peeled off. Padded shackles around his wrists and ankles at least prevented him from tearing off any more. His pupils had dilated, consuming his irises, so that it looked as if black holes had been drilled into the whites of his eyes. He babbled unintelligibly when he wasn't screaming and he didn't recognise her or even his own name. Jacin had said he'd spent a year working on a tonic that would reverse the effects of the ilanxis worm. Noah marvelled at his audacity in even attempting it. She'd happily give her piece of firestone to the cause but even with the power of dragonscale, would it be possible to reverse that much damage?

A key scraped in the lock. Unwilling to let anyone see her cowering under the covers, Noah threw back the blankets and sat up. The door opened. Nerili and Montana stood in the entranceway. The king beckoned to her.

'Come,' he said. 'We're going outside.'

'To the surface?'

'Yes.'

'Why?'

'Because when we get back to Leninstar, you're going to describe what you see up there.'

Noah shuddered. 'Please tell me there are no more bodies.'

Montana craned her neck so she could see inside Noah's dorm. 'Come on, Noah. We'll do it together.'

Noah stood up, blew out the candle and walked to the door. Montana took her hand. Allowing her friend to lead her, Noah focused on putting one foot in front of the other. Nerili set the pace while Shar brought up the rear. When they reached the lift platform, Noah took a deep breath. They were an hour from sunlight – if it was daytime. She assumed it was. Nerili wouldn't take her to witness something she needed to recount in detail if it were dark.

Shar set the pulleys and shifted the lever. Noah braced herself as the lift lurched. Once the initial jolt passed, the lift settled to a consistent speed, the gentle whirring of the pulley the only sound until Nerili spoke.

'Who is Alan?' he asked.

'Alan?' Noah and Montana said in unison.

Nerili nodded. 'He called through and left me a message. He had a bit to say about me returning Noah safely. What is the nature of *that* relationship?'

'It's not what you think,' Noah said.

'How do you know what I think?'

'I don't,' she admitted. 'But whatever it is – you're wrong.'

'Perhaps you'd care to explain it then? He seems overly protective of you. I think I am in more danger from him than from Emir.'

Noah snorted as Montana smiled. 'Alan's as harmless as he is nauseating,' Noah said. 'He wants me to team up with him to do a project and he's *really* persistent.'

'What sort of project?' Nerili asked, rubbing his chin.

'A raiki project,' Noah said.

'Why is he so interested in you?'

'Because I'm just that interesting,' she replied.

'I know you're a professor,' he said, 'but surely if this Alan is serious about his project, he'd find someone with more qualifications than you.'

'No doubt he's tried,' Montana said, 'but he *is* nauseating. Finding someone who is talented *and* tolerant is a big ask.'

'Mmm, possibly,' Nerili said, 'but I think there is more to it.'

'You're overthinking it,' Montana said.

'Really?' Nerili said. 'Noah is a royal tailor who is partnered with the king's adviser – now Regent – and whose brother is Commander of Leninstar's Royal Guard. She is a Professor of Raiki, a Dragonsbane of Talisker and is a close confidante of the high priestess. This is not something I would expect of someone who has been here such a short time. What makes her *so* special, I wonder?'

He paused and Noah hoped her face didn't betray her.

'And something haunts you,' Nerili said. 'Something disturbs your dreams. I have heard it several nights.'

Montana guffawed. 'Something disturbs her dreams, alright,' she said, giving Noah time to compose herself. 'Mine too. After what we've been through this past week, you shouldn't be surprised that we're not sleeping peacefully. We're hostages; our lives were under constant threat in Carai. Noah has been set upon by an angry goblin mob, our comrades are infected with ilanxis worm, her king is dead – tell me, where is the surprise in troubled sleep?'

'Your dreams are not so troubled, Priestess,' Nerili said.

'I'm over eight hundred years old,' Montana said. 'I have perfected the art of sleeping despite what troubles me.'

Nerili cocked his head to one side. 'There is more to you than meets the eye, Noah Chord,' he said, 'and I will find out what that is.'

Noah stared at him but didn't respond. To forestall any further conversation, she sat down on the lift floor. Crossing her legs, she rested her elbows on her knees and then her head in her hands. She thought about the sun. *I need sunlight,* she thought. It had been over a week since she'd felt its warmth on her skin. Despite the beauty she'd seen in Carai and indeed in the Desceran city below Leninstar, life underground held no appeal for her.

When the lift finally began to slow, Noah looked up. The bright hole above her beckoned. She shielded her eyes; it would take time for them to adjust.

'Prepare yourselves,' Nerili said.

Noah stood up, shaking her legs to get the blood flowing again. In the last few metres of the ride, the heat reached her. In spite of the carnage that no doubt awaited them, Noah revelled in the sun's delicate kiss.

The lift stopped and Shar opened the gate.

'It doesn't take much imagination to describe this,' Montana said grimly. 'What hasn't been incinerated has been levelled.'

'If I'd said those words to you,' Nerili said, 'is this what you'd have pictured?'

'No,' Montana admitted.

Noah surveyed the remains of the fort. The perimeter fence was gone, all the buildings obliterated. *There's nothing left here to cast a shadow,* she thought. Whatever had destroyed the fort had eradicated the insects too. Silence had replaced the lazy drone of horse flies.

'This isn't boulders and burning oil,' Noah said, eyeing the lone catapult in the distance. 'What have they fired in here to do this?'

'Whatever it was, it looks like it was one thing ... and it landed over there,' Montana said, pointing to a large black crater near where the front gate of the fort had stood. 'Come on.'

Flanked by Nerili and Shar, Noah and Montana wound their way through the debris to the impact site. As Noah studied one blackened patch of earth with a clump of metal next to it, she said, 'Tell me that's not what I think it is.'

'What do you think it is?' Nerili asked.

'Well, the metal looks like it might have been a sword ...'

'Agreed,' Nerili said. 'So the ash?'

'A soldier,' Noah whispered.

'That is what I think too.'

Noah looked around her. 'So many ... what could do this?'

'And the fort, too, is ash,' Nerili said.

'Not charcoal,' Shar clarified, surprising Noah with his uncharacteristic intrusion into the conversation. 'Ash.'

'That was elderwood,' Montana said. 'What could turn an entire elderwood fort to ash?'

'All that's left are the metal hinges and fittings,' Shar said, 'though they're all melted – like the swords.'

The thatched roofs of the stone buildings had disappeared – they'd stood no chance against a fire that could destroy an elderwood fort. And as for the stones, they'd been pulverised and scattered – gravel now carpeted the ground.

They reached the impact site and Noah felt lightheaded. The crater was a metre or so in diameter, though shallow. Something had exploded here. Something thrown in from the catapult in the distance. Something that had contained firestone.

'Someone's used firestone in this explosion,' Noah said.

Nerili's eyes narrowed. 'So are you saying it's been destroyed?'

'The big piece?' Noah said.

Nerili nodded.

'No. I think what was used here was just a very small piece. Either cut from the large stone or maybe it was one of the existing small pieces – from one of the twelve keys.'

Sweat that had nothing to do with the sun broke out of every pore on Noah's body. She scanned the site, expecting to see a stripy feline lurking nearby. Brinn would be very unhappy that the large piece of dragonscale had been stolen. Noah sighed. *When she told me to get rid of it, at least I knew where it was,* Noah thought. *Then it was just impossible. Now it's more impossible.*

Chapter 16

As the railcar slowed, Noah braced herself to stand. Across the aisle, Montana did the same. The track repairs in Leninstar's subterranean terminal had taken longer than expected. They'd spent three excruciating days at t'Amos with decomposing bodies, ilanxis-infected hostages and dwindling food supplies. Though she was glad to be home, there'd be little to celebrate.

Through the soot haze in the carriage, Noah looked at the shrouded body of the late King of Leninstar lying on the centre bench seat. At least the clatter of the railcar meant she couldn't hear the infected miners' screams from the last carriage. *This isn't right,* she thought. *Someone will pay for this.*

Nerili picked up Tambian's sword and handed it to Noah. 'I will wait in the next carriage for your summons as we agreed,' he said.

Noah nodded and exhaled slowly as the goblin king turned and made his way to the door between the carriages.

'I'm not ready for this,' Noah said when he was gone.

'Me neither,' Montana replied, 'but we need to do it all the same. I can go out first if you'd like.'

'No,' Noah said. 'I'll do it.'

The railcar's whistle sounded.

'Here we go,' Noah said as the railcar stopped.

She walked to the outer door, wrenched the handle and pushed. Leninstar's soldiers stood shoulder to shoulder along the length of the platform. Noah's heart pounded at the sight of Emir standing amid a squadron of soldiers near the engine-car. Nothing in his dress distinguished Leninstar's new regent from his army commander who stood at his side. Raven smiled at her. Noah jumped down from the railcar as they walked towards her.

'Montana is with Tambian's body in this car,' Noah said, pointing behind her as she wrestled down her urge to hug her favourite men. 'Nerili's in the second car, the hostages are in the third. Nerili's three guards are in the engine-car. I suggest you remove the king's body quickly and clear the platform, the hostages'—a shrill cacophony of cries erupted from the third carriage of the railcar—'are in a bad way.'

'Yes, Ma'am,' Raven said, putting out his hand to take Tambian's sword. Turning to his soldiers, he gave his orders. 'Retrieve the king's body and escort the royal family back to the palace. When the platform is clear, we'll deal with our people and then the goblins.'

The soldiers saluted. Two bearing a stretcher entered the railcar first.

Raven looked at Noah. 'Glad to see you, Sister.'

Noah smiled. 'Glad to see you too, Brother.'

Ignoring protocol, Raven embraced her with his free arm, resting his cheek on her head momentarily. When he released her, he steered her in Emir's direction as he returned his attention to the soldiers.

Emir took a step forward and took her hands in his. 'I'm glad you're back,' he said. 'I need you here.'

'I'm *very* glad to be back,' Noah said.

Frowning, he put his hand to her temple. 'What happened to your head?'

'I'm fine,' she assured him. 'I'll tell you later.'

She peered down the platform to where Tambian's grieving family stood with the three Taliskeran kings who remained in Leninstar City. King Tara stood at Queen Rosemary's side while Kings Henrik and Mallory stood behind Princess Catriona, who nursed her two-year-old brother. Prince Vernon sucked his thumb under the watchful eyes of a squadron of soldiers.

Though they were Talisker's elite, the royals seemed small in the cavern of the Desceran city. It was as if the ornate houses carved into the mountainsides of the underground valley ignored them, dismissing them as biological oddities, while the colossal stepped pyramid hunkered on the floor with its back to them. Likewise, the lava river that wended its way through deep chasms in the valley floor exalted in its own warmth and light, and paid the humans no mind.

But not everything in the city was as Noah remembered it. Scraps of twisted metal lay piled up at the entrance to the tunnel that led north to Seychelles. The workmen had done enough repairs to give railcars access again but the debris and their tools suggested there was still more to do.

With a nod in the Queen's direction, Noah said, 'How are they doing?'

'They're doing what needs to be done,' Emir said as the soldiers emerged with their king's body on the stretcher.

The hostages shrieked again, their tortured cries echoing around the city. Even Emir flinched.

Montana jumped down to stand beside Noah.

'Regent,' Montana said as she curtseyed.

'Stop that,' Emir said. 'I'm not the king.'

'Even if you *were* the king, you couldn't order me around,' Montana said with a smile. 'But I am greatly relieved to be back and unless you want me to hug you …'

Emir put up his hands. 'A curtsey is fine,' he said, adding, 'I'm glad you're back safely.'

As the soldiers escorted the king's body to his family, Noah and Montana fell in behind them. Queen Rosemary stepped forward. When the soldiers stopped before her, she reached out and turned back the cloak concealing her husband's face. The queen laid her hand on Tambian's brow and closed her eyes. When she took her hand away, she scooped her toddler from Catriona's arms so she could pay her respects.

Noah stepped forward and bowed her head. 'I am so sorry for your loss, Your Majesty,' she said.

Queen Rosemary nodded. 'Thank you for bringing him home, Noah,' she said. Looking to Montana, she added, 'And I thank you too, High Priestess.'

Montana curtseyed as Raven stepped forward. Bearing the king's sword on his open palms, he offered it to the queen. Rosemary nodded and took the sword before motioning to the stretcher-bearers to take Tambian's body to the lift.

'How are the hostages?' Queen Rosemary asked.

'They're in an appalling state,' Montana said. 'They'd have been better off if they hadn't survived.'

'Take them to the infirmary, they'll have the best of care,' Rosemary said.

'Yes, Ma'am,' Montana said.

As the queen led her children to the lift, King Henrik said, 'We will wait upstairs. Will you be ready to meet in an hour?'

Emir deferred to Noah and Montana. 'Ladies?'

'I need to bathe,' Noah said, 'and I really need something to eat.'

'Fine,' Henrik said. 'We'll start when you're both ready.' To Raven, he said, 'Make sure Nerili and his cronies are well secured.'

Raven nodded.

'I'll accompany the kings now,' Montana said. 'I'll see you upstairs, Noah.'

Noah nodded. 'Yep. I'll join you when I finish up here.'

Once Montana and the royals had cleared the platform, Noah said, 'Why was Tambian there?'

Emir shrugged. 'I don't know, but nothing he said to me indicated that he intended to storm the mine to retrieve the firestone.'

Noah sighed. 'I don't want to believe he'd do that – especially since the hostages weren't rescued.'

Raven said, 'Let's see the hostages.'

'They look worse than they sound,' Noah said grimly. 'Do *not* take them to the infirmary. Keep them in the dungeons down here.'

Emir looked at her as they walked. 'In the dungeons? Really?'

'From what you've *heard*, do you think it's a good idea to have them in the infirmary?'

Another tortured scream tore through the underground, reverberating vociferously off the stone walls. The first cry precipitated a chorus of others. Within seconds, the city again rang with the subhuman wailing.

'I guess not,' Emir said.

As they neared the end carriage, Noah said, 'Will Catriona be king?'

'Eventually.'

'I don't imagine that stunt she pulled stowing away on the railcar did her any favours.'

Emir shook his head. 'There's more to it than that.'

When they arrived at the carriage door, Noah steeled herself.

'Stand back,' Raven said before nodding to one of his soldiers to open the door.

Noah gagged at the stench of putrid flesh and human excrement when the door opened. In the dim interior was a tangle of shackled bodies.

'Get them out,' Emir said.

One by one, the hostages were extracted from the railcar. Jaxon was the last. He squirmed free of the soldiers and fell to the dusty ground, writhing desperately – like a wounded snake – while the guards tried to contain him.

Stepping forward, Emir said, 'Jaxon!'

Without a flicker of recognition at the sound of his name, Jaxon continued his thrashing, now enveloped in a cloud of dirt.

Raven moved in front of his regent. 'Stay back,' he said.

Splatters of blood on the platform showed where Jaxon had banged his head against the floor. Noah glanced at Emir. A slight puckering between his eyebrows marred his usually flawless façade. As the stricken hostages were wrestled away by Raven's squadron, Emir stood motionless.

'What were they poisoned with?' he asked. 'What could do that to my brother?'

'Ilanxis worm,' Noah replied. 'It's a parasite found in the sulphur pools deep underground.'

'They're barely human anymore,' Raven said.

Shaking his head, Emir said, 'We need to secure Nerili and his guards.'

Raven drew his sword. 'Yes, we do.'

Noah followed as Emir and Raven strode to the carriage where Nerili waited. Raven opened the door. The goblin king stood waiting.

'Time to go,' Emir said.

Nerili stepped down onto the platform. 'Greetings, Regent,' he said to Emir. With a nod towards Raven, he added, 'Commander. I am sorry for your loss.'

Both men nodded.

'Thank you,' Emir said as Raven signalled to his guards at the engine-car to escort Nerili's three guards to where they waited. When the guards arrived, Emir addressed the goblins.

'You will be escorted to secure quarters,' he said. 'You will remain there until you are summoned to a meeting. If your actions in any way threaten the safety of anyone in Leninstar, my promise to protect you is void. Do you understand?'

'We will not instigate any harm,' Nerili said, 'but we reserve the right to defend ourselves if we are attacked.'

'I don't anticipate that will be necessary,' Emir said.

Nerili shrugged. 'We shall see.'

As Raven's soldiers led the goblins away, Noah took Emir's hand. 'Seen Brinn around lately?' she asked.

'Brinn?' he said.

'Yes, Brinn. You know … small, stripy, furry and with all the subtlety of a supermassive black hole.'

'I remember her,' Emir said, 'but I haven't seen her since that night with Orville. Can we expect a visit?'

'Yep. She's got her knickers in a knot about the firestone.'

'You've seen her?'

Noah nodded. 'She came to visit me at the mine – before we went to Carai.'

'That's interesting.'

'Interesting for you, maybe,' Noah said. 'Excruciating for me.'

♪♫

Just a few minutes, Noah thought as she slid down into the bath water's warm embrace. She tilted her head back and closed her eyes. There was nothing like having warm water caress one's scalp. As she indulged she inhaled deeply, enjoying the scent of lime and lavender in the water. The muscles of her neck and shoulders surrendered some of their tension, though Noah knew she'd need several refills of the copper tub before they'd loosen completely. No time for that though. King Henrik had said they'd wait for her to eat and bathe, but she couldn't keep them waiting too long.

But as she lay there, her skin pricked into goosebumps despite the warm water.

Someone was watching her.

Thankful for the froth that protected her modesty, Noah opened her eyes. Two soulful brown eyes and a slobbery pink tongue confronted her.

'Kane!' she scolded. 'Can't you just lie on the floor like a normal dog?'

The Alsatian panted as his toenails scrabbled on the curved lip of the bath.

'NO!' she cried, sitting up instantly to barricade her watery real estate from canine intrusion.

A wave of water sloshed over the bath and onto the delighted pooch. He barked and jumped around in circles before splaying his legs. Noah knew that pose. She ducked her head as he shook himself luxuriantly.

'He missed you,' a voice said.

Noah peeked over the edge of the bath. Princess Catriona leaned against the doorframe. Noah looked at the princess and then at the bathrobe that lay tantalisingly out of reach over a wrought-iron chair.

'I won't keep you, Noah.'

'It's probably time I got out anyway,' Noah said, stifling a sigh. 'Would you mind passing me my robe?'

The princess obliged before turning to Kane.

'Sit.'

The dog complied, his tail swishing across the floor without a shred of remorse at showering the room in suds.

'I'm sorry for your loss, Princess,' Noah said once she was appropriately covered. 'Your father was a great man and a great king. How are you keeping?'

'I am keeping well, thank you, Noah,' Catriona said. 'And yes, my father was a great man and a great king.'

The silence that followed stretched like warm, newly-worked dough. Only Kane seemed happy to be in the room. At last, Noah said, 'What can I do for you, Princess?'

Patting Kane's head, Catriona said, 'I want you to make Emir make me king.'

Wary of igniting one of Catriona's indulgent tantrums, Noah chose her words carefully. 'If he's not of a mind to do it, there is nothing I can say to change his mind.'

The princess' face remained calm. 'But he'll listen to you.'

'He'll listen,' Noah agreed, 'but then he'll do whatever he damn well pleases anyway. You know how stubborn he is.'

'I do know how stubborn he is, yes. But I am old enough to be king and he is being unreasonable.'

'Can I assume you've told him that?'

'Yes.'

'You know, *sometimes* honesty is the best policy but not always. I think a little more tact was probably required there.'

'Well, I can't change that conversation now,' Catriona said. 'What's done is done. Will you help me or not?'

Noah wished Raven was here. At least with him around, Noah could be sure the princess would remain calm. Having the unchaperoned heir-in-waiting in her bath chamber made Noah feel as though she were walking on eggs. One careless word would see her on the wrong end of an unholy fit of rage. Clearly, telling her to stop behaving like a spoilt brat was not going to be considered 'helping'.

'I'm not going to talk to Emir about it,' Noah said calmly, 'because that won't work. To be king you have to demonstrate that you're capable of leading Leninstar.'

'How am I supposed to do that if I'm not king?'

Taking her life in her hands, Noah said, 'If you have to ask that, you're probably not ready to be king.'

Catriona's eyes widened momentarily but she kept her composure. Barely. 'Then what do you suggest?'

Noah retied her robe while her mind struggled with the fact that Catriona was asking for her advice. An image of Brinn appeared in her mind. Noah shivered. Firestone.

'You could give some thought to recovering the firestone,' Noah said. 'That's the kings' priority.'

'Hmmm,' Catriona said.

Did I really just suggest that? Noah wondered. *Has Brinn taken over my mind?*

Rolling with the idea, Noah said, 'You're coming to the meeting?'

Princess Catriona nodded.

'Right,' Noah said, 'speak little, listen lots.'

'How am I supposed to demonstrate authority if I can't say anything?'

'I didn't say you couldn't say anything, but you need to be brief *at* the meeting.'

Catriona eyed her like a cobra eyed its charmer. 'And *after* the meeting?'

'When the meeting is over, speak to Emir alone but don't ask him to make you king. Tell him one thing you saw him do that you are going to try. Show him that you want to learn.'

Catriona nodded thoughtfully. 'I can do that.'

'Okay, so I'll see you there then,' Noah said.

Catriona continued nodding but made no other move. Noah looked at Kane, wondering what cue she needed to move the princess on.

'Do you think I was reckless going to t'Amos?' Catriona asked.

'Does it matter what I think?'

'It doesn't *really* matter,' Catriona said, 'but if I can get an insight into the mind of a commoner, I might better be able to prepare myself to deal with Emir and get this king issue sorted out.'

What does my brother see in this woman? Noah wondered. Resisting the temptation to set her dog on the princess, and mustering all the calm in her that she could find, Noah said, 'You said yourself that your father was a great man and a great king. If he gave you an order, you should think he had good reason for doing so. I think if *you* can't follow the orders of your king, you can't expect others to follow your orders when you become king. *Commoners* expect their kings to lead by example.'

Catriona's cheeks flushed red but she held her tongue. Eventually she said, 'I guess I did ask.'

'Have you discussed this with Raven?' Noah said.

'No.'

'Good,' Noah said. 'Don't.'

Chapter 17

'I call this meeting to order,' King Tara said.

It was a quaint way to start a meeting and one that seemed out of place today. The sombre mood around the table didn't need taming. Kings Henrik and Mallory flanked King Tara who'd taken responsibility for chairing the emergency meeting. Emir and Catriona sat together beside the three Majors from Mellifont. Sachin was sandwiched between Major Maggie and Major Anok, whose combined experience of raiki exceeded Sachin's lifespan by five times. *If they think that's going to keep him quiet they're wrong,* Noah thought. For her part, Noah was thankful to be seated between Anok and Montana. Alan had been overlooked again, she noticed. He was in the palace and no doubt would be miffed that he'd been excluded.

King Tara spoke again. 'We have several items on our agenda today,' she said. 'For those of you recently arrived or returned, we will update you on events here in Leninstar City since goblins invaded the mine at t'Amos. After that, we will discuss the matter of recovering the firestone. We will then hear about Noah's and Montana's experience in Carai. Finally, we will discuss King Tambian's death and the current state of the Sovereign States Alliance.'

'Which appears at the moment to be the *Southern* States Alliance,' Sachin said.

Though used to his breathtaking boldness, Noah winced.

'Emir,' Tara said. 'Could you please give a summary of events since the raid?'

Emir nodded. 'You are all aware that goblins invaded the mine and commandeered the firestone, taking twenty of our people hostage in the process. A contingent from Leninstar went to t'Amos to meet with King Nerili to negotiate the release of the hostages and return of the firestone. We offered the goblins access to our electricity network though not a physical share of the firestone. Nerili requested amendments to the offer which required ratification at a full meeting of the Alliance. Apart from Noah and Montana, the contingent returned to Leninstar with fifteen of the hostages.

'The amendments Nerili requested were not accepted by the Alliance. Kings Arissa, Franco and Ulster did not agree to granting Carai a physical share of the firestone. Negotiations continued for a week – until goblins invaded the palace.'

'Goblins have been *here*?' Noah said.

Emir nodded. 'The fighting was intense, though brief. The goblins were disorganised and quickly overwhelmed. During the commotion, King Ulster claims to have been the victim of an assassination attempt.'

'*Claims* to have been?' Montana said.

'It is difficult to understand how,' King Tara said, 'given the fighting throughout the palace, Ulster could conclude that he was being specifically targeted.'

Montana nodded.

'King Ulster, along with Arissa and Franco, fled Leninstar City in the wake of the attack. After their departure, damage to the rail lines at the terminal was noted, as was Tambian's absence. We suspected the mine could be targeted and tried to contact the mine; however, there was no response until a day later when we received word that Nerili had returned there with Noah and Montana.'

'What made you suspect another raid on the mine?' Montana asked.

King Henrik drummed his fingers on the table. 'Arissa, Franco and Ulster wanted to raid the mine from the beginning to retake the firestone from Nerili's mob. We think they let goblins into Leninstar as a smokescreen. It gave them an excuse to leave *and* goblins could easily be blamed for the damage to the rail lines as well.'

'Which conveniently prevented any pursuit,' Montana said.

'Precisely,' Henrik said.

'Considering how much they didn't want to negotiate with goblins, would they really do a deal with them like that?' Noah asked.

'They want the firestone,' King Mallory said, 'and we think they'd do *anything* to get it. We believe King Tambian went to stop them.'

Noah's relief that Tambian wasn't a suspected traitor was overshadowed by her anger that Arissa, Franco and Ulster had likely caused his death. She clenched her fists as Emir reported on the condition of the poisoned hostages.

'This is ill news,' Major Maggie said gravely. 'The Academy stands ready to assist Jaxon and his companions, Emir. My colleagues and I will do whatever we can to help their recovery.'

'Thank you,' Emir said, 'We've never seen anything like this, so your help would be greatly appreciated.'

The three Majors nodded in unison.

'The firestone is our next problem,' Tara said. 'We believe that Arissa, Franco and Ulster have the firestone. On that basis we can assume it's heading north.'

'Tchuganni City,' Noah said.

'Ah. Thank you, Noah,' Tara said. 'I was going to ask if you could narrow down which of the three northern capitals it was heading for.'

'So obviously our priority is to recover the firestone,' King Henrik said.

Noah scanned the room, hoping to see Brinn. This was the perfect forum for the cat to share her plan to get rid of the dragonscale permanently. Annoyed though not surprised the room was feline-free, Noah resolved to ignore Brinn's directive until the cat was willing to speak about it publicly.

'I can coordinate the recovery operation,' Princess Catriona said.

Tara looked at her. 'This is too big a responsibility for one person.'

'Nerili will help.'

In lesser company there might have been stunned silence, but not here.

'Can I assume you've spoken to him then?' King Tara said.

'Yes,' Catriona replied.

That was fast, Noah thought. *How did she even have time to visit Nerili before coming here? She must* really *want to be king.*

'What is your plan, Princess?' King Mallory asked.

Catriona glanced at Noah before turning her attention to Melwick's king. 'Take a small force and liberate the firestone from Tchuganni City,' she said.

'Why would you need Nerili?' Tara asked.

'I believe Nerili's … tactical experience in commandeering firestone would be an asset. And it's a test – if he wants a seat on the Alliance he's going to have to prove himself worthy.'

The three kings looked at each other. Noah wondered if they were communicating telepathically. They exchanged no gestures or facial expressions that she could discern.

At length, Tara spoke. 'We shall discuss it and get back to you, Princess Catriona.'

'As you wish, Your Majesty,' Catriona said, bowing her head slightly.

'To enable us to do that,' Tara said, 'I guess we need more of an insight into Nerili's motivations. Perhaps now would be the appropriate time for Noah and the high priestess to share their experiences of Carai.'

Montana nodded. 'Carai is an ancient Desceran city near Orian's border with Tchuganni,' she began. 'About half a million goblins live there now. From what we saw, their society functions much as ours does – good and bad. They maintain a temple honouring Xan and Elani. It is immaculate – all the stained-glass windows and jewels are intact. They have a perfectly preserved copy of the Score as well. We observed a service where a goblin elder read the freedom story.'

As Montana recounted her experience of the temple, its profound impact on her was obvious.

'I find it difficult to believe that a temple could survive goblin occupation,' King Mallory said. 'I thought they'd just tear something like that apart.'

'I thought the same,' Montana said, 'but it stands and it is intact.'

'What else did you see?' King Tara asked.

'We visited their parliament,' Montana said, 'and they appear to have a democratic style of government.'

Noah held up her folio of fabric samples. 'This is from a textile factory. They are keen to trade with us.'

Tara motioned for the folio to be brought to her. 'May I?'

'Of course, Your Highness,' Noah said as she handed the book to Tara's adviser.

As the king commenced her perusal of the book, Noah said, 'We also toured a raiki facility. They're making instruments using the same slider technology we have.'

'How's that possible?' Major Maggie asked.

'There's at least one adept in Carai,' Noah said.

Anok put his hand on her arm. 'Who?'

'His name is Jacin,' Noah said, hoping that 'is' was the correct verb. With another stab of guilt that she'd led the murderous mob to his family's home, she continued, 'Flautist – he left Mellifont a year ago.'

'Why would he leave Mellifont and go to Carai?' Sachin asked.

'He went home,' Noah said.

Silence saturated the room.

Emir recovered first. 'There are humans living in Carai?'

'Well, yes there are,' Noah said, 'but he's not exactly one of them.'

'Not *exactly* one of them?'

Noah took a deep breath. 'Goblins and humans are breeding in Carai,' she said. 'Their offspring are called gomans. Jacin is a goman. He *looks* human but he is in fact a hybrid.'

'You're sure about that?' Anok said.

'I tested him,' Noah said. 'His signature is part human, part goblin.'

Mallory said something Noah didn't understand. Noah assumed she was swearing in one of Melwick's tribal dialects.

'Is it not bad enough that they abduct and rape our women?' Mallory said. 'But there are offspring?'

'It does get worse,' Noah said.

Mallory's dark eyes flashed dangerously. 'How could it get worse?'

'Apparently not all of the women are there against their will,' Noah explained. 'I visited Jacin's home, met his parents. His mother – Amy – is from Leninstar originally. She went to Carai to escape an abusive human husband. She now has eight children with her goblin husband and says she is perfectly happy. According to her, there are many like her who have *chosen* a life in Carai.'

King Henrik sat back in his chair. 'If Amy's story is true – that she chose to go to a goblin city for a better life – it is deeply disturbing.'

'There are many goblin cities,' Tara reminded him. 'Carai is only one. It would be dangerous to read this as a general trend.'

'That's true,' Montana said.

'I think the matter of – gomans – can be deferred to another time,' Tara said. 'We've other things to deal with today.'

'You're right. You don't need to deal with gomans today,' Montana said, 'but the fact that they exist – and the *way* they exist in Carai – speaks for Nerili's motivation. From what I saw in their temple, in their parliament and in their raiki facility – there is a morality in this goblin society that should give us pause. I don't think you should dismiss Nerili's application to join the Alliance lightly.'

'What if he's playing us?' Henrik said. 'What if this is all a sham?'

'Then he is outrageously cunning. Perhaps someone you'd rather have *with* you than against you?'

'Keep your friends close but your enemies closer, High Priestess?'

Montana shrugged. 'Something like that. But I think you could trust him to retrieve that firestone.'

Tara interlaced her arthritis-ridden fingers and leaned forward. 'We do need that firestone back as a matter of urgency. I hate to think what Franco and Arissa have in store.'

'Weapons,' Noah said.

All eyes went to her.

'What we saw at the mine site when we returned, could have been what Franco and Arissa have in store.'

Between them, Noah and Montana described the destruction they'd seen at the fort.

'Such progress is surprising,' Henrik said.

166

Major Maggie put up her hand. 'We at the Academy believe that Ylestar and Remenov have been up to no good for some time,' she said. 'The Council has been suspicious of some of their adepts. Their interest in raiki doesn't seem to stem from a desire to contribute to the common good.'

'How do you mean?' Noah asked.

'They seek tonics to splinter wood rather than heal it, to shatter stone rather than soothe it, to create earthquakes rather than quell them. They attempt to explain their interest in such things by saying "only by understanding the nature of destruction, can we understand healing". But the Council is not comfortable with this. Several applications for firestone sliders have been … stalled on the basis of such concerns.'

'Why only stalled?' Mallory asked. 'Why not denied altogether?'

Anok ran his hand over the dark, glossy skin on his head. 'There is no option in our processes to deny applications outright,' he said. 'If people pass the exams, they're entitled to a share in a firestone slider. Until recently, we've had no reason to want to deny anyone a key.'

King Tara shifted in her seat. 'Thank you, High Priestess and thank you, Noah for your testimony. We're all grateful that you are home safely. Perhaps now is a good time to take a break. We kings will consider what we have heard.'

Noah stood up, glad to leave the kings to matters of state.

'Sit down, Emir,' Henrik said. 'You will speak on Tambian's behalf.'

'I'm not a king,' Emir said.

'So you cannot fail to take orders from one then,' Henrik said.

Noah put her hand over her mouth to conceal her smile.

♪♫

'Noah,' Sachin said as they left the stateroom. 'Where are you off to now?'

'To see Gillette,' she said.

'Want me to come?'

Was he kidding? Sachin was only one place in front of 'nobody' in the line of people Noah might have considered to take with her for moral support, and 'nobody' was a better option.

'No, I'm fine,' Noah lied.

'Shouldn't you wait for Emir?'

'Probably, but who knows how long he'll be stuck in there.'

'I'll walk you there.'

As they set off for the west wing, Sachin rubbed his chin. 'We need to see the hostages asap,' he said. 'What have they been poisoned with?'

'Ilanxis worm,' Noah said. 'It's a parasite found in eels.'

'Never heard of it,' Sachin said. 'What's your diagnosis?'

'It's going to be a hell of a thing,' she said. 'I don't even know that it's possible to reverse the effects of it.'

'Bad attitude, Noah.'

'Just wait until you see them. Jacin has already spent a year working on a cure …'

'Jacin? The adept in Carai?'

Noah nodded. 'He has fond memories of the night you killed me actually.'

'*Half*-killed you,' Sachin said absently. 'Jacin. Mmm. Maybe you should have brought him back with you. His knowledge might be useful.'

'Perhaps you could go and visit him,' Noah said.

Unfazed, he said, 'I think I'll just send for him if we need him.'

Unable to bring herself to tell him Jacin might not still be alive, she said, 'We'll go to the dungeons once I'm finished talking to Gillette. You organise an escort with Raven.'

'They're in the dungeons?'

'I told you they're in a bad way. We can't have them in the infirmary.'

Sachin whistled. 'We'll have to do a *thorough* analysis.'

'Yes,' said Noah, wondering why he'd felt the need to point out something so obvious.

'*Very* thorough.'

Noah glanced at him as they turned left into another of the palace's vaulted corridors. 'Why the sudden fascination with thoroughness?'

'Being *thorough* is an essential skill for anyone wanting to be Chief Examiner at the Academy.'

'And *you* want to be Chief Examiner someday?'

'The position is currently vacant,' he said. 'I've applied.'

'Really?'

'Really.'

'You're twelve years old – surely they won't take your application seriously.'

'Noah, I'm thirteen next week.'

Noah stared at him. 'Have you had an interview?'

'Yep. Should find out within the month.'

'Well,' Noah said. 'Good luck.'

'Thank you.'

They'd only taken a dozen more steps when Sachin stopped. Noah turned. He was looking at the ceiling.

'What is it?' Noah said, certain that now wasn't the time to be admiring the mural.

Not taking his eyes from the frieze, Sachin said, 'You should do your doctorate on reversing the effects of the ilanxis worm.' After another long moment he looked at her, his eyes ablaze. 'Yep. I'll sponsor you.'

'Thesis, you mean. I need to complete my *thesis* to become a doctor.'

'If this thing is as extreme as you say, curing it is *doctorate* material. You do this, you'll be a Major.'

Noah stared at him. 'Surely I have to do a thesis first.'

'Noah,' he said, rolling his eyes, 'it's me.'

'If you're going for the position of Chief Examiner, do you think it's wise to flout the rules like that?'

'Please don't use the f-word, Noah. It's not "flouting", it's being "expedient".'

Noah frowned. 'Expedient?'

'Look,' Sachin said, 'if we have the skills to do it now, why should we wait?'

'We have to include Alan,' Noah said. 'He will make our lives a misery if we don't.'

Sachin winked. 'That's my girl. I'll go and organise us an escort to the dungeons.'

He didn't wait for a reply. Noah watched him go and shook her head. She'd deal with him later. Gillette was her priority now.

♪♫

'*Noah!*' Gillette cried from across the green.

Shielding her eyes from the late afternoon sun, Noah waved to him and watched as the boy raced her Alsatian across the lawn and back to the cobblestone courtyard outside her studio. Kane won paws down. Now dry after Noah had soaked him in her bathroom, Kane barked and ran circles around her.

'Hey Boy,' Noah said, kneeling to hug her dog. 'I missed you too.'

He licked her face.

'*That,*' she said, pushing his silky face away playfully, 'I did not miss.'

When Gillette arrived moments later, he bumped the canine out of the way.

'Did you bring Dad back?' he asked.

Noah hugged him. 'He is back, Gillette – but he's very sick.'

Gillette stiffened. 'How sick? Is he going to die?'

'I think so,' she said as she released him. She sat down on the stone bench. 'Come and sit here with me.'

Gillette settled himself on the seat while Noah tried to calm her excited pooch.

'Can I see him?' Gillette asked.

'No,' Noah said. 'I don't think that's a good idea.'

Gillette's eyes were glassy but he didn't cry. 'Why not?'

'Because he's very sick, Gillette and I don't want you to remember him how he is now. I want you to remember him as he was before.'

'You're just saying that because I'm a kid – but I trained with Raven and I'm a soldier now. I can handle it.'

Noah took quiet breaths, regretting her decision not to wait for Emir.

'Maybe you can handle it,' she said, 'but that's not a risk we're willing to take. We're making this decision for you because – soldier or not – you *are* still a kid. Your father expects us to take care of you and that's what we're doing.'

Gillette folded his arms across his chest. 'It's not fair! I want to see him.'

'Life isn't fair, Gillette,' Noah said. 'If it was, this would never have happened in the first place.'

'I still want to see him.'

'Sometimes,' Noah said, 'when we lose something precious, we want it back no matter what. And sometimes we do get it back and we're happy again. But sometimes, when we get our precious thing back, it is badly damaged or broken – and that's worse than not getting it back at all. And Gillette, your dad is very broken.'

Gillette's voice dropped to a whisper. 'Broken how?'

'His body is covered in sores and he's in a lot of pain. But what is worse is that his mind is broken too. He doesn't know any of us – he doesn't even recognise his own name. You need to remember him the way he was, not the way he is now.'

Kane sat in front of Gillette, resting his head on the boy's lap. With eyes that melted Noah's heart, Kane looked up at his human playmate.

As Gillette stroked the dog's ears, he said, 'But he must feel so alone.'

'His mind is so broken, he doesn't understand feelings anymore, Gillette. And you know what, we're not just doing this to protect *you*, we're doing it for your dad too. He wouldn't want you to see him like this. This is to protect you *and* to respect your dad.'

Gillette continued patting Kane's head. A single tear rolled down his cheek and dropped onto the dog's rust-coloured fur. 'What happened to him? How did he get broken?'

'It's a worm,' Noah said. 'A very small parasite that gets into the body and releases a poison.'

Gillette looked at Noah. 'Can't you fix it?'

'I don't know that it can be fixed.'

'But you'll try?'

'I'll definitely try,' Noah said. 'I've already talked to Major Sachin about it. He's going to help.'

Gillette frowned. 'Major Sachin is really important, isn't he?'

Noah nodded. 'Don't tell him I said this, but he's the cleverest Major in Mellifont.'

'I want to talk to him,' Gillette declared.

Noah smothered a look of horror … she hoped. Before she could stop him, Gillette raced across the lawn towards the palace. With a silent prayer that Sachin would not be himself while he talked to Gillette, Noah followed the boy inside.

Chapter 18

Noah adjusted her shoulder-sack as she followed the soldiers down the narrow stone staircase to the dungeons. Though her shoulders ached, the burden of the fruit she carried was slight compared to the plight of the stricken mine workers who languished beneath the Desceran palace under Leninstar City. Alan lumbered behind her bearing a sack of salted pork while Sachin, Maggie and Anok brought up the rear with bags of boiled potatoes and seed bread. The oil lamps on the wall, called into active service for the first time in over a century, glared balefully as they passed.

'How much further, Noah?' Alan asked. 'My legs are turning to jelly.'

'Not far,' Noah replied. She'd only been to the dungeons once before and had no idea how far they still had to go, but she thought it best not to share that with Alan.

'There have been one hundred and seventy-eight steps so far. How many are there altogether?'

'Not being an auditor, I never counted them,' Noah said. 'How about you let me know when we get to the bottom.'

Alan made a noise that sounded like a goat with a digestive complaint. 'It's got nothing to do with being an auditor,' he said, panting. 'Everyone counts stairs when they walk up and down them.'

'I don't,' said Sachin. 'And since we've established that Noah doesn't either, I think we can safely conclude that only auditors count stairs when they walk up and down them.'

Had he the breath to do so, Alan would have asked the soldiers if they counted steps but he followed the rest of the way in silence. Noah was grateful for the reprieve.

When they reached the dungeons, all was quiet but Noah knew that would soon change. She unshouldered her pack, moving her head slowly from side to side to stretch her neck muscles. A soldier gave her a curt nod as he took the sack from her. As he and his troop sorted the contents of the sacks into individual portions, Noah motioned to Sachin.

'Jaxon is in the end cell,' she said.

Maggie and Anok joined them.

'Maggie and I could examine Jaxon if you like,' Anok offered.

Noah was tempted, but loyalty won out over her distress.

'It's okay. I can do it,' she said. 'How about Sachin and I work from the far end and you and Maggie work from this end. We can meet in the middle and then compare notes.'

'That sounds good,' Anok said.

'What can I do?' Alan asked.

'You'll come with us,' Sachin said.

As the soldiers laid loaded trays of food outside the miners' doors, the gibbering started.

'Come on,' Noah said. 'Let's get started.'

Sachin nodded and motioned for her to lead the way. Keeping her eyes straight ahead, Noah walked along the uneven stone floor, her heart hammering. When she got to Jaxon's cell she curled her hands around the bars on the door and pulled. The doors weren't locked.

She stepped inside and then to her right, staying in the light that spilled in from the oil lamps in the corridor behind her. Sachin followed her in with a tray of food and placed it on the floor. Jaxon howled and scrambled forward as far as his chains allowed, stirring up a cloud of dust as he did so. Noah stepped back and reached for the pole beside the door. Carefully, she nudged the tray towards her friend who was almost unrecognisable under the sores and contusions that blighted his skin.

But it was his eyes that upset Noah most. Not a flicker of humanity remained in them.

Jaxon shovelled the food into his mouth, most of it bypassing his yellowed teeth unscathed on its way to his stomach. While he was occupied, Noah reached into one of the many pockets on her trousers to retrieve her viola. Sachin had said that if they succeeded in their quest to reverse the effects of the ilanxis worm, they'd have achieved the greatest raiki feat ever. She wasn't sure about that though. The trousers that Anok had invented were brilliant. The pockets, which appeared as required, could hold anything. Noah had carted around a harpsichord, a sewing machine and a horse saddle for weeks without any trouble at all. She'd even survived a trip in a pocket of Raven's trousers without any ill-effects.

Keeping her eye on Jaxon, Noah removed her firestone slider from her locket and inserted it into the bridge of her instrument. She tucked the viola under her chin.

Sachin took out his flute. 'Ready?'

'Yes,' Noah said. She looked at Alan. 'Are you okay?'

Staring at Jaxon, Alan nodded.

'You sure?' she asked.

Alan looked at her, eyes wide. 'Let's just get started.'

Drawing her bow across the strings, Noah played a few testing notes to gauge Jaxon's reaction. He ignored her, intent on devouring everything on the tray. Knowing that food wouldn't distract him for long, Noah set about her first task in what promised to be a complicated problem. Her first job was to test just how deep the affliction was.

Confident Jaxon's shackles would hold, Noah closed her eyes. The first note of her tonic was long and as she drew the bow across the strings she focused her mind. Aligning her consciousness to the music, she probed Jaxon's body, rigorously applying a diagnostic tonic Sachin had taught her. The young Major added his own melody to Noah's and as the music wound its way through their subject, the notes alternately reflected, refracted and harmonised with Jaxon's musical signature, giving them an insight into the seriousness of his condition. By the time she was done, her faith in their ability to cure the ailment had taken a severe hit.

When Jaxon had finished with the tray, he scurried back into the far corner of the cell. Since there was nothing to hide behind after Raven's guards had cleared the rooms, he curled up in the foetal position and gibbered to himself.

'It's going to be tricky,' Sachin said.

'Tricky?' Noah echoed. 'The worm has affected every fibre of his being. As far as I can see, we'd have to rebuild every cell – one by one – which we couldn't possibly do. I think we're biting off more than we can chew.'

'Well, if *we* can't do it,' he said, 'at least we'll know it can't be done.'

Noah frowned. 'What do you mean?'

'What do you mean what do I mean?' Sachin said. 'I'm brilliant and you're a living key. If we can't resolve this, then it can't be done. But we've got a lot of work to do before we come to that conclusion.'

'But there are squillions of cells in the body that are replicating constantly,' Noah said. 'How can we get on top of them?'

Alan pointed a pudgy finger at Noah. 'Squillions isn't a real number.'

'It's more descriptive than "lots",' Noah said. 'I could've said *lots* of cells.'

'*Squillions* might be more lyrically pleasing but it doesn't quantify any better than *lots*,' the auditor said.

Sachin's eyes widened.

Noah said, 'What are you thinking?'

'I do believe I've just found a use for you, Alan,' the Major said.

Alan's brow furrowed in suspicion. 'What would that be?'

'We're going to need a series of cell-replication algorithms,' Sachin said, absently pushing his fringe from his eyes, 'that take into account the variety of cell types as well as the diversity of organelles inside the cells. Ultimately, I think we'll need an equation whereby we can calculate the required frequencies and the atonal progression.'

Noah jumped to support Alan who began to swoon.

'You know you should make him sit down before you start talking like that,' Noah said. 'If he falls, he'll do himself an injury.'

'Nonsense,' Sachin said. 'Look at him. He's well-padded.'

In his rapturous state, Alan ignored the jibe at his weight. His mouth opened and closed several times before any intelligible words came out. 'Some cells work based on trigonometric functions while others follow quadratic routines. I can see my recent work with universal numbers coming in handy here ...'

He trailed off, apparently lost in thought. Then, without warning, he grabbed at one of his pockets and pulled at a stylus and paper.

Noah and Sachin flinched. As they watched Alan scribble indecipherable symbols on his paper, Noah said, 'I didn't know he could move that fast.'

'Me neither,' Sachin said. Tucking his flute under his arm he added, 'If Jacin's spent some time working on this, we should bring him in on it.'

Alan looked up from his notebook. 'Any chance we could get this Jacin character here?'

Unwilling to tell them Jacin might be dead, Noah said, 'War's about to start. I don't think we'll get him here anytime soon.'

'Hmmm, we'll see,' Sachin murmured. 'Anyway, we can't sort that out right now so let's get on with what we're doing here. We need to examine the others.'

Noah nodded. Confident that Jaxon would stay where he was, Noah collected the empty dinner tray. Nothing remained. She sighed, wishing she'd peeled the banana he'd been given.

'I'll see you soon, Jaxon,' she said.

By the time they'd examined the other patients, Maggie and Anok were waiting for them.

'I think,' Maggie said gently, 'that we can make them comfortable but I don't think there's any chance of returning them to health.'

'If you and Anok can make them comfortable,' Sachin said, 'Noah and I will work on a cure.'

'And me,' Alan said, raising his hand.

Maggie grimaced. 'But Sachin—'

'Until we're *sure* we can't fix this,' Sachin interrupted, 'we're going to try for a cure.'

Looking at Alan, Noah said, 'This needs to stay just between us. What these men are going through cannot become general knowledge.'

A soldier who was loading extra food stores on wooden racks stopped what he was doing. Addressing the group, he said, 'That's true, Ma'am. The Commander says this operation is secret. If news of this gets out there'll be more panic – and the Royal Guard has more than enough to deal with at the moment.'

Alan sighed. 'Leninstar's people don't need more bad news,' he said. 'Their king is dead and they're about to go to war with the northern neighbours who stole their firestone.'

'Yes,' Sachin agreed. 'It's pretty grim.'

♪♫

Noah rubbed the oil-imbued rag over the back of her viola, the subtle scent of saffron calming her as she went about her task. She'd had little time to relax lately and tending her beloved instrument was the perfect way to avoid thinking about Leninstar's woes. They'd wait – at least until Emir returned from his meeting. Noah glanced at the sideboard. The cheese and fruit platter beckoned.

Emir's lucky my hands are dirty, Noah thought, *otherwise he'd miss out on the salted peaches.*

When the bedchamber door opened, it wasn't who Noah expected.

'Montana,' Noah said, putting her viola aside and wiping her hands on a damp cloth.

'The kings' meeting has finished,' Montana said. 'I passed Emir on my way here. He'll be along shortly.'

'That's good.'

'How is Jaxon – and the others?'

'They've got an appetite,' Noah said, 'but there's no improvement in their condition. Maggie and Anok are going to sedate them but they're not optimistic we can cure them.'

'It does look like a tough case.'

'It's more than tough,' Noah said. Gesturing towards the platter, she added, 'You hungry?'

Montana smiled. 'No, I'm fine.'

When Emir entered the bedchamber he looked weary but found a smile for Noah. He bowed his head to the high priestess.

'The kings have declared war?' Montana asked as Emir unstrapped his sword and kissed Noah on the forehead.

'The northern kings have,' Emir clarified.

'The *northern* kings?' Noah echoed. 'Which meeting were you at?'

'The southern kings consider the theft of the firestone as the northern kings' declaration of war.'

'Ah,' Montana said. 'Technicalities.'

'It may be an important distinction later,' Emir said with a shrug.

'When they try to re-negotiate the Alliance, you mean?' Noah said.

'Among other things, yes,' Emir replied.

For a few moments, no one spoke. Noah watched Emir as he absorbed Montana's unflinching scrutiny.

At last Montana said, 'They're going to need you, Emir. In Tambian's absence, you're the one who can bring the Alliance back together.'

'I'm just a regent,' he said. 'They don't take me too seriously.'

'I'm sure you'll sort them out, Regent,' Montana said. 'You'll just have to charm them.'

'Charm them?' Noah said. 'That'll never work – they know him too well.'

'Hey, what's that supposed to mean?' he said, raising an eyebrow.

Noah grinned. 'They know how heartless, arrogant, dismissive and untrusting you can be.'

'Well, at least I'm not shallow, fickle, selfish and conceited,' he said.

Montana rolled her eyes and groaned. 'Do we have to go through this *again*?' she said. 'I can't believe you keep bringing that up – you should be too embarrassed.'

'It's funny,' Noah said.

Montana folded her arms across her chest. 'It's not funny – it's sad,' she said. 'You know, in my very long life, I have never met a more clueless couple. You should be embarrassed that it took a megalomaniacal sociopath trying to destroy the world to make you realise you loved each other.'

'Okay, so it was an unconventional courtship,' Emir said.

'An unconventional courtship?' Montana spluttered. 'Emir Delorian, you might not be King of Leninstar but you are the undisputed King of the Understatement. An unconventional courtship, indeed!'

'Well, it was,' Noah said. 'How many girls are threatened at sword point before their first kiss?'

Emir winced. 'I wish you wouldn't say it like that.'

'How else can I say it?' Noah pulled up her sleeve to reveal the scar that ran from bicep to wrist. 'You sliced my arm, then you said, "Take another step and I'll slit your throat." Lucky for me, Chase was there.'

'Well, if I'd known about the blood spell you were under, I would never have said that. And if I'd known that you were the 13th key, I certainly would never have said that. But no one told me those things – and you wonder why I'm untrusting!' he said, shaking his head.

'You know everything now,' Noah said.

'Do I?'

Noah tapped her cheek, considering his question. At last, she said, 'Well, all the important stuff anyway.'

Montana threw her hands in the air. 'Leninstar is lucky that you two are better at your jobs than figuring out your own hearts.'

'I'll say,' Brinn said.

All heads snapped to the sideboard where the cat was cleaning her whiskers.

Glancing at the platter, Noah said, 'Did you eat the cheddar?'

Brinn purred. 'No one else seemed interested in it.'

'To what do we owe this pleasure?' Emir said as Montana approached the cat.

'As usual, I'm checking up on Noah,' Brinn said.

Montana stroked the feline, who rubbed up against the high priestess affectionately. 'It's good to see you, Brinn.'

'It's good to see you too, Montana,' Brinn said. 'I don't suppose you've got any cat treats?'

Smiling, Montana said, 'If you'd let me know you were coming …'

'You don't need treats,' Noah said. 'You just had cheese!'

'Why are you checking up on Noah?' Emir asked.

'I gave her a little task,' Brinn said, 'and I wanted to see how it's progressing.'

Emir turned to Noah. 'What kind of task?'

'You haven't told them?' Brinn said.

Glaring at the cat, Noah said, 'I've been busy. We've *all* been busy.'

Brinn's tail twitched. 'Busy?'

'Is that so hard to believe?' Noah said. 'How long have you been busy for?'

'That's different,' Brinn said.

'Yes, it is different,' Noah replied. 'You haven't been dragged around a goblin city as a hostage.' She gestured towards Emir. '*And* you're not Regent of Leninstar. We *are* busy.'

'What's the task?' Emir said.

Brinn stretched. 'Disposing of the firestone.'

Emir frowned. 'Did you say—'

'Yes,' Brinn said. 'I said the firestone needs to go.'

'Go where?' Emir asked.

'Somewhere out of reach of humans – and goblins,' Brinn replied. Turning to Noah, she added, 'You couldn't even find time to tell them I'd talked to you?'

Rather than speaking aloud, Noah mouthed the word, 'Busy.'

The cat jumped down from the sideboard and up onto the bed. 'So can I assume you've been too busy to tell them who else you've been talking to?'

'Yes,' Noah said.

'Noah?' Emir prompted.

'I spoke to Xan – briefly,' Noah said.

Emir's brow furrowed. 'How?'

'After you left the minesite, while I was waiting in my dorm before going to Carai, she talked to me.'

Taking Noah's hand, Emir said, 'And what did she say?'

'She said "hello", then she asked *who* I was, then *what* I was.'

'And what did you say?'

'I told her my name was Noah and that I was human. Then she asked me if I was *sure* that I was human and when I said I *was* sure, she didn't want to talk to me anymore.'

'That's odd,' Emir said.

'I know,' Noah said, 'who wouldn't want to talk to me?'

Emir folded her hand between his and studied her, the dark bands under his eyes betraying his fatigue. 'You need to get over yourself.'

Noah shrugged. 'It's been said.'

'Anyway,' Brinn said, 'the point is that Xan talking to *anyone* is clearly a problem and the firestone is the trigger.'

Emir's shoulders sagged slightly. 'That's vexing.' He shook his head. 'Please excuse me while I wash my face – hopefully it might clear my mind.'

As Emir headed for the washstand in the corner, Montana said, 'This information might have been easier to digest if we'd had it earlier, Brinn.'

'No doubt,' Brinn said, 'but I've had other things to deal with.'

Rubbing the feline's ears, Montana said, 'Couldn't we cut a piece off? Keep a portion of it?'

'No. *That* piece must be put out of reach – permanently.'

'But the Alliance is counting on having firestone for the electricity network,' Montana argued as Emir towelled his face.

Brinn growled. 'If the Alliance uses that firestone to power their electricity network, they won't be doing it for long. Waking Xan ...'

'Is there any *other* firestone we could use?' Emir asked.

Brinn's ears flattened. After a long pause, she said, 'Yes.'

'So if we agree to get rid of this piece, as you ask, you'd help us find a suitable replacement?'

'This isn't a negotiation,' Brinn said testily. 'I'm not "asking" you to get rid of it. I'm telling you that your survival – and that of this world – depends on it.'

'Why does Noah have to do it?' Emir said.

'Because she's Dragonsbane and the 13th key – it's her job.'

'It will make her an enemy of the state.'

'That is unfortunate,' Brinn said.

Unfortunate? Anger flushed through every fibre in Noah's body. Unable to contain herself she dashed to the bed and scooped up the cat. Keeping the struggling feline at arm's length, Noah raced to the washstand and dumped Brinn in the tepid water. Brinn yowled as she scrambled out of the porcelain basin. She fell, twisted and landed on her feet – crouching, motionless. Water dripped from her fur onto the stone tiles. Her body trembled. She glared at Noah.

Noah's heart thumped in her chest and she fought to keep her breathing steady. 'You're so … *mean* and … bossy,' Noah said. 'If the large piece needs to go then it's going to be better for *everyone* if we can replace it with something more appropriate. Why won't you help us do that?'

As Montana swaddled the soggy feline in a towel, Brinn kept her eyes on Noah. 'Because you don't *need* my help.'

Was that a compliment? Noah wondered, as Brinn turned her attention to Emir.

'Make Catriona king,' Brinn said.

'Queen Rosemary wants to hold over the kingship until Catriona recovers the firestone,' Emir said.

'Tambian's dead. Catriona's his heir and she's of age. Why wait?' Brinn asked.

Noah said, 'Have you not met her?'

Ignoring Noah, Brinn said, 'Princess Catriona will need every bit of her tenacity to fill Tambian's shoes.'

Noah guffawed. 'Tenacity? Is that the new word for—'

'Be quiet, Noah,' Brinn said. 'If Catriona's going to bring the rebel kings to account for the theft of the firestone, she needs to be king – not an heir-in-waiting. Why should *they* take her seriously if her own household doesn't?'

'We're at war,' Emir said. 'Catriona isn't trained for that.'

'You and Raven will take care of that. Catriona's job is bringing in the rebel kings.'

'Tara, Henrik and Mallory have only authorised her to recover the firestone,' Emir said.

'Yes,' Brinn said, 'but *we* know that's not going to happen. You're going to send Noah with Catriona. Noah will get rid of the firestone and Catriona will arrest whoever took it.'

'She'll never agree to that,' Noah said.

Brinn sniffed. 'Of course she won't. That's why, as far as she's concerned, your job is to help *find* the firestone. She doesn't need to know everything.'

Chapter 19

Noah took her foot off the sewing machine's treadle and reached for her scissors. After a long night with Brinn, it was good to enjoy a bit of routine. The morning sun streaming in through the casement windows always lifted her spirits. For a few days at least, she could focus on her job as Royal Tailor.

'So where did the ilanxis worm come from?' Sachin said.

'Originally, you mean?' Noah said, as she snipped the dark thread.

'No,' Sachin said, 'the ones the goblins infected Jaxon and his friends with.'

Noah thought back to what Nerili had told her. 'Nerili said that the goblins at the mine had infected them without his knowledge'—she bit at her lip, struggling to remember his exact words—'or did he say permission? I just can't remember now exactly what he said.'

'The question is, was the ilanxis worm *brought in* to t'Amos or did they *find* some close by?' Sachin said.

Alan tapped on the table with his stylus. 'If it was brought in, that would show Nerili's intention to use it on the hostages.'

'That's logical,' Noah said. 'If we could prove that, it would lessen his chance of joining the Alliance.'

'But if it was opportunistic, as Nerili claims,' Sachin said, 'that would suggest that maybe there is a supply somewhere near the mine …'

'Somewhere we could get to and catch some ourselves for our research,' Alan finished. He looked at the Major. 'That is brilliant thinking!'

'Of course it is,' Sachin said loftily. 'It's me.'

Noah rolled her eyes. 'Aren't we lucky my studio is big enough to accommodate his head.'

'If you say so,' Alan said with a smile.

Sachin feigned indignation. 'Hey, *Doctor* Alan, you're supposed to be on my side. Do you want to be a Major or not?'

Noah looked at Alan. 'I'd get in quick if I were you – just in case he *does* get the Chief Examiner's job,' she said.

Sachin snorted. 'What do you mean *if*? There isn't anyone better qualified for the position than me.'

'I don't doubt that,' Noah said, 'but maybe they're looking for more than just technical skills.'

Folding his arms across his chest, Sachin said, 'Like what?'

'Modesty, charm, empathy?' Noah suggested.

'I want to be Chief Examiner,' he said, 'not a priest.'

'Anyway,' Alan said, 'we need to get our hands on that ilanxis worm. We need to go to t'Amos.'

'We?' Noah said. 'Here's an idea … I'll have a chat with Princess Catriona and see if she'll send *you* there.'

A voice intruded from the doorway. 'Send who where?'

Noah, Sachin and Alan all spun round to see the princess striding into Noah's studio. All three jumped to their feet.

'Morning, Princess,' they chorused.

Catriona wore her military regalia like she was born to it. Noah reminded herself that Catriona was, in fact, born to it.

'Morning all,' the princess said. 'Who wants to go where?'

'Noah was just kidding,' Alan said. 'I don't need to go to t'Amos.'

Catriona fixed him with a level stare. 'Noah wouldn't joke around at a time like this.'

Noah suppressed a smile as Alan's eyes widened. 'W-we can do everyth-thing we n-need to here,' he stammered.

'I'm glad to hear it,' Catriona said, 'but you'll have to do it without Noah because I need to borrow her.'

'We'll soldier on,' Sachin assured her.

'Good,' she said. 'Noah?'

'Coming,' Noah said.

Noah hurriedly folded the garment she'd been hemming and dropped it on the table before following Catriona. She caught up with her halfway down the corridor.

Without preamble, Catriona said, 'We're going to talk to Nerili.'

'Oh … right.'

'Emir will be there too.'

Relief washed through her that Emir would be present, but she wondered why Catriona had come personally to collect her. It would have been easier to send a runner. As they wound their way through the long halls of the palace, Catriona said, 'How's the ilanxis cure coming along?'

'Slowly. I don't know if it *can* be done.'

'If you can't find a cure, we need to figure out a way to eradicate the worm altogether,' Catriona said grimly.

'Why is that?'

'It's a biological weapon, Noah. One we can't afford to have used against us.'

'You've seen Jaxon?'

'I've seen them all.'

'You think the goblins are planning to use it in a large-scale attack?' Noah said.

Catriona shook her head. 'I'm more worried about the rebel kings.'

'Do they even know about it?'

'I'm not sure, but it's possible,' Catriona said. 'I don't know the sequence of events. Maybe Arissa and Franco discovered what had happened and that's why they left them there.'

'Or maybe,' Noah said, 'they had no intention of rescuing them and know nothing about it.'

'Also possible. I can't decide which of those options I think is worse.'

'Where are we meeting?'

'On the railcar,' Catriona said. 'Once we're done, Nerili will be on his way.'

They walked the rest of the way to the lift in silence. Once on the lift, Noah studied the princess. Catriona would know now that she'd be crowned king. Despite Queen Rosemary's reservations, Emir would have seen to it that Brinn's wish became reality. Anger coursed through Noah again. *That cat's going to be the death of me,* she thought. Then sadness followed the anger. *I won't be able to work here anymore. Even if I don't steal the firestone, I couldn't work for Catriona. She's had it in for me ever since I arrived.*

When they reached the underground platform, Catriona led Noah to the second carriage of the railcar where Nerili and Emir waited. The men stood as the young women entered.

'Please sit,' Catriona said.

Nerili sat on the seat opposite Catriona while Noah and Emir flanked the princess.

'Good to see you again, Noah,' Nerili said with a nod in her direction.

'It's good to see you are safe,' Noah replied.

'As our regent has no doubt told you,' Catriona began, 'the kings have affirmed my recommendation that you and I recover the firestone.'

'Yes, he has,' Nerili said. He stared at her for a long moment. 'It is curious … they don't trust you to be king but they trust you with such an important mission?'

Catriona smiled. 'Yes.'

There was probably a good reason for Catriona keeping her impending coronation a secret, but Noah couldn't fathom what it was.

'You need this – to become king,' Nerili surmised. 'You need *my* help to get your crown.'

'You need this – for a chance to show your worth,' Catriona countered calmly. 'You need *my* help for a seat on the Alliance.'

'For a *chance* for a seat on the Alliance,' Emir said.

'For a chance for a seat on an Alliance which doesn't exist at the moment,' Noah added.

Nerili nodded, not taking his eyes from Catriona. 'I think we understand each other,' he said. 'So let us see if you are worthy of a crown, Princess Catriona. What is your plan?'

'We will recover the firestone – which is currently in Tchuganni City – and return it to Mellifont.'

'Mellifont?'

'Neutral territory,' Catriona said. 'The adepts at the Academy will keep it until the situation with the Alliance is resolved.'

'You're sure it's in Tchuganni?' Nerili asked.

'*I'm* sure,' Noah said.

Nerili looked at her. 'I want you along on this mission, Noah.'

'Noah will accompany us,' Catriona said. 'You will leave Leninstar on this railcar after this meeting and return to Carai. I will grant you safe passage to the Seychelles exchange and King Henrik has agreed to give you safe passage west on his line.'

'We're about halfway between Seychelles and Orian,' Nerili said. 'It's a waste of time to take the railcar to Orian City.'

'There are three intermediate stations between Seychelles and Orian,' Catriona said. 'Using one of them will save you some overland travel time. Collect your personnel and provisions and I will meet you in Orian City a week from today. I will bring eight soldiers with me.'

'We won't be able take the railcar from Orian to Tchuganni though,' Nerili said. 'Ulster will have boosted security on that line.

Catriona nodded. 'We'll have to ride overland most of the way, but I'm hoping we can get north of Skycleaver at least.'

'That sounds workable,' Nerili replied, tapping his talons on the wooden seat, 'but I'm wondering if a squadron of soldiers might be useful. I know you won't fight alongside us but we can still fight. Taking out a few enemy outposts on the way might improve our chances for a seat on the Alliance?'

'No,' Noah said.

Everyone looked at her. 'This has to be a PR exercise for you,' she continued. 'If you attack humans, you're not going to win any support.'

'But if they're the enemy?'

'They're still human. Even if humans are fighting each other – they'll unite against goblins every time. Number one priority for you is to recover the firestone and return it to Mellifont. That will get people's attention – especially if you can do it without bloodshed.'

The goblin king was quiet for nearly a full minute. 'I like this plan. I hope I can trust you to keep your side of the arrangement.'

'You and your guards will be leaving with your lives,' Catriona said. 'Take that as a show of our good faith.'

♪♫

In the pulpit of Leninstar's oldest church stood the High Priestess Montana, dressed in a simple yet striking emerald silk gown. Noah was happy with the dress. The princess neckline, trimmed with a pearl brocade, was modest and befitting of the highest office of the Order of Elani on Talisker. From her seat in the front pew, Noah admired the bell sleeves and the A-line skirt that fell from under the bust to the floor in loose folds. Montana's hair was braided and coiled at her nape, and she wore a garland of Leninstar's magenta and gold olbera flowers on her head in deference to the state's slain king who lay in the coffin beside her.

The official party had taken their seats and Noah hoped the service would soon get underway.

'Queen Rosemary looks tired,' Sachin said.

'Of course she does,' Noah murmured.

The queen's gold-trimmed magenta tunic did nothing to lift her sallow complexion. Noah would have preferred a different colour outfit but tradition dictated that the queen wear her military regalia.

At a nod from Emir, Montana began the funerary service.

'Welcome one and all to today's service,' she said sombrely. 'May Elani bless us today and always.'

The gathered mourners chorused, 'May Elani bless us today and always.'

Montana cleared her throat. 'Today we return King Tambian to his maker. After a lifetime of service to his kingdom, Tambian can stand tall before the great god, Elani. We gather here today to celebrate his life and honour his achievements.

'At his coronation, fifty years ago, Prince Tambian was a willful teenager with ambition and a strong sense of justice. During his reign he laboured to better the lives of his people. He had a vision that everyone would have food, shelter and healthcare. He wanted jobs for all and to build wealth throughout the kingdom. He wanted electricity – clean energy that would make his people's lives easier.

'He built an army to not only protect but to serve. His soldiers are as renowned for their valour on the battlefield as they are for their assistance in times of need. Who can forget their efforts in evacuating the eastern district when the dam wall gave way? Leninstar's losses would have been significantly higher had it not been for the tireless efforts of the men and women who risked their own lives to get others out of harm's way.

'In my humble opinion though, King Tambian will be best remembered for his unwavering dedication to the Sovereign States Alliance. His focus was not solely on advancing his own people, but all people. His commitment to the Alliance will be sorely missed. I hope that as I commend Tambian's soul to Elani, that Leninstar will stay true to his ideals and continue his legacy of progress through collaboration.'

Tears slid down Noah's cheeks as Montana moved to Tambian's casket. Sachin offered her a handkerchief. Although Noah already had one, she accepted his. As Montana placed a single olbera flower on Tambian's chest, Emir rose from his seat and moved to the pulpit.

Noah's pulse quickened as Emir prepared to perform his last role as regent.

'Though not customary,' he began, 'today we will crown the new King of Leninstar. We forgo the usual mourning period, not out of disrespect, but out of practicality. Extraordinary times call for extraordinary measures. And these are extraordinary times. The Alliance is in disarray and war is upon us. The high priestess has charged us with continuing Tambian's legacy. To do this, we must get our house in order. We need a strong king.'

Emir turned and gestured towards Catriona, who stood up.

'Today,' he continued, 'Princess Catriona becomes King Catriona. I relinquish the regency and return to my position as the king's adviser, if it is Her will.'

Catriona stepped forward, and Noah held her breath. The princess looked calm and confident in her military attire. Noah hoped she wasn't so confident she thought she could do without an adviser.

Sachin leaned in close to Noah and said, 'Gee, if she accepts his offer, Emir is going to have his work cut out for him, isn't he.'

Noah stared at him, incredulous. 'I doubt it would be any tougher than the gig he had trying to keep *you* in line.'

Sachin recoiled. 'I am not as bad as she is.'

'Not now maybe,' Noah said under her breath.

In a clear voice, Catriona said, 'People of Leninstar, it is a great honour to take my father's place as your king. I give you my pledge that I will serve you faithfully and act in the best interests of the Sovereign States Alliance. As I strive to continue my father's good work, I will accept counsel from my adviser, Emir Delorian and army commander, Raven Chord.'

Emir reached for the sword that lay beside Tambian's casket and presented it to Catriona on open palms.

'By the authority vested in me,' he said, 'I present you with the king's sword and name you King Catriona, sixty-seventh King of Leninstar.'

King Catriona nodded her head as she accepted the sword. Emir put his fist over his heart and bowed to the king.

In a loud voice, Emir said, 'Hail to the king.'

As one, the people stood and echoed his words. 'Hail to the king.'

Once Catriona had strapped the sword around her waist, the crowd waited in hushed anticipation. The king moved to the head of her father's casket and placed an olbera flower on his chest. Queen Rosemary came to stand at her daughter's side to offer a flower also. Raven led Prince Vernon to the casket and lifted him up to place the last flower. When her young brother had completed his task, King Catriona closed the lid of the coffin.

To her audience, she said, 'Please be seated.'

With much shuffling and murmuring, people took their seats. King Catriona moved to the front of the dais.

'I regret that today we have not honoured my father's passing in the tradition way,' she said, 'but I promise to celebrate his life, as is our custom, once the current crisis is resolved.'

She paused briefly to a smattering of applause. What began as a smattering, swelled into a raucous ovation. People whistled and cheered as Catriona stood patiently waiting for order to return. Eventually, it did.

'My first job is to update you on the current state of affairs. As Emir said, the Alliance is in disarray and unfortunately, war with our northern neighbours is upon us.'

'She's a confident speaker, isn't she,' Sachin whispered to Noah.

Noah nodded. *A little too confident,* she thought. *There's a fine line between confidence and arrogance.*

'I wonder how much information she will give away,' Sachin said.

Without looking at him, Noah said, 'If you listen, you might find out.'

Catriona rested her hand on the hilt of her sword. 'The northern kings would have us believe that they took the firestone to rescue it from the goblins. But the truth is – they want it for themselves. Despite my father giving his life trying to stop them, the rebels have taken the dragonscale to Tchuganni. My priority is retrieving the firestone and returning it to Mellifont. It will remain there until the Alliance can be renegotiated.'

'How are you going to do that?' someone called out.

'Well, for obvious reasons, I can't share the *details* of the plan,' Catriona said, 'but I can promise you this – the firestone *will be* recovered and returned to Mellifont. Anyone who gets in the way of that happening will wish they'd never been born.'

'I don't reckon I'd want to cross her,' Sachin whispered.

Noah shivered. *Bloody cat,* she thought. *If I have to get rid of this piece of firestone, I'll be damned if I'm coming back empty handed. Brinn is going to help me find a replacement or I'll…*

A vortex of helplessness threatened to consume her. What could she do? Brinn claimed that Noah didn't need her help, but Noah suspected Brinn just didn't want to help her. And trying to *make* Brinn do something was like nailing jelly to a tree. Noah looked down at her hands.

Maybe I'm getting ahead of myself. First, I've got to steal the firestone from Catriona and Nerili. How am I supposed to make off with a piece of rock I can't possibly lift?

She thought about confiding in Sachin. Arguably the most talented adept on Talisker, he'd surely have a suggestion, and he was sitting right next to her. But she couldn't do it. He'd applied to be Chief Examiner and she had no right to compromise him. It was bad enough that Montana, Emir and now Raven knew the plan. If she did manage to do as Brinn asked, they'd be in as much trouble as her.

Chapter 20

'Turn around and face me,' Noah said as she took another pin from the pincushion to secure the hem of Gillette's tunic.

Gillette spun round a half turn. 'Do I look like a real soldier now?'

Noah stepped back to assess her handiwork. Happy that the hem was now straight, she said, 'You will once I've *sewn* the hem. The pins do detract from the look a bit.'

He stroked the gold, embroidered *infini* symbol over his heart. Noah watched him with a mix of sadness and pride. Ten-year-old boys should not wear the trappings of war but she admired his commitment to the cause. At least it gave him a distraction from his father's plight.

Noah had hoped that sewing would distract her from *her* mission, but it hadn't. She could sew tunics in her sleep. Though her hands were busy, her mind was free to imagine her fate. In the morning she'd leave with King Catriona to track down the firestone, and if she *were* to return to Leninstar, it would likely be in chains.

'Can I sew it?' Gillette asked.

Noah motioned towards her stool. 'All yours,' she said. 'Not too fast on the treadle, remember?'

'Yes, Ma'am,' Gillette said, rolling his eyes. 'Lucky for you, my legs are a bit sore from training with Raven so I won't be able to go too fast.'

'Lucky,' Noah said.

Emir had bought the machine for her and it remained her favourite. It had served her faithfully, due in no small part to the attention she lavished on it. It was regularly cleaned, serviced and oiled. Anok had suggested modifying the machine so it was powered by dragonscale rather than a treadle. However, despite her love of firestone, Noah had so far resisted the upgrade. She loved the machine as it was.

Wriggling carefully out of his tunic, Gillette sat up on Noah's stool and placed his garment on the sewing plate. He set to work, the machine doing his bidding noiselessly. As the boy laboured, Noah tidied her workspace. Her measuring tape, pins and chalks went back in the top drawer on the left side of the sewing table; the four pairs of scissors she had out went in the drawer on the right. When everything was away, Noah still felt that something was out of place. She stood, hands on hips, trying to figure out what it was.

'Kane,' she said at last.

Gillette looked around. 'Where?'

'Exactly,' Noah said, heading for the outer door. 'I haven't seen him for hours.'

'He's probably chasing wildcats again,' Gillette said as he returned to his sewing.

'Probably,' Noah replied, 'but it's getting late. He should be in by now.'

As she let herself out into the courtyard, the sun was resting on the horizon. Noah whistled and called as she walked towards the olbery. When she reached the trees with no response, she resigned herself to the fact that Kane was indeed up to no good chasing wildcats, and she would have to scour the gardens. Wildcats were small but vicious. After a concerted cull, there weren't many left on the palace grounds but the few that remained were the wiliest of them all. Kane was an agile dog but the crafty felines often found a way to slash him. Noah worried that one day he'd lose an eye.

When twilight stole the day, her search had yielded nothing. She made her way back to the palace hoping that her dog had sneaked back in of his own accord. Closing the studio door behind her, she first saw the empty sewing stool and then the unfinished tunic on the table.

Noah frowned. Gillette wouldn't abandon his endeavour. Something was wrong.

The door behind her slammed against her back, knocking her forward. She landed heavily on her hands and knees, gasping for air. The world turned grey as her assailant pulled a cloth bag over her head. Rough hands clamped around her arms.

A man's voice, low and menacing, penetrated her panic. 'Come quietly or the boy will suffer a bloody end.'

Still battling to recover her breath, Noah nodded.

'Right,' another voice said. 'Let's go.'

The men dragged Noah outside. The kerosene smell of her hood compounded her light-headedness and she stumbled on the soft grass, the men's grip on her arms tightening as they hauled her along. Though her mind was hazy, she knew they were staying close to the palace wall – the grass underfoot was a giveaway – but they hadn't gone far when they stopped. A chain rattled and a hinge creaked. Noah guessed it was the cellar door. Now just an antiquated palace oddity, the cellar was once used as a refuge in times of war. It offered protection, storage and a passage that led to more underground chambers.

Noah's captors pulled her forward. Negotiating the steps blindfolded was difficult and Noah missed the second step. The man behind her wrenched her right arm painfully but it saved her from tumbling down the stairs. The door slammed shut. Ultimately, this passage led to the Desceran city below Leninstar – an alternative for those not of a mind to use the lift – but to Noah's knowledge no one had used it in years.

When she'd recovered her breath, she said, 'Where are we going?'

'For a little walk,' one of the men said.

'Where to?'

'That is not for me to say,' he answered.

'Then who will say?'

'Not me. And if you can't keep quiet, your young friend dies.'

Gillette. Noah was desperate to know where he was but she didn't ask. Her mind raced. Raven had scaled back the underground patrols to minimise the number of palace staff coming in contact with Jaxon and his friends. The trusted dinner servers were done for the day and the railcar platform would be deserted until morning. Her captors knew the palace routines.

To focus her mind, Noah tried Alan's technique of counting steps. She knew the Desceran city was four hundred metres down so she'd be counting for a while. The zigzagging staircase turned back on itself after every two dozen steps, and when she got to a thousand steps she congratulated herself.

Now for the next thousand, she thought. At twelve hundred and fifteen, one of her captors called a halt.

Twelve hundred and fifteen ... twelve hundred and fifteen ... Noah repeated the number to herself as she fought to ignore the burning in her legs.

'How much further?' she asked.

'We're about halfway,' came the reply.

The man didn't sound out of breath. It wasn't much of a clue to his identity but Noah knew to stay alert to any information that might be helpful. The rest didn't last long. They were soon moving again.

At two thousand three hundred steps, the sound of a railcar engine penetrated her hood. Had Nerili returned? Surely not. As far as she knew, no one was due to visit Leninstar. *Trouble,* Noah thought. *Trouble is visiting Leninstar.* Pushing negative thoughts aside, she concentrated on counting. When she next saw Alan, she wanted to be able to report back a faithful final count.

'Stop,' a man said.

'Two thousand three hundred and fifty-two,' Noah said.

'You missed a few,' the other voice said. 'There are actually two thousand three hundred and seventy-four.'

Noah didn't respond. She hoped he was a braggart. She detested braggarts but on this occasion, it was better than the alternative. If he did know how many steps there were on this little-used passage, he was probably a regular in Leninstar's palace.

Noah felt rope around her wrists and wrestled to get loose.

'Is this really necessary?' she said. 'Can't two of you keep one girl under control?'

'We have orders,' a man replied.

'Who's giving the orders?'

'You'll see soon enough.'

'If I must be tied, could we lose the hood?'

'No.'

'It smells awful in here,' Noah said. 'It's making me feel sick.'

'Sad,' the man said, 'but trust me, you've got bigger problems than that. Let's go.'

'All aboard,' said the other.

They dragged her along the platform. As the noise of the railcar engine grew, Noah wondered what had happened to Gillette.

'Stop.'

Noah did.

'Step up.'

Noah coaxed one leg into action and her captors did the rest, manhandling her aboard.

'Gillette?' Noah said.

'Not in this carriage,' came the gruff reply. 'You'll wait here alone until our liege sends for you.'

'Can the hood come off now?'

'No.'

Noah gasped when something struck the back of her knees. She dropped, landing on her backside. As the men wound rope around her ankles, Noah kicked out at them but it only delayed the inevitable.

The railcar lurched.

'Enjoy your ride,' one of the men said.

Noah didn't answer. She heard the inter-carriage door slam but she wasn't sure they'd left her alone. As the railcar rattled away from Leninstar, she considered her predicament. Whoever had orchestrated this was doing their best to unsettle her. She couldn't identify her assailants. The hood was not only disorienting but the fumes were making her woozy. Her wrists and ankles were bound. Maybe they had Gillette, maybe they didn't. And now, the wait for a summons.

By the time they came for her again, her head was pounding. They hauled her onto a seat and pulled off the hood.

King Franco sat across from her, flanked by two of Leninstar's soldiers.

Noah frowned.

'Lovely to see you again, Noah,' Ylestar's king said.

'I'd be lying if I said the same,' Noah replied coolly. 'You need to take me back to Leninstar.'

'I can't do that,' Franco said.

Wriggling her fingers, numb from the ropes binding her wrists, Noah said, 'Of course you can. You're a king. You give the orders.'

'Indeed I do,' he said, 'but before I start giving more orders, allow me to introduce my newest recruits—'

'Don't bother,' Noah said. 'I know who they are.' She didn't know the soldiers by name but she'd seen them around Leninstar's palace. Glaring at one soldier and then the other she added, 'I hope you enjoy what little time you have left. *My* new king has no time for traitors.'

'Well, at least *our* new king won't sell us out to the goblins,' one of them said, bowing to Franco.

Anger burned in Noah's chest. 'Well, since you've *shown* your true colours,' she retorted, 'perhaps you should start *wearing* them too and stop dishonouring Leninstar's uniform.'

'All in good time, Noah,' Franco said. 'All in good time.'

Noah inhaled slowly, returning her gaze to the king. As she eased the air from her lungs, she relaxed her shoulders. Composure was everything.

'So what do you want from me?' she asked. 'A new suit?'

Franco smiled. 'While you're probably a fabulous tailor—'

'I *am* a fabulous tailor,' Noah interrupted.

'—there is something else I need from you,' Franco finished.

The king stood up, turned and took a seat next to her. Franco raised his hand and touched her face lightly with his fingers. He brushed her cheek and traced her jawbone, then slid his fingers down over her throat to her collarbone. Noah glowered at him as he drew her locket out from under her top and placed it on his palm. Ignoring Noah's gaze, he opened the silver casing to reveal her firestone slider.

'Truly beautiful,' Franco said, removing the firestone from the locket to study it more closely. 'And I think with the right leverage, you might find a way to be of use to us.' He looked to one of his soldiers. 'Bring him.'

The soldier saluted before leaving the carriage. Seeing her piece of firestone in Franco's hand, made Noah's heart pound against the inside of her chest like a prisoner beating on their cell door. Adrenaline surged through her veins. She couldn't let him take it. Noah pictured herself head-butting Franco. In her mind, she saw the look of disbelief on his face and while it would be gratifying, she knew it would not be to her advantage. For now, she needed to play along.

The inter-carriage door opened again. Gillette marched into the carriage, hands behind his back but head high. He looked at Noah, his face grim but composed, and nodded once.

'Ah,' Franco said. 'My leverage.'

The soldier pushed Gillette onto the seat opposite Noah and sat down beside him. Gillette looked small sandwiched between the two soldiers but he was not cowed.

'Now, Noah,' Franco continued, 'I need you to help me—'

'She won't help you,' Gillette said. 'Neither of us will help you. We'd die first.'

'A noble sentiment,' Franco said, 'and one I hope you remember if it becomes necessary for me to run a sword through you both.'

'Like you did to Tambian?' Noah said.

Franco's eyebrows arched. 'That's a bold accusation, Noah.'

'So did you?'

'I did not,' he said.

'Who did?'

'I don't know, but if I had to *guess*,' he said, 'I'd say he was most likely done in by a goblin. You can't trust them – that's what Arissa, Ulster and I have said all along – but Tambian went ahead and tried to negotiate with them anyway.'

'He *negotiated* for the safe return of his people,' Noah said. 'A noble act – and what people expect of their kings.'

'Spoken like the commoner that you are, Noah,' he said. 'You have no idea what it takes to be a king. There is no greater challenge than balancing the needs of individuals against the needs of the collective. And sometimes, sacrifices have to be made. We can't save everyone.'

'You might not be able to *save* everyone,' Noah said, 'but you don't get to risk people's lives to serve your own agenda. You let goblins into the palace to make it look like Tambian had brought it on himself—'

'We had contingencies to manage the raid,' Franco said calmly.

Noah stared at him. 'Meaning you planned to kill the goblins you let in?'

Franco nodded. 'And it worked. Nobody died in the palace.'

'Except Tambian.'

'He didn't die in the palace,' Franco countered.

'He died *because of you*.'

'That's debatable, but you know what? I'm not going to debate it with you.' He held her piece of firestone close to her face. 'As you well know, this dragonscale represents awesome power – power that cannot fall into the hands of the barbarians under any circumstances. Our actions were necessary to protect the firestone from falling into the wrong hands.'

'So what is your plan now?' Noah asked.

'The plan has not changed. We will use the firestone to wipe out the barbarians.'

Noah snorted in disgust. 'You *can't* use firestone in weapons.'

'We *can* actually,' Franco said. 'How do you think we got the firestone back?'

Unwilling to admit she'd seen his handiwork at t'Amos, Noah said, 'As a Professor of Raiki and a Dragonsbane, I am telling you that using firestone in weapons will upset the natural order of Talisker. Messing with the symphony of this world has dire consequences.'

'Ridding the world of goblins will balance things out,' Franco said.

Noah bowed her head, anger boiling inside her.

'And everyone has their part to play in that,' Franco continued cheerfully. 'Noah, you are going to help us cut up the firestone.'

When he didn't add anything else, Noah said, 'Is that it?'

'Well, unless you'd like to volunteer to make the weapons as well?'

'No,' she said. 'And actually I'm not keen to cut up the firestone either. I rather like it the way it is.'

Franco curled his fingers, trapping the firestone in his fist. 'Well, that's where Gillette comes in.'

'I'm not cutting it up,' Gillette said.

'Of course you're not,' Franco said. 'You have no talent for it. *You* get to be the spit hog.'

'What do you mean the "spit hog"?' Gillette asked.

'I'm going to cut pieces off *you* until Noah starts cutting pieces off the firestone.'

'Don't worry, Gillette,' Noah said. 'We will soon be missed and they'll send a search party after us.'

Franco smiled. 'If they can even figure out that you've been taken through the tunnels, they'll be hours behind us.'

'They'll figure it out,' Noah assured him.

'You should have more faith in me, Noah,' Franco said. 'Look at what I've managed to do under your noses. Your king, your boyfriend, your brother – none of them has any idea that I'm even here, let alone what I'm doing.'

Noah wondered how long it would be until she and Gillette were missed. Then a chill ran through her.

'What did you do to my dog?' she asked.

'Nothing permanent,' Franco said. 'I wouldn't hurt an animal. He'll sleep for a while though.'

Noah wasn't sure she believed him – she didn't know why she'd even bothered to ask.

Chapter 21

Under King Franco's watchful gaze, Noah settled herself on the bed of spruce needles she'd raked together. Her shackles had been upgraded from ropes to irons, but at least her hands were in front of her rather than behind her now. It gave her a chance to get comfortable enough to sleep, but she held out little hope of peaceful slumber.

'Get a good night's sleep, Noah,' Franco said. 'We've got a long ride tomorrow.'

Noah didn't answer. She'd spent only twenty-four hours with Ylestar's king, but in that time, Franco had managed to make Brinn look like pleasant company.

'Do you want to know where we're going?' Franco said.

'Not really,' Noah said, 'but I get the idea you're going to tell me anyway.'

Franco chuckled. 'Indeed I am. We're going to Sandeep Lake.'

'Fishing?' Noah asked.

'Well, if you like fishing, there'll be time for you to do that while we wait for the firestone to arrive.'

Noah sighed. 'How long?'

'It'll take about twelve days to get there. It's a long, slow ride overland from Tchuganni City with a heavy load.'

'Why there?' Noah asked.

'Because now that I've kidnapped you,' Franco said, 'you can't tell Catriona that it's moved. She'll still head to Tchuganni City – and she'll be captured. Brilliant, hey?'

'If you say so,' Noah said, relieved that Franco was moving the stone. She still had no idea how to fulfil Brinn's wish of stealing the dragonscale, but with Catriona and Nerili following a false lead, she had only to outwit one king instead of three.

'I do say so,' Franco said. 'And now, I bid you goodnight.'

He turned and walked away without waiting for her response.

Noah nestled her hands between her cheek and one of the rolled up blankets that had been left for her, and stared into the fire. The soldiers had taken Gillette for a toilet stop. *I hope he keeps his mouth shut this time,* she thought. He already had one black eye for speaking out of turn.

She knew the guards were watching her too, waiting for some ill-conceived escape attempt, but she wasn't going anywhere tonight. Tonight she'd survey her surroundings and when she understood the countryside, then she would plan their escape.

Gillette signalled his return with, 'Night, Noah.'

Raising her head from her makeshift pillow, she called, 'Night, Gillette. Sleep tight.'

'You too,' he called back.

Now that he was back, Noah could settle to her task.

She inhaled deeply, the smell of wood smoke in the outdoors was a welcome change from the sooty confines of the railcar but it evoked haunting memories of camping trips with her parents. Worries past and present collided and tangled in her mind; reaching her trance state was going to be a challenge. *One thought at a time,* she told herself. *One thought at a time.* She started with her firestone slider. *Franco has my firestone.* Noah acknowledged the thought and set it aside. Next, her trousers. *Franco has my adept's trousers with my possessions in the pockets.* She acknowledged that thought too and then put it aside. *The large piece of dragonscale could expose the firestone in my blood.* That one was more difficult to ignore, but Noah pushed on.

The trance was slow to come but quick to give way to sleep. After several hours of nothingness, her dream began. Stirring deep in her subconscious, it soon spiralled its way up – wispy, snaking tendrils that curled and coiled. Out of the twisting threads, order eventually emerged.

Noah lay on her back on a cloud, gazing out into the night sky. While the cloud gave her some protection from the chill, she longed for the sun's warmth. The heavens turned in their own time though, ponderously slow to her human eyes. A tingling sensation on her chest drew her attention. Her locket. Noah sat up. Opening the locket, she removed the slider that contained her precious firestone. On impulse, she held it monocle-like over one eye and the heavens exploded into life.

Noah gasped. No longer was there a dome of black, punctuated by silver pricks of light. Colours fountained and swirled wherever she looked and she could see depth. *She wasn't looking* at *space; she was looking* into *it.*

Noah peered into the sky, deeper and deeper. She picked out the two stars in the middle of the Caspar constellation and focused on a point between them. Suddenly, the cloud she was sitting on disappeared and she was floating between the two Casparian stars. A wave of exhilaration and apprehension swept through her as she looked back at Talisker which was now a speck in the distance.

I need to move slowly, *she thought,* or I won't find my way back. *With careful experimentation she found the best way to move at a measured pace.*

She continued on her way. There was so much to see, it was difficult to know where to look. A way away – way back in time – a flicker of dazzling light caught her attention. Abandoning caution, Noah stared intently through her slider and was swept through eons of time.

She came face to face with a gigantic dragon.

The beast was a kaleidoscope of colour and Noah knew instantly who it was. This was the dragon upon whose bones Talisker was made. Xan, still free in the beginning of time, flashed here and there like a playful puppy. The multi-coloured scales of the living dragon defied description. Though Talisker's firestone was as potent as it was magnificent, it was a mere shadow of what Noah witnessed here.

The dragon spoke. 'Who are you?'

'I am Noah.'

The dragon nodded. 'Greetings, Noah. What are you?'

Noah hesitated. Keen to avoid her last mistake, she said, 'You tell me.'

The dragon swooped and circled and came to hover in front of Noah. Noah thought she could have hosted a small party inside her eye socket. With her massive snout almost touching Noah's nose, Xan studied the puny intruder.

'You *are* here,' Xan said at last. 'As I am.'

'I'm just dreaming,' Noah said. 'I'm actually on Talisker, and so are you.'

'In another time, I am part of Talisker's story,' Xan said. 'But not in this *time.*'

Noah was confused. 'How can you know that? How can you know your future?'

'I am a dragon,' she said simply. 'I know what I know. But the question is, what do *you* know?'

'I know I'm dreaming,' Noah said.

'So you said. But I'm a dragon and I know more than you and I'm telling you that you *are* here.'

'But how can I be here?'

In a puff of smoke, Xan said, 'Wrong question. Don't worry about *how* you got here – you should be more concerned about *why* you are here.'

'Why am I here?'

'How should I know?'

'I thought you said you knew everything.'

'I know everything about *me* – but I don't know everything about *you.*'

'But you know something,' Noah said.

'Yes.'

The dragon's magnificence overwhelmed her but she forced herself to concentrate.

'I need to look at your scales,' Noah said at last.

The dragon's eyes gleamed. 'Be my guest.'

With her firestone monocle, Noah began her inspection. Suddenly conscious of the size of her task, she worked quickly. If she *was* dreaming, she couldn't afford to sleep too long – she had things to do. If she *wasn't dreaming* … she decided now was not the time to worry about that.

Noah floated around the dragon, scouring her massive scales. With her slider over her eye she looked deep into the coloured scales. Gold and *azure; ruby, orange, and mauve; emerald and black – the colours cascaded in elegant waves. It would have been so easy to lose herself in the miasmic depths but she stuck to her task.*

Near the tip of the dragon's mighty tail, Noah found her answer. A match. In a miniscule corner of one of Xan's gargantuan scales, Noah's piece of firestone matched perfectly. The stone she held in her hand was part of this beast. The stone in her hand held part of the dragon's consciousness. The essence of the stone was in her blood.

'You are part of me,' Noah said. 'I'm part dragon?'

'Yes,' Xan replied. 'I do not know how this happened – you are a strange-looking beast – but you are my child.'

Noah opened her eyes. The coals in the fire pit winked at her. When she'd been close to the firestone at the mine, Xan had spoken to her. Was the dream Xan's way of talking to her again or was it really just a dream? Was she really part dragon? Beads of sweat trickled down Noah's forehead.

According to Franco, six people, including two adepts from Mellifont, had died trying to cut the firestone. The stone seemed able to defend itself. Noah shuddered. There was a chance the dragonscale in her blood would protect her. But there was also a chance it might amplify the problem.

♪♫

'I thought it would be bigger,' Gillette said.

'Still your tongue,' a soldier said as he slapped the boy across the back of the head.

As Gillette recovered his balance and was about to speak again, Noah took his arm and pulled him close to her. 'Remember what Raven taught you,' she said.

Gillette's eyes focused. He nodded slowly. 'Yes, Ma'am,' he said at last.

Noah turned her attention to the stone. In the fortnight since Franco had kidnapped her, she'd made three failed attempts to escape. Gillette had complicated things. It would have been easy enough for her to get away, but springing Gillette as well had proven to be a problem. But now wasn't the time to worry about that.

With Franco and a dozen guards looking on, Noah walked around the pear-shaped piece of firestone. Like at t'Amos, she felt the heat rising inside her as the firestone in her blood reacted to the piece before her.

Hello again, Noah, the stone said.

Hello, Xan, Noah thought.

Good, Xan said. *Let's keep this conversation just between us.*

'Any ideas?' Franco asked.

'Not yet,' Noah replied. 'What tools do you have?'

'Come and see for yourself,' Franco invited, turning on his heel.

Noah followed him towards the bench at the far end of the lodge. The stone building was long, about half the length of a jousting track, Noah guessed. Centuries ago it would have accommodated Tchuganni's royal family during their winter retreat but it obviously hadn't been used in generations. Noah doubted King Ulster had even seen it.

Its stonework appeared not to have noticed the passage of time and the exposed hardwood beams and struts of the pitched roof would petrify before they rotted. But despite the steadfast durability that had delivered it through the ages, the firestone gave the ancient lodge an odd fragility. Noah thought Franco's choice to hide the dragonscale here was an odd one. *It's like trying to hide an angry bear under a lace bedcover,* she thought.

On a wooden workbench, Noah found a selection of iron tools. Saws, chisels, nails, forceps, clamps, spanners and chains of varying sizes were neatly arranged. She shuddered. When it wasn't being used as a workshop, it could double as a torture chamber.

What are you doing? Xan asked.

Procrastinating, Noah thought.

'Noah?' Franco prompted.

Noah picked up a chisel. 'Tell me what happened to the adepts who tried to cut it.'

'The first adept tried the large chisel with the mallet,' Franco said. 'He struck it once and fell down dead.'

Noah winced. 'And the second?'

'The small saw – same outcome,' Franco said. 'Power on this scale obviously needs a subtle approach.'

'Obviously,' Noah murmured. 'Or maybe it's a warning – power on this scale should be left alone.'

Franco's eyebrows arched. 'Left alone? What about electricity?'

'It's a great idea in theory,' Noah said, 'but if we can't cut the stone …'

Franco frowned. 'Don't be such a defeatist, Noah. We were able to recover the stone. We must be able to cut it up.'

Noah looked at Franco. 'I'm not sure that we can.'

'Well, *something* in here is going to be cut up,' Franco replied, glancing at Gillette. 'I'll leave it to you to decide which it is, Noah.'

Eyeing the implements on the table, Noah said, 'Who's next in line after me?'

'You're planning to fail?'

'Not *planning* to fail but I'm not brimming with confidence.'

To Noah's surprise and disgust, Franco walked towards her and put his arm around her shoulder. 'Sachin is my next candidate,' he whispered. 'I have people inside Catriona's palace who are awaiting my orders. I can take who I like, when I like – as I did with you and Gillette. Something you'd do well to remember.'

A cold hard knot tightened in Noah's stomach. Franco could be lying but she couldn't be sure that he was. Her own abduction had been swift and methodical. If his spies were still there, anyone could be a target – Emir, Raven, Catriona.

Noah, Xan said, *focus.*

Noah looked at the tools again, then back at the firestone. 'I need time to think about this,' she said.

'Fine,' Franco said, drawing a dagger from its scabbard. 'You have an hour'—he glanced at Gillette—'and then I start carving.'

'I want Gillette to sit with me,' Noah said.

Franco nodded. 'As you wish. The guards will be watching – and listening.'

Noah walked to the stone with Gillette at her side. As they settled themselves on the compacted dirt floor, she said, 'Now just sit quietly and let me think.'

Gillette patted her knee. 'You got it.'

Taking a deep breath, Noah straightened her spine and let her hands rest in her lap. She stared into the firestone and the colours started to swirl. The last time this had happened she had been disoriented, but today she was ready for it.

Brinn says I need to rebury this firestone, Noah thought.

Who's Brinn? Xan asked.

A cat.

A cat? Xan echoed. *You talk to cats?*

Only this cat, Noah replied. *And only because she's* very *persistent.*

That's odd, Xan said, *but the cat's right. This piece of dragonscale could destroy this world.*

Noah drummed her fingers against her knees. *I don't suppose you know of a smaller piece we could use instead?*

There are thirteen pieces of acceptable size in Tisaan.

Noah's heart beat faster. Even though she had no idea where Tisaan was, Noah said, *And I could take those?*

Yes, Xan replied.

Then what are we waiting for?

We're waiting for you to deal with this piece, Xan said.

Noah frowned as she stared at the swirling colours inside the stone, and as had happened at t'Amos, her blood ran faster and hotter inside her. How was she to get such a massive piece of rock away from Franco and his henchman? Even if she could distract or overpower them, how would she and Gillette move it? And where would they hide it?

When half an hour of contemplation had yielded nothing, Noah got to her feet. She took a long, slow breath in as she approached the stone. Ignoring the stares of Franco and the guards, she stopped before the glowing dragonscale and reached out a tentative hand. And again, as had happened at the mine, her hand was invisible in front of the stone. All she could see was the whirling colours within the firestone. But as she studied the phenomenon, she realised that that wasn't quite right. There were now two layers of colour. Though she couldn't see her skin, she could see the firestone in her blood above the surface of the stone.

A fragment from last night's dream floated through her mind. *I am part dragon. The stone and I are one.*

Finally, Xan said.

You knew this was the answer? Noah asked.

Yes.

Then why didn't you tell me?

Because you had the answer.

Pulling her hand away from the stone, Noah turned to look at Gillette. *And him?* she asked.

No, Xan said.

Buoyed by her first good idea, Noah sifted through her mind for another. She wouldn't leave Gillette behind. She *couldn't* leave him behind. There had to be a way.

And the idea, when it came, brought a smile to her lips.

Noah signalled to Franco. 'I need my trousers.'

Franco studied her for a long moment. 'Why?'

'I want to try something.'

'What?'

'I want to see if the firestone will fit into one of the pockets,' she said.

A look of wonder wandered across the king's face. No doubt he recognised the ease with which he'd be able to move the firestone if such a feat could be achieved. Noah was banking on the fact that this would win him over.

Franco clicked his fingers. 'Trousers.'

When the guards handed her the trousers, Noah said, 'A little privacy?'

'You need to put them on?' Franco asked.

'Yes.'

'Guards turn,' he ordered. As his soldiers complied, Franco said, 'I'm not prepared to turn my back on you though. Change.'

Noah undid the rope drawstring on the cotton trousers she'd been given and let them drop to the ground. She stepped into her own trousers and pulled them up quickly. Once she fastened the buttons, she said, 'I'm ready.'

'Just remember,' Franco said, 'that the boy bleeds if you try anything clever.'

Noah nodded. 'I remember.'

Turning her back on Gillette and the guard, Noah faced the dragonscale.

She stood staring at the stone until Franco said, 'Noah?'

'Yes, okay,' she said, opening a pocket on her right thigh. 'Let's see if this works.'

With her free hand, Noah grabbed Gillette's hand and yanked him towards her.

'Hey!' the boy yelled.

Noah looked down to see Gillette disappear inside the open pocket. As she buttoned it closed, a guard charged, sword at chest height.

'Stand down!' Franco yelled.

The guard paid no attention and Noah crouched at the last moment, letting the soldier's momentum carry him past her. She closed her eyes as his sword sheared the stone and light exploded inside the lodge. Screams echoed around the room as the light burned unprotected eyes. With her eyes still tightly closed, Noah launched herself at the firestone. When her body made contact with the stone, it yielded to her instantly. It was like diving into a lake.

I've got you, Noah, Xan said. *You're safe now. Look!*

Noah opened her eyes. She'd done it. She was inside the firestone. Outside, King Franco of Ylestar looked to be standing on his head. Noah wriggled around to right herself. It was like swimming in jelly but she managed it. Bracing her feet against the shell she eyeballed the king from the safety of her dragonscale cocoon. He did not look pleased.

'What's your plan now?' he growled.

'This dragonscale is going back to the depths,' Noah said. 'Its power is too great for us.'

'Says who?' Franco demanded.

'Says me,' Noah replied.

'Well, perhaps I could come in there,' Franco said, 'and talk you out of this nonsense.'

'You can't come in here,' Noah said.

'Why not? You're in there. Why can't I join you?'

Butterflies fluttered in Noah's stomach. 'I'm a Dragonsbane of Talisker,' she said, 'and I bear a piece of firestone.'

Franco smiled as he plucked something from his fob pocket. 'I think you'll find that *I* bear your piece of firestone, Dragonsbane so perhaps you'd best move over.'

Anger quelled the butterflies. Though the piece of firestone she commanded now made her little piece look like a trinket, it had been in her family for six hundred years and it galled her to see it in Franco's hands.

'If you try to breach the stone, you'll die,' Noah said.

'Is that a threat?'

'You've seen what the stone can do.'

'Yes, but now you seem to be … in command. If anything were to happen to me'—he looked around at his guards—'you would be held responsible.'

'Well, let's make sure nothing happens to you then,' Noah said, throwing her weight to her right.

The stone toppled surprisingly easily. Now horizontal, Noah braced her hands and feet against the inside of the stone and rolled. Though slow at first, she soon picked up speed. Franco jumped aside as the stone tumbled towards him. Noah concentrated hard. When she hit the wall at the far end of the lodge, she needed enough momentum to punch through it. Noah had never been overly fond of rolling down hills as a child but at least it didn't make her ill; luckily, because if her plan worked, there was plenty more rolling to come.

Chapter 22

The plan did work and Noah's head was spinning – faster and faster – as the firestone barrelled down the steep hillside beyond the lodge. Though the walking track from the lodge to the lake below zigzagged down the hill, the firestone took the most direct route. As the stone tumbled over and over, Noah prayed they'd hit the lake soon. At least they'd roll slower then. She braced herself for impact. She didn't want her momentum to slam her against the stone's shell. Either she'd break like the yolk inside an egg or she'd smash through the shell and end up in the icy water. Neither option was appealing.

The frantic spinning came to an abrupt halt.

We're in the lake, Xan confirmed.

Now that their conversation was private, Noah dispensed with telepathic communication. 'Yep. I figured that,' she said aloud. 'Now what?'

You need sinking sand.

Noah shuddered. 'Sinking sand,' she murmured. 'Because no one will be able to dig up the stone if it's buried in sinking sand at the bottom of a lake.'

Correct.

Sandeep Lake was vast. Even from the lodge's elevated position Noah hadn't been able to see the far shore. Noah knew it was deep. Very deep. And there was no telling how deep the sinking sand was. She wondered how *she* would get out.

Don't worry about that, Xan said. *I will return you to the surface.*

'Maybe it would be better if I didn't return to the surface,' Noah said.

Why?

'Because everyone's going to be after me for stealing the firestone. Everyone. There'll be nowhere for me to hide.'

You can replace this piece. I told you there is firestone in Tisaan.

'Where is Tisaan? I've never heard of it.'

It's a Pyranhi city.

'The Pyranhi cities are deep underground. We have no way to access them.'

Countless expeditions had gone in search of the ancient cities over the centuries. Of those that returned, none had found what they were looking for. And of the many ill-fated expeditions, rumours of their fates were at the heart of many of Talisker's poems, ballads and plays. Whether the long-lost explorers had perished, or prospered in secret in the bowels of the world, was still a point of conjecture. To Noah's knowledge no one had ventured there recently.

And you call yourself a Dragonsbane of Talisker? Have you been to Dragonhall?

Noah frowned. 'Of course I have.'

Did you not sense that some of the doors lead to deep places?

'I sensed that some of the doors lead to *dark* places,' Noah replied. 'Places that no one should go.'

Deep, dark … call them what you will. It is true that some of these cities can no longer be accessed using physical routes. Only through one of those doors will you find Tisaan.

'And there are thirteen pieces of firestone?'

Yes. They belonged to the Pyranhi. When their race declined, they cut a small piece from each and gave them to the Descera.

Noah chewed her lip. 'Franco has my small piece. I need to get *that* back. How big are the pieces in Tisaan?'

Put both your fists together – about that big.

Noah clenched her fists and pressed them together. Compared to the pieces they had now, the pieces in Tisaan were significantly bigger. Yet would it be enough to satisfy Talisker's kings?

'How much further until we get to the sinking sand?' Noah asked.

I have found my preferred spot. You steer – I will guide you.

Noah discovered she didn't have to turn with the stone. She floated in the centre and let the shell rotate around her like a mouse-wheel. At Xan's instruction she would shift her body weight to alter the firestone's direction. As she rolled along the rocky lakebed, fish flashed by her, trails of light whipping around like twirling gymnasts' ribbons. But the aquatic spectacle wasn't enough to stop her fretting. Gillette's dwindling air supply, the fractured Alliance, the war, ilanxis worm, the firestone …

Noah.

'Yes?'

Concentrate.

Noah sighed. 'Easy for you to say.'

Oblivious to the crushing weight of icy water above her, Noah rolled on. Her firestone shell bounced over rocks, sending luminous, bottom-dwelling crustaceans scurrying in all directions. When they approached a weedy underwater forest, Noah sensed rather than saw the hairy, ropey vines that swayed in the current as they stretched for the light far above.

Not far now.

Even as Xan's words floated through her mind, Noah felt the firestone slow. Her heart beat faster. Though the stone shielded her, there was something about the inescapable inevitability of sinking sand that still inspired panic.

I will release you now, Noah.

'What do I need to do?'

Walk. I'm going to create a bridge back to the lodge.

'Does it have to be there?'

It is the safest place.

'Franco will probably still be there. Surely there are safer places.'

There are safer places for you to be, *but that's different. It's the safest place for me to send you because that's where you entered the stone. There's a marker there – an anchor point for my bridge.*

'And without an anchor point, your bridge might collapse?'

Yes.

'Can I let Gillette out on the bridge or do I have to wait until I get back to the lodge?'

He will be fine on the bridge.

Noah nodded, thankful that she'd have company for the walk back. 'So this is goodbye?'

For now, but I suspect we'll meet again.

'Sleep well, Xan,' Noah said.

Thank you, Noah.

The colours of the firestone disappeared and the light faded until all that remained was … beige. Noah turned. The only blemish on the beige was a thin dark line that streaked away to a vanishing point far behind her. Keeping the line on her left, Noah took a few steps. As she walked forward, the line behind her faded. She took a few more steps.

I guess this is the bridge, she thought.

Noah unbuttoned her trouser pocket and scooped out her charge.

Gillette crouched, clutching his stomach. 'Where are we?'

'On our way back to the lodge,' Noah said. 'How do you feel?'

'Like I want to vomit.'

'It'll pass, but it'll take a little while. We need to get moving though. Can you walk?'

Gillette nodded. 'I think so, but … what is this place? Where's the lodge? And where's the firestone?'

'We escaped from the lodge inside the firestone,' Noah said, heaving him to his feet, 'and I rolled it into sinking sand at the bottom of the lake.'

'You did *what*?'

'I got rid of it.'

'Why?'

'It's too big. Too dangerous.'

Gillette whistled. 'The kings won't be happy. You're going to be in deep sh—'

'Yes,' Noah said. 'I *know*.'

'So if you know you're going to get in trouble for it, why did you do it?'

Because a cat told me to wasn't the answer Noah was prepared to give. Instead she said, 'Sometimes things just need to be done, Gillette and it doesn't matter if you *want* to do them or not.'

Gillette stared at her. 'How'd we get inside the firestone?'

Though she omitted some details, Noah explained that Xan had allowed her to dive into the stone.

His eyes narrowed. 'Xan? As in the dragon, Xan?'

Noah nodded.

'You can talk to—'

Before Gillette could finish, the beige was torn asunder. A gaping diagonal tear leered at them.

'Something's coming,' Noah whispered.

'What is it?'

Noah shook her head. 'I don't know.'

Xan hadn't warned her of danger. What could be here that the dragon hadn't foreseen? It would have to be something immensely powerful to slip into Xan's consciousness undetected.

'Have you got any swords in those trousers of yours?' Gillette asked.

As a red mist poured through the breach, Noah said, 'Swords won't do us any good here.'

Swirls of red twisted and whirled around her but strangely, created no draught. Ignoring the mist, she peered into the breach. A figure floated into view. A man. Waves of dark hair cascaded to his shoulders, framing his pale, angular face. Noah admired the cut of his high-necked emerald robe, cinched at the waist with a scarlet belt, but she winced at his choice of shoes. His black knee-high boots were a bit much; she'd have preferred suede to the glossy finish.

'Hello, Noah,' he said. 'I'm Jong.'

Noah sighed. 'Of course you are. And what do you want?'

Gillette put his hands to his temples. 'Hang on a minute,' he said to the man. 'Did you say your name was Jong?'

'I said my name *is* Jong,' the man said.

'As in …?'

'Yes, Gillette,' Noah said, 'he's *that* Jong.'

'I've been waiting for you, Noah,' Jong said. 'What took you so long?'

Meeting the god's gaze, she said, 'I've been busy.'

'Noah,' Gillette whispered, 'is that any way to talk to a *god*?'

Noah frowned at the boy. 'What?'

'Could you be a bit more polite? I'd like to get his autograph.'

'*What?*'

Gillette clasped his hands. 'Well, I got a great mark for that story I wrote about him and Elani and Xan for my homework and if I could get his autograph, that'd be pretty awesome.'

Glaring at him, Noah said, 'I'm *never* helping you with your homework again.'

'Fine,' Gillette said, folding his arms across his chest.

Jong waved his hands. 'Noah?'

'Yes?'

'I need you to do something for me,' Jong said.

Take a number, Noah thought. 'What is it?'

'I need to get out. I'm tired of being captive here.'

Noah recoiled. 'You deserve to be captive,' she said. 'You're evil.'

'Evil?' Jong echoed. 'I don't know about that.'

'Really?' Noah said. 'You destroyed so many of Elani's wonderful creations that your own dragon fought you and ate you to stop you. Can you really not take a hint?'

'Evil is something humans made up, Noah,' Jong said. 'You need to think of me, not as evil, but as ... change.'

'Change? How do you figure that?'

'My brother's creations that I "destroyed" ... did you see them?'

'Of course not,' Noah said.

Jong shook his head. 'Most of them *weren't* wonderful,' he said. 'My purpose in destroying them was to free up the matter that had gone into making them, so that it could be used to make something that *was* actually wonderful. Elani had great potential, but in the beginning, it was just that – potential. Each one was an improvement on the last, but still ...'

'So you were doing him a favour?' Gillette said. 'Is that how you see it?'

'Doing the universe a favour,' Jong corrected. 'Each particle is precious and deserves to be used in the best way possible. When Elani moulded things that didn't do justice to its component parts, I simply *changed* things – put them back the way they were – to be used better next time.'

The logic was seductive but Noah clung to her indignation.

'Think of me as a butterfly,' Jong said.

While Gillette stared in disbelief, Noah tried to decipher the god's thinking. If she could understand how his mind worked, might she have a chance of defeating him?

'So when you were destroying your brother's creations – you were like a caterpillar?' Noah guessed. 'Now you're here, in your chrysalis, completing your metamorphosis. And your plan is what? To break free of your cocoon – our world – and flutter about the universe?'

Jong smiled. 'Something like that.'

'You can't do that!' Gillette cried. 'You'll kill us all if you destroy Talisker. How is that not evil?'

'Were you not listening?' the god asked. 'The matter of this world could be – should be – used for a greater purpose. Human arrogance is astounding. Do you *actually* believe that *humans* are the epitome of evolution?'

Noah indulged in a deep, steadying breath. 'Our lives might not be important to you, but they're important to us.'

'I understand that,' Jong said condescendingly, 'but I have a higher purpose.'

'And you call *us* arrogant,' Noah said.

'You're lucky I still need you, Noah, else I'd smite you where you stand,' Jong said.

'I won't do it.'

Jong smiled. 'You *will* do it.'

'I'd die before I'd break you out of here.'

'I won't let that happen,' Jong said.

Noah shrugged. 'Then you leave me no option but to kill you.'

'Well, lucky for me, you can't *actually* do that.'

'You're bluffing,' Noah said. 'If I have the power to get you out of here – as you claim – then I have the power to destroy you.'

'Go Noah!' Gillette cheered. 'You tell him!'

Jong floated towards Noah, stopping only a few centimetres from her, the red mist enveloping them both.

'You have the power – yes,' he said, 'but not the knowledge. Though it is remotely possible that you *could* kill me, you would *definitely* destroy Talisker in the process. Is that what you want?'

'No.'

'I didn't think so.'

Seizing Gillette's arm, Jong said, 'But enough for now. You have work to do, Noah.'

By the time Noah had blinked, Jong was floating in the blackness beyond the breach clutching his prize.

'I will not harm him,' Jong said. 'When you return to free me, he will be hale. I promise you this – as proof to you that I am not evil.'

As Gillette squirmed to get free of his captor's grasp, Noah's heart pounded painfully. 'Manipulating me so you can destroy us doesn't prove you're not evil!' she yelled. 'Quite the opposite!'

'You have a higher purpose, Noah,' Jong said, 'and you will fulfil it. Releasing me will make the universe a greater place and you will make sure it happens.'

Noah clenched her fists.

'Go,' Jong said, 'fight your little war. Save your friends if you can. Then you will return for him.'

Jong ruffled Gillette's hair, smiled at Noah and disappeared.

Chapter 23

Noah cursed aloud, her dirty words turning to pristine vapour in the night air. As she clung to the spruce branch, she searched for somewhere to plant her feet. At least the sliver of moon high above wouldn't betray her to Franco's guards who'd now be patrolling the grounds. She swung gently, hooked her knees over a nearby branch, and eased herself onto it. Rubbing her stinging, cold hands on her trousers she fought for calm. The bridge was supposed to take her *inside* the lodge, not land her in a tree outside it. Xan had messed up, but that wasn't the dragon's worst mistake. How could she not have foreseen the danger? Gillette should have been here with her, not in Jong's clutches.

Taking deep breaths to slow her racing heart, Noah stared down at the lodge. Her vantage point gave her a clear view of the structure at least. It was as she'd left it – with a gaping hole at one end where she'd punched through the wall with the rolling piece of firestone. She strained to see inside. Four soldiers dressed in Leninstar's livery lay bound on the floor. King Catriona sat among them.

'Oh no,' Noah breathed, sending more plumes of white into the night. 'How did they find this place? And how am I going to get them out?'

She frowned and chewed her bottom lip. Was Nerili in there too? He'd planned to meet up with Catriona to reclaim the firestone. If Noah could calm herself, she could use her perception to see how many musical signatures – human and goblin – she could find. She leaned against the trunk of the tree to steady herself and closed her eyes, skin tingling as she called on the firestone in her veins. Noah raked her senses through the lodge. She counted three goblins and eleven humans.

'Right,' she said, 'now I just need a plan.'

Her viola was in a pocket of her trousers but Franco had her firestone. The other sliders she carried wouldn't be up to this task. Equally, her sword would be of no use. She was hopelessly outnumbered. Could she create a diversion? Draw the unbound occupants from the lodge? At least that way she could isolate the prisoners. It *might* buy her enough time to release them.

As the night chill pressed in on her, Noah continued assessing her options. She scanned the ground below for signs of perimeter guards. After several minutes of intense evaluation, Noah climbed down the tree. She walked to the lodge and strode through the hole in the wall without breaking stride.

All eyes turned to her.

Franco spoke first. 'Noah,' he said, 'I didn't expect you to come back here – not after what you did.'

Noah had pinned her hopes on the element of surprise, so she needed to act quickly. She scanned the room. Liah and Frost lay either side of King Nerili while Leninstar's four soldiers flanked King Catriona. As her eyes met Catriona's, Noah bowed her head. Her king returned the gesture.

Looking at Franco, Noah said, 'You need to release these prisoners.'

'No I don't,' he replied. 'In fact, you need to join them. I'm sure your king will be fascinated to hear what you've done with the firestone since you *stole* it.'

'It's gone,' Noah said simply. 'No one can get it now.'

'Noah?' Catriona said.

Deciding not to mention Brinn, Noah turned to her king. 'Your Highness, it was Xan's will that the piece of firestone be reburied. It was too powerful and too dangerous for us.'

'Xan's will? How do you know?' Nerili said.

'I'm a Dragonsbane. I can communicate with her.'

'Where is it?' Nerili asked.

'Gone,' Noah said.

'I'm not sure that it *is* gone,' Franco said. '*I* think you've hidden it for yourself.'

'It's gone,' Noah insisted.

'It's in the lake,' Franco said. 'We'll find it.'

'Good luck,' Noah said. Keen to avoid prickly questions about the manner of her return she continued, 'But in the meantime, I do know where we could source firestone that Xan does approve of.'

'If that's true,' Nerili growled, glaring at Franco, 'perhaps now isn't the time to reveal it.'

'As Dragonsbane, I act in Talisker's best interests,' Noah said. 'I will share the information I have honestly and openly.'

'It doesn't change the fact that *you* stole the firestone, Noah,' Franco said, with a glance at Catriona.

'After *you* stole it, Franco,' Catriona said.

'I would have kept it safe and shared it with my *like-minded* colleagues,' Franco said. 'Unlike Noah, who says she's lost it – which really means she's taken it for herself. And where is Gillette? Did you dispose of him to keep your secret?'

'He's safe,' Noah said.

'Perhaps your little minion is guarding the stone?' Franco said.

With her composure threatening to unravel, Noah said, 'Do you want to hear where we can get more firestone or not?'

With a wave of his hand, Franco said, 'Go ahead.'

Ignoring withering looks from Catriona and Nerili, Noah said, 'The thirteen pieces of firestone that were given to the Descera by the Pyranhi, were cut from thirteen bigger pieces. According to Xan, the original pieces – which she would allow us to have – can be found in the Pyranhi city of Tisaan.'

Franco reached into his fob pocket and drew out Noah's piece of firestone. Holding it in front of his eyes, he said, 'Are you saying this was cut from a bigger piece?'

Noah nodded.

'How big?'

Wanting to sidestep a conversation about size, Noah said, 'I don't know.'

'Did you not ask?'

'Believe it or not,' Noah said, 'it's tricky to communicate with the consciousness of a sleeping dragon.'

Franco smiled. 'So where is Tisaan, Noah? How do we get there?'

'Noah,' Catriona warned.

Noah glanced at her king with a look she hoped said, *Trust me, I know what I'm doing.* Turning her attention back to Franco, she said, 'It can only be accessed via the crypts in Dragonhall.'

'And you know the way?'

Noah shrugged. 'I know the way to Dragonhall but not the specific doorway to Tisaan.'

Franco's eyes gleamed as he considered her words. 'Guards, clear the compound and surrounds. Make ready to leave.'

The soldiers saluted and set to work.

'You think you can find it?' Noah said. 'You do know that only those with the Dragonsbane's mark can enter Dragonhall, don't you?'

'Oh, there are always ways around these things, Noah. I'm a king after all,' Franco replied. 'Would you like to join me?'

'No,' Noah said.

Franco waved dismissively. 'You can watch me find the firestone or die here with your friends. Your choice.'

'None of us is going to die here,' Noah said. 'You're going to let us go – and it's going to be a race to see who can find the firestone first …'

Still toying with Noah's firestone, Franco said, 'Well, that *does* sound interesting. Tell you what, since I'm such a good sport, here's what I'll do …'

He walked across the room and picked up a black satchel. Drawing out a dark metal sphere, he returned to stand before Noah.

'This,' Franco said, 'is what Arissa, Ulster and I have been working on to eradicate the scourge of the goblins. We used one of these to great effect on the fort at t'Amos on our last visit.'

A bead of sweat ran down Noah's back. 'You *can't* use firestone for weapons.'

'Wrong, Noah. You're about to see *firsthand* that I can. But as I said, I'm a good sport, which means that when I leave here … you'll have about a minute to save as many of your friends as you can before I toss this in and obliterate the place.'

'Don't do it, Franco,' Catriona said, straining against her bonds. 'You still have a chance to do the right thing.'

Franco spat. 'Getting rid of goblins is the right thing,' he said. '*You* still have a chance to do the right thing, Catriona. Don't make the same mistake your father did.'

Anger flashed in Catriona's eyes.

Franco gestured to one of his guards. 'Tie her up,' he said, pointing to Noah.

'Yeah,' Noah said, as her arms were pulled behind her, 'you're a real sport.'

'You single-handedly stole a huge piece of firestone,' Franco said with a dismissive wave. 'Getting out of this should be no problem for you, Wonder Girl. Now, if you'll excuse me, I have to go and prepare my … equipment.'

With his metal ball in one hand and Noah's firestone in the other, Franco turned and walked away.

Once the guard was done tying Noah's bonds, he shoved her to the floor beside Catriona.

'When we get back to Leninstar,' Catriona hissed, 'I'm going to lock you in the dungeon for a *very* long time, Noah.'

'Well, it'll have to wait,' Noah said brazenly. 'I need to go to Dragonhall first.'

'Can I presume you have a plan?'

'Yes – get out of here before that bomb goes off.'

'Your plan's a little light on detail,' Catriona said. 'Maybe you should have done something *before* they tied you up.'

'Just roll with it,' Noah said, turning her attention to Franco.

She watched as he raised a hammer above his head. '*No!*' she cried.

King Franco ignored her. He slammed the hammer onto the end of the chisel atop the anvil. Light burst through the lodge, followed by a thunderclap.

Noah wailed in agony as her piece of firestone splintered. Her pain went beyond loss. Though the firestone had been in her family for six centuries and was one of her late mother's treasures, her suffering was not simply sentimental. And her pain went beyond the supreme injustice of Franco using the firestone for death and destruction. Compounding her loss and indignation, was her physical pain. That sliver of firestone made her the 13th key. The essence of that piece of firestone was in her blood. Now it felt like all the shattered fragments coursed through her veins, shredding her insides.

'Noah!'

She heard her name as if from a distance, but couldn't respond. An image of Emir's face formed in her mind. *I need you,* it said.

'I can't,' she whimpered. 'It *hurts* ... I can't.'

She felt a hot breath on her ear. *'Noah! Sit up! That's an order!'*

Noah groaned, but Catriona persisted. 'Noah, sit up *NOW!'*

Noah opened her eyes and tried to focus on the workbench. Franco was gone.

'Roll,' was all Noah managed to say.

Figuring it couldn't be any more painful to move, Noah rolled towards the opening in the wall. It was certainly more difficult without her firestone cocoon but they needed to get out before Franco detonated his weapon.

'Follow me!' she yelled.

Ignoring the cuts and bruises she accumulated on her way across the littered threshold, Noah concentrated on keeping her head from hitting the ground. An inglorious end it would be if she avoided getting blown to bits only to die from self-inflicted concussion. She was wrong about it not being any more painful to move. Rolling with one's hands tied behind one's back was incredibly painful. She wondered how the others fared with their feet bound as well. They just had to get clear of the lodge.

BOOOOOM!

Noah lay on her stomach and squeezed her eyes closed, praying that she would not be hit by flying debris. When the concussive blast had passed, she wriggled around until she could sit up. She scanned the hillside. Eight bodies. Seven of which showed movement. Head pounding, she edged her way to a rock nearby, using its jagged edge to saw through her bonds. Once free she pushed to her feet and stumbled towards Nerili. Noah dropped to her knees beside him as Frost arrived. A long wooden stake protruded from the king's stomach.

'Your Highness,' Frost said, leaning forward over his liege. He'd managed to cut his own bonds already and placed one hand on Nerili's forehead.

The king's eyes fluttered open as Liah squatted beside Frost. He groaned.

'That hurts,' Nerili wheezed, looking at the faces around him. 'Where's Catriona?'

'I'm here,' Catriona said as she took a place next to Noah.

'Good,' he said. 'I have one last job to do and not a lot of time to do it, so listen up.'

Liah cut his king's bonds so Nerili could at least move one of his arms. The stake that impaled him made moving the other arm impossible.

Nerili grunted as he rested his free hand against the stake. 'Thank you.'

Liah nodded but said nothing.

'Noah,' Nerili said, 'I want you to accompany Frost and Liah to Carai.'

'Ah, I was actually planning to go to Tisaan to pick up some firestone—'

'Yes, yes,' Nerili said impatiently, 'but I need you to go via Carai.'

'Why?'

'For your coronation,' he said.

Sure she has misheard him, she said, 'What?'

He tapped the stake. 'You know I won't survive this. I want you to be the next goblin king.'

'I could try to heal your wound.'

'No,' Nerili said. 'You can't.'

Noah dropped her head. 'If I had my firestone, I could try.'

Nerili closed his eyes briefly. 'Well, you don't, so you can't. You need to be the next King of Carai.'

'You can't be serious,' Noah said. 'That's utterly ridiculous! I'm not a goblin.'

'So you'd be king of the goblins rather than the goblin king,' he said.

Noah stared at him. 'They'd never accept me as their king.'

Nerili's expression didn't alter. 'I have only to sign a decree in front of three witnesses. I can do that now, if someone can find parchment and ink.'

Noah looked at Liah and Frost. They at least had the grace to mirror her shock.

Nerili said, 'I know it is unorthodox—'

'*Unorthodox?*' Noah sputtered. 'It's totally ludicrous!'

'Unorthodox,' he repeated. 'But this would give us a better chance of joining the Alliance.' He glanced at Catriona. 'Talisker's kings will listen to you, Noah.'

King Catriona stared at Nerili. 'There are some who would question her ability to perform this role.'

'You being one of them?' Nerili asked.

Catriona nodded. 'Yes.'

Nerili coughed, wincing in pain as he did so. 'It's a shame you have such little faith in her,' he said. 'Am I the only one who can see her talent?'

'Noah's *talent*,' Catriona said, 'is for raiki and dressmaking, *not* matters of state. I can appreciate your strategy, Nerili but I cannot support it.'

'What of your children?' Noah said. 'I recall that Princess Severine was looking forward to being the next King of Carai.'

'My daughter is too young,' Nerili said. 'She needs to be mentored for a few more years. She could not negotiate for a place on the Alliance.'

Noah frowned. 'What if I were just regent – for a short period?'

'Noah!' Catriona said. 'You can't seriously be considering this!'

'She'd have to survive Carai first,' Frost added. 'I don't think the parliament will accept this.'

'They have to,' Nerili said. 'It is the law.'

'Many will be unhappy,' Liah said. 'They will try to kill her.'

'It is your job to protect the king,' Nerili countered.

'What's your king's oath?' Noah asked.

Nerili rested his hand over his heart. 'I will rule for the safety and prosperity of all my kin; with honour, humility and valour I serve.'

Noah absorbed the words. 'Short and sweet,' she said.

'It says what needs saying,' Nerili said. 'Will you do it?'

'Noah,' Catriona said, 'what are you doing?'

'Thinking about it,' Noah answered.

'Why?'

Noah looked Catriona in the eye. 'Because Emir would.'

'Might I remind you that I can order you not to,' she said.

'I don't want to defy you, Your Highness but as Dragonsbane I serve Talisker first. The future of the Sovereign States Alliance might depend on this.'

Noah looked at the sky. If she accepted this job, she'd really have to do it. She'd be expected to fight for a place for them on the Alliance. And she'd have to live in Carai. Noah baulked at the thought. What would Emir say? And Raven? Catriona certainly didn't like the idea.

And what if she refused the position? Nerili's injury would soon claim him. The king's job was going to be vacant. Severine and Sandor were too young. Was there another Nerili in the ranks? Another goblin who wanted peace? Could she step away from a chance to resolve the conflict between humans and goblins?

'Alright,' Noah said. 'Write your decree and I will take it back to Carai. I will accept the position *if* it is endorsed by a majority in your parliament. In the event it is not supported, the parliament should be authorised to elect the new king.'

Nerili's lips pressed together into a thin line. 'That is highly irregular,' he said.

'And trying to appoint a human tailor as the goblin king isn't irregular?' she countered.

'A fair point,' Nerili conceded. Turning to his soldiers, he said, 'Is this suggestion acceptable to you?'

Liah and Frost exchanged a look.

'Yes, Your Highness,' Frost said. 'We accept this.'

♪♫

'Noah, this is a bloody mess,' Catriona said.

Without taking her eyes from the lake's shiny, moonlit surface, Noah replied, 'You don't say.'

'They'll never accept you in Carai. The goblins will think the Alliance has planned this – to bring them down from within.'

'Funny,' Noah said. 'That's what the Alliance thought Nerili was trying to do to us.'

'Some would argue that it's working,' Catriona said grimly. 'The Alliance is in tatters. We're fighting among ourselves. Maybe that was his goal all along.'

Noah turned to her king. As the forest around them slumbered, she searched for the right words. 'If destroying the Alliance was his goal,' Noah said, 'his job is done. What's to be gained from making me King of Carai?'

'He wants the firestone,' Catriona said. '*You're* the one who can get the firestone from Tisaan, Noah, and as Carai's king, you'd be obliged to take it there.'

'But Nerili knows I'll fight for a place on the Alliance for them – I'm obliged to share it. The firestone's a bargaining tool – he still wants to join the Alliance.'

Catriona stared at her. 'I never thought I'd have to deal with you as an equal,' she said at last.

Noah turned her attention back to the lake. 'Well, you might not have to. There's a good chance Carai's parliament will vote against it.'

'Personally, I hope they do.'

'Same here,' Noah whispered.

A ferret scampered past within metres of the girls as they courted their own thoughts. *What business does a ferret have scurrying about at this hour,* Noah thought, thankful for a distraction. The rest of the forest was still, as if in shock from the afternoon's explosion, which had left a black wound on the escarpment. Nerili still lay where he'd fallen, the stake through his abdomen. Frost and Liah would maintain their vigil until death finally came for their king. Four of Catriona's soldiers had spent the afternoon preparing the funeral pyre; all they needed now was the guest of honour.

'Whether you're King of Carai or not, you're going to have to go to Tisaan – and get there before Franco,' Catriona said.

'Franco can't get into Dragonhall to access the secret door. Only those with the mark of the Dragonsbane can enter Dragonhall. He'll have to wait until I've found it and ambush me on the way out.'

'I'll send Raven to Ironside,' Catriona said. 'You'll have Leninstar's assistance to get any firestone you find to Mellifont.'

Noah shivered. 'If I can't con Dr Grainger into accompanying me, I'll have to go to Tisaan on my own. I can't say I'm looking forward to that.'

'Though it'll probably be a picnic compared to Carai,' Catriona said.

Heavy footsteps approached from behind – the footsteps of a soldier not wanting to startle his liege.

Noah and Catriona got to their feet.

'Your Highness,' the soldier said, bowing his head.

'What news?' Catriona said.

'The goblins have returned. Nerili is dead,' he said. 'They await your presence.'

She nodded and fell in step beside him as he turned on his heel. 'And our scouts?' Catriona said.

'Everyone is accounted for,' he reported. 'They found several of our horses so we have some weapons and supplies.'

'At least Franco didn't kill the horses,' Noah said. 'That's always something.'

'We recovered nothing from the lodge,' the soldier continued. 'That bomb was powerful – everything was destroyed. All the weapons Franco confiscated from us – all gone.'

'That's what the fort at t'Amos looked like too,' Noah said. 'We can't let them keep setting those things off.'

Mesmerised by the fire ahead, Noah walked the rest of the way back to camp in silence. The flames leapt with freedom and joy that seemed out of place. Nerili, King of Carai, was dead. Noah sighed. Only a month ago, that would have been cause for celebration for her. Now, having experienced Carai, her heart was sore. Her anti-goblin stance had clearly softened, but how much? Could she overcome her ingrained prejudice of goblins to fight for a place for them on the Alliance?

Leninstar's soldiers formed up on either side of the funeral pyre. Catriona stood at the head of one row while Noah took her place at the head of the other. Nerili's body lay on wooden braces that his guards would use to manoeuvre his body into place on the fire.

Frost cleared his throat. 'It is with great sorrow and solemnity that I commit King Nerili of Carai to the flames this day,' he said. 'His body will return to the earth but his soul will now be free. Those of us who remain will honour his memory and tell tales of his great deeds.'

The goblin bowed his head as his compatriot took over.

'King Nerili served goblinkind with distinction,' Liah said. 'He was a visionary and a statesman. His high ideals and desire for peace and prosperity for his kin should serve as a lesson to all. Those who follow in his footsteps'—he looked at Noah—'should seek to emulate his example with sincerity and courage.'

Noah avoided his gaze, focusing instead on the quiver that hung across his chest. Rather than arrows, the quiver contained Nerili's decree that Noah be his successor. She was a parliamentary vote away from being King of Carai – a king of Talisker. It was no good going with the hope of being rejected – even though that would likely be the outcome. Liah was right. She had to approach the task with sincerity and courage.

As Liah and Frost lifted Nerili's body, Noah fought to steady her breathing. She closed her eyes and bowed her head. She'd seen bodies consumed by flames. The skin blistered and blackened before melting away. The face was horrifying to watch. Noah had had nightmares of noses and eyeballs collapsing in pools of goo before sizzling away. But the smell was the worst. The stench of burnt hair turned Noah's stomach.

She turned her thoughts instead to the letters she needed to write before morning – one to Emir and one to Raven. Noah's stomach churned at the thought of admitting to Emir that she'd lost Gillette. With any luck, she'd find something in Dragonhall that could help her rescue him from Jong, but that was a slim hope. Nothing – not even a lifetime in the dungeon with Franco as her cellmate – could be worse than Emir being disappointed in her.

Chapter 24

'I'll be back in an hour to collect you,' Frost said.

Noah nodded. 'Take your time.'

I'm probably safer in the dungeons than anywhere else in Carai, she thought. Once word of Noah's return got out, and the reason for it, the city would be in uproar. She was determined to make the most of her last hour of peace and anonymity, before she met with Nerili's advisers.

'Ready?' the cell block captain asked.

'Yes,' Noah said.

'Follow me,' the goblin said, 'and don't look sideways.'

'Got it.'

By the time they reached Jacin's cell, Noah had added another three profanities to her vocabulary but was thankful she hadn't been spat on.

She thought Jacin had been joking when he'd referred to his cell in the dungeons as 'his room', but it certainly had the 'lived in' look. The clutter of books, parchments, instruments and clothes made it difficult to determine what furnishings the cell contained, but Noah suspected a bed, desk and bookshelves lurked amongst the mess. In fact, until her goblin escort rattled the keys and Jacin looked up, she hadn't been able to pick him out of the chaos either.

'Noah!' he cried as he leapt off the bed. 'Gee, it's *great* to see you.'

'You really do spend a good deal of time here, don't you,' she said as the guard unlocked the door.

The guard frowned at the mess before looking at Noah. 'Watch your step.'

'Will do.'

'Here, let me help you,' Jacin said, reaching out to take the stack of books she carried. 'Are these for me?'

'They're for us,' Noah said. 'We have some research to do.'

Jacin's eyes widened. 'Sounds exciting! But surely you have news for me. How long have you been back?'

'I've been back long enough to visit the library to collect these,' she said.

Jacin garnished the mayhem on the table with the books Noah had brought before clearing off a chair for her. 'Well, I'm honoured you came to see me first. Please, make yourself comfortable.'

Noah sat. 'You should sit too,' she said. 'I have bad news.'

Jacin's shoulders sagged. 'Oh. Okay.' He shuffled some parchments aside and settled himself on the bed. 'I'm ready.'

'Nerili's dead and the firestone's lost,' she said.

Jacin stared at her. 'How?'

Noah told him everything that had happened since she'd left Carai.

Jacin picked up his flute and laid it across his lap. He sighed. 'I can't believe Nerili is dead.'

Noah said nothing.

'And the other advisers don't know?' he asked.

'They probably do now. Liah and Frost are arranging a meeting.'

'Gisa will be devastated.'

'I'm very sorry for your loss,' Noah said.

Jacin bowed his head. 'Wily old bugger.'

'What?'

'Nerili,' Jacin said, looking up. 'I never would have guessed he'd pick you as his successor.'

'I don't reckon you'd be alone there.'

'It's brilliant.'

'Well, don't get too excited. Parliament has to approve it yet.'

Fingering the keys on his flute, Jacin said, 'So I guess whether you're King of Carai or not – you'll go after the replacement firestone?'

Noah nodded.

'I'm with you either way,' he said.

Noah raised an eyebrow.

Jacin said, 'If you're my king, I present myself for duty. If not … I'll come as your apprentice.'

'Apprentice what?'

'Apprentice Professor of Raiki,' he replied. 'I'm currently a Master, I would like to be a Professor – like you.'

'Let's do our research first,' Noah suggested, 'then you can decide if you want to come along.'

'I don't care how dangerous it is,' he said. 'I'm coming.'

'And what about your family?'

Jacin shrugged. 'Well, they'll slow us down but I'm happy to ask them along if you want.'

Noah rubbed her eyes and shook her head wearily. 'That's not what I meant.'

Jacin took half the books from the pile and handed the rest to her. 'How do you spell Tisaan?'

'I believe it's T-i-s-a-a-n,' she replied, 'but look for anything that's close.'

Noah settled herself to read. She opened the first musty tome and leafed through it, skimming the ancient faded scrawl for any reference to Tisaan. To her surprise, the goblin text was neat and coherent, similar to what she would have expected from Leninstar's library books. Noah found herself distracted by the illustrations and archaic penmanship. The simple act of leafing through a book was great therapy – a distraction from the danger that stalked her. She had to remind herself that she had a purpose here.

'I think I've got something here,' Jacin said.

Noah looked up from her book. 'What is it?'

'An old goblin legend.'

Noah put her own book aside. 'What does it say?'

'When the Pyranhi civilisation went into decline,' Jacin said, studying the text, 'they split into two main groups. Some – who worshipped Elani – populated Tisaan and others – who idolised Jong – moved to

Somyni. The Jong worshippers, according to this account, were zealots who wanted to release Jong from his prison so he could take his loyal followers to a new world where they could have a fresh start and the chance of a better life. Those who worshipped Elani on the other hand, took great pains to stop them – knowing that their success meant the end of Talisker.'

'What happened?'

'There was a great battle and Somyni was defeated,' Jacin said. He looked at Noah. 'Lucky they didn't release Jong, hey? We wouldn't be here if they did.'

Thinking of Gillette and her own encounter with Jong, Noah shuddered. 'What happened to Tisaan?'

'Okay,' Jacin said, pointing to the relevant section of the text, 'so before the war there were thirteen pieces of firestone in Tisaan. The Pyranhi, sensing their doom, cut a small portion from each and gave them to the Descera. Twelve pieces were to be used in the formation of twelve keys – instruments which would heal the land. The last piece was to be held in trust, to make a thirteenth key should it be needed to save the world from a great evil.'

Jacin paused.

Noah tried in vain to swallow the knot of despair that lodged in her throat. She'd met the Descera who'd entrusted that piece of firestone to her family and he'd helped her make the 13th key with it. Franco now had that piece of dragonscale – what remained of it. Anger welled inside her, freeing her vocal cords.

'And then?' Noah said.

'Then they built Dragonhall,' Jacin continued, 'a place where Xan's consciousness could be monitored to make sure Jong stayed imprisoned. Apparently, it took a hundred years to build.'

'It's an impressive building,' Noah said. 'I'm surprised it only took that long to build.'

'Interestingly, neither the Pyranhi nor the Descera used it,' Jacin said. 'Talisker's first Dragonsbane was human.'

'And what about Tisaan?' Noah said, steering him back to the topic at hand.

'After the war with Somyni, Tisaan was … cut off. Somyni was defeated, decimated, and it seems Tisaan counted it as a hollow victory. In fact, it *wasn't* a victory in their eyes. To them, the Pyranhi race had failed. In their long history, there'd never been a war. Only when the doom of their race was upon them had it come to that. That they'd slaughtered their brethren was the ultimate failure and in shame, they sealed off their city by magical means.'

'They used the firestone to set their city outside of time,' Noah guessed, 'so that no one would be able to get there.'

'Yes,' Jacin said.

'But there is a way – through Dragonhall.'

Jacin frowned. 'It doesn't say that here.'

Rubbing her temples, Noah said, 'That's the thing about legends, they don't tell the whole story. It's pretty difficult to get all the facts – especially when you can't talk to the people – or Pyranhi – involved.'

'I guess you're right,' Jacin said, closing the book. 'So we're going to Dragonhall?'

'*I'm* going to Dragonhall,' Noah said. 'Only those with the Dragonsbane's mark can enter Dragonhall.'

Jacin smiled and unbuttoned his shirt. Noah stared at the small crescent-shaped mark on his chest.

'*We're* going to Dragonhall,' he said.

'Did you do that—'

Folding his arms across his chest, he said, 'How could you even suggest such a thing? Of course I didn't do it. I came by this honestly I'll have you know.'

Noah raised her hands in surrender, but before she could reply the goblin guard returned.

'Frost is here to collect you,' he said.

Noah sighed. 'Where'd that hour go?'

Keys jangled in the lock.

To Jacin, she said, 'I'll come back when I'm done.'

Jacin smiled. 'I look forward to it.'

♪♫

'Are you ready?' Frost asked.

No, she thought, *I've only been back in Carai for two hours. I'm not ready to face Nerili's children and confidantes.*

Aloud, she said, 'No, but let's do it anyway.'

The goblin held her gaze. 'This needs to be done right,' he said, shifting the urn into the crook of his left arm. 'Just let me run the meeting.'

'Happy for you to do that,' Noah said.

'Your seat will be between Liah and Gisa. The only two goblins you haven't met are Graze and Iron – the two army captains.'

'Right,' Noah said.

'You remember the king's advisers?'

'Gisa, Rankin and Ulan,' Noah said.

Shar's head appeared around the doorway at the end of the corridor. He waved to Frost, who returned the gesture.

With a nod, Shar withdrew into the king's stateroom.

Looking at Noah, Frost said, 'Follow me.'

He strode down the hallway and Noah felt as though she was being dragged along in his wake. She kept her eyes on the quiver containing Nerili's decree, which hung across Frost's back. As the senior guard, he had the dubious honour of presenting the decree to the Council and the king's ashes to the orphaned children. It promised to be a harrowing meeting. For the time being, Noah was less worried about her own fate. Her heart was raw thinking about Severine and Sandor.

Everyone stood as Frost and Noah entered the room. Frost took his place at the head of the polished stone table while Noah walked around to take her place between Liah and Gisa. When Noah reached her spot, she took the goman's hand and squeezed it gently. Gisa looked at her through bloodshot eyes.

Noah scanned the group, relieved that there were just two goblins she hadn't met. The army captains stood across from her, with Shar on one side and Sandor and Ulan on the other. Severine and Rankin were beside Gisa.

Frost placed the urn containing Nerili's ashes on the table before him. He bowed his head and everyone present followed his lead. After a minute's silence, Frost said, 'Please be seated.'

The cushioned feet of the chairs left the silence intact as everyone took their seats.

'None of us expected that this is how our king would return to us,' Frost said, gesturing towards the urn. 'We have much to discuss today, but first we will honour the king who gave his life for his kin.'

'I want to know the *whole* story,' Sandor demanded. 'Everything that has happened since my father left Carai with *her*'—he pointed an accusing finger at Noah—'and I also want to know why *she* isn't dead – or at least in the dungeon!'

Because Noah understood his anger, she made no move to placate the young prince. There was nothing she could say to Sandor right now that would give him any relief. Her own anger at losing her parents was still a part of her. She could control it now, but it would always be there.

'We will give a full account of everything we know,' Frost assured him, 'and we will also need to hear what has transpired here in Carai in our absence.'

Severine leaned forward and clasped her hands on the table. 'Did my father die in battle?'

'Yes,' Frost said without hesitation. 'Let me tell you what happened.'

Noah listened as Frost related the events from the evening they left Carai after the attack on Jacin's and Gisa's home. He detailed the destruction at t'Amos, the theft of the firestone by the rebel kings and Tambian's death. Everyone at the table was quiet as he told of their stay in Leninstar and of Nerili's meeting with Catriona. Frost's vivid description of the palace and its machinations made Noah homesick. His eloquence surprised her – she'd never heard him string so many words together.

Any thoughts of indulging in memories of home were dispelled quickly. The story of what happened after Nerili and his three guards left Leninstar was new to her. She was keen to hear how they'd tracked the firestone to the lodge.

'Catriona said we would have safe passage to Seychelles and then along the western corridor to Orian City,' Frost said. 'When Catriona arrived with her soldiers we rode north to Tchuganni City, but on arrival we found that the firestone was gone. Since Noah had been kidnapped by Franco, we had no way of knowing where the stone was.'

Noah shook her head. 'I'm surprised you escaped Tchuganni. Franco's intention was that anyone attempting to track the firestone there would be captured.'

'We were attacked,' Frost said, 'but we prevailed. We were a week behind the firestone but we set out to track it, while Shar returned here to advise of the change in circumstances. Since the firestone had to be moved by cart, and we were travelling lighter, we'd hoped to catch up to it before it reached its destination.'

Noah drummed her fingers on the table, appreciating the strategy. Snatching the firestone on the road would be easier that trying to retrieve it from a secure location.

Gisa spoke up. 'So what happened with Franco? Did you find the firestone?'

Frost glanced at Noah before looking to Gisa. 'We tracked Franco and his company to a lakeside lodge. When we arrived, we saw the firestone ... roll into the lake. Noah's the best person to explain what happened there. Noah?'

She'd been dreading this moment, having to admit responsibility for losing Talisker's precious piece of firestone. And she knew this wouldn't be the last time she'd have to tell her story. It was just a question of whether or not she'd stay free long enough to try to find the replacement stones Xan had told her about. There'd be no end of people – and goblins – wanting to lock her up for her crime.

Rather than cower in her seat, Noah stood up. 'I rolled it into the lake,' she said calmly. 'It is lost ... for good.'

Ulan leapt to his feet. *'Why?'* he demanded.

'Its power is too great,' Noah explained. 'I am a Dragonsbane of Talisker and being so close to a piece of firestone that size gave me access to Xan's consciousness. I could listen to her, and talk to her. She told me what to do. She told me to rebury the stone.'

Iron spoke. 'So you just pushed it down the hill and it rolled into the lake?' she asked. 'Surely we can pull it out of the lake.'

Noah studied the army captain. 'No,' she said. 'The firestone has been reburied – in sinking sand. It's not coming back.'

'How do you know it's in sinking sand?' Iron asked.

Noah took a deep breath. 'I steered the firestone … from inside'—
she put her hands up to deflect interruption—'Xan allowed me to enter
the firestone. For a short time, she allowed me inside the stone so I could
do what she wanted done. She wanted me to roll the firestone into the
lake and lodge it in some sinking sand so that no one … *no one* … could
get it out. I did it. It's done.'

'If you buried it in sinking sand,' Rankin ventured, 'how did *you*
get out?'

'Yeah,' Sandor said, 'how *did* you get out?'

'Xan's magic,' Noah said simply. 'I did what she asked and in return
she spared my life.'

Sandor snorted. 'How convenient.'

'It's more than convenient,' Noah said. 'She wants me to find
replacement firestone.' Again, she held up her hands to forestall interruption. 'In the ancient Pyranhi city of Tisaan, there are thirteen pieces
of firestone that Xan is happy for us to have.'

'Who's *us*?' Iron asked. 'Goblins? Humans?'

Noah looked at her. 'Taliskerans.'

'I say you tell us where it is … and we'll go and get it,' Iron said.

Frost interrupted. 'Now is not the time for a detailed discussion
about the firestone,' he said. 'At this time, we are honouring our late
king.'

The army captain bowed her head. 'Of course.'

Noah sat down and tried to ignore her heart hammering on the
inside of her chest. She kept her eyes on Frost but only half listened as
he related what had transpired after they'd been captured by Franco's
forces. As he told them about Franco's bomb, Noah put her hand to her
chest, feeling for her empty locket. Her own precious piece of firestone
was gone – splintered and used to fuel a monstrous weapon.

Failure weighed heavily on her. Her ancestors had kept the firestone
safe for six hundred years and now she had lost it and had it used against
her. Nerili had died because of her failure to protect her piece of dragonscale. The goblins would hold her responsible and rightly so. They'd
never accept her as their king. Fear crawled through her like a tsunami
of angry ants, scouring her insides.

Princess Severine stood up. Her bearing reminded Noah of Catriona. *It must be something princesses are born with,* Noah thought.

'My father was a humble goblin but a brave king,' Severine said. 'His funeral will be spectacular – celebrating his greatness.'

'And who will succeed him?' Ulan asked.

Frost unhooked the quiver from his chest and opened the cap. He upended the cylinder on the table and let the rolled parchment slide out.

'What's that?' Iron asked.

'King Nerili's decree regarding his successor,' Frost answered. 'I will read it.'

As Frost untied the brown cord that bound the scroll, Grave made his first contribution to the meeting. 'Is now the time?' he asked.

Noah looked across the table at the army captain whose pockmarked face betrayed no emotion.

'Speculation and rumour are our enemies,' Frost said. 'All here have a right to know.'

Noah bowed her head as Frost read Nerili's decree.

'I, King Nerili of Carai, bid farewell to my kin and give my last instructions,' Frost read. 'To my children, Severine and Sandor I say … be strong and be fair. I love you both and I will miss you. Your mother and I will watch over you from beyond.'

As Frost continued, Noah wondered what her parents might have written to her if they'd had the opportunity.

'To my advisers, army captains and guards,' Frost said, 'I have valued your advice, protection and companionship. It was a privilege to work with you. I ask of you now, one last service. I ask you to support my successor … Noah Chord.'

Frost paused.

'No,' Ulan said flatly as he put his hand on Sandor's arm. 'I cannot support this.'

Rankin stood up. 'This is deeply concerning,' she said. 'If King Nerili has given his reasons for this, I would be keen to hear them. Why would he want a human to be our king?'

'A fair question,' Frost replied. 'I will read on … Although I am authorised to appoint my successor, Noah has requested that her appointment be conditional upon a parliamentary vote. Her primary function would be to gain Carai a seat on the Sovereign States Alliance – after she has secured replacement firestone. Her tenure would last for one year after Carai has attained a seat on the Alliance. After this time, the throne will go to Severine.'

Rankin sat down, a frown creasing her face. 'This is highly irregular,' she murmured.

'Indeed it is,' Gisa agreed. 'But how like King Nerili – he was always surprising.'

'And he *really* wanted a seat on the Alliance,' Iron said. She looked at Noah. 'Could you get us that?'

'Not without the support of you'—she gestured to those around the table—'and your kin,' Noah said. 'If you want a seat on the Alliance because you want *peace* … I will fight for a place for you.'

'And if we don't want that?' Ulan challenged.

'If your *parliament* decides they don't want that, then I return to Leninstar.'

Grave spoke again. 'And if you return to Leninstar, what of the firestone?'

Noah met his gaze. 'I will recover the firestone for the Alliance. If you choose not to join, you will have no firestone and no access to electricity.'

'You're holding us to ransom,' Ulan accused.

'The choice is yours,' Noah said calmly. 'If you want in on the Alliance and access to the benefits it brings, then let me do my job. If you don't want that, I'll happily go home. No ransom. It's simply your choice.'

'Why can we not fight for a place on the Alliance with our own king?' Iron said.

'You can,' Noah said. She looked at Severine. 'Are you up for it, Princess?'

Severine lifted her chin proudly. 'I could appoint a regent,' she said.

'Yes, you could,' Noah said, 'but do you think the Alliance will take your application seriously if you send a messenger?'

A prickly hush saturated the room.

'We don't need your arrogance,' Ulan growled.

As Noah's eyes flicked to the disgruntled adviser, something inside her snapped. *I don't need to take this,* she thought. *I'd rather go home anyway.* She stood up and leant forward, resting her fingertips on the table.

'I'm not going to address your parliament to beg for this position,' Noah said. 'You think I want your validation? Think again. Yes, you and your kin can decide if you want me to lobby for you or not, but I have a choice too. If I don't think your motivation is appropriate, I won't fight for you. I'm not doing this for Nerili or for you – my goal is peace. If that's not what you're after, well … I'm going home.'

Noah turned her attention to Frost. 'I'll be in my quarters. Let me know whether you want me to address your parliament or not.'

She didn't wait for a response. She walked out of the meeting room and strode down the corridor, the tide of her anger carrying her along. *I don't have to take this,* she thought again. *I'd rather get on with finding the replacement firestone … and Gillette.*

Chapter 25

'Will I show her in?' Frost asked.

Noah scanned her bedchamber. Everything appeared to be in order. 'Yes, show her in.'

Frost opened the door and beckoned. He stood aside as Liah came through with another goblin bearing a large book. Noah's heart fluttered. At least she'd have a distraction while the parliament voted on Nerili's decree.

The young goblin smiled broadly at her. 'Rarely does anyone get a second one of these,' she said, patting the book of fabric samples. 'I'm Rainy, by the way.'

Noah returned her smile. 'It's nice to meet you Rainy, and thank you for bringing me another copy. My original catalogue is back in Leninstar.'

'That's okay. The boss didn't mind at all. He's keen to get a deal with the royal family in Leninstar.' She handed the book to Noah. 'Now, could I take the liberty of drawing your attention to a couple of new swatches we've included in this edition for you?'

'Certainly,' Noah said as she settled herself on the chaise lounge near the window. With the sample book in her lap, she ran her fingers over the olluka wood cover, savouring the delicate music that still trickled through the timber.

The young goblin sat beside her while Frost and Liah assumed their positions either side. Noah hoped they liked fabric; the parliament didn't look like resolving the vote anytime soon so she was fully intending to spend a couple of hours studying the samples.

Noah opened the cover. 'Anything new in the baltik silk?'

'As luck would have it, yes,' Rainy replied.

Leafing through to the silk section, Noah felt the familiar tingle of excitement that fabric always gave her.

'This one's new,' Noah said. 'I'd definitely have remembered if I'd seen it before.'

'Well spotted,' the goblin replied. 'We are particularly proud of this one. It's called *Peacock bronze* – for obvious reasons – and we think it absolutely captures the essence of the magnificent bird. See the way it shimmers when you move it? It's like millions of beads of late afternoon autumn sunlight reflecting off a waterfall, don't you think?'

'It's mesmerising,' Noah agreed.

The pair spent the next half hour pouring through the book discussing the colours and textures of the samples. When they reached the back cover, Rainy said, 'Well, that's probably my cue to leave. I thank you for your time, Noah, but I think it's time I returned to the factory.'

'Thank you for delivering this so promptly,' Noah said. 'I'll have a more thorough look through it this afternoon.'

Running her hand over the inside of the book's back cover, Rainy said, 'There is just one thing I haven't shown you yet—'

In a blur of movement, Rainy ripped away the silk backing and retrieved a small knife. Before the guards could react, the goblin jammed the blade into the top of Noah's leg. Searing pain exploded in her groin. As she stared in disbelief at the handle protruding from her flesh, she was vaguely aware of Frost grabbing the goblin and throwing her to the floor, landing on top of her with his knee in the middle of her back and pushing her face into the stone.

When Liah moved towards her, Noah found her voice. 'Don't touch it!'

'We need to get it out,' Liah said. 'It's probably poisoned.'

Fighting through the haze of pain and shock, she said, 'I don't think so. She's gone for an artery. Trust me, unless you want blood everywhere – leave it where it is.'

She took several deep breaths to stave off the panic that threatened.

'What can I do?' Liah asked.

'Get me my viola,' she whispered.

He reacted instantly, crossing the room in half a dozen urgent strides. By the time he returned, Frost's unconscious captive was securely bound and he was at her side too.

'Frost,' Liah said, 'get the doctor.'

'No,' Noah said, shaking her head. 'I don't want anyone else in here. Frost, guard the door. No one enters. No one.'

'Yes, Ma'am,' Frost replied.

Noah looked at the knife handle. Fear paralysed her. She knew she needed to act quickly but she couldn't. If the knife had severed her artery, she didn't have long to try to repair it. Leaving the blade in bought her some time but not much. She'd repaired muscle tissue and small blood vessels before. However, arteries were notoriously tricky to deal with and with no firestone slider it would be almost impossible.

A picture of Emir's face flashed in her mind. Then Raven's. And it quickly became a movie reel of everyone she held dear … family, friends, pets … every reason she had to stop procrastinating. But still, she stared at the knife. Though irrelevant to resolving the situation, she catalogued every detail on the hilt. The olluka wood was oiled to a deep brown and intricately carved with a series of interlinked circular glyphs. The glyphs looked vaguely familiar but Noah couldn't place them. *Sachin would know what they are,* she thought.

'And if I want a chance to ask him, I'm going to have to live that long,' she muttered aloud.

'Pardon?' Liah said.

Noah glanced at him. 'Nothing. I'm ready.'

He thrust the open viola case in her direction. 'You've done this before then?'

'Never.'

'But it's relatively straightforward?'

'No. I'm not aware of it ever having been done successfully.'

'Right. I'll stop talking.'

'Thank you.'

In the absence of her firestone, she selected an obsidian slider from her viola case and with shaking hands, inserted it into the bridge. She tucked the viola under her chin as Liah passed her the bow. While she tuned her instrument, she assessed the internal damage to her groin with her natural perception. Ignoring the muscles and nerves, Noah hunted for the artery, which she found easily. She was not surprised to find it severed. This assassin knew her stuff – and it was how Noah knew there'd be no poison. It was a matter of pride among assassins. Using poison took little skill; hitting an artery though, required talent.

Noah strove for detachment. She needed to analyse the situation objectively. Pushing panic aside, she focused on the blood seeping into the tissue around the severed blood vessel.

I need to slow my heart rate to minimise the blood loss, she thought. *Deep breaths …*

She knew a tonic to constrict blood vessels, but for an artery her obsidian slider wouldn't be enough. She'd need to use the firestone inside her to make the tonic work. Confident that neither Liah nor Frost would discover her secret, she set to her task. Within the first few bars of the tonic, she could feel all her arteries begin to constrict.

'Liah,' she said.

'Yes?'

'When I say "start", you're going to drag the knife to my right. Don't pull it out and don't change the angle of the blade. Just drag it slowly to my right. Understand?'

'That will cut you even more.'

'Correct but that's what has to happen. The artery is in two pieces and I need to move the blade aside while I try to reconnect the ends. If you disturb the ends too much when you move the blade, I might not be able to get them lined up again.'

'There's going to be a lot of blood?'

'A fair bit, I'd say. But ignore that. Focus on maintaining the angle of the blade and dragging it slowly to the right. I'll probably scream – but ignore that too. Start when I say "start" and keep dragging until I say "stop".'

'Got it.'

As her blood pressure rose and the amount of blood leaking into her groin decreased, she braced herself and said, 'Start.'

Liah didn't hesitate. As the blade sliced more muscle and flesh, Noah nearly fainted from the pain. Instead, she focused her awareness on the severed ends of her artery so she knew when the blade had cleared the area.

'Stop!'

Ignoring the warmth on her leg as blood escaped from the wound, she changed her melody. At least the blood wasn't spurting from the wound. Using a tonic that Sachin had taught her, she attempted to re-join the artery. Though she'd reduced the flow of blood, some still escaped, hampering her efforts.

She needed to stop the flow altogether, which meant constricting the artery further. But she couldn't isolate the artery, so she made another attempt to re-attach the loose ends.

After the third attempt, the ends aligned.

'Okay, now just stay there,' she whispered as she plucked her way through a series of notes to help the tissue bind. With such a big vessel, she needed to repeat the series over and over again. When she was sure it would hold she lowered her viola.

Though not finished yet, Noah opened her eyes. Liah was still beside her, his hand still on the knife. 'Can you take the covers off the cushions, please?' she said.

Bowing his head, he said, 'Of course.'

Her bidding was done within moments. 'When I pull the knife out, you press those over the wound,' Noah said.

He nodded.

Clenching her teeth so she didn't scream, Noah extracted the knife carefully. As Liah pressed the cloth onto the gash, Noah wiped the bloody blade on her sleeve then inspected the four-inch steel with morbid fascination. The blade at least looked clean, which minimised the chance of infection.

'Someone should stitch that,' Liah said.

'Yes,' Noah agreed. 'I'm not quite finished yet though. Just keep holding that.'

While Liah plugged the wound, Noah played to dilate her blood vessels again. Exhausted though she was, she concentrated hard. She needed enough blood flow to replenish all her muscles and organs but not so much that she damaged the artery she'd just repaired. When she was done she returned her instrument to its case on the lounge beside her, along with her bow.

'I'm done for the moment,' she said. 'I can hold that now.'

Liah took his bloody hands away from the wad of cloth. 'Should I get the doctor now?'

'Get Jacin. Don't tell him what's wrong – just bring him and a medical bag.'

'Yes, Ma'am.' He saluted and glanced at Frost. 'Once I have performed this task, you will be relieved of our service. There are others more competent than us to provide security for you.'

Noah's chest tightened. 'No.'

'You cannot argue our failure tonight,' Frost said. 'We're not worthy to serve.'

'Rubbish,' Noah said. 'Quite the contrary, in my view. You have proved your trustworthiness beyond doubt tonight – and trust is not something I feel a lot of around here. You could easily have let me bleed to death or even have finished what she started.'

Liah pointed to her viola. 'That is what saved you. It's lucky you have such skill.'

'Lucky? I don't know about that. If I didn't have such skills, I doubt I'd have got myself into this position in the first place.'

Liah nodded thoughtfully. 'Great gifts bring great responsibility.'

'Something like that,' Noah said.

'What would you have us do with the prisoner?'

'Put her in a cell and watch her. I want her alive.'

'Why?'

'I'd like her to live with the shame of knowing she failed.'

'We'll question her when she wakes up,' Frost said. 'See if we can find out who she's working for.'

No chance of that, Noah thought. *Assassins don't snitch.*

♪♫

Noah studied her reflection in the mirror. She didn't look like a king. Despite her crown, sword, cloak and tunic bearing Carai's olluka tree emblem, Noah didn't see royalty. She saw a costume. *How the hell am I supposed to do this?* she wondered. The vote in parliament had been close – thirty-eight to thirty-three. *They don't believe in me,* I *don't believe in me,* she thought, *how can I expect the other kings to take me seriously?*

She sighed before turning to the guards at the door to her bedchamber.

'How long until show-time?' she asked.

'Your coronation begins in an hour,' Shar said.

Noah nodded.

Amy, who'd been quietly observing Noah's preparations, poured a glass of water and walked over to stand beside Noah. 'You'll be fine,' she said. 'Just be yourself.'

Accepting the glass, Noah said, 'I don't think that's a good idea.'

A knock at the door interrupted the conversation.

'Who's there?' Noah called.

Frost answered. 'I bring Jacin, Gisa and Rankin.'

Noah nodded to Shar and Liah, who opened the door to admit the three advisers.

Jacin walked towards her, arms outstretched. Noah drew her dagger.

'Don't even think about it,' she said.

'Oh come on,' Jacin said. 'Can't I even give you a congratulatory hug?'

'No.'

Amy sighed. 'Sorry, Noah,' she said. 'Gisa got all the subtle out of those two.'

'Who needs subtle?' Jacin said. 'I do just fine without it.'

Gisa grimaced. 'If you say so.'

Despite the circumstances, Noah smiled as she looked at each of the advisers. Only Ulan had decided he couldn't work for her.

'I thank you all once again for agreeing to stay on in service of Carai's king,' she said.

The three bowed in unison.

'We will serve with honour,' Rankin said.

Noah clicked her fingers. '*That's* what I had to do,' she said. Looking at Liah, she said, 'Remind me ... what's the king's oath?'

'I will rule for the safety and prosperity of all my kin; with honour, humility and valour I serve,' Liah replied.

After a moment's pause, Noah said, 'Can I change it?'

Frost's eyes narrowed. 'Change it how?'

Noah chose her words carefully. 'I don't know that I should say "kin". I don't feel comfortable saying it and I don't think most goblins will either.'

'What are you going to say then?' Shar said.

'Subjects?' Noah suggested.

'No,' Liah said flatly.

'Why not?'

'Because it makes you sound superior – like you're trying to be above us. "Kin" is meant to sound like the king is actually one of us.'

'Yes, but I'm *not* one of you. That's the point, isn't it?'

'You can't refer to us as subjects,' Shar said.

'Goblins?' Noah said. 'How about – *I will rule for the safety and prosperity of all goblins; with honour, humility and valour I serve.*'

Jacin said, 'We're not all goblins here. What about the humans ... and the gomans?'

'People?' Noah said.

'No,' Liah said. '*People* sounds too human.'

'Residents?' Noah suggested.

Shar winced. 'No. Sounds too ... impersonal.'

'Inhabitants?'

The guards shook their heads in unison.

Exasperated, Noah looked at her three advisers, 'What am I paying you all for? Please feel free to *advise* on this.'

'May I make a suggestion?' Amy said.

'Please do,' Noah said.

'What about – *I will rule for the safety and prosperity of all in Carai; with honour, humility and valour I serve.*'

Noah looked at the guards. 'Would that be acceptable?'

'I have no objection,' Frost said.

'Nor I,' Shar added.

Liah shrugged. 'It's your oath.'

Noah's eyes widened. 'I beg your pardon? You've just spent the last few minutes telling me what I can't say! How is it now "my oath"?'

Unflappable, Liah said, 'We're here to offer advice but ultimately the decision is yours.'

'Thanks. Good to know,' she said.

'Is there anything else you need, Your Highness?' Gisa said.

'No,' Noah said. 'I don't think so.'

'How's the leg?'

'Healing well,' Noah replied.

'That's good,' Rankin said. 'Everyone knows about the assassination attempt and if you can walk without limping – you'll earn some serious respect.'

'I wasn't going to mention it.'

'Good. Don't,' Rankin advised.

Noah could feel Jacin's gaze on her but she ignored him.

'Well, we'd best go and get ready,' Gisa said. 'We just stopped in to see if there was anything you needed.'

Noah nodded. 'I'm fine. I'll see you soon.'

Gisa, Rankin and Amy all bowed before leaving. Only Jacin remained.

'Dismissed,' Noah said.

'But—'

'Dismissed,' Noah repeated.

Frost took Jacin's elbow and turned him towards the door.

'I have a raiki question,' Jacin said over his shoulder.

'Which can wait,' Noah finished, turning back to her mirror.

Jacin continued to grumble as Frost escorted him out of her chamber.

Noah took a measured breath. In desperation, she'd sought Jacin's help in the aftermath of the assassination attempt. And while his skills had proved useful in aiding her recovery, his curiosity about her quick recovery was now a problem. A problem that she'd have to deal with. Jacin knew that the obsidian she'd used wasn't powerful enough for the tonic that had healed her wound. He had lots of questions. Uncomfortable questions.

Jacin was a talented adept who bore the mark of the Dragonsbane. *He's either going to be my biggest asset or my biggest liability,* she thought. Either way, she needed to watch him.

♪♫

Noah scanned the amphitheatre as the last goblins took their seats. This was the second coronation she'd attended in a month. Catriona's had been a surprise. She wasn't sure how to categorise this one. There were more archers around the perimeter of the stage than there were officials on it. Soldiers punctuated the end of every row of seats. The cache of weapons that had been confiscated at the door would have been the envy of many a small town.

Nerili's twins sat either side of Noah – Princess Severine on her left and Prince Sandor on her right. Army captains Iron and Grave plugged the ends of the row. Noah's guards and advisers sat behind them.

Frost leaned forward and whispered to Noah. 'Ready?'

Noah stood up and walked to the dais, followed by her guards who carried the ceremonial pieces she'd be presented with.

She looked at the sea of disfigured faces and took a deep breath.

'Hail to the King!' Frost said.

The crowd echoed his words. *'Hail to the King!'*

Noah bowed to the crowd.

Frost took charge of the ceremony. 'Welcome all,' he said. 'As you know, tonight's coronation is far from usual. King Nerili's death was unexpected and his choice of successor has surprised many. I am happy to say that Carai's parliament has shown great wisdom, and respect for Nerili's legacy. King Nerili's goal was to gain a seat on the Sovereign

States Alliance – to bring peace and the benefits of firestone and electricity to Carai. With Noah as our king, this hope remains. And when her job is fulfilled, she will relinquish the throne.'

Noah nodded. 'I will rule for the safety and prosperity of all in Carai,' she said. 'With honour, humility and valour I serve.'

Frost stepped forward. 'To remind you of the honour of serving Carai, I present you with this crown.'

Noah held her head high as he placed the coiled silver crown over her brow.

As Frost retreated, Shar took his place. 'Let this simple cloak remind you of humility,' Shar said as he draped the pale blue cloak around her shoulders.

Liah was last to present his piece. 'With this sword,' he said, 'let all see the valour with which you defend us.'

Noah accepted the plain black sheath and drew the sword from it. She held it in front of her, inspecting the blade. The polished steel reflected the light as she tested the edge with her thumb. *Definitely sharp,* she thought. She swung the blade in a figure of eight. *And well balanced.*

'I accept these gifts of office,' Noah said, 'and reaffirm my commitment to securing the replacement firestone and lobbying for a place on the Alliance.'

A tense silence stretched out for several long moments before someone at the back called out, 'Is that it?'

'These things will not be easily achieved,' Noah said. 'It will take a concerted effort and this isn't to say they are the only things that will be done – but they are my priorities.'

'Will we keep our jobs?'

Noah didn't hesitate. 'You'll keep them if you want to work for me and as long as you don't get in my way. Anyone who thinks they *can't* work for me, I am happy to help them find work somewhere else.'

'What about the war between the north and south?' another asked. 'Are you going to send a fighting force?'

Noah shook her head emphatically. 'It is not our war,' she said, 'and besides, any military involvement on our part would only serve to compromise a place on the Alliance.'

'Surely demonstrating our willingness to fight would stand us in good stead!' one declared.

'Goblins' willingness to fight is not in question,' Noah said bluntly. 'The goal of a place on the Alliance is about achieving peace. We need to refrain from killing Alliance members if we are to succeed.'

'They will still kill us!'

'We will defend ourselves, but we will not attack.'

'And what will you do if Leninstar attacks? Do you really expect us to believe that your allegiance lies here?'

'I would be truly conflicted, obviously but I would hope, with my connections in Leninstar, that that situation will not arise.'

Chapter 26

Noah kept her eyes on Raven as she approached the bridge to Dragonhall. The *infini* symbol on her brother's breastplate made her heart swell under her new, foreign regalia. She pushed thoughts of her mission to Tisaan aside for the moment and focused on Leninstar's soldiers. Under the blazing midday sun, twenty of Leninstar's finest flanked the state's army commander. Relief washed through her that Catriona had kept her promise. There'd been no sign of Franco since she'd left Carai but Noah was sure that he'd be waiting for her if she found the firestone.

She stopped a kingly distance from her brother as her soldiers formed up around her. Raven put his clenched fist over his heart and Noah returned Leninstar's traditional salute with a nod.

Raven bowed his head. 'Your Majesty,' he said.

'Knock it off,' Noah said as she stepped forward and put her arms around him.

Raven returned her embrace. 'Is this allowed?' he whispered.

'I say it is,' Noah answered, 'so they won't draw their swords. I warned them.'

Kissing the top of her head, he said, 'They don't look happy about it.'

'This is the least of what they're unhappy about.'

'I can imagine.' He released her. 'It's good to see you.'

'It's good to see you too. How's Emir?'

Raven grinned. 'Surprised.'

Noah smiled but didn't get a chance to answer.

'Ahem.'

Noah looked sideways. Jacin inclined his head towards Raven. 'Are you going to introduce me?'

'All in good time,' Noah said. Turning back to her brother she said, 'I think we should eat and discuss our plans.'

'Our camp is beyond the ridge,' Raven said.

Frost spoke up. 'You lead,' he said. 'We will escort our king.'

Raven's eyes flicked to Noah. She nodded.

'To camp,' he ordered.

Leninstar's soldiers turned and marched. Shar and Liah fell in behind Raven with ten of their goblin comrades. Frost and Jacin flanked Noah with her remaining soldiers behind her.

Looking back over his shoulder towards Dragonhall, Jacin said, 'That building is amazing. I can't wait to go in there.'

'It is amazing,' Noah agreed.

'I thought our temple in Carai was impressive,' he continued, 'but this makes it look … kind of ordinary.'

'I wouldn't say that,' Noah said, thinking of the massive dragon carved out of olluka wood.

'It's hundreds of times the size,' he said, 'and look at all those bronze shingles. They're perfectly aligned. They look like real scales.'

As they trekked across the dusty plain to Raven's campsite, Noah tuned out to Jacin's wonderment and reviewed what she'd learned of Dragonhall in Carai's library. It wasn't a Desceran construction as she'd previously believed. The Pyranhi had built it. Noah shuddered again at the thought. She'd spent a good deal of time in Dragonhall and had a deep respect for the place. But somehow, the fact that it had been built by the Pyranhi rather than the Descera made it more ethereal. Perhaps because she'd met some of the Descera, she reasoned. They'd been real to her so the place was too, but the Pyranhi were an ancient and mysterious race. Something built by them was therefore ancient and mysterious too.

Noah pushed such thoughts aside. She needed to focus on the task at hand. Scanning the small island of Ironside, she wondered where Franco was. The island was relatively flat barring the mountains to the north. There weren't many places to hide. If he was here, Raven would find him.

As Shar marshalled Carai's soldiers to set up camp, Raven invited Noah to take a seat on a log. Frost and Jacin sat either side of her while Raven dragged a stump over and sat in front of her. He glanced at Jacin before returning his attention to Noah.

'Are you going to introduce me to your new friend?' he said.

Noah nodded. 'This is Jacin, one of my advisers.'

Raven bowed his head. 'Raven Chord,' he said. 'Leninstar's Army Commander.'

'So nice to meet you,' Jacin said, thrusting his hand towards Raven.

'And you,' Raven said, accepting the handshake.

'And you remember Frost?' Noah said, gesturing to her left.

Raven nodded. 'One of Nerili's guards.'

'So what's your plan here?' Frost said.

'Officially,' Raven said, 'I'm here to make sure that any firestone recovered is returned to Mellifont, and to deter or detain any other interested parties along the way.'

'Franco, you mean?' Jacin said.

'Yes,' Raven replied.

'And unofficially?' Frost said.

'Unofficially, I'm here to make sure my sister's safe.'

Frost nodded. 'That's our job now.'

'Then it seems we have a common purpose,' Raven said. 'No reason we'd be getting in each other's way.'

'So you haven't seen any sign of Franco or the others?' Noah said.

Raven shook his head. 'Not yet. I think it's more likely he'd strike after the firestone is found.'

'Assuming we can find it – and retrieve it,' Noah said.

'So what's your plan there?' Raven asked.

'Jacin and I are going in.'

Raven looked at the goman and then at his sister. 'Jacin's going in? He has the mark?'

Noah nodded. 'We'll talk to Dr Grainger and his apprentice first. I'm hoping they'll help us.'

'Is there any reason they wouldn't?' Raven said. 'Surely they'd jump at the chance to find firestone.'

'I think there's a good chance they'll try to *stop* us,' Noah said. 'They were never keen on the first piece – for the same reason Xan isn't, as it turns out – but I don't think they're going to like this any better. Venturing into places outside of time is bound to ring warning bells for those charged with keeping the great dragon sleeping.'

'But you think it's okay?' Raven said.

'I think if Xan told me to do it … then it's okay.'

'Then surely, they'd accept the same logic.'

'I wouldn't count on it,' Noah said.

'And then,' Jacin said, 'we just need to find the doorway to Tisaan, survive a place that doesn't exist in our time, retrieve the firestone and get back here.'

Raven frowned as he stared at his sister. 'Do you want me to keep your dinner warm?'

Three soldiers bearing food interrupted the conversation. The soldier from Leninstar delivered bread and salted pork while Shar and Liah distributed nuts and dried fruit.

'Thank you,' Noah said.

The soldiers bowed and left.

As Noah took a handful of nuts and fruit from the bag Frost offered, she said, 'From our research in Carai, we know that the Pyranhi were masters of firestone. They were the ones that built Dragonhall and created the role of Dragonsbane. But they didn't trust the Descera with the pieces of firestones they had, so they cut off small flecks and left instructions for the twelve keys, which the Descera made and used to maintain Talisker's dragonsong. The idea to *hide* the city was to ensure that only those with an appropriate level of skill could access the rest of the dragonscale.'

'Right,' Raven said.

'Your concern for your sister weighs heavily on you,' Frost said.

'Yes,' Raven said.

'Do you doubt her ability?'

Raven looked at the goblin. 'No,' he said evenly. 'I doubt the world will judge her fairly – regardless of what she achieves here.'

'We believe in her,' Jacin said, patting Noah's knee.

Raven's gaze returned to Noah. 'I would like to talk to my sister alone.'

'Your Highness?' Frost said.

'Yes,' Noah said. 'Leave us.'

'Yell if you need anything,' Jacin said as he stood up.

'Sure,' Noah replied.

When Frost and Jacin were out of earshot, Raven sighed. 'Noah, you're limping,' he said. 'What happened?'

'Someone tried to kill me.'

The colour drained from his face but he said nothing. Noah didn't speak either. For nearly a minute they sat in silence. Noah wondered whether Raven didn't know what to say or whether, like her, he didn't trust his voice to stay steady.

Eventually, he said, 'Do you want me to get you out of here? Take you back to Leninstar? Just say the word … we're ready.'

'I want to come home more than anything,' she said quietly, 'but I have to do this.'

'We want you home too,' he replied, 'but you know that we'll support you in what you're doing.'

'We?' Noah said. 'Who is "we"?'

'Emir and Cate and me.'

'Catriona? Really? She said that?'

Raven nodded. 'Of course.'

'That's not the impression I got from her.'

Tapping his knees, Raven said, 'She's jealous of you, you know.'

Noah snorted. 'Yeah right.'

'*That's* why she gives you such a hard time,' Raven said.

'You noticed? You could try sticking up for me occasionally.'

'I do,' he said. 'She *was* taken aback by your decision, Noah, but she's got your back on this one. Trust me.'

Noah looked at the cloudless sky. She hoped there'd be a few more that supported her. The kings of the southern states would probably back her. Tara, Henrik and Mallory had supported Tambian's move to negotiate with Nerili in respect of the Alliance so they should be behind her. Sachin would stand by her too, she was sure. Anok and Maggie too. In fact, she'd probably get more support in Mellifont than anywhere else.

'Do you trust your guards?' Raven asked.

Noah nodded. 'Frost, Shar and Liah – yes. The others'—she waved her hand towards those setting up camp—'were hand-picked by them.'

'And Jacin? Did you say he's one of your advisers?'

'I have three. Nerili had four but one resigned with my appointment.'

Raven looked across the campsite at Jacin. 'There's something about him I don't like.'

'He's an outrageous flirt,' Noah said.

Raven put his hand on his sword hilt. 'Has he—'

Noah put up her hands. 'I can handle that,' she said. 'That is the least of my problems.'

Raven smiled ruefully. 'Yeah okay. Sorry. It's just ...'

'I know,' Noah said. 'But there is something ...'

When Raven leaned forward, Noah did the same. 'What is it?' he said.

'I think he's onto me,' she whispered.

'Onto you? How?'

'When I was stabbed, the knife cut an artery. I didn't have any firestone – Franco took my piece – so I used an obsidian slider. The guards didn't suspect anything but Jacin has studied in Mellifont. He knows that obsidian couldn't heal a wound like that.'

'So he knows you used firestone ... somehow.'

'He's definitely suspicious, yes.'

'Noah if he figures out you're the 13th key ...'

'I know. I *know*,' she said.

Raven tapped on his leg. 'And diving in and out of a massive piece of firestone didn't help either, I imagine.'

'You heard about that?'

'Cate told us. Do you think it's a good idea to take him with you to Tisaan?'

Noah thought about Grainger and his apprentice. 'I think I'm going to need all the help I can get.'

Chapter 27

'I don't suppose there is another bridge?' Jacin asked.

'No,' Noah said.

'How does a rickety wooden bridge survive the heat from the lava in the moat anyway?'

'I think the wood has petrified.'

'And the ropes?'

'Also petrified,' Noah said glibly.

'Convenient,' Jacin said.

A screech – familiar to Noah but clearly not to Jacin – rent the air. A shimmering blue and copper phoenix darted up from the moat and hovered above them, showering sparks into the chasm.

'Cecil,' Noah said, 'I was wondering where you'd gotten to.'

'Well, wonder no longer,' the phoenix cried as he came to land beside her. Standing a head taller than her, the bird looked down on her. 'Who's your friend?'

'This is my apprentice, Jacin,' Noah said with a wink.

'Your apprentice, you say?' Cecil said. 'Something tells me there is more to this story …'

Noah lowered her voice. 'Only if you promise to keep it to yourself.'

Cecil burst into flame. 'You can count on me. I'll hear the story once we get the formalities out of the way.' The phoenix turned to Jacin. 'Show me your mark.'

Jacin unbuttoned his shirt to reveal his brand.

Cecil waved a dismissive wing. 'Fine,' he said. 'Put it away. Are we ready to go?'

'You seem to be in a hurry today,' Noah said. 'Are we keeping you from something?'

The phoenix fixed her with a burning stare. 'Keeping me from something? Really?' Cecil looked around. 'What else have I got to do? The Descera are gone, Priscilla has gone, Brinn never comes to visit anymore, you're always off with your friends in Leninstar …'

Noah reached up and scratched Cecil's neck affectionately. 'You know I'd love to come and see you more often,' she said, 'but there's a lot going on in the world at the moment.'

'Which is why you need to be *here*,' the phoenix said, nuzzling his head against her neck. 'Things haven't been the same here since you left.'

'You just miss my cooking,' Noah said.

'I do miss your cooking,' Cecil conceded, 'but it's more than that. We had good times together here, you and me.'

What Jacin thought of the flaming guardian of Dragonhall lamenting the loss of his playmate was anyone's guess and Noah ignored him for the moment. She and Grainger had worked together successfully in Dragonhall after the destruction of the twelve keys but things hadn't always been rosy. Dr Grainger was an exceedingly talented practitioner of raiki but had limited people skills – or bird skills. Cecil had never warmed to him. Noah had hoped that when Grainger took on his apprentice that Cecil would find a companion in her, but Yeti had proven even more aloof than Grainger.

'Well,' Noah said, 'let's make the most of the time we have now. Shall we go?'

Cecil shook himself, sending sparks flying. 'Yes. We'll go. Now remember, there's no running on the bridge … just follow me.'

'Will do,' Noah said.

'And you owe me a story, Noah,' Cecil said.

'Of course,' she said. 'I'll be right behind you.'

Cecil nodded and walked onto the bridge.

'Stay close behind me,' Noah said to Jacin.

Jacin nodded, his face pale.

As they made their way across the bridge over the moat, Noah began the tale of her recent escapades. She continued her story as they entered the curved corridor of the dragon's tail that marked the entrance to the ancient building. Jacin's terror-induced silence turned to awestruck silence as the main hall came into view.

'Impressive, isn't it?' Noah said, taking a break from her narrative.

Jacin nodded.

Noah stroked Cecil's wing. 'Did you want to tell Jacin about the frescos and the stained glass?'

Warming to his task, the phoenix nodded. 'This is the main hall,' Cecil said. 'You'll see the frescos on the walls and ceiling show Talisker's creation. You can see Elani and Jong and Xan.'

'And who's that in the stained glass?' Jacin asked, finally finding his voice.

'That's Trixit – Talisker's first Dragonsbane.'

'Wow!' Jacin said. 'This place is amazing.'

'And this is probably the least impressive part,' Cecil said. 'There is a labyrinth of corridors and passageways on this level and above us, and then there are the crypts and dungeons below us.'

'Crypts?' Jacin echoed. 'Is that where we'll find the doorway to Tisaan?'

'Actually no,' Cecil said. 'That's on one of the upper levels if my memory serves me correctly.'

'You *know* where it is?' Noah said.

'I'm pretty sure I'd know it if I saw it,' the phoenix said slowly.

Noah poked the bird gently in the chest. 'Right. So you have no idea where it is!'

'I used to know,' Cecil said, 'but I suppose you'll have to talk with Grainger about it.'

Noah nodded.

With a flick of his head, Cecil said, 'I'll catch up with you once you're done.'

'That's fine,' Noah said.

'I'll take you to his office, though,' the bird said, 'so you can finish your story on the way.'

♪♫

Noah knocked on the olluka wood door, then wiped her palms on her Academy trousers.

'Nervous?' Jacin whispered.

'A little,' Noah conceded. 'This will be unpleasant.'

Jacin took her hand and squeezed it.

'You shouldn't do that, you know,' Noah said.

'Why? You think Emir will find out?'

'No,' she said slowly. 'You shouldn't hold my hand because I'm your king. Would you have done that to Nerili?'

'Ah,' Jacin said. 'No.'

'Right then.'

'I don't suppose you'd believe that I temporarily forgot you were my king?'

Noah frowned. 'If you're going to *forget* when I'm out of uniform, you're going to be out of a job.'

'Harsh,' he said, shaking his head. 'Anyway, since we're pretending that we're here on Mellifont's behalf rather than Carai's – I'd have thought my *forgetting* was a good thing.'

Noah sighed.

'Do you think you should knock again?' Jacin said. 'Maybe Dr Grainger didn't hear you.'

'I'm sure he *did* hear,' Noah said, 'but this is part of the game.'

She knocked again. Louder this time.

'Come in,' said a voice from the other side – an invitation devoid of enthusiasm.

Noah looked at Jacin. 'Remember what I said?' she whispered.

Jacin nodded. 'I don't speak unless spoken to.'

'Right.'

Noah opened the door and walked into the office. Behind the fortress that served as a desk, Dr Grainger leaned back in his seat, interlacing skeletal fingers over his abdomen. For the moment, Noah ignored his young apprentice, who sat on a low footstool among a sea of parchments on the floor to Grainger's right.

Grainger glanced briefly at Jacin before turning his attention to Noah. 'I take it you've come to apologise and beg forgiveness?' he said.

'For?' Noah prompted.

'Disturbing the dragon's dream,' Yeti said.

All eyes went to the apprentice whose dark eyes burned with defiance. 'You are arrogant and reckless, Noah Chord,' the young woman said. 'How dare you—'

'Thank you, Yeti,' Grainger said, without looking at her. 'Let's give our visitor a chance to apologise.'

'No chance of that,' Noah said. 'This is just a courtesy call.'

'What do you know of courtesy?' Yeti said.

Noah turned to Grainger's apprentice. 'You do know that the more you interrupt, the longer this is going to take? Do you enjoy my company so much that you want to prolong this meeting?'

From beneath her helmet of dark ringlets, Yeti's eyes flashed again. 'Don't flatter yourself.'

'We know you've been communicating with Xan, Noah,' Grainger said. 'Explain yourself.'

'She spoke to me through the piece of firestone from t'Amos,' Noah said. 'She told me to rebury it.'

Grainger leaned forward on his seat. 'And you did?'

Noah nodded. 'Yes. As per Xan's instructions, it's buried in a patch of sinking sand at the bottom of Sandeep Lake.'

When the corner of Grainger's mouth twitched, Noah knew he was summoning a trademark 'I told you so' – he'd been vehemently against digging up the firestone in the first place – so she hurriedly added, 'And now, she wants us to get other pieces of firestone to replace it.'

'Other pieces?' Grainger said.

'Thirteen other pieces, in fact,' Noah replied. 'From Tisaan.'

'Tisaan?' Grainger said.

'Tisaan,' Noah confirmed.

As if the word itself had power over the inhabitants of Dragonhall, Grainger and Yeti remained silent. All Noah could hear was her own heart beating.

After several long moments, Grainger said, 'I can't allow it.'

'It's Xan's order,' Noah said.

Grainger frowned. 'Noah, are you listening to yourself? Going to Tisaan? At best – it's foolish, at worst – reckless. As if what you've done so far isn't bad enough!'

Noah cocked her head. 'What have I done?'

Grainger's eyes widened. '*You're* the reason the Alliance dug up that massive piece of firestone in the first place – against my advice.'

'*Our* advice,' Yeti said.

'Against ... advice,' Grainger said without looking at his apprentice. 'And to what end? The firestone – according to you – is gone and what have we got to show for it? I'll tell you what we've got to show for it – a restless dragon. That's great, Noah. Thanks for giving us more work to do. You're supposed to be on our side for goodness sake! Not making our job more difficult. And now you want to go to Tisaan, presumably so the Alliance has a good supply of firestone so they can really mess with the natural order of things. But that's not even the worst part of your plan. Oh, no! Do you actually think Xan will sleep through your planned adventure to Tisaan? *Do* you?'

Noah felt the growing heat in her cheeks. After all this time, how could he think so little of her? Did he honestly believe it was her intention to wake the dragon? She decided not to tell him that if she'd wanted to destroy Talisker, she'd had many opportunities to do so before this. She needed to be diplomatic. For Jacin's sake, she needed to behave like a king. For her sake, she had to make sure Grainger didn't find out she was one.

'I was hoping that *with your help*,' Noah said, 'we could retrieve the firestone and leave Xan sleeping peacefully.'

'But she's not sleeping peacefully now, Noah,' Grainger said. 'That's the point. The firestone got her attention. *You've* got her attention. She's communicating with you! Did you stop to think that *maybe* she's keen to wake up and that's *why* she wants you to go to Tisaan? To finish the job?'

Noah hadn't thought of that but she was reluctant to admit it. Instead, she said, 'I think you're giving me way too much credit.'

Grainger scowled.

Noah added, 'If the great dragon wants to wake up, I'm sure she doesn't need me going to Tisaan to do that. She could have just let us keep the piece we had.'

Grainger tapped his fingers on the table as he considered Noah's words.

Yeti stood up. 'Dr Grainger, you're not seriously thinking about this, are you?'

'This is a serious business, Yeti,' Grainger said. 'I must think about it very seriously.'

Turning his attention to Jacin, Grainger said, 'Your face is familiar. Who are you?'

'I am Master Jacin – Professor Noah's apprentice.'

'Hmmm. I must have seen you in Mellifont at some point. What house?'

'Wind, sir,' Jacin said. 'I'm a flautist.'

'Apprenticed to a viola player. Interesting,' Grainger said. 'And you're willing to follow your mentor into almost certain death? Is that what you signed up for?'

'Yes, Doctor,' Jacin replied. 'I trust her. Any opportunity to learn – I'm there.'

Grainger drummed his fingers on the table again. 'Tisaan,' he murmured. 'One of the great Pyranhi cities.'

'Sealed off,' Yeti reminded him. 'Strong Pyranhi magic was needed to move the city to another realm. They must have had a good reason to do that. They wanted to stop anyone going there again.'

'But they didn't seal it off,' Noah said. 'They left one avenue open. The only way into Tisaan is through here – Dragonhall. Why did they leave that one avenue? Because they foresaw a time when the world was ready for the firestone they kept there. But they didn't want just anyone going there. Only certain people. Only people who can get in *here*.'

'People who should know better than to put the world at risk to power some lights,' Yeti countered.

Noah didn't respond. Yeti had never been a fan of the Alliance's proposed electricity network but Noah wouldn't be distracted arguing about that again. She kept her attention on Grainger. He wasn't her biggest fan either but he wouldn't do things simply to spite her. Though she didn't always agree with his methods, Grainger would act in what he thought was Talisker's best interest. But she knew better than to pour too many words into the conversation. She couldn't afford to sound like she was pleading. Grainger didn't respond well to that.

'This is an important decision and one that can't be rushed,' Grainger said at last. 'I will sleep on it and we will reconvene tomorrow. Until then Noah, you may show Jacin around Dragonhall.' He looked at the goman. 'I hope you live long enough to regret your decision to apprentice yourself to Noah.'

Chapter 28

Noah stared at the stained-glass window, humbled by the image of the great Xan bowing before Talisker's first Dragonsbane. Being a Dragonsbane of Talisker was a tremendous honour as well as a frightening responsibility and as Grainger wrestled with his decision about the venture to Tisaan, Noah searched for inspiration in Dragonhall's great window. She'd persuaded Cecil to take Jacin on a tour of the precinct so she had a precious couple of hours to herself.

How will I find the doorway? she wondered.

None of the books in Dragonhall's library had yielded any clues. Noah wasn't surprised. The Pyranhi had gone to such great lengths to hide their city, it didn't make sense for them to leave directions on how to get there. It reinforced her theory that finding the ancient city was the first test for retrieving the firestone.

Noah took a few steps back from the window and sat down on the floor. Settling herself into a meditative pose, she gazed at the dragon's multi-coloured scales. When something brushed against her back, she froze.

'What are you doing?' Brinn asked.

'I *was* enjoying some "me" time,' Noah said. 'What are you doing here?'

'I'm here to see you.'

Lucky me, Noah thought. Aloud, she said, 'To thank me?'

'To thank you? For what?'

'For getting rid of the firestone.'

'No,' Brinn said. 'That was your job. I'm not thanking you for doing your job.'

Noah sighed. 'Then what do you want?'

'I'm here to say goodbye.'

'You're going somewhere?'

'No. You are. Or have you changed your mind about going to Tisaan?'

Unsurprised Brinn knew her plan, Noah said, 'No, still going … *if* we can find the doorway.'

Brinn scratched her ear. '*Obviously* it will be tricky to get there if you can't find the doorway, Noah.'

'You're not going to help me out?'

'No.'

Noah drummed her fingers on her knee. 'Why not? You're usually keen to give me a task that's likely to get me killed.'

Brinn flattened her ears and hissed.

Noah recoiled. 'What was *that* for?'

Ears twitching, Brinn said, '*That* was for whining. It doesn't suit you, Noah. Don't do it.'

Noah's heart thumped against her ribcage. 'Whining? Really?'

'Yes, really,' Brinn said. 'These "tasks" that I "give" you are *yours* to do. You're the 13th key, Dragonsbane and a Professor of Raiki. If you would just *do* your job, I wouldn't have to keep telling you what to do.'

'I *do* do my job,' Noah retorted, 'but would it kill you to give me a bit of help?'

Brinn growled. 'You don't need my help. You're quite capable.'

Again, Noah recoiled. After staring at the cat for several seconds, Noah dropped her head and closed her eyes, frustration boiling inside her.

'If you have nothing to offer but "goodbye" then please get it over with and leave,' she said without looking up, 'so I can get back to doing *my job*.'

To Noah's horror, she felt a paw on her knee. She opened her eyes. Brinn's nose almost touched hers. The feline's eyes blazed hypnotically.

'I can't tell you where the door is, Noah,' Brinn said, 'but I will help you.' The cat settled herself in Noah's lap and purred softly. 'I'll stay with you until you figure out where the door is.'

'How can I do that sitting here?'

'Trust your instincts,' Brinn said. 'You're in the right place to find your answer.'

Noah glanced at the stained-glass frieze. 'The window?'

Resting her head on Noah's thigh, Brinn said, 'Yes, Noah. The window.'

Noah returned her attention to the artwork depicting Talisker's creation. As her eyes followed the narrative, she thought of the story Gillette had written for his homework. Her gaze lingered on the figure of Jong. *If you hurt Gillette you'll be sorry,* she thought. She moved on, absorbing details and trying to sift out any clues to Tisaan's location. Nothing. Moving past the creation story, Noah studied the image of Xan bowing down before the hooded figure of the Dragonsbane. Still nothing.

Beyond that, an olluka tree dominated the scene. Noah's skin tingled. *The answer must be here,* she thought. There was so much to look at though that it was difficult to know where to start. Mystical Pyranhi symbols adorned the myriad branches. If the answer lay in the ancient script, Noah had no chance of deciphering the clues. She focused on the pictures instead. Near the top of the tree, a phoenix clutched a broken chain in one claw. On another branch an hourglass lay on its side. *Time standing still?* Noah wondered. A sloth with a padlock, a snake biting its own tail, a cluster of rats huddled in a fork ... the images became a blur.

'Anything?' Brinn said.

'Not yet,' Noah murmured as she contemplated a porcupine at the base of the tree.

The mammal sat on its haunches, bristling with sharp spines. It clutched a dagger in its delicate paws. *What are you guarding?* Noah wondered. Behind the porcupine was a knothole in the trunk. Though nothing was visible in the cavity, Noah was sure this was her answer. Her skin puckered into goosebumps.

'Oh crap!' she said.

Brinn's ear twitched. 'Got it?'

'Yes,' Noah said. 'I know which door I need, but I don't want to go there.'

'Mmm?'

'Turns out, *finding* the door might actually be the easiest part.'

'Which door is it?'

Noah shivered. 'The one to the olluka portal cluster.'

'Are you sure?'

Noah nodded. 'I'm sure.'

Brinn rubbed her head against Noah's leg. 'Been nice knowing you, Noah.'

'Thanks for the vote of confidence.'

'No one's opened that door in over a thousand years,' Brinn said, 'and with good reason. The cluster is unstable.'

'Yeah, I know that.'

'Do you know *how* unstable it is?'

Noah's eyes narrowed. 'Do you?'

'I haven't been in there,' Brinn said, 'and there's *nothing* that would get me in there.'

Stroking the cat's fur, Noah contemplated the mission ahead. Negotiating the portal cluster was a huge risk.

'At least Grainger will be happy if he decides to come,' she said. 'He's been itching for an excuse to check out the cluster.'

'It's suicide. The Pyranhi magic is failing down there. Grainger's a fool if he thinks he can fix it.'

'We don't know enough about Pyranhi magic to fix it,' Noah admitted, 'but there's only one way to study it.'

Brinn growled. 'There are plenty of portals you could study – one of the ones to Earth for instance.'

'That's different.'

'Yes,' Brinn said. 'That's actually *my* point. The Pyranhi should have known better. Creating so many portals in such a small section of an olluka tree was reckless. Having the portals so close together creates too much interference and the deterioration …'

'Will someday be catastrophic,' Noah finished.

'Correct.'

'But not today.'

'That depends on what you consider to be catastrophic,' Brinn said as she stepped out of Noah's lap and stretched.

Noah smiled. 'You'd miss me if I didn't come back.'

'It's not all about you,' Brinn said with a sniff. 'Talisker can't afford to lose two Dragonsbanes now. If that happens, we'll be in Yeti's hands.'

That would be catastrophic, Noah thought. 'Got it,' she said. 'We'll be extra careful.'

'Well, let's hope that's enough,' Brinn said.

♪♫

'Shall we?' Dr Grainger said.

Noah didn't answer immediately. She was glad Grainger had decided to accompany her to Tisaan – and grateful he'd left Yeti behind – but she didn't want him taking charge. Stalling, she studied the wooden door before her. Its innocuous façade indicated nothing of the danger beyond. Opening this door would change Talisker forever. It was just a question of whether it would be great or disastrous.

'There's no handle,' Jacin said.

Noah put her hand on the smooth wood. The door vanished.

'Security could do with an upgrade,' he said.

Darkness cascaded through the doorway like a waterfall, swamping Noah and her companions and obliterating the corridor in moments.

'Well,' Noah said, as she scanned the dank woodland around them, 'here goes nothing.'

Jacin whistled softly as he looked up. 'Is that … lightning?'

Noah nodded as she fought to take in their new surroundings. The air in the tunnel sizzled with static electricity and when it built up, lightning snaked across the ceiling. Rather than dazzling white though, the lightning here took on the gloomy green-brown hue of the plants. *We're inside an olluka branch,* Noah thought. *This forest is inside a* massive *olluka branch.*

'How many portals are in here?' Jacin asked.

'Twenty-three,' Grainger said.

His gaze still on the ceiling, Jacin said, 'Where do they all go?'

'Can we talk about this later?' Noah said. 'We need to get moving.'

'Of course,' Jacin said. 'Lead on.'

Noah looked to her left and then to her right but the gloom made it difficult to see far. There was no way of knowing which direction to go to find the portal she needed. *I'll just have to guess,* she thought.

Turning to her right, Noah said, 'This way.'

As they picked their way through the mossy undergrowth, Jacin said, 'So we're looking for a porcupine?'

'A symbol of a porcupine,' Noah replied. 'I hope there aren't any real ones down here.'

'How are we supposed to find anything in this gloom?' Jacin asked. 'I'm having enough trouble just seeing where I'm going.'

'Be quiet,' Grainger said. 'The more you yabber, the more chance you'll draw *unwanted* attention.'

Jacin nodded but said nothing.

Noah scanned the immediate area, wary of the unwanted attention Grainger had mentioned. The failing Pyranhi magic made the portals unstable. Who knew what kind of creatures might have found their way here in the years since anyone on Talisker had ventured down here. Sweat trickled down Noah's back. Apart from the lightning, nothing else appeared to be moving, but they had to remain vigilant.

Like the olluka trees, the plants that grew here had no leaves. Mosses and lichens covered the twisted woody trunks and branches. On closer inspection, Noah realised that it was the glowing fungi that were responsible for the feeble light in the tunnel. *I hope they're not radioactive,* she thought. In daylight the array of moulds and mildews might have been impressive, but down here they were menacing.

Their colours were as varied as their shapes. Hairy clusters surrounded multi-coloured cups of different sizes. Some fungi were spiky, while the mosses were velvety. Up ahead wide, kelp-like ribbons hung from the interlaced branches high above. Dark pods dangled from some of the lower branches and Noah hoped they weren't bats.

A buzzing behind them made Noah turn. The air shimmered like heat haze in a desert.

'Unwanted attention?' Jacin asked.

'Yes,' Grainger said. *'Run!'*

Grainger sprinted away with Jacin and Noah close behind.

'Don't look back,' Noah said when Jacin glanced over his shoulder.

'It's gaining—'

'Just run!'

Noah pumped her arms as fast as she could as she scanned the tunnel for a hiding spot. Grainger veered towards the dangling straps of seaweed-like fungi. *It's a start,* Noah thought, *but we need better cover than that.*

Grainger cried out as he swatted the first strap aside. 'Ahhhh! Don't touch—'

But his warning was too late. Noah and Jacin crashed into the fungi.

Searing pain burned along Noah's upper arm where she'd made contact. She spun away, hitting another piece in the process. Pain exploded in her back this time.

'I'm stuck!' Grainger cried.

'Me too!' Jacin yelled. 'Ah! It stings!'

Panting, Noah said, 'Try not to move ... you'll just get more tangled.' Carefully she turned her head, looking for whatever it was that pursued them. She caught a glimpse out of the corner of her eye. It had passed by. Straining to see through her pain, Noah fought to focus. It paid off. She watched the ball of shimmering air slam into a tree trunk further down the tunnel.

Relief did nothing to ease the pain though. She looked at her companions. Both were well tangled in the stinging vines. Noah's sword was across her back and now out of play, but if she could get the knife from her boot she could cut them loose. As she lifted her right leg and reached down carefully, her brain registered a new sound. Galloping!

Beside her, Grainger whispered, 'Oh no.'

Noah risked a glance to her left. Six cat-sized beetles with the heads of hyenas lumbered towards them.

'What are *those?*' Jacin said.

'It's a dundar,' Grainger replied.

Not taking his eyes off the gruesome creatures, Jacin said, 'What do you mean "*it* is" a dundar? There are six of them.'

'The shimmering ball that chased us,' Grainger wheezed, 'was a dundar. It's a kind of … spirit energy and it can take on any physical form it chooses once it has organic material to work with.'

Suspending her quest for her knife, Noah studied the motley creatures. 'They're made of wood.'

Grainger tried to nod but it was difficult with his head stuck to the fungal strap at his back. 'Yes. The dundar has used wood from the tree down there. It can remain as one creature or split into many.'

As the oversized insectoids encircled the trio, Noah said, 'And now what?'

'It needs to feed. Consuming lifeforms with a soul increases its spirit energy.'

'It gets bigger?' Jacin said.

'Stronger is probably a better description,' Grainger replied.

One of the creatures climbed the fungal strand beside Jacin. The small surface area of its pincer-like feet meant it didn't stick to the ribbon. And being wooden, it suffered no ill-effects from the stinging hairs.

Noah's heart hammered as the creature opened its canine jaws centimetres from Jacin's arm. Its teeth would crush bone as effectively as they'd tear flesh. Ignoring the critters that stalked her, she made another reach for the knife in her boot.

'*NOOOOOOOOOOOOO!*' Jacin screamed.

Noah cringed. *Focus,* she told herself. *Just get the knife.*

As her fingers found the handle, Grainger shrieked in pain.

They're going to eat us alive, Noah thought. Predators normally went for the throat first. Severing the jugular made for a quicker death. But these weren't normal predators. Noah pulled the knife from her boot as teeth sank into her thigh.

Light exploded in the tunnel and Noah crashed to the floor. She dropped her knife as searing pain in her leg overwhelmed her. Panting, she rolled onto her hands and knees. *I can't see.* Noah blinked several times, but the panorama of white persisted.

When her retinas recovered enough for her to see grey rather than white, five blurry shapes squatted before her. Noah squeezed her eyes closed and then opened them again. There had been six creatures.

'I'll be back for you,' a voice said, as the five insectoid hyenas scurried back towards the tree they'd come from.

Shivering, Noah looked for her companions. Both Jacin and Grainger lay on the ground, unmoving. Noah crawled to Jacin and put two fingers to his throat, searching for a pulse. *Thank goodness,* she thought. Leaving him, she found Grainger and administered the same test. Again rewarded with a pulse, she sighed in relief.

Noah delved into a pocket on her trousers for camphor balls, wincing as the fabric rubbed against the bite wound on her thigh.

'There's more to you than meets the eye,' a voice said.

Noah spun round to find an enormous wooden snake coiled before her.

'So now what?' she said.

'Now I eat you,' the snake said. 'What a prize *you* are. I don't know where you get your energy from, but I will grow much stronger because of it.'

'Do you think that's wise?' Noah asked, retrieving her knife before getting to her feet. 'Look what happened when you bit me before. Part of you was destroyed.'

'Ah. Yes,' the snake said. 'Well, this time, I won't bite you. I'll just *swallow* you whole.'

Behind her, Jacin groaned.

Noah gripped her knife tighter. If the secret of the firestone in her blood were to remain a secret, she needed to dispense with the snake before Jacin and Grainger awoke. The dundar slithered free of its coils. Noah studied its girth. Human-sized prey would present no challenge. Noah tucked her knife back into her boot and drew her sword instead.

'Come and get me then,' she said.

The snake lowered its head towards Jacin and hissed. 'I might need an appetiser first.'

Noah lunged towards the snake and swung her sword, connecting with one of its fangs. The wooden tooth dropped and wedged in the loamy soil. The snake hissed in fury.

'You do not understand what you're up against, little human,' the snake said.

'I'm more than just a "little human",' Noah said, 'and you know it.'

'You have power but not wisdom,' the dundar replied. 'You are no threat to me.'

Jong had said much the same thing, Noah remembered. Anger stewed within her. Maybe she didn't know everything, but she was sick of having it pointed out to her. She inhaled deeply. *Its goading me,* she realised. *When it bit me, its energy reacted with my firestone and it came off second best. I've just chopped off one of its fangs. If I chop off another one, it won't be able to bite me. It needs to swallow me whole…*

As Noah contemplated her next move, the dundar scooped Jacin up in its mouth. Jacin moaned. Noah watched, eyes wide, as the snake dislocated its jaw to accommodate the goman's limp body. Jamming her sword back in its sheath, Noah ran towards the snake's massive head. At the last moment she launched herself at its gaping jaws. Clutching the reptile's lower jaw, she flipped herself up into its mouth. The snake shook its head, but Noah was ready. She jumped and wrapped her arms and legs around the remaining wooden fang.

The snake hissed but Noah held tight. With a glance towards Jacin, she released her grip slightly and slid down the fang. Clenching her jaws in anticipation of the pain she lifted her leg, impaling her already-injured thigh on the end of the snake's tooth.

Again, light exploded inside the olluka branch.

Noah twisted as she fell, landing on her feet this time. Opening her eyes, she dived to her left over the mossy ground to cushion Jacin's fall.

'Ouch!' she said, as he landed on top of her.

Pushing him onto the ground, Noah rolled onto her side and propped herself up on one elbow. The snake was nowhere in sight.

She eased herself back onto the spongy ground. Breathing heavily, Noah closed her eyes.

An image of Brinn's face floated into her mind. *I told you it's too unstable.*

Yes, you did, Noah thought, *but we're here now and we're going to find that portal.*

Then get up and do it before something else finds you.

Noah groaned. Reluctantly, she sat up. She rummaged through the pockets on her trousers until she found some camphor balls. Waving them under Jacin's nose, she prayed they'd do the trick.

Jacin screwed up his nose and shook his head. 'What happened?'

'The dundar's gone,' Noah said. 'We need to move and find the portal.'

Opening his eyes, Jacin said, 'How did you—'

'I'll tell you later,' Noah said. 'We need to go.'

Jacin nodded. 'Grainger?'

Noah tossed some camphor balls to him. 'Your job.'

'Yes, Your Highness,' he said.

Noah scowled. 'Knock it off. Grainger can't find out about that.'

'Of course ... *Professor,*' Jacin said, bowing his head before crawling towards Grainger.

Why did I rescue him? Noah wondered. *He's going to be the death of me.*

Chapter 29

Noah stared at the carving of the porcupine in the tunnel wall. 'Are we ready?'

'I'm ready for anything that gets me out of this portal cluster,' Jacin said.

Grainger nodded curtly. 'After you.'

Though they'd sustained no further injuries since they'd encountered the dundar, tempers were stretched. Grainger was particularly tetchy. He hadn't liked Noah's explanation of the dundar's demise. Noah wasn't happy with her sketchy version of the story either, but there was no way she'd admit to what triggered the explosion that had shrivelled the stinging fungus straps and knocked Grainger and Jacin unconscious.

Like in the stained-glass window in Dragonhall, the porcupine carved into the olluka branch here clutched its sword defensively. Beside the critter, a dark knothole in the trunk pulsed eerily. It was no bigger than a bowling ball but size didn't matter. Once she was close enough Noah knew the portal would do its job.

Noah walked through the knothole … and onto a short pier. A gleaming lake dominated this subterranean landscape. A solitary wooden boat tethered to the end of the jetty was untroubled by the faint ripples on the water. *It's an underground ravine,* Noah thought.

'Where's the city?' Jacin asked as he appeared beside her.

Noah craned her neck and peered up, but darkness swallowed the tops of the gorge's rocky walls. She scanned the scene as far as the light allowed. No danger was immediately obvious but Noah knew they had to be wary. There were likely other safeguards the Pyranhi had put in place to protect their precious city – wherever it was.

'Looks like we need to take a little cruise,' Noah said.

Grainger snorted. 'I'm not rowing.'

Noah strode towards the skiff. Footsteps behind her told her that Jacin and Grainger were following her. When she reached the end of the pier, she took the mooring rope in both hands.

'I'll untie it,' Jacin offered. 'You two get in.'

Surrendering the rope, Noah jumped down lightly. She braced herself as the craft swayed beneath her. She sat in the middle of the boat with her back to the bow and took up the oars while Grainger settled himself at the stern.

Jacin tossed the rope into the boat and stepped onto the bow. 'I'll navigate.'

'Right,' Noah said. 'Let's hope the boat holds together long enough for us to reach our destination. I hate to think how long it's been sitting here.'

'It'll be fine,' Grainger said. 'Pyranhi craftsmanship and magic – they knew how to make things last.'

Noah sighed and heaved on the oars. She rowed until her palms sported four blisters – her only means of measuring time here. Relinquishing the task to Jacin, Noah replaced Grainger at the stern. The Dragonsbane moved to the bow to assume navigation duties.

As they glided along with the gentle current, she studied the shimmering surface. *What lurks beneath that silver sheen?* she wondered. Without taking her gaze from the water, she drew her sword.

'Expecting trouble?' Jacin said as he pulled on the oars.

'Always,' Noah replied.

'And you think you can deal with it with a sword?'

'You've got a better idea?'

'No,' Jacin admitted. 'It just seems a bit … primitive.'

'I agree,' Grainger said. 'For any adventurers who made it this far, I'm sure the Pyranhi would have tested their worthiness by means of *sophistication* rather than their *strength*.'

Noah bristled. 'If an enormous tentacle looms up out of the water, I'll take my chances with my sword. Feel free to be as sophisticated as you want about that.'

Grainger drew his baton from his pocket. 'I will.'

Noah eyed his device briefly before returning her attention to the water.

Jacin still didn't have any blisters by the time they rounded the last bend where the gorge bulged, straining to contain an enormous lake. A glowing city perched atop a sheer column of rock that protruded from the lake's centre. Enveloped in silence, nothing moved.

'This must be it,' Noah said. 'Tisaan.'

Resting his weary arms as he drank in the view, Jacin said, 'That's going to be fun to climb.'

'The Pyranhi were keen fishers,' Grainger said. 'There'll be an entrance to the column at water level. I can't see one from here. We'll row around to the other side.'

'Totally happy for you to do that,' Jacin said. 'Thanks for offering.'

'I wasn't offering,' Grainger said. 'I don't—'

A loud *thud* sounded under the boat and the craft rocked violently. Noah gripped her sword tight and shifted her weight to the left to compensate.

'What was *that*?' Jacin said.

Visions of tentacles whirled through Noah's mind.

Thud. Thud. Thud.

'I don't know,' Noah said, 'but Grainger – I hope you're ready to be sophisticated.'

Movement in the bottom of the boat beside her foot caught her eye. A small hole appeared.

'Something's drilling through the hull!' she said.

Noah watched in horror as a bulbous brown knob bored its way through the wood. Rather than spinning, it twisted back and forth but it was ruthlessly effective. When the hole was about the diameter of her thumb, the knob retracted. Noah held her breath as an eel-like creature slithered through the hole.

Resisting the urge to squeal, Noah said, 'What *is* that?'

'Lamprey,' Grainger said. 'Stay away! If it attaches to you, it'll bore into your flesh just like it did to the boat.'

Whisking her feet out of range, Noah clutched her knees to her chest. Another lamprey wriggled through the hole in the boat. And then another.

'They're hideous,' she whispered.

'And we're going to end up with a boatful of them if we don't do something,' Grainger said. Slicing off a piece of rope from the bowline, he added, 'Cut this into pieces and plug the holes.'

He tossed the rope, hitting Noah in the side of the head. She snatched at the rope, stashed her sword and grabbed the knife from her boot. Hacking through the Pyranhi cord was difficult but once she had a finger-length piece she jammed it in the hole and then stomped on it with her boot heel.

'Take that,' she said, panting.

Heaving on the oars, Jacin said, 'More to do, Noah.'

Scanning the hull, she found four more holes. Water streamed in, bringing more lamprey with it. 'Bloody hell!' she said.

Noah glanced at Grainger. He'd found a bucket in his trousers and was bailing. Turning her attention back to the rope, she hacked off several more pieces. Despite Grainger's efforts, the water level in the boat was rising. Noah shivered. To get to the holes, she had to put her hands in the water where knots of lamprey now wriggled and churned. Kneeling on the seat, she bent forward and plunged her hands into the icy water.

'Crap, crap, crap, crap,' Noah chanted as she plugged another hole.

When she pulled her hand up this time a lamprey dangled from her wrist. Though the chilly water had numbed her, Noah still felt its suction. She stared into one of its bulging eyes and gagged.

'Get off me!' she cried, flapping her arm wildly to dislodge it.

'Noah!' Grainger yelled. 'Stop that! Use your blade to scrape it off!'

Fighting for calm, Noah sucked in a ragged breath. *Steady,* she thought as she put the blade against her skin. With one smooth motion she scraped the lamprey off.

Noah risked at peek at the column. 'We're almost there, Jacin. *Row faster!'*

Jacin grunted. 'Easy for you to say.'

Noah saw his difficulty. To keep his legs away from the lampreys, he now knelt on the seat rather than sitting on it – severely hampering his rowing action.

Noah swore under her breath. 'Grainger,' she said, 'have you got another bucket?'

He threw his to her and rummaged in his pocket for another. Noah caught the pail with one hand as she sheathed her blade. Water half-filled the boat now. She planted her feet on the seat and started bailing – nothing else mattered now. Ignoring the lamprey slithering in the water, Noah focused on her motion and rhythm. She scooped the bucket through the water rather than dipping and filling it. Not only could she bail faster, but she minimised the chance of another lamprey latching onto her.

As they closed in on the column, more of the boat under the water than above it, the lamprey thrashed voraciously in the water around them. The boat had only to sink another couple of centimetres and the fish could save themselves the trouble of boring into the boat. They could simply jump aboard.

'No time to look for an entrance,' Noah said as she scooped another bucketful of water out of the boat. 'Jacin just get us close enough to the column so we can jump onto it.'

Wrenching precariously on the oars, Jacin nodded.

Heart racing, Noah bailed faster. *Just a bit further,* she prayed. Eyes fixed on the column, she surveyed the stone facade. It wasn't as smooth as she'd initially thought. Its craggy surface promised plenty of hand-holds and footholds – if they could get there.

As they came alongside the column, lampreys slithered around Noah's ankles. She dropped the bucket and jumped onto the seat next to Jacin.

'Time to go!' she said, launching herself at the rock. As her hands slammed onto the jagged surface, Noah winced in pain. But grazed hands weren't her biggest problem. Her wet boots made finding a foothold near impossible. As she scrambled to secure her position, Jacin landed alongside her.

Breathing hard, Jacin said, 'You're awfully fun to be around, Your Highness. Nerili never took me on adventures like this.'

Noah frowned. 'Shut up.'

'As you wish, Your Highness.'

'*Stop it!* If Grainger hears you …'

'He's still in the boat.'

Straining to look behind her, she called, '*Jump,* Grainger. Jump *now!*'

She turned back to face the rock and took a couple of deep breaths as she waited for Grainger. *I hope there's an entrance close by,* she thought. *I don't fancy climbing to the top.*

Grainger landed beside her. 'If you want to wait here, I'll go and look for an entrance?' he said.

'You lead,' Noah said, 'we'll follow.'

'As you wish.'

Grainger didn't hesitate. As he scaled the rock face with apparent ease, Noah felt a twinge of embarrassment. He was almost three times her age.

'Is he part spider, do you think?' Jacin said.

Ignoring the question, Noah said, 'You go next.'

'Got it,' he said.

Noah took her time. The last thing she needed was to slip and end up in the lamprey-infested lake. The curve of the rocky pillar made it difficult to see too far ahead, so rather than fixating on the destination, she focused on each transition. By the time she spied the archway, her arms and shoulders ached and her hands were raw. *Not much further,* she thought.

Jacin was waiting for her. He held out his hand to her as she reached the entryway. Clutching his wrist, Noah let him help her swing around onto the ledge inside the cave.

'Wow!' she said.

Jacin smiled. 'Pretty impressive, hey?'

'That's an understatement. Where's Grainger?'

'He's looking for a way up to the city. Come on.'

Water lapped against the stone only half a metre below the walkway. Noah followed Jacin along the path, keeping her shoulder close to the wall to stop her from straying too close to the edge as she studied the harbour. The thought of the lamprey that lurked beneath the surface sharpened her focus.

Like many of Talisker's deep magic places, the inside of the stone column glowed with its own natural ambience. This cathedral-like cave, hollowed out of the rock, was now eerily quiet. Small boats floated among larger fishing vessels, nets rather than sails strapped to their masts. Noah shook her head in wonder. The Pyranhi magic that sustained this place was beyond her comprehension.

When they reached the boats, Noah scanned the cave's rear wall. She shuddered – lampreys painted on the walls peered out at her from between the nets, ropes and baskets that hung from hooks all around.

'The Pyranhi fished for lamprey,' Noah said.

'It seems so,' Jacin replied.

Noah walked to a grand old net that cascaded from a pulley set high above. The room was silent now but she tried to imagine what it had been like when the Pyranhi fishermen had been unloading their catch.

'We're probably the first humans ever to be in here,' Noah said.

'You and Grainger are the first humans,' Jacin said from the far side of the room. '*I'm* the first goman.'

'Right.'

Grainger reappeared. 'I've found a lift,' he said. 'Follow me.'

Jacin gestured for Noah to go first. Thankful that she wasn't going to have to climb the column, Noah fell in behind Grainger.

'Look familiar?' Grainger said when the lift came into view.

Noah nodded. 'It's the same kind the Descera built – the same kind we built in the mine at t'Amos. It's amazing that the technology hasn't changed much in all this time.'

'Well, let's see if it still works,' Jacin said. 'I'm keen to get up top to the city.'

Noah stepped onto the wooden platform and adjusted the levers. 'Ready?'

'Ready,' Jacin said.

Grainger nodded.

Noah pulled the lever. The gears and pulleys whined in protest as the chain tightened. The platform inched its way upward, and Noah prayed they'd make it to the top. Might the Pyranhi have rigged the lift to fail?

Noah hid her relief when she finally stepped off the lift.

'Amazing!' Jacin said as he looked around the city.

Noah couldn't tell if he was talking about the lift ride or what he saw of the ancient city, but it didn't matter. They had a job to do.

Chapter 30

As they wound their way through Tisaan's silent streets, Noah's nerves tingled. The Pyranhi love of art and design was evident. Their affinity with the natural world gave their city an air of grandeur that was unmatched in any human city Noah had seen. It looked like Tisaan had evolved from the rock rather than being built upon it. Had their mission not been so dire, Noah might have taken the time to enter some of the dwellings and appreciate the lavish designs and fine furnishings of the Pyranhi. But it was too dangerous. Cities in unknown dimensions were not places to loiter.

'The Pyranhi must have been smaller than I thought,' Jacin said. 'I'd have difficulty standing up inside those buildings.'

'They were small,' Grainger confirmed. 'Perhaps some of the taller ones might come up to my ribs, but most were probably about hip-height on me. They had luxuriant manes that stretched all the way down their backs, then cascaded in wonderful horse-like tails.'

'Do you think we'll find any … remains?' Jacin asked.

'No,' Noah said. 'Even if there *are* any here – we are *not* going looking for them.'

'But if we were to come across some …'

'No,' Noah said. 'Just no.'

'Do you hear running water?' Grainger asked.

Noah listened. 'Yes.'

Grainger pointed to his right. 'It's coming from that direction.'

'That's odd,' Noah said. 'Nothing else in this city is moving …'

'We should see what it is,' Jacin said.

Winding their way through a cobbled laneway packed with boarded up shops, they walked in the direction Grainger had indicated. As the sound grew louder, Noah's heart raced. The firestone was close. She felt it.

Around the bend at the end of the laneway they found a large plaza and at its centre, the most frightening fountain Noah had ever seen. The bronze reptile that dominated the massive pool stood over four metres tall. Its perfectly-crafted armoured scales were the size of Noah's hands and the long, barbed spines that protruded from its back had a myriad of other fierce creatures impaled upon them. Though frozen in a moment of rage eons ago, the beast's ferocity was undiminished. It roared its silent challenge to any that dared confront it.

'What is that?' Jacin said. 'I've never heard of a creature like it.'

Grainger cleared his throat. 'If it *does* have a name, I think it would be best not to utter it here.'

'It's not a great likeness,' Jacin said, frowning.

'What?' Noah said.

'To the portal marker,' Jacin said. 'Remember the porcupine with the sword?'

A likeness of the porcupine carved into the olluka branch as well as the one in the stained-glass window in Dragonhall flashed in Noah's mind. 'They got the spines right,' she said.

'Yeah,' Jacin conceded, 'but they missed the crocodilian head and tail?'

The Guardian, Noah thought. Staring at the statue, she said. 'It's here. The firestone is here – in the fountain.'

Grainger frowned. 'Are you sure? I don't see any.'

'Well, unlike you, I don't have to *see* it to know it's here,' Noah answered testily.

Grainger glared at her. 'Are you communicating with Xan again?'

'No,' Noah said. 'I don't need to.'

'Maybe you two could argue later?' Jacin suggested. 'Or would you like me to nip in and get the firestone while you finish up here?'

'No one's getting anything yet,' Grainger said. 'We need to be *very* careful now.'

'Right,' Jacin said.

Again, Noah looked at the statue. *So Guardian,* she thought, *where is the firestone you're guarding?*

The thought was no sooner loose in her mind than light exploded inside her skull and her legs crumpled beneath her.

'Noah!' Jacin cried.

Hands gripped her arms on both sides.

'Noah!' Jacin hissed into her ear. 'What's wrong? What do I do?'

Noah fought to answer him over the maelstrom inside her. The firestone here was protected, as she'd expected, and its protector did not appreciate her intrusion. With her perceptions, she'd woken … something.

'Let me down,' she whispered.

When she was safely on her hands and knees, the dizziness subsided. She opened her eyes and a grey haze greeted her. She squeezed her eyes closed again and took a deep breath. *Come on,* she thought, *I need to see what's happening.* Opening her eyes again, she strained to make sense of the blurred scene.

One detail struck her. Movement.

'Um … Noah,' Jacin said. 'The beast is *moving.*'

A wretched, keening shrill punctured the air. Noah clamped her hands over her ears, but the futility of such a move was immediately obvious. She blinked twice more and the beast came into focus. It reared on its hind legs, screeching into the gloom overhead. The carcasses on its back dangled lifelessly as its body trembled with rage.

Grainger leaned in close to Noah. 'What's your grand plan now?'

Unable to tear her gaze from the enormous reptile, she said, 'Just have your baton ready.'

The Dragonsbane snorted. 'You don't have a plan.'

'Not yet,' Noah admitted.

The conversation attracted the beast's attention. It turned to face them, beating powerful fists against its plated chest. When it roared, the column trembled.

'What is this?' it said. 'Three puny beasts come to challenge the Guardian?'

'Xan sent us,' Noah said.

It shook its snout, snapping its jaws twice. 'I know no Xan.'

Hiding her disappointment, Noah said, 'Who made you the Guardian?'

The creature's eyes widened. 'Who made me the Guardian? What an unusual question. Who wants to know?'

'I do,' Noah said.

'And who are you?'

'I am Noah Chord.'

The creature waded through the water in the fountain towards her. It stopped just short of the wall and crouched down. '*What* are you, Noah Chord?'

Deciding to keep things simple, she said, 'I am human.'

'Human,' it repeated. 'I've never heard of humans.'

Noah frowned. 'Who made you Guardian of the firestone?'

'Goh,' he said. 'Goh of the Pyranhi.'

'And where is the firestone?'

'Inside me,' the creature said, patting its chest. 'Completely safe.'

'And no one has ever got any from you?' Grainger asked.

The creature turned its head, eyes gleaming. 'That is correct. Are you ready to do battle for it now? Or would you like to rest after your long journey?'

Noah held the creature's eye. 'You're stalling. What are you afraid of?'

The creature roared again. Noah, Jacin and Grainger all jumped. '*Afraid?* Me?' It turned around. 'All these,' it said, pointing to the carcasses impaled on it spines, 'all these came for the firestone. Look at *you*. What have I got to be afraid of?'

Noah swallowed with difficulty. The trophies on its back could have filled an encyclopaedia of the most hideous intergalactic monsters.

Without looking at Noah, Grainger said, 'We haven't decided yet if we will fight you or not.'

'Oh? You've come all this way and you haven't decided if you'll fight me? That is very odd.'

'Humans can be a bit odd,' Jacin said.

Noah made a mental note to give Jacin a week in the dungeon for his comment if they made it back to Carai.

'Well, I might go for a wander to stretch my legs,' the beast said. 'As you can imagine, I don't get out much. Take as much time as you like. When you're ready to die … just let me know.'

'Hang on,' Jacin said. 'Ready to die? What if we decide not to fight you for the firestone?'

The Guardian put his snout within centimetres of Jacin's face. 'You can't leave,' it said. 'I assume the lamprey took care of your boat?'

'There are more in the harbour,' Jacin said. 'We'll take one of those.'

'You could try,' the Guardian said, 'but your presence will draw the lamprey again. You cannot escape this place now. At least fighting me, your end will be gloriously quick.'

Without giving them a chance to answer, the Guardian leapt out of the pool and stalked away on all fours towards the portion of the city to their left.

'Right,' Jacin said. 'That was weird.'

'Do you have a plan yet, Noah?' Grainger asked.

Noah chewed at her bottom lip. 'Magic,' she said at last.

Grainger rubbed his temples. 'Magic? What do you mean?'

'The Guardian,' she said.

'You want to use *magic* to destroy the Guardian? Noah, what are you talking about? What do you know about *magic*?'

'Not a lot,' Noah conceded, 'but I don't think we have to destroy the Guardian.'

Grainger frowned. 'You don't *think* so?'

'I *think*,' Noah said slowly, 'that he's our way out.'

'What? How?'

'Think about it,' Noah said, 'maybe *this* is the test we've been waiting for.'

'It's a test alright,' Grainger said, rolling his eyes. 'Did you see how big that thing is? How many trophies he's got on his back already?'

'But that's the point. Every other creature has tried to destroy the Guardian. Maybe that's the test. Did you wonder why we can understand what it's saying?'

Jacin's eyes lit up. 'We don't speak ancient Pyranhi any more than he speaks our language. We shouldn't be able to understand it.'

'Correct,' Noah said. 'He said that Goh made him the Guardian. I think that Goh *made* him – conjured him up. The Guardian is magic – a spell.'

'A spell cast by the Pyranhi to protect the firestone,' Jacin finished.

Noah nodded. 'So the test is … are we reckless enough to destroy on sight, something we don't understand, or do we use our brains and our wits to get what we came for?'

'He said we needed to do battle,' Jacin said.

'It doesn't have to be a physical battle,' Noah said.

Grainger stroked his baton thoughtfully. 'If we can't use a boat – there's no way we're going back the way we came. You think we can use the beast's power to get out of here?'

'You got a better plan?' Noah asked.

The old man shook his head. 'No.'

'So,' Jacin said, clapping his hands twice, 'let's find our friend.'

♪♫

They scoured the city until they were footsore before finding their quarry swimming in the lake far below. The giant reptile was lying on its back, swishing its tail from side to side to propel it through the water.

'Well, at least the lamprey won't bother him,' Grainger noted.

'I expect not,' Noah said. 'Jacin, get his attention, would you?'

'Right you are,' he replied with unquenchable enthusiasm.

Leaning out over the brick wall and waving his arms above his head, he cried, 'Hey! Guardian! Can you come up here, please?'

'How about you come down here?' the beast said.

'Not so keen on the lamprey,' Jacin called. 'We're happy to—'

The Guardian screeched and the wall Jacin was leaning against gave way.

Noah grabbed for him as he fell with the wall. She caught his trouser-leg and tried to wrench him back. *'AHHHHHHH!'* she cried as she fell forward and skidded over the edge.

Tumbling as she plummeted towards the water, she released her grip on Jacin and fought to steady her descent. She stretched out her arms and legs. Wind whipped her face, but Noah fixed her attention on the Guardian. He wanted them down here. Would he save them? He didn't get many visitors. The prospect of a fight – considering he usually won – probably weighed in their favour.

The Guardian shifted position. One of its massive feet loomed under her. She braced herself, drawing her legs under her torso. Crashing hard onto the beast's scaly foot, Noah groaned. 'Ouch!'

Rolling onto her knees, she looked to her right. As Noah had hoped, the Guardian had caught all of them. She clambered down on the Guardian's underbelly to join Jacin and Grainger.

'And what have you decided?' the Guardian asked. 'Are you ready to do battle for the firestone?'

'No,' Noah said. 'We've decided we want to go home. Will you take us back to the portal, please?'

The Guardian snapped its jaws. 'What? You're not going to fight?'

'No,' Noah said, shaking her head. 'We want to go home.'

'Really?' the Guardian said. 'That's very strange. No one has ever done that before.'

'I did try to tell you that humans were odd,' Jacin said. 'Will you take us?'

'I don't know,' the Guardian said. 'I need to think about this. I'm supposed to stay in Tisaan and guard the firestone. That is my purpose.'

'You'll still be guarding the firestone,' Noah said, *'and* you'll be removing a potential threat at the same time.'

The Guardian growled. 'A threat? I thought you said you wouldn't fight for the firestone.'

'We won't,' Noah promised. Turning to Grainger, she said, 'May I borrow your baton?'

'Since you're using its proper name …' he said, handing the slender olluka stick to her.

She knew if she'd called it a 'wand' now, he'd likely stab her in the eye with it.

Clutching the Dragonsbane's device, Noah trod carefully on the beast's scaly belly and kneeled on his chest.

'We are not here to do battle,' Noah assured him, 'but may I show you something?'

'What?' the Guardian said.

'Do you know of olluka wood?'

Shaking its spiny head, the Guardian said, 'No. Can I eat it? I'm a bit hungry.'

'If you're hungry, eat lamprey,' Noah suggested, suddenly more worried about becoming a meal than dying in battle.

'I do *like* lamprey,' the beast said, rolling to his side.

Noah and her companions clutched at whatever scales or spines they could to avoid being tipped into the water with the slippery fish.

'Could you wait just a few minutes more?' Noah asked, scrambling free of the icy water and doing a quick scan for any wriggling parasites.

'Oh alright,' the creature said as it rolled back. 'You were saying?'

'Olluka trees,' Noah continued, as she rested the bulbous end of Grainger's baton between two of the beast's scales, 'are very precious to us humans because they are rooted in the lava that flows through this world. Nourished by lava – dragon blood – its wood has magical properties that we use to maintain the natural order of our environment.'

'It feels warm,' the Guardian said.

Noah held her breath as she angled the baton and pushed gently until it disappeared under one of the scales.

The Guardian hissed sharply. 'What are you doing?'

'Just relax,' Noah said, her hand trembling. 'I want to show you something.'

As she withdrew the baton, the scale lifted noticeably. The Guardian cocked its head for a better view of Noah's operation, its saucer-like eye full of menace.

When the baton came out, Noah was the only one not to gasp. She smiled. On the end of Grainger's baton was a lump of firestone about the size of a human brain.

'Have you ever seen the firestone you're guarding?' she asked.

'Thief!' the Guardian hissed. 'You're stealing the firestone!'

'*NO!*' Noah cried as the creature lurched to one side. '*STOP!*'

Clutching Grainger's baton in one hand, Noah grabbed at the Guardian's scales with the other as she slid towards the water. Unable to find a handhold, Noah splashed into the icy lake. She kicked hard with her legs, hoping to keep her head above water. The last thing she wanted was lamprey boring into her face.

With any luck the firestone will keep them away, Noah thought. Fighting for breath, she yelled, 'I'm not trying to *steal* it. I just want to *show* it to you.'

'You'll put it back?'

'If you want … *yes!*'

The Guardian plucked them all out of the water. Noah watched in horror as the creature dangled Jacin over its toothy snout.

'*NO!*' she screamed.

The creature ignored her. Instead it nipped at a lamprey attached to Jacin's ankle and then another on his backside. After it had cleared Jacin of lamprey, it moved onto Grainger. Once it had eaten all the lamprey, the Guardian put them down on its belly again. Noah shivered. Partly from the cold and partly for the job ahead.

She held up the firestone attached to Grainger's baton. 'Do you want me to put it back now?'

'Yes. Put it back now.'

Noah nodded. 'I'll just remove the baton first.'

She closed her eyes as she clasped the ball of firestone between her hands. Ignoring everything else, she summonsed the firestone in her veins to assist her in her task. Working quickly, she knitted the firestone in her hands to the olluka wood. Combining dragonscale and dragon-blood would create a potent instrument.

Twisting the baton gently, Noah extracted it from the lump of firestone and passed it to Grainger, who stared at the glittering firestone that now coated the bulb of his baton.

'Noah,' he breathed, 'what have you done?'

'You're welcome,' she said.

'*This*,' he declared when he recovered his wits, 'is a suitable replacement.'

Noah turned to him. 'Replacement for what?'

'The 13th key,' he said. 'You made the 13th key out of the Dragonsbane's staff and then you destroyed it in your battle with Orville. This is a fitting replacement – finally.'

'I'm glad you like it,' Noah said.

'That's cool, Noah,' Jacin said. 'I don't suppose ...'

'You know I'm kind of busy right now,' she said. 'One miracle at a time – do you want to go home or not?'

Jacin smiled. 'Oh yes, that'd be great.'

Turning back to the Guardian, Noah said, 'Ready for me to put this back?'

The beast's eyes narrowed as he studied the lump of firestone. 'Should it be pulsing like that?'

Noah shrugged. 'It's not uncommon.'

'Maybe you could have that *one* piece,' the Guardian said.

'It won't hurt you,' Noah said. 'You're special. You're made of magic. You can handle this.'

'Magic?' the Guardian repeated. 'Special?'

'Yes,' Noah said.

'No one ever said I was special,' the Guardian said. 'All the creatures that come here just try to kill me.'

Noah stepped forward and stroked the creature's jaw. 'Well, we don't want to do that,' she said. 'I will take this piece of firestone though, if you're happy with that?'

'Yes. That is fine.'

'So,' Noah said, 'if you'd like to take us back to the portal, you can get back to the fountain.'

'You know, I quite like swimming in the water here. I don't want to go back to the fountain ... just yet.'

'Well, we've got no pressing engagements,' Jacin said. 'We're happy to wait here awhile right, Noah? Grainger?'

Noah nodded. 'Absolutely.'

'Sure,' Grainger said.

'I'd like to eat some more lamprey,' the Guardian said.

'Ah,' Noah said.

'I could drop you off at the harbour while I fish?'

Noah patted its belly. 'Sounds great.'

With a swish of its long tail, the Guardian set off. The ride back to the harbour was smoother than Noah had imagined. *At least it's better than rowing,* she thought. He let them off at the wharf with a promise to return.

As they watched him duck under the water, Grainger said, 'Are you sure he'll come back?'

Noah perched herself on a flat stone and smiled. 'He'll come back. May I borrow your baton?'

Grainger hesitated before handing it over. 'What are you up to?'

Closing her eyes, she said, 'You'll see.'

Noah cradled the piece of firestone in her one hand and Grainger's baton in the other. She didn't need the baton for her task – only to stop Grainger asking questions later. Noah inhaled deeply. *Answer me.* She focused on the firestone in her veins, trying to draw a reaction from the dragonscale she held. Her heart beat faster as her blood temperature rose. *Don't swim too far away,* she thought. *I can't do this if you're too far away.*

Familiar pain coursed through her but she ignored it. She'd done this before – on a much smaller scale – the night she defeated Orville in Leninstar. Thirteen small pieces of firestone had done her bidding that night. One of those pieces had been cut from the piece she held now. The other twelve, from the chunks the Guardian still held in its chest.

Noah felt her heart swell with the effort of beating harder. She opened her eyes and touched the tip of the baton onto the piece of dragonscale.

'Noah?' Jacin said. Putting his hand on her arm, he said, 'Cripes! You're burning up.'

Noah shrugged him off. The stone in her hand pulsed in time with her heartbeat. *Keep beating. Harder. I need the others.*

Jacin knelt in front of her. 'How can I help?'

She pushed the firestone into his hands. 'Hold that,' she whispered. Passing the baton back to Grainger, she said, 'Put that away.'

'You've called the Guardian back?' Grainger guessed as he stashed his olluka rod in a pocket.

Noah exhaled slowly. 'Yes.'

Within a minute, a ripple marred the water in the harbour. It snaked towards them hypnotically.

'Jacin,' Noah said, 'pretend to tell us a joke. Grainger – we're going to laugh at whatever he says.'

'I don't have to pretend,' Jacin said indignantly. 'I can tell you a *real* joke.'

'Sorry – I just didn't want to put you on the spot. If you know one, get *on* with it.'

Jacin cleared his throat. 'What do you call something that is unrelated to elephants?'

Noah and Grainger both shrugged.

'Irrelephant,' Jacin said.

Grainger clapped and chuckled. 'That is *actually* funny. Good one!'

Jacin grinned as the Guardian's snout appeared out of the water.

'Having a lovely time are we?' the creature said.

'Yes,' Noah said, continuing the charade. 'We're excited about going home. Are you ready to take us back to the portal?'

The Guardian glanced at the pulsing firestone in Jacin's hand. 'Well, I don't feel so good. I might need a rest first.'

'Oh?' Noah said. 'What's wrong?'

'My chest feels like it's burning.'

'That's never happened to you before?'

Its eyes narrowed into slits as it climbed out of the water. 'You've done this to me,' it said. 'You *are* trying to kill me!'

Noah put her hands in the air as she retreated from the approaching monster. 'No, I'm not,' she said. 'Have you ever been away from the fountain this long?'

The creature stopped. Water dripping from its armoured body into the growing puddle beneath it echoed ominously in the cavern. 'I don't think so,' it said at last.

'That'll be it,' Grainger said, stroking his chin.

'That'll be what?' the Guardian asked.

'When you're a statue in the fountain, the Pyranhi magic keeps the firestone dormant,' the Dragonsbane replied. 'When you're moving about though, it becomes unstable. The pain you're feeling is from the pieces of firestone reacting with each other.'

Noah held her breath while the monster considered Grainger's words. Grainger had lied masterfully to cover her tampering with the firestone, but if the creature didn't believe it … *we're going to die here,* she thought.

The Guardian roared, its spines quivering as its body trembled. Noah couldn't tell if it roared from pain or frustration, but she backed further away. She gestured to Jacin to do the same.

Grainger stood his ground. *'STOP THAT!'* he yelled.

The beast recoiled. Noah stared at Grainger.

'That's enough of that rot, Guardian,' Grainger said. 'You need to stop carrying on and make your decision.'

'What decision?' it said.

Grainger wagged his finger at the creature. 'You need to get yourself back to the fountain or let Noah remove the firestone from your chest.'

'You *do* want to steal it!' the Guardian cried.

'We want to *help* you by taking it out of you,' Grainger said with a glance at Noah, 'and if we do, we all get what we want. We get the firestone and you don't have to be stuck in the fountain for eternity.'

The Guardian hissed. 'How does that work?'

'Your purpose is to guard the firestone,' Noah explained. 'That's why Goh made you. To guard the firestone, you need to stay in the fountain until someone challenges you. Until now, the creatures that have challenged you, have tried to kill you. But now, as you've seen, I can remove the firestone without killing you.'

'But you'll take away my purpose for being,' the Guardian protested.

'Exactly,' Noah said. 'Which is why you won't have to return to the fountain. You can swim around down here and eat lamprey as long as you like.'

Cocking its head, the Guardian said, 'I'd be free?'

For as long as Goh's magic lasts, Noah thought. Aloud, she said, 'Yes.'

'So you remove all the firestone and I can stay swimming down here?'

'After you swim us back to the portal – yes,' Noah confirmed.

Noah's pulse raced as the Guardian's little brain grappled with the choice.

Finally, it bobbed its snout up and down. 'I accept.'

Chapter 31

The thirteen pieces of firestone twinkled benignly in the candlelight. Across the desk from Noah, Grainger nursed his baton as he contemplated the stones.

'Are you sure they'll be safe in Mellifont?' he said at last.

'As long as we can keep Franco and his cronies out of the city they will be,' Noah said, keeping her attention on her sewing. *And if we can't keep him out,* she thought, *these stitches are going to be the most important ones I ever do.* Outwitting the northern kings with needle and thread seemed a long shot but it was all she had. Despite the task ahead of her, Noah's hands remained steady.

Grainger sighed. 'Though these smaller stones are safer than the large one, this still weighs heavily upon me. It will be a terrible burden if things go wrong ...'

'Yes,' Noah said.

Grainger held the bejewelled end of his baton in front of his eyes. 'I don't know what to make of this ... enhancement. I am thrilled by the possibilities but terrified of the dangers.'

'You'll master it,' Noah said.

The Dragonsbane's eyes flicked to her. 'How can you be so sure?'

'You consider all options, weigh all the dangers – you always have.'

Grainger nodded slowly. Placing his baton on the desk, he said, 'I used to envy you, Noah. When Sachin first endorsed you as his candidate to find the 13th key, I couldn't understand it. And when you were appointed Dragonsbane ahead of me, well then … I hated you.'

Noah let her hands rest in her lap.

'But I don't envy you anymore,' Grainger said. 'I think I finally understand you.'

In her peripheral vision, Noah saw Jacin lean forward and rest his elbows on the table.

Grainger said, 'In your time here, I came to understand that you were a gifted adept. I came to respect you. But after you left and wanted to dig up that firestone – I just saw a reckless glory-hound. I thought the power had gone to your head and that you craved recognition of your talent. I thought that you wanted the masses to bow down to you – worship you for the gift of firestone you'd bestowed upon them.'

Despite her best efforts to not react, Noah winced.

Grainger put his hand over his heart. 'But I was wrong, Noah. Very wrong,' he said. 'I could not have done what you did in Tisaan. I don't believe there is anyone else on this world who could have done it. I watched you work and I think I finally got it. Your talent means that this world asks a lot of you. What I saw in Tisaan was a girl who stepped up to do what was asked of her – not someone driven by ambition and power – and you did it masterfully.'

And I hope you remember that when you find out I'm King of the goblins, she thought.

Aloud, she said, 'Thanks for giving me the chance.'

Jacin sat back in his seat wearing a smug grin. 'Well, aren't I lucky to have such a great mentor,' he said. 'I should be a Major in no time.'

Grainger frowned at him. 'If you live long enough.'

'I'm pretty hard to kill,' Jacin declared.

'You've found yourself a cocky young apprentice there, Noah,' Grainger said. 'Could you not have found one that was a little nicer?'

Thinking of Yeti and thankful she'd been excluded from this meeting, Noah said, 'I could ask the same of you.'

Grainger flinched. 'Okay. I guess I deserved that.'

'Yes, you did,' Noah replied, returning to her sewing. 'Now would you like to choose the piece of firestone to keep here in Dragonhall?'

'Which piece did you use to enhance my baton?'

'I know this,' Jacin said. He stood and reached across the table. 'This one,' he said as he passed the stone to Grainger.

Noah glanced up. 'No. Not that one.'

'Ah,' Jacin said, selecting another piece, 'then it was *definitely* this one.'

Noah shook her head.

His enthusiasm undented, Jacin chose another piece. 'This one?'

'Oh, for goodness' sake,' Noah said, dropping her sewing. 'Do I have to do everything?'

'This one!' Jacin cried.

Rolling her eyes, Noah said, 'Yeah, you're gifted.'

'That's perfect,' Grainger said, accepting the stone from Jacin.

When Noah finished her alterations she packed all her implements away in the pockets of her trousers. She stood and pushed her seat under the desk. 'We'll take our leave now. The sooner we get to Mellifont, the better.'

Grainger got to his feet. 'Do you think the Alliance will accept these stones in lieu of the one that you … returned to the depths?'

'They'll accept them,' Noah said confidently, 'but that doesn't mean there won't be a further price to pay.'

'What do you think they'll do to you?'

Noah shook her head. 'I'd rather not think about.'

♪♪

Raven looked up as Noah and Jacin entered his command tent. Rising to his feet, he strode over to Noah and hugged her tightly.

Her head against his chest, Noah said, 'Miss me?'

'I'm so glad you're back,' he said. 'I had a bad feeling. Are you okay?'

'I'm fine … now.'

'I'm fine too,' Jacin added.

Without releasing his sister, Raven said, 'Do I want to know what happened in there?'

'Later,' Noah said. 'We need to get to Mellifont.'

A commotion at the entrance to the tent made Noah turn.

'Your Highness,' Frost said.

Liah and Shar followed close behind the senior goblin soldier. They all nodded in her direction.

'Did you get the firestone?' Frost asked.

Raven's eyes narrowed. 'She's fine, by the way,' he said.

'My eyes tell me that is so,' Frost said. 'We have no time for redundant questions.'

Though grateful her brother was protective of her, Noah knew they had a job to do.

'I have the firestone,' she said, patting the pockets on her trousers. 'Now we have to get it to Mellifont.'

'May we see it?' Liah said.

Noah settled herself on a hessian cushion on the dirt floor as her companions settled themselves around her. One by one, she extracted the pieces of firestone.

'I thought there were supposed to be thirteen,' Shar said.

'There were,' Noah said. 'I left one in Dragonhall.'

'And one will go to Carai?' Frost said.

'Initially, all these go to Mellifont,' Noah said. 'When the situation with the Alliance is resolved, the firestone will be distributed.'

'It is likely that Franco is already in Mellifont – or will be soon,' Raven said. 'I don't think it's a good idea for you *or* the firestone to go there.'

'It's neutral territory,' Noah argued. 'We have to get the firestone there.'

'Why not leave it here?' Raven said. 'Surely it's safer inside Dragonhall?'

'Safer, maybe,' Noah said, 'but I need to prove that there *is* firestone. The only way I can do that is to take it to Mellifont. What's the latest news on Franco?'

'We had word yesterday that armies from the north crossed Skycleaver a week ago,' Raven said. 'If they haven't surrounded Mellifont yet, they soon will.'

'And the adepts?' Jacin asked.

'The city's been evacuated,' Raven said. 'Only a few adepts remain.'

'And what of *your* army?' Frost said.

Raven glanced at Noah. 'Emir leads them to Mellifont in my absence.'

Noah frowned at her brother. 'You weren't going to tell me?'

'I was hoping it wouldn't come up,' Raven said.

'But *you're* planning to go to Mellifont?'

Raven nodded. 'Of course. I am expected to show up at some point and command my army.'

Tapping her fingers on her knees, Noah said, 'When you're finished babysitting me, you mean?'

'Don't be like that,' Raven said.

'Like what?' she asked.

'Like *you*,' he replied.

'Are you really asking me not to be me?'

'Yes.'

'Well, that's going to be awkward,' she said.

'Noah,' Raven said. 'You need to stay here – in Dragonhall – where you'll be safe.'

Liah came to her rescue. 'Noah is the King of Carai. She does not have to take orders from you.'

Raven threw his hands in the air. 'I'm cursed,' he declared. 'The two women dearest to me are bloody-minded kings! What have I done to deserve this?'

'I'm going to Mellifont,' Noah said. 'We can go together, or I can meet you there. What's it to be?'

Jacin cleared his throat. 'May I make a suggestion?'

Everyone turned to the goman.

'Speak,' Frost said.

'It's late and we're all tired,' Jacin said. 'How about we get some sleep and reconvene in the morning? We need a tight plan from here – something best done with clear heads.'

'I can live with that,' Raven said.

Noah turned to her guards. 'Go. I'll be along shortly.'

The three goblins stood, bowed and left.

To Jacin, she said, 'Take your own advice. Go and get some rest.'

'Right you are,' he said. 'See you in the morning.'

Noah watched him go. When the tent flap fell shut, she turned to her twin. 'Don't try to sneak off without me.'

Raven smiled. 'Funny, that's exactly what I was just about to say to you.'

'I have as much right to be there as you and Emir.'

'I'm not trying to deny you your rights, Noah. I just want you to be safe.'

Noah put her hand on his. 'I want you to be safe too, but *I* wouldn't tell *you* not to go.'

Squeezing her hand, he said, 'You're more important than me, Noah. You're the 13th key, you're—'

'*Don't* start!' she said, jumping to her feet. 'I don't need this from you too.'

'Noah—'

Heat raced through her veins. 'I am *not* an object – I'm your *sister*.'

'Yes,' Raven said slowly, 'and I have *always* been your protector – even before you were the 13th key.'

Noah squeezed her eyes shut to stop the tears that threatened. She regretted her outburst. Since she was a baby, Raven had been her loyal companion. He deserved better from her.

'I don't see you as an object,' he continued, 'but I can't ignore the fact that the fate of this world is tied to you, Sister. I wish it wasn't that way, but it is. We all have a duty here. *I* can't save this world, but I can protect the one who can. That's you, Noah.'

Noah hung her head. 'No pressure.'

'Get some rest. We'll sort out a plan in the morning.'

With her heart hammering in her chest, Noah nodded and walked out of the tent.

♪♫

Noah kept her eyes on the dark smudge of hills to the north as she stole out of camp and into the moonlit night. She didn't bother deluding herself that she'd evade her guards but she wanted a head start. As she walked, she relished the silence that would make her evening's task easier. She reached the hills within half an hour and set about looking for a good spot. *Just on the other side of this hill will be perfect,* she thought. Crunching her way up a gravelly incline, she was confident that when her guards came, she'd hear them.

Noah cleared the loose stones from a patch of ground with her boot and sat cross-legged on the dirt. The night air was cool on her skin. She closed her eyes and took several deep, slow breaths to start her routine. Her mind needed to be as still as the hills around her. After the drama of the past few days, Noah knew it would take her some time to achieve her trance tonight.

A voice startled her.

'What are you doing?' Liah asked.

'Besides having a heart attack, you mean?' she asked.

'How am I supposed to protect you when you sneak off like that?'

'The only thing I need protection from at the moment is you scaring the life out me,' Noah said, 'and anyway – how did you get here so quickly?'

'I was with you the whole way,' he said.

Noah shook her head. 'Just sit on the other side of the hill and make sure I don't get any *more* visitors. I need some peace and quiet.'

'Yes, Your Highness.'

She listened for his retreating footsteps but heard nothing. No wonder he'd surprised her. She didn't imagine there were many people who could walk silently on the rocky terrain. *I should probably have just brought him along in the first place,* she thought as she resettled herself. In hindsight, her charade had served only to waste time. She drew the silence into her mind to smother the random thoughts that taunted her.

When all was still, Noah commenced her task.

From a deep and precious vault in her mind, she drew out a trea-sured memory of her mother. *Arms outstretched, Isla Chord beckoned to her daughter from the other side of a small stream. Noah – only three years old – stared intently at the four stepping stones between them. She stepped onto the first one no trouble. The second one was also easy. Confidence soaring, Noah stepped onto the third one. She looked up and her mother smiled. Unable to contain her pride and excitement, Noah leapt onto the last stone, but lost her footing. Before the disappointment of failure took hold, Isla grabbed her daughter's hands and swung her onto the sandy bank. The thrill of the looping swing at the end eclipsed the walk across the stones and Noah's heart raced as she clung to her mother's hands.*

Love and grief tangled in Noah's chest and she channelled those feelings as she pictured her mother's ring. The silver dragon curled protectively around its precious stone. The firestone that had been in Noah's family for hundreds of years had been taken. Taken and shattered. Anger coursed through her but she controlled it. If she could focus her perceptions, she'd find her firestone. She'd find Franco.

It didn't take her long. *Damn it,* she thought. *He's already in Mellifont.*

Noah's stomach tightened. How would she get there? With war raging, the thousand-kilometre journey overland was out of the question. *We need to get there fast. The longer Franco is there, the more danger Emir is in.* The railcar lines? She shook her head. *They'll be dangerous too.* No planes on Talisker so flying was out of the question.

The moon glided silently overhead as Noah wrestled with her dilemma. Her bottom was numb by the time a solution presented itself. She scrambled to her feet.

'Liah!' she said as she crested the hill.

'What's your plan?' he asked.

'We're going to Mellifont ... via Earth.'

The goblin stared at her. 'Say again?'

'We're going to Mellifont ... via Earth.'

'That's what I thought you said. How's that going to work?'

'There are many portals between Earth and Talisker,' Noah explained. 'With a few ... connections ... we can land ourselves right inside Mellifont.'

'Sounds risky.'

'It is.'

'Your brother won't like that.'

'No,' Noah said. 'He won't.'

Liah stopped walking.

'What?' Noah said.

'Nerili was right about you,' Liah said. 'You'll make a great king. You listen to advice but you make your own decisions. That shows strength.'

'If I live long enough perhaps,' she said, uncomfortable with the praise.

Without warning, Liah wrapped his arms around her. She froze.

'We'll make sure you live long enough,' he said.

Recovering slightly, she returned his embrace awkwardly. 'Well, if you don't, I won't pay you.'

The goblin laughed and released her. 'We should return to camp and get some rest. We have a difficult journey ahead of us.'

Chapter 32

Noah frowned. 'Where's Jacin?'

Liah and Frost shook their heads.

'He was right behind me,' Shar said. 'He should be along any—'

'Ta-da!' Jacin said as he appeared from the olluka branch.

'Shush!' Raven said. 'We're right underneath Elani's chamber. You need to be quiet.'

'I thought the city had been evacuated,' Jacin said.

'*Mostly* evacuated,' Raven said. 'We need to be careful.'

Inhaling deeply, Noah looked at her companions. It was a miracle they'd all made it through the portals. After two days of scampering from olluka branch to olluka branch across swathes of Talisker and Earth, Noah's nerves were raw. Disguising three goblins on a bus from Sayle to Kallide had been the biggest challenge and it hadn't gone well. It had ended in a foot chase with police. If Earth's constabulary decided to investigate the group's sudden disappearance more closely, they'd likely end up wandering around in the prickly north end of Maldine Forest.

Making her way towards the door, Noah said. 'Let's check out the chamber.'

'You think Franco will be there?' Raven asked.

Noah nodded. 'I'd put money on it.'

They approached the chamber in silence, Noah's trepidation growing with every step. Mellifont's uncharacteristic quiet unsettled her. When they reached the chamber's giant timber doors, Noah opened them without hesitation and strode down the aisle towards the central dais. Twenty thousand vacant seats ringed the amphitheatre, but it was the thrones on the dais that captured Noah's attention. Emir, Sachin and Montana occupied three of them.

The instant she saw Emir's face, Noah knew she'd walked into a trap. Hand on her sword hilt, she bolted. Anger surged through her at the sight of the shackles that confined him to the ornate chair. Montana and Sachin sat either side of him, their expressions grim.

Franco stepped out from behind one of the thrones as Noah reached the polished stone table.

'Noah,' he said. 'About time.' Grimacing at her, he added, 'What is that you're wearing?'

'Noah is our king,' Frost said.

Franco guffawed loudly. 'You've got to be kidding!'

No one spoke as Franco's soldiers filed into the chamber, surrounding Noah and her companions.

'I'm surprised, Noah,' Franco said. 'Did you kill the last king to steal his crown?'

'*You* killed him,' Noah said, 'when you set off that bomb in Tchuganni.'

Franco scratched his head. 'So you're here to thank me then?'

'Hardly. We're actually here to take you into custody.'

Franco raised an eyebrow as his soldiers laughed. 'Well, let's see how that goes.'

Noah drew her sword and the resounding metal *schwing* around the chamber told her that she wasn't the only one. She turned and swung her blade at a soldier's neck. He ducked to dodge the blow as the guard beside him kicked out at her. His boot slammed into her thigh where the dundar had bitten her. Ignoring the pain, Noah reset her sword. Before she could strike again, Shar leapt in front of her.

'I want them alive,' Franco said.

Shar lunged.

'*Ahhhhhhhh!*' a soldier screamed.

As the soldier sank to the floor, Shar pulled his sword from the man's stomach. Three of the stricken man's companions jumped on Shar and wrestled him to the floor. A series of sickening thuds followed as the soldiers pummelled the goblin. Noah jumped on a soldier's back.

'Right!' Franco yelled. 'That's enough.'

Someone yanked on Noah's collar, dragging her free of the melee. As her hands were tied behind her back, Noah glanced at her allies; all were squirming under multiple captors.

When satisfied that his prisoners were securely bound, Franco said, 'Now, you're all going to listen to me. This is officially the end of the Sovereign States Alliance. The northern states will not tolerate the southern states' treachery any longer. If you want goblins as your bedfellows'—he glowered at Noah—'then you're welcome to them. You deserve each other.'

Montana spoke up. 'You're quick to point out the treachery of others, Franco. What about your own?'

'My allegiance is to Talisker,' Franco said, 'and I'll do whatever it takes to rid this world of goblins *and* their sympathisers.'

'So what do you plan to do with us?' Noah asked.

Franco snorted. 'You're all going to die here.'

'Noah's a king,' Sachin said. 'If you kill her, there'll be serious consequences.'

'Yes,' Emir said. 'That'll be three kings you've killed. The charges are mounting.'

'*Goblin* kings don't count,' Franco said.

Noah glared at him. 'So you admit that you killed King Tambian?'

With his hand over his heart, Franco said, 'Proudly!'

Silence engulfed the chamber. Though she'd suspected his involvement, Noah hadn't believed he'd confess. And his admission brought mixed feelings. She'd identified Tambian's killer but there'd be no justice. *There's definitely no way he's letting us out of here alive now,* Noah thought.

'Even if you kill all of us,' Raven said, 'you won't win. The southern kings will hunt you down.'

Franco waved his hand dismissively. 'They can try,' he said, 'but my comrades and I will have the advantage.'

'Which is?' Raven said.

'The firestone, of course,' Franco replied. Turning to Noah, he said, 'I'll be taking that now. I'm assuming it's in your trousers somewhere?'

'I left it in Dragonhall,' Noah said.

'Liar!' Franco retorted. 'Guards, take her trousers.' He pointed to Jacin. 'And take his too – just in case.'

As Jacin protested, three soldiers converged on Noah. Though the outcome was assured, she struggled valiantly, kicking and wriggling to make the soldiers' job as difficult as possible. At least it got the blood flowing to her painful corked thigh. If she did somehow get free, she needed to be able to run.

Noah looked over at Emir. His eyes smouldered under his creased brow. She sucked in a sharp breath. *I don't think I've ever seen him look so angry,* she thought.

Turning her attention back to Franco, Noah said, 'So now what? What's your plan to take over the world?'

'I'm so glad you asked, Noah,' Franco said. 'Believe it or not – Arissa, Ulster and I have given this much thought. I think you'll appreciate the elegance of our plan.'

'I'll be astonished if there's even a *shred* of elegance in your plan,' Sachin said.

Ignoring the Major, Franco focused on Noah. 'You came here to Mellifont because it's "neutral" territory. But the problem is, that it isn't neutral anymore. The adepts here are in league with the southern kings and as such – like the Sovereign States Alliance – the apparatus of the Academy needs to be dismantled as well. And I'm here to see that that happens.'

The King of Ylestar sauntered over to Noah and squatted in front of her. He reached into his breast pocket and pulled out a velvet pouch. Opening the drawstring, he emptied the contents onto his palm. Noah's splintered firestone twinkled in the chamber's warm light.

'You recall what I did in Tchuganni with just a small sliver of your dragonscale?' he said. 'Well, I've recovered three firestone sliders—'

'Stole!' Sachin yelled. 'You *stole* three firestone sliders, you filthy thief!'

'—from Sachin, Maggie and Anok,' Franco continued, 'and I'm going to use them to fuel three more bombs, right here in Mellifont.'

'Firestone cannot be used in weapons,' Noah said. 'As Dragonsbane of Talisker—'

'Shhhh … don't interrupt, Noah,' Franco said, tapping the olluka tree on her breastplate. 'I think we've already established that our weapons work *exceptionally* well. The three that I've brought here though, are extra special.'

Franco clicked his fingers. Noah shuddered.

One of the king's soldiers reached under the stone table and retrieved a black duffel bag. He placed it on the floor beside Franco.

'Ah,' Franco said, opening the bag reverently.

Inside the bag was a dark metal ball, similar to the one Noah had seen in the lodge in Tchuganni, but with a coil of thin rope attached to it.

'A fuse,' Franco said, 'which I can cut to any length I like. There's probably thirty metres or so on this one. I could leave it that long or I can cut it shorter, depending on how long I need.'

'To run away?' Raven said. 'You bloody coward.'

'I'm going to leave this one here in this grand old chamber, Noah,' Franco said. 'When I blow it to hell, I'll have ripped the heart out of Mellifont. I have a second one ready in the reservoir. With no water, there can be no life here. And the last one, is in the library. The ancient superstitions of this … cult need to be eradicated too. By the time these devices have done their jobs – the life, heart and mind of Mellifont will be no more. Poetic, don't you think?'

Frost growled. 'So you're going to blow us up too?'

'Yes,' Franco said. 'And I'd greatly appreciate it if you'd all stay put this time.'

'Don't count on it,' Noah said. 'We got out last time. We'll do it again.'

Franco smirked. 'Well, since you *are* trouble when you're together, I am going to split you up a bit.'

'Oh yes?' Noah said.

Nodding, Franco said, 'Noah, I'm going to leave *you* here with Emir, Montana and Sachin. Raven and two goblins will join Anok in the reservoir, and the other goblin and your little pet'—he waved in Jacin's direction—'can join Maggie and Alan in the library.'

'You're an evil bastard,' Noah said.

Franco wagged his finger at her. 'Hang on – you haven't heard the best part yet.'

Noah waited, heart pounding.

'None of you will know how long the fuse is at your location or when I will actually light it. It might be minutes … or it might be hours. You might hear another bomb detonate … or you might be first. Exciting, hey?'

'I don't know about "exciting",' Noah said, 'but it certainly sounds more fun than listening to you babble on and on. How about you just get on with it?'

Franco's eyes narrowed. 'As you wish.' Turning to his guards, he said, 'Take them away.'

Noah fought to keep her breathing steady as a soldier hauled Raven to his feet. *Not my brother,* she thought. *I can't lose him.* As if he'd read her mind, Raven winked at her. Noah managed a smile before the soldier led him away.

'We'll be back for you, Your Highness,' Frost said as he was escorted away.

Liah and Shar nodded their intention to do the same.

'If you get loose,' she said to Jacin, 'just get the hell out of here.'

'Yes, Your Highness,' he said.

Noah glared at him. 'I mean it.'

Jacin grinned. 'You certainly sound like you mean it.'

'Touching,' Franco said, as Jacin was ushered away. 'And you know, that's your biggest problem, Noah.'

'No, *you're* my biggest problem,' Noah said.

Shaking his head, Franco said, 'No, *your* biggest problem is that you're a *commoner,* Noah. You don't want to upset anyone. You want people to like you. That's not what being a king is about. It's not a popularity contest. Being a king is about making tough choices – balancing the good of many against the good of the individual.'

'Do you really think I became King of Carai to be *popular*?' Noah said. 'Are you *serious*? I just about can't think of a way to make more enemies. And I *am* balancing the good of many against the good of the individual. Trying to anyway. I am actually trying to balance the good of all Taliskerans – not just my own state – against my own wellbeing.

'I don't need lots of people to like me,' she continued, 'but there are *select* people whose opinions matter. There are *select* people whose respect I want to earn. People like those sitting at that table over there'—she nodded towards Emir, Montana and Sachin—'people who want to do what's *right*. At the moment, I have their respect and I intend to keep it. I actually pity you because you won't have that.'

'I will leave a legacy,' Franco said. 'Talisker will remember me.'

'Yes,' Noah agreed, 'as a traitor and a murderer.'

Franco sneered. 'You think you've got what it takes to be a king, Noah?'

'Not really,' Noah said, 'but I'm going to do it anyway. Working for King Tambian, I have seen what a good king does. And now having worked with you, though briefly, I have seen what a bad king does. You are the perfect non-example, Franco. Everything I do will be the exact opposite of what I think you would do.'

Franco snorted. 'Well, since you'll only have a couple of hours at best to *play* at being a king, Noah – I'll leave you to it.'

Chapter 33

The double doors slammed shut and the echo reverberated around the chamber.

'Well, the bomb is inside, but the fuse is outside,' Sachin noted.

Trying to ignore the dead soldier Franco had left behind, Noah said, 'Franco doesn't want us to know how long we've got.'

'Noah,' Emir said, 'how long do *you* think we've got?'

Noah looked at him. Franco had put her in the chair next to Emir so they were close enough that they could have held hands – if their arms hadn't been tied to their chairs. 'We'll be last,' she said. 'He'll want me to hear the other two blasts.'

'Then we've got time to act,' Montana said.

Emir tugged at his restraints. 'Only if we can get free.'

Wriggling in his seat, Sachin said, 'I want to get my slider back – I can't stand to think it's going to be used to power a bomb. I don't care what Franco says. It's not *poetic*, it's *perverse*.'

'We have to get free first,' Montana said. 'Then we need to defuse this bomb, as well as the other two, before capturing Franco.'

'Lots to do,' Emir said. 'Ideas anyone?'

Noah closed her eyes. 'Give me a minute …'

Pushing all other thoughts aside, she called on the firestone in her blood. *My wrists,* she thought, *dragonscale, I need your fire in my wrists.*

Noah clenched her jaws as the heat intensified. When the burning was almost unbearable she opened her eyes. Her skin glowed orange and delicate tendrils of smoke curled into the air from ropes that bound her. She needed to work quickly or the muscles in her forearms would cook.

'Noah!' Emir said. 'What are you doing?'

'Nearly done,' she replied, hoping it was true.

Noah pulled against the ropes, trying to speed up the process. *Burn,* she thought, *just burn already.* When the flames did take hold, Noah screamed. She wrenched and twisted her arms until the ropes finally broke.

A quick inspection of her wrists showed they were red and blistered but there were no flames.

'Ouch!' Sachin said.

'You got that right,' Noah said, ripping off her breastplate and unbuttoning her vest.

Once her vest was off she turned it inside out. She opened a pocket and pulled out her dagger.

'That's my girl,' Emir said as she sliced the ropes at her ankles before moving onto his bonds.

'How long have you had pockets in there?' Montana said.

'Since I got back from Tisaan,' Noah replied. 'I figured Franco would take my trousers if I happened to run into him, so I removed a few pockets and sewed them into my vest. I've got my most precious stuff hidden here.'

'Like the firestone?' Sachin said.

Noah nodded. 'Yes – and a spare pair of pants.'

She slipped into her replacement trousers before Emir wrapped his arms around her. 'You're amazing,' he whispered.

'I'm so glad you're alive,' she said. 'I was scared I wouldn't see you again.'

Emir kissed her tenderly. 'Cut the others loose,' he said. 'I'll start on the bomb.'

'No, *you* cut the others loose. *I'll* start on the bomb,' Noah said.

Sachin cleared his throat. 'Can *someone* cut us loose, please?'

'Emir will do it,' Noah said. 'I'm king. I give the orders.'

Noah did take a moment to enjoy the look on Emir's face before pushing the handle of her dagger into his hands.

As she raced down the aisle towards the doors, Noah sifted through her options. Franco wouldn't have lit the fuse for this bomb yet. Surely all she had to do was cut the fuse. But should she try to retrieve Sachin's firestone slider? Could she afford to leave the bomb here? She knelt before the device and cupped her hands around it.

'I want my slider back,' Sachin said.

'Hmmm. Not right now,' Noah said. 'This can't stay here.'

'Where should we put it?' Montana asked.

Noah thought for a moment. 'Take it to one of the portals, send it somewhere else until we're done here.'

'I'll do that,' Sachin offered.

Looking at Montana, Noah said, 'Both of you go. Emir and I will go to the reservoir – it's closer – then hopefully we'll get to the library before …'

'We'll meet you at the library,' Montana said, scooping up the bomb.

Squeezing Emir's hand, Noah said, 'Let's go.'

He took off and Noah fought to keep pace with him. As they ran through Mellifont's deserted streets, Noah heard fighting beyond the city. All Talisker's armies had converged on Mellifont but none had yet broached the perimeter. Apart from Franco's surreptitious incursion, it seemed everyone else respected Mellifont's neutrality. But Noah wondered how long that would last.

When they reached the domed hillock that sheltered the city's subterranean lake, they found the door open.

Emir sprinted into the tunnel, Noah pumping her arms hard to stay with him. If Franco was true to his word, Raven and Anok would be here. *Please give me time, please give me time,* she thought. Noah pinned her hopes on the fact that Franco would want to draw things out to torture her, but every second that passed without an explosion was a second less she had to save her friends.

Around the last bend, the silver lake came into view. Raven, Anok, Frost and Shar lay bound on a raft in the middle of the lake.

'Raven!' Noah called.

'Hey Sister!' Raven yelled back. 'Little help?'

'Coming!' she said. To Emir, she said, 'You get them, I'm going to find the bomb.'

Emir pointed to the wall to their right. 'There.'

The bomb sat on a rocky outcrop about halfway up the wall. Noah tracked the fuse line to the far side of the lagoon. Her stomach knotted painfully at the sight of a sparkling light in the tunnel across the lake from her.

'We don't have much time,' she said. *'Go!'*

'What are you going to do?'

'Just get them out of the water,' Noah said.

Emir nodded. 'We can't afford to fail here.'

'I know,' she said. 'Cut them loose and make them swim back to shore. I'm going to climb that wall. Bring the raft to me.'

Noah heard the splash as Emir dived into the water but her eyes were on the burning fuse. She looked to the bomb on the wall again. *Blowing out the wall will drain the lake,* she thought. *No one can live here if there's no water.*

Noah ran to the wall and launched herself at it. Difficult as it was to not look at the burning fuse, Noah kept her focus on the climb. She just needed to get to the bomb before the fuse ran out. Scaling Tisaan's rock wall had been good training. Thankfully the wall here was still vertical. Further up, the ceiling sloped towards a central point which would have been impossible to climb. Noah reached the bomb with a handful of seconds to spare. She snipped the fuse.

'Good job, Noah!' Raven called from the bank.

'Not done yet,' she called back. 'We need to detonate this one.'

'Why?' Emir said.

'I want to send Franco a message,' she said.

'Do you—'

'Catch!' she said as she dropped the bomb down to him.

Noah pushed off the wall, following the metal ball. The raft rocked violently as she landed.

'I thought I'd be bringing *you* back, Noah – not *this* thing,' Emir said.

'We need to get back to the middle,' she said.

Emir placed the bomb on the raft and lowered himself onto his stomach. 'You going to help?'

Dropping down, she said, 'Of course.'

They both kicked, steering the raft back to the middle of the lake. 'Leave it here,' Noah said. 'Let's get back to shore.'

'Are you going to tell me your plan?' Emir asked as he slid into the water.

'No,' Noah said. 'No time. Just trust me.'

The cool water brought some relief to her burnt wrists but Noah was keen to get to shore. When they reached the water's edge, Raven and Frost grabbed her arms and dragged her onto land.

'Hey Sis—'

Swatting their hands away, Noah struggled to her feet. 'Not done yet,' she panted as she reached into a pocket inside her vest. Pulling out her viola and bow, she added, 'Go to the library while I finish up here.'

'What are you going to do?' Raven said.

She glared at him. 'Just go!'

'No!' he said. 'I'm not one of your subjects. You can't order me around!'

Exasperated, Noah turned to her goblin guards, 'Go to the library—'

'We don't know where it is,' Frost said.

Noah pointed her bow at Anok. 'Please take them to the library. If you see Montana and Sachin on the way, tell them to leave the city.'

Anok nodded. 'Follow me,' he said to the goblins.

Noah didn't wait to see if her guards obeyed her order. She put her viola under her chin and channelled the firestone within her. Closing her eyes, she visualised a spot on the ceiling high above. Drawing her bow across the strings she employed a tonic she'd learned as a new Master at the Academy.

'Noah,' Raven said, 'I think the ceiling is caving in.'

'Good,' Noah said without opening her eyes. 'That's the plan.'

She played for another few heartbeats before opening her eyes. She glanced at the hole in the ceiling high above and smiled. 'Perfect.'

'Now what?' Emir said.

'Watch,' Noah said, turning her attention to the raft.

She started a new tonic, one for water this time rather than stone. Monitoring the raft as she played, Noah coaxed the water into action. A small wave quickly became a fountain. The spire of water inched higher and higher with the raft teetering on top of it.

Raven applauded. 'You're going to detonate the bomb above the city!'

'That's the plan,' Noah said as she plucked her way through a staccato element of the tonic.

'Franco will hear the explosion and think his plan is on track, but the bomb won't do the damage he intended,' Emir said.

Noah nodded.

'I can't wait to see what you've got planned for the next one,' Raven said.

'Let's just hope we make it there in time,' Noah said, thinking of Maggie, Alan, Jacin and her guards.

Tempting as it was to rush through the tonic, Noah measured her pace. It needed to be done properly or she risked collapsing the entire structure. She pushed the water column higher and higher until the bomb was clear of the ceiling. *How much further?* she wondered. Focusing on the firestone slider inside the device, Noah tracked the bomb's progress until she thought it was high enough. With a final flurry of notes, Noah connected the firestone inside her to the slider inside the bomb.

BOOM!

The cavern trembled. Noah held her breath, but it stayed intact.

Emir put his arm around her shoulder. 'You did it.'

Lowering her viola, she nodded. 'One more to go.'

Jamming her instrument back into her vest pocket, she ran back up the tunnel. She prayed the explosion would buy them the time they needed to save the others. Surely Franco would want to maximise her distress by leaving a significant amount of time between blasts. Noah's thigh ached but she ran on. She had to get to the library.

'Made it!' Raven said as he approached the threshold.

Noah followed him with Emir close behind her. Frost and Shar waited at the entrance with Montana and Sachin. She hadn't really expected that they'd leave the city.

Slowing down, Noah said, 'There's no time to argue.' She looked at Sachin and Montana. 'If you want to do something useful, find Franco. You'll only be collateral damage here.'

Without waiting for a response, Noah ran inside.

'This library is on twenty-four levels,' Emir said. 'Where do you think he's put the bomb?'

'Bottom level,' Noah said.

'You have a plan for this one?' Raven asked.

'Almost,' Noah lied as they reached the central stairway.

Although there were only twelve flights of stairs to the basement, Noah wished the librarian had installed the fireman's pole she'd suggested. Each hurried step on the spiral staircase abraded her nerves further. Instead of fretting about her potential failure, Noah focused on a plan for the final device. *It depends how much time I've got,* she thought. *Getting it out of here is going to be the problem.*

By the time she reached the bottom level, she still didn't have a plan.

'Noah!' Alan cried. 'Am I glad to see you!'

'And me,' Maggie said.

'Your Highness,' Jacin and Liah said in unison, bowing their heads.

The bomb made a grotesque centrepiece to the table they sat around.

Franco's really got a thing for tying people to chairs, Noah thought as she looked for the end of the fuse. The sputtering flame was only about four metres from the device. Noah shuddered.

Drawing her blade, Noah crouched down.

'NO!' Jacin yelled. 'DON'T!'

Noah looked at him. 'Why not?'

Eyes wide, Jacin said, 'Franco said you can't cut this one!'

'Because?' she said.

'Because wherever you cut it,' he said, 'the spark will restart from there.'

Noah frowned.

'If you cut the cord,' Jacin said, 'you are shortening the fuse and the bomb will go off sooner.'

Noah chewed her bottom lip. 'Surely he can't do that.'

'He sounded pretty convincing to me,' Alan said.

'Test it,' Emir said. 'Cut it near the lit end.'

Thankful for a sensible suggestion, Noah did as he said. To her horror, the fuse sparked back to life where she'd cut it.

'How is that possible?' Maggie said.

Noah gave her dagger to Raven. 'Get them out of here.'

Emir knelt beside her. 'What are you thinking?'

'Just get them out of here – and hurry,' she whispered.

'I'm not going anywhere,' Emir said. 'You can tell me your plan or I'll just watch it unfold. Up to you.'

Noah tried in vain to swallow the lump in her throat. If the bomb detonated with her here, the twelve pieces of firestone from Tisaan in her vest would … Noah didn't want to think about it.

'The firestone,' she said.

Emir put his arm around her. 'What about it?'

What about it? The words echoed inside her head. *What about it?*

An image of Xan flashed in her mind. She turned to Emir and kissed him hard on the lips.

'You're a genius,' she said. 'I love you.'

Instantly suspicious, Emir said, 'Noah, what are you doing?'

She reached into a pocket inside her vest and rummaged around for the stone she wanted. Drawing out one piece, she said, '*This* is what I'm doing.'

Noah stood up.

'Noah?' Raven said.

'Run!' Noah said.

Raven cocked his head. 'But—'

Noah glanced at the fuse. There was no more time to argue. If they wouldn't go, she couldn't make them.

She placed the brain-sized piece of firestone on the table. The piece from which her sliver had been cut. The piece that – as the 13th key – she was connected to. Noah wasn't totally sure this would work but she had no other option.

Noah stepped up onto the chair that Jacin had vacated and then leapt lightly onto the table beside the bomb. Only a metre of fuse remained now and the spark moved relentlessly towards its destination.

Just one more time, she thought.

With that thought in her mind, Noah stepped on the firestone. This piece was tiny compared to the one she'd entered last time but … it worked. Noah watched the dragonscale give way and swallow her foot.

And the rest, she thought.

At her bidding, the firestone relinquished its solid form. Molten firestone coursed up her leg, her skin tingling under the firestone shield. *I need full body armour,* she told it.

'I don't believe it,' Raven said.

Emir frowned. 'I don't *want* to believe it.'

Noah ignored them. Her eyes darted between the firestone and the fuse. It looked like the fuse would beat her. She swore.

'I'm out of time,' she said.

'Noah!' Emir said as he grabbed for her arm.

Noah twisted, slipping free of Emir's grip, and dropped down onto the table. She curled herself around the bomb, clutching it against her stomach. Closing her eyes, she prayed that the firestone shield would be enough to protect her friends.

BOOOOOOM!

White heat blasted through her like an exploding star. The detonation was so strong, Noah's body rocketed off the table and slammed into the far wall. As she sank to the floor, she fought for enough breath to scream. Pain consumed her, a tsunami of aftershocks scouring every nerve. She was vaguely aware that someone had lifted her from the floor but the concussive tremors disoriented her.

'Noah!'

Though her eyelids burned, she forced them open. Her eyes were slow to adjust but she felt a familiar hand on her cheek.

'Emir?' she whispered.

'Yes,' he said, cradling her against his chest. 'What can I do?'

'Is Montana back yet?'

'Not yet … but I'm more worried about you at the moment.'

'And so am I,' Raven added. 'Geez, Noah! Do you reckon you could warn us before you do something like that?'

'If I had warned you, you would have tried to stop me,' she said.

'Damn right,' Raven said. 'That was bloody reckless.'

Noah attempted a smile. 'But it worked.'

'How do you feel?' Alan asked.

'A bit shaky,' Noah said, 'but I'll be fine. We need to find Franco.'

'*You* need to rest,' Emir said. '*We'll* find Franco.'

'Franco and I have some unfinished business,' Noah said.

Emir sighed. 'You're impossible.'

'But you love me anyway,' Noah said.

'Yes.'

'So you'll help me?'

Emir released her and stood up. 'If you can stand up on your own, Your Highness, I'll think about it.'

Noah groaned. 'Don't you "Your Highness" me.'

She looked at Liah.

'I'm with him,' Liah said, cocking his thumb at Emir. 'If you can't stand up, you're going nowhere.'

What's the use being king if you can't order people around? she thought.

'And the firestone bodysuit's a bit much,' Jacin added.

'Fine!' Noah said, closing her eyes.

Thank you, Xan, she thought. *This job is finished.*

As the firestone melted from her, Noah felt instantly cooler. When it was solid stone again, she picked it up from the floor and returned it to her vest pocket. She rolled onto her hands and knees wondering if it was possible to have full-body concussion. Slowly, she stood up.

Once on her feet, Alan and Jacin threw themselves on the floor before her.

'At your service,' they said.

'Did you two rehearse that?' Noah said.

Raven rolled his eyes. 'Hardly,' he said as he tugged on Alan's shirt collar. 'They're competing for your affection. I hope you've got the stomach for it.'

Noah winced but before she could reply, she heard a commotion on the staircase above. She looked up and saw Frost and Shar taking the stairs two at a time with Sachin and Montana behind them.

Montana's first question was for Noah. 'Bomb's sorted?'

Noah nodded. 'Do you know where Franco is?'

'Yes, we found him … but you don't look so well. Are you okay?'

'No, she isn't,' Emir said, before giving the high priestess an account of Noah's handling of Franco's last bomb.

Montana frowned. 'It sounds to me like you should rest, Noah.'

'I'll rest when Franco's in chains,' Noah said. 'How many soldiers does he have?'

'Twenty,' Montana said.

'Well, there are twelve of us,' Raven said. 'The odds aren't too bad.'

'Thirteen,' Anok said.

Alan patted Anok on the shoulder. 'Definitely twelve, my good man. As Mellifont's chief auditor, I can assure you there are *twelve* of us.'

Anok kept his eyes on Noah. 'Juno watches over Franco now. She will help us when we get there.'

'Who's Juno?' Jacin asked.

'Anok's hawk,' Maggie said.

Anok turned to Alan. 'Thirteen.'

Alan wagged a finger at him. 'So there *will be* thirteen, but right now … there *are* twelve.'

Losing patience with the numerical bickering, Noah spun on her heel and strode to the stairway.

'Noah?' Alan called. 'Where are you going?'

'I'm going to the armoury,' she said as she mounted the staircase, 'and then I'm going to find Franco. Count on that.'

Chapter 34

'Are you at all worried that one of them might actually burst?' Sachin said.

Noah frowned at him. 'As long as they do it quietly, I'm happy.'

Sachin folded his arms across his chest as he returned his gaze to the silent combatants. Jacin and Alan's battle to out-quiet each other to win Noah's favour had been in progress for close to an hour. So far it had achieved its purpose. As the group awaited Franco's return, stealth was paramount.

'Are you sure Franco will come back here?' Maggie asked.

Noah nodded. 'He'll want to know where the firestone is – before he kills me.'

'We can't let him get his hands on the dragonscale,' Anok said.

'No,' Noah said. 'We can't.'

Raven grimaced. 'And we can't let him kill you either, Sister.'

'We will make sure that doesn't happen,' Frost said.

'The bomb is secure?' Raven asked.

Montana tested the blade she'd borrowed from the armoury, swinging it in successive figures of eight. 'We sent it offsite,' she said.

'Where?' Raven said.

Sachin smiled. 'Earth.'

Raven rubbed his chin. 'Could it detonate?'

'I think that would be unlikely,' Sachin said. 'I hope it doesn't. I want to retrieve my slider from inside it once this is over.'

Noah leapt to her feet. 'Shush. Someone's coming.'

Emir stood at her side as footsteps disturbed the silence in the corridor beyond the antechamber. 'I hear them.'

'About time!' Alan blurted.

A triumphant smile split Jacin's face. 'I win!' he declared. 'I was quiet the longest!'

Drawing his sword, Raven put the point at Jacin's throat. 'I can make it permanent.'

'Everyone behind me,' Noah said as she walked to the door.

Frost took his place at her side. 'We'll protect you, Your Highness.'

Noah reached for the door handle and listened. Though it was difficult to hear the footsteps outside over the sound of her heartbeat pounding in her ears, she waited until they'd passed.

Wrenching the door open, she stepped into the corridor. Franco and six guards scooted down the passageway away from them.

As her entourage flanked her, Noah called out, 'Looking for something?'

Franco spun round. His soldiers drew their swords. Ylestar's king smiled and sauntered towards her.

'Noah,' he said. 'This is getting tiresome. Where is the firestone?'

'There's no firestone for you,' Noah replied. 'I'm taking you into custody – you will face Mellifont's court for your crimes.'

Franco snorted. 'No. You will stop this nonsense right now. You're a *tailor,* Noah not a *king. I* am a king though, and I order you to hand over the firestone.'

Noah's companions encircled Ylestar's king and his soldiers. 'If you don't surrender,' Noah said, 'we will take you by force.'

Laughing, Franco said, 'That's one of your many problems, Noah. You talk too much.' He put his hand into the pocket of his tunic and pulled out what looked like a small metal pear. 'And I'm done listening to you.'

He drew back his arm and lobbed the object over Noah's head. As soon as he'd released it, he turned and bolted. 'Soldiers! Retrieve the firestone!' he yelled as he disappeared up the passageway. 'Bring it to me!'

Franco's guards dropped to their stomachs as Noah spun around.

'Down!' Frost yelled.

Shar appeared in front of Noah as the miniature bomb detonated.

Bang!

Noah crumpled to the floor. The pain inside her was unbearable. Razor blades raced through her veins. *My slider,* she thought. *He used my firestone for that.*

Strong hands gripped her shoulders.

'Noah!' Emir said. 'Noah! Look at me!'

'Help me up,' she panted.

'You're hurt,' Emir said.

Clutching his arm, she said, 'I *need* to stand up! Help me!'

The clang of clashing swords reverberated along the corridor as Emir dragged Noah to her feet. She scanned the hall. Five bodies lay on the floor. Before she could identify them, Emir scooped her up in his arms.

To Frost, he said, 'Cover us.'

The goblin soldier nodded and barked an order to Liah.

Emir raced after Franco, dodging frantic fighting in the confined space.

'Put me down,' Noah said. 'I can run.'

'Are you—'

'Just *do* it!' Noah snapped.

Emir did as she said, but kept hold of her hand as they ran.

'Who was down?' she asked.

Emir shook his head. 'Noah, don't. We need to get Franco. Trust in your friends that they can deal with the guards.'

'But who was down?' she demanded.

'Montana, Maggie, Shar and Alan,' he said.

Noah's knees threatened to fail her, but she said, 'I saw five.'

'One of Franco's soldiers was also down.'

Noah stopped. 'They can't ... die because of me. We have to go back!'

'At this stage they are injured, Noah – not dead. It's still six of us against five of them. Once the soldiers are neutralised, Sachin and Anok can tend to any injuries.'

'Jacin can too,' Noah murmured.

'Then let's get Franco before he unleashes any more bombs.'

Noah looked into his eyes and nodded. 'Okay.'

Footsteps behind them made her turn.

'Raven!' she called.

He barely slowed down as he got to them. 'Come on. We need to get Franco.'

The trio raced down the passageway after the renegade king. Despite the pain inside her, Noah ran as fast as she could. If Franco made it out of the city, his army would conceal him. He'd escape justice.

Emir reached the door first. He shoved it open, holding it for Noah and Raven. At the end of the narrow ravine, she saw Franco skidding around a corner.

'I see him,' Noah said.

Sword in hand, she ran after him as a series of screeches echoed through the ravine.

'Juno!' Raven yelled.

Noah nodded as another scream followed. A human scream.

As Noah rounded the next bend, Franco came into view. Arms overhead, he swatted wildly at the hawk that swooped him as he ran.

'Go away!' Franco screamed.

'Anok's got her well trained,' Emir said as he came alongside Noah.

Short of breath, Noah just nodded.

Franco drew his sword

Noah whistled. 'Juno! Look out!'

Franco swiped at the hawk, but she avoided the blade. Juno dived again, tearing a gash in Franco's cheek with her claw.

'Ahhhhhhhhh! Bloody bird!' Franco screamed.

'We're closing on him,' Raven said.

With her eyes on Franco, Noah focused on her feet. The sandy ground in the gorges made running treacherous.

'He's headed for the tunnel,' Emir said.

Up ahead, the walls either side of the gorge converged. The tunnel, forged by ancient rains, connected the east and west sides of the city. Noah glanced at the entranceway. It looked like a crumpled wizard's hat. Though they'd made up ground on him, Franco disappeared into the entrance ahead of them.

Bracing herself for the stench that awaited them, Noah slipped her hand under her breastplate and reached into her vest to extract a piece of firestone.

'Do you think that's wise?' Emir asked.

'I'd like to see where I'm going,' Noah said as the darkness swallowed them.

'But the bats ...'

Noah squeezed her eyes shut, concentrating hard. Light exploded from the rock in her hand. The shrieking and gibbering of a million startled bats ricocheted off the walls.

Though the fluttering mammals obscured her vision, Noah saw Franco fall to his knees. Only just within range of her light, Franco scrambled on all fours towards the exit.

Noah smiled despite the suffocating stink of aeons of bat faeces. *That ought to slow him down,* she thought as she dragged her feet through the sticky guano that carpeted the tunnel floor.

When she reached the exit herself, Noah found Franco still a good way ahead of them.

'Franco!' she yelled.

The king turned around. Blood streaked his face and his uniform was smeared with bat poo.

'I will get the firestone!' he screamed as he dashed away again.

'He could be leading us into an ambush,' Raven said. 'We need to catch him.'

'Rockfall should slow him up,' Emir said.

Noah took off. 'Well, we need to catch him before he gets there,' she called back over her shoulder.

Here the gorge was narrow. The walls stretched up nearly a hundred metres either side but there was only room to run single file. And it

FIRESTONE

twisted and coiled like a ball of yarn that had been at the mercy of a playful kitten.

When the ravine finally widened, Rockfall came into view. A prehistoric avalanche had plugged the gorge with stones, rocks and boulders. Franco was more than halfway up the face.

'You two go over the top,' Noah said. 'I'll take the shortcut.'

Emir and Raven saluted before clambering up the rock wall. Noah stripped off her breastplate and dropped it on the ground. She ran to her right. When she'd found the small gap she sought, she wriggled into it. *There has to be some advantage to being small,* she thought.

Generations of diminutive adepts had squirmed their way through this narrow capillary in the natural cairn, always with the associated risk that the rocks might one day shift and collapse. Noah prayed that today wasn't that day.

She threaded her way through the opening, ignoring the scrapes and bruises she accumulated on the way. When she reached the other side, Franco was nowhere in sight. Noah poked her head out and risked a peek towards the top of Rockfall. Ylestar's king was halfway down.

Tucking her head back inside, Noah waited. She counted to twenty before struggling free of the rocks.

'You!' Franco said as he dropped to the ground. 'Did my soldiers get the firestone?'

Noah smiled. 'No. They didn't.'

Sighing, Franco drew his sword. 'Then I guess I'll have to do it myself.' He'd taken only two steps towards her when Raven called out.

'Franco!' Raven yelled. 'Surrender – and maybe you won't be hurt.'

Franco scowled. Glaring at Noah, he said, 'My soldiers *will* catch you. They *will* get that firestone.'

With a glance up at Raven and Emir, Franco bolted. Noah launched herself at him. Wrapping her arms around his knees, they both crashed to the rocky ground.

Franco swore. 'Let go!' He twisted and kicked, his boot connecting with Noah's jaw.

As dizziness swamped her, she clung to the one leg still in her grasp. But Franco was too strong. He was up and off again.

Bastard! Noah thought as she pushed to her feet. She stumbled but kept after him. *He could be leading us into an ambush.* Raven's words bounced around in her head. Ignoring that danger, Noah ran on. She kept Franco in sight as he negotiated the twisting trail between Mellifont's stone megaliths.

The path curved left and ended.

Noah pulled her sword from its sheath. Fighting to catch her breath, she said, 'Dead end, Franco. What's your plan now?'

Franco scanned the walls before jumping onto a low ledge. Finding handholds, he began his ascent.

Noah shook her head. 'You've got to be kidding.'

I can't climb that, she thought. *And I don't want Emir or Raven climbing it either.*

Noah scooped up a handful of stones from the ground and selected the biggest one. She pegged it at Franco, hitting him on the back. It bounced off harmlessly. Noah threw another, missing him altogether this time.

'These are too small,' she said aloud.

Dropping the stones, she brushed her hands on her tunic and reached for a piece of firestone. She cradled the rock in her hand, admiring it for a moment. She looked back at Franco and took careful aim.

The firestone hit his elbow.

Franco grunted. 'Really, Noah? Is that the best you can do?'

'I thought you wanted firestone,' she said, retrieving the glittering rock from the ground.

Franco looked down on her, eyes widening at the sight of the dragonscale. Noah stepped back and lined up her next shot.

Franco caught the rock in his left hand. 'Aha! That's one – only twelve to go.' He stuffed the firestone inside his shirt. 'Give the next one your best shot.'

'I will,' Noah said.

She pulled two more projectiles from her vest as Emir and Raven arrived.

'Perfect timing,' she said, handing them a piece a firestone each.

Staring at the sparkling rock, Raven said, 'So what do you want me to do with this?'

'Target practice,' Noah said as she organised the ammunition. 'Let's knock him off that wall.'

Glancing at the firestone, Emir said, 'Only eleven pieces?'

'One's in Dragonhall and Franco has one,' Noah said. 'If we get him down, we get that one back.'

Raven didn't wait for a further invitation. He pitched a rock at Franco, hitting him in the head.

Franco grunted but was undeterred.

Emir and Noah set to work, bombarding their climbing quarry with a volley of shots.

'He's getting away,' Noah said as Franco continued his ascent despite the barrage.

Raven threw another stone. 'You collect the rocks, Sis – we'll throw them.'

Noah nodded. Franco was almost out of range of her weary arms. It made sense to leave the throwing to stronger arms. If she supplied the ammunition in a timely manner, they had the best chance of bringing the king down.

Emir and Raven continued pitching stones. With two successive strikes to Franco's head, the king slipped down the rock face.

'No!' Franco yelled as he scrabbled for a handhold.

He found none, and hit the ground with a thud.

Raven got to him first, flipping the king onto his stomach and wrenching one arm behind his back.

Franco spat. Blood sprayed across the ground. 'You'll regret this,' he panted.

Noah shook her head as Raven and Emir hauled the bound and dishevelled king to his knees.

Looking down on him, Noah said, 'I regret nothing.' Reaching her hand inside his shirt, she retrieved the firestone he'd caught.

'Take a good look,' she said, holding the rock in front of his face, 'because it's the last piece of firestone you'll ever see.'

Chapter 35

Flanked by two of Montana's warriors, Noah walked down the corridor towards Elani's chamber. Franco strode ahead of her, also under escort. When they reached the chamber, Franco stopped in front of the doors. He looked at one of the warriors.

'You going to open the door?'

'The door will be opened when the high priestess is ready,' the warrior replied.

Franco turned around to face Noah. Raking his eyes over her, he said, 'You're still pretending to be a king, I see.'

One of the warriors drew a short blade from his scabbard and held the blade against Franco's throat. 'By the high priestess' decree, the prisoners will not exchange words,' he said.

Anger flashed in Franco's eyes but he said nothing more. His uniform was clean and his hair had been washed and combed, but even after two days in custody, his injuries were glaringly prominent. A gashed cheek, split lip and black eye diminished his regal demeanour.

In the twenty minutes they waited at the door, Noah watched the skin on Franco's neck flush with colour. *He's like a thermometer,* she thought. *As his anger rises, his skin shows the temperature change.*

When the doors finally opened, Montana stood in the entryway. Noah again gave silent thanks that the high priestess had survived the blast that had claimed two others. Shar and one of Franco's soldiers had succumbed to their injuries. Alan had lost a foot but would be able to continue his duties in Mellifont.

Montana stepped aside. 'Enter.'

Sachin and Anok stood at the table on the dais. Alan, scrawling furiously on a sheet of parchment, remained seated. When Franco and Noah were seated, the judges resumed their seats.

Montana's warriors fanned out around the table as the high priestess began proceedings.

'I am Montana, High Priestess of Talisker and today I preside over an extraordinary trial. Judges assisting are Majors Anok and Sachin of Mellifont. Dr Alan will keep the record of account. At this time, we acknowledge two prisoners – King Franco of Ylestar and King Noah of Carai. Prisoners are advised that at all times you will remain seated and not threaten the safety of anyone in this room. I remind you that my warriors are highly trained and will use whatever force is necessary to restrain you if you fail to adhere to this directive. Are there any questions in regards to the process?'

'Where is the audience?' Franco asked.

'There is no audience,' Montana said. 'For today, this is a courtroom, not a concert hall.'

'You have something to hide, High Priestess?'

'My position is above reproach, King Franco. Have care how you speak.'

'I have another question,' Franco said. 'How is it that all judges on the panel are friends of my co-accused?'

'Circumstance,' Montana said.

'Circumstance?'

'In the course of our duties, members of the panel – including myself – have had various opportunities to encounter, and in some cases work closely with, your co-accused. As a result of those interactions, those circumstances, we have become friends.'

'So you don't deny you are friends with her?' he asked, stabbing a finger in Noah's direction.

'No, I do not deny it,' Montana said. To Alan, she said, 'Dr Alan. Please let the record reflect that fact that there is a friendly relationship between the judges and King Noah of Carai.'

'In the interest of equity, should I not have friends on the panel?' Franco said.

Holding his gaze, Montana said, 'I interviewed widely here in Mellifont and I found no one to fit that criteria. Are there any further questions? Or could we get started?'

Franco scowled. 'No further questions.'

'None here,' Noah said.

Montana nodded and placed one hand on each of the piles of parchment before her. 'I have read your accounts of your actions since goblins raided the mine at t'Amos two months ago. My fellow judges have also read the accounts and we are all deeply disturbed by the contents. It is clear to us that the Sovereign States Alliance is completely dysfunctional and that the current war is a result of that dysfunction. What is also clear is that your actions have escalated the conflict.'

'You can't be serious,' Franco said. 'I have at all times acted in Talisker's best interests – trying to *save* the firestone from goblins.'

'I am not interested in your motives – only your actions,' Montana said. 'Regardless of your *intentions* – and I mean both of you – your combined *actions* have triggered this war. You are both accountable.'

'I am trying to save our world from this maniac,' Franco argued. 'She's stolen firestone, she's consorting with goblins … her crimes are many. Did you read my whole report? It is *very* detailed.'

'Detailed, yes,' Montana agreed. 'And I would also add, full of lies.'

Franco's eyes bulged. 'Are you calling me a liar?'

'If you wrote this report,' she patted the sheets under her left hand, 'then yes.'

'I have witnesses,' he declared.

'Your ability to conjure up witnesses to corroborate your lies is not in question, King Franco,' Montana said. 'I have no doubt we could spend several weeks listening to the false testimonies of your accomplices.'

'Accomplices? I thought you said this was a court,' Franco said. 'I don't think I'm getting a fair trial. I think you've already made up your mind.'

'You are quite correct,' Montana said. '*We* have made up our minds.'

Franco scowled. 'So what is your decree?'

'You will both be detained in Mellifont until all the issues identified in your respective accounts have been addressed with due process.'

Franco leapt to his feet. 'You mean I'm *stuck* here?'

Two warriors shoved him back in his seat.

'Until *all* these matters have been *thoroughly* investigated and addressed, yes,' Montana said. 'This is only the first step, King Franco.'

'You *can't* do that!' he said.

'She *can* do that,' Sachin said.

'I have a kingdom to run,' Franco said.

'Word will be sent to Ylestar that a regent should be appointed in your stead,' Anok said. 'The same will happen for Carai.'

Franco shook his head, his face reddening with every passing second. 'You have no idea what you're doing,' he said. 'The southern states will give firestone to the goblins and they'll use it against us. *When* the slaughter begins – let it be on your heads.'

'At the moment, men are slaughtering men in the war you've started. *That's* on your head.'

'No!' Franco said. 'The southern states' kings can wear that. *They* are the ones conspiring with goblins. The northern states are simply championing the Alliance's long-held view that goblins should be eradicated from Talisker.'

'The Alliance,' Montana said. 'It is the view of this court that – due to the deep division between north and south – the Sovereign States Alliance has dissolved. It is no more.'

'How convenient,' Franco sneered.

'It is also the will of this court,' Montana continued, 'that – until a new Alliance is forged – *no one* will be getting any firestone.'

'*And* the Alliance's new charter must be acceptable to the Council here in Mellifont in terms of how firestone is used,' Major Anok said.

'I will never be part of an Alliance that gives firestone to goblins,' Franco said.

'Actually,' Montana said, 'it is the view of this court that you are unlikely to be *permitted* to be part of any future Alliance.'

'Oh really? Why is that?'

'As I said earlier, there are many issues to be addressed in both your accounts,' Montana said, leafing through a sheaf of parchments, 'and the one this court will prioritise is the matter of King Tambian's death at t'Amos.'

The colour drained from Franco's face.

'Your confession here – in this very chamber, in front of several witnesses,' Montana said, 'pretty well settles that matter.'

With blinding speed, Franco swiped a blade from the warrior nearest him and launched himself at Noah.

'*Stop!*' Montana cried, leaping to her feet.

A warrior yanked Noah's seat aside while another tackled Franco. Ruthlessly efficient, Montana's warriors disarmed and bound the disgraced king in seconds.

'Dr Alan,' Montana said. 'Please update the record of account to reflect the attempted murder of King Noah of Carai by Franco of Ylestar.'

'Yes, High Priestess,' he said, reaching for a fresh sheet of parchment.

'That's *King* Franco of Ylestar,' Franco said.

Montana looked at him. 'No,' she said. 'You are no longer a king. For the murder of King Tambian of Leninstar, I hereby strip you of your title. You will rot in a cell here in Mellifont for that crime alone. Whatever else we find you guilty of,' she placed her hands on the parchments before her, 'we will add to your sentence.'

'What's the point of that?' Franco said.

'It does seem pointless,' Montana conceded, 'but we follow the rules here.'

Glaring at the high priestess, Franco said, 'And what about Noah?'

Montana smiled and turned to Noah. 'You may return to your suite when you're ready, Noah,' she said, 'so you can continue work on your doctorate. The sooner you find how to reverse the effects of the ilanxis worm, the better.'

'You've got to be joking!' Franco said.

'Take him away,' Montana said with a dismissive wave. 'This court is adjourned.'

Chapter 36

'You look tired, Noah,' Catriona said.

Noah put her cutlery on her plate and dabbed the corners of her mouth with her napkin. 'I am tired.'

She surveyed her dinner companions, and thought they all looked tired. After a fortnight negotiating terms for the new Firestone Alliance, anyone who still looked fresh probably wasn't doing their job.

'Have you made any progress on a cure for Jaxon?' Catriona asked.

'No,' Noah said. 'If it *is* actually possible, it's going to take us a while.'

Catriona nodded. 'Well, you've certainly got your work cut out for you, don't you?'

'You can say that again,' Noah said.

'How are you planning to balance your roles?'

Noah resisted the urge to shrug. Montana had told her countless times in the past fortnight that shrugging was not regal. While Noah had managed to balance her responsibilities as Dragonsbane and King Tambian's tailor, this was different. Much different. Delivering a cure for ilanxis symptoms while discharging her duties to Carai promised to truly test her.

'I don't know yet,' Noah said. 'I've got some negotiating to do when I get back to Carai.'

'I could help you with that,' Catriona offered.

Noah turned to face Leninstar's king. 'You're going to come to Carai?'

Catriona raised an eyebrow. 'Don't be ridiculous, Noah.'

Frowning, Noah said, 'Perhaps you just tell me exactly what you're offering?'

'Emir.'

Noah's heart beat faster. 'On what terms?'

'You can have him – as your adviser in Carai.'

'For how long?'

'For as long as you require.'

Noah sat back in her chair, folding her hands in her lap. She looked across the table to where Emir was talking to Jacin.

Without taking her gaze from him, Noah said, 'Have you discussed this with him?'

'Yes,' Catriona said. 'He is keen to go with you.'

'You have a suitable replacement?'

'I have a *workable* replacement,' Catriona said. 'I would prefer to have Emir continue as my adviser, but I think the new Alliance is better served if he is in Carai.'

Noah nodded, relief flooding through her. She'd expected that her beloved Alsatian would be the only one accompanying her to Carai. If Emir were to accompany her too though … life in Carai might just be bearable. Jacin wouldn't like the competition, but he'd have to live with it.

'I accept,' Noah said.

Skewering a potato from the platter on the table, Catriona said, 'Just don't be getting any ideas about poaching anyone else. Raven is mine.'

Sachin elbowed Noah. 'Are you two done gossiping?'

Turning to him, she said, 'We were discussing matters of state, I'll have you know.'

'You were talking about your boyfriend, Noah,' he said, rolling his eyes. 'Don't give me that "matters of state" crap.'

'So when are *you* going to come and visit us in Carai?'

Swallowing a mouthful of salted peaches, Sachin said, 'Pencil me in for the fourth of never. Does that work for you?'

'As sponsor for my doctorate, shouldn't you come and check up on me occasionally?'

'Alan will come and check up on you.'

'Don't be mean,' Noah said, nudging him. 'He's going to find it pretty difficult to get around now that he's got only one foot.'

'Noah,' Sachin said, 'you should check your luggage before you leave. He'll try to stow away, I guarantee it.'

'Sachin, you're terrible.'

Sachin smiled. 'No. I'm a realist. Alan is so worried that Jacin is going to "steal you" from him. He'll be glad that Emir is there to chaperone you, but I'm telling you, Noah – you won't be able to keep Alan away.'

'He hates goblins,' Noah said. 'He won't last long in Carai.'

Putting up his hands in surrender, Sachin said, 'Believe what you want. Just don't say I didn't warn you.'

'Duly noted,' Noah said.

Mopping up his gravy with a chunk of bread, Sachin frowned thoughtfully. 'And what about Gillette?'

Noah's stomach tightened. 'Rescuing Gillette will be a very delicate operation.'

'But you think it can be done?'

'If it's possible to get him *in* there, it must be possible to get him out again. I'll have to talk to Grainger about that.'

Sachin frowned. 'Do you think he'll help you?'

Noah tapped her fingers on the table. 'As I said, it will be a *very* delicate operation.'

♪♫

From her perch on top of Rockfall, Noah watched Emir's approach. Kane jabbed his wet nose at her face to get her attention, but she deflected him. Whatever Franco had done to him when she and Gillette were abducted had had no lasting effect. Kane was back to his usual boisterous antics.

'Noah, I've been looking everywhere for you,' Emir said. 'What are you doing?'

'Teaching Kane sign language.'

Emir climbed the rocks with ease and took a seat next to her. 'You think that's a good use of your time, Your Highness?'

'Yes,' she said, ignoring the royal title. 'I taught Raven sign language when he was a dog and you've seen how good he is at it.'

'You think Kane is going to turn into a person too?'

Noah rolled her eyes. 'I bloody hope not.'

'Language,' he said, elbowing her playfully.

'When it's just you and me, I can say what I like.'

Kane flopped across Noah's lap.

Patting the dog's head, Emir said, 'He has a thing or two to learn about subtlety.'

'You can teach him that.'

Emir glanced at her. 'I think we've got enough to do in Carai without adding *that* to the list.'

'You're probably right.'

'I'm definitely right.'

Now that a full meeting of Mellifont's Council had approved Noah's release from custody, they'd travel to Carai within the week.

'We need to negotiate for Carai to have a seat on the Firestone Alliance,' Emir said.

'Yep.'

'And you need to find how to reverse the effects of the ilanxis worm.'

'Yep.'

'And we need to find Gillette.'

'Yes,' Noah whispered.

'You have a plan?'

Noah frowned. 'I have an idea.'

'Which is?'

'I think we need to find Somyni.'

'Who?'

'Somyni – it's a place. A Pyranhi city. It's where Jong's followers lived.'

Emir rubbed his chin. 'Right.'

'I figure between Dragonhall's records and Carai's archives, I should be able to find out where it is.'

'Yes, but it sounds like a trap. That's what Jong wants, right? He wants you to free him?'

'That's *his* plan, yes.'

'How are you going to deny him? Are you planning to destroy him?'

Noah shook her head. 'He's a god. I don't think he can be destroyed.'

'Not even by the 13th key?'

'No.'

'So, you're going to sweet-talk him into giving up Gillette then?'

'Something like that.'

Emir put his hand on her knee. 'I think you've a better chance of destroying him.'

'Thanks for the vote of confidence.'

'Noah, let's face it … diplomacy is not really what you're known for.'

Noah winked at him. 'That's what I've got you for.'

Noah's adventures continue in *Redemption*

Temperance sipped her tea while Elani massaged his temples. The prolonged silence as he fretted eroded her patience.

'What troubles you, Brother dear?' Temperance asked.

Elani sighed. 'The vortex is growing much faster than I'd anticipated.'

'Yes,' Temperance said. 'Comets and asteroids won't appease it for much longer. It's going to have an appetite for bigger things.'

'Talisker,' Elani said. 'It's going to swallow Talisker.'

Temperance placed her teacup on the saucer. 'Yes.'

'You know I don't want to sacrifice Talisker, Temp,' Elani said, 'but it's the only way.'

Temperance shook her head, setting her brown ringlets jiggling. 'No it isn't.'

Elani drummed his fingers on the table but said nothing.

'The Pyranhi foresaw this,' Temperance said. *'The thirteenth key the world shall need, for evil to be brought to heel – One of two, the Dragon's bane must rise; and the music wield.* The 13th key has been made.'

'The human?'

'Her name is Noah.'

'She's not ready.'

Temperance sniffed. 'Of course she's not … but she will be.'

'Temp, you can't help her. *We* can't intervene.'

Eyes smouldering with ageless wisdom, Temperance smiled. 'Not *directly.*'

Elani stood up and strode to the archway. Temperance took a deep breath before joining him. Beyond their celestial palace, the galaxies sprawled gloriously across the universe. All Elani's wonderful creations. But the shimmering tapestry of star-studded gas clouds, fountaining quasars and swirling planetary clusters brought Temperance no joy today. In a distant galaxy, Talisker – her favourite of all Elani's worlds – sailed through the heavens on a collision course with a rapidly expanding vortex.

Talisker was a paradox. Both a shrine and a prison. The mighty dragon, Xan had been mortally wounded when she'd battled the destructive god, Jong – and then devoured him – to end his campaign to destroy all Elani's creations. Elani had built a world around her; a protective cocoon in which the injured dragon could continue to contain the vanquished god. It was a precarious situation though. Jong still lived, waiting for his chance to break free.

Talisker must be saved, Temperance thought, *and we're desperately short of time.*

'What if Noah were to find the illestial?' she said.

Elani spun round. 'No! That'd be playing into Jong's hands. That's exactly what our brother wants.'

'But with the illestial, Noah could extract Jong from Talisker and rehome him in the vortex. That's what we need, isn't it? We've got a voracious vortex and a delinquent god – a perfect match.'

Elani frowned. 'I agree it's a perfect match, Temp. Xan cannot contain Jong much longer. The vortex is definitely the solution. Jong's power wouldn't be enough to break free of the vortex, but he'll suck enough energy from it to stop it growing.' He sighed. 'It weighs heavily on me that the vortex will consume Talisker, but it's the safest way to get Jong in there.'

Temperance glared at her brother. 'How can you talk like that? Noah could do this. Talisker could be saved.'

'The human is brave and well-meaning,' Elani said, 'but no match for Jong.'

'Noah is part dragon. Xan's power is in her veins.'

'She is mortal.'

'So because her life – *human* life – is fleeting, it is meaningless?' Temperance said. 'We should just let them all die?'

Elani faced her. 'Don't do that.' He put his hands on her shoulders. 'You know that's not what I meant.'

Temperance waited.

'Temp, Xan was a mighty dragon,' Elani said. 'The mightiest. She fought Jong and ...'

'Contained him,' Temperance said. 'With the illestial, Noah could do the same. She wouldn't have to do it for long – just long enough to get Jong into the vortex.'

Elani returned his gaze to the cosmic landscape. 'The illestial was designed to free Jong. We can't risk that. If Jong is free – he will destroy everything. Not just Talisker ... *everything*.'

Titles by Sarah Fisher:

The 13th Key

Firestone

For the latest news on new releases, sign up to Sarah's website:
www.sarahfisherauthor.com

Or follow Sarah Fisher – Author on
Facebook @sfisher9 or Twitter @WhatTheFish9

About the Author

Sarah Fisher lives west of Brisbane, Australia. When she's not corralling her collection of unruly fictional characters, she teaches real characters at local schools. She is living proof that while growing older is compulsory, growing up is not.